There goes the bride

ly McQueen has wanted to be a writer ever since
overing that the nuns at her junior school would
her off maths homework if she wrote a story
ad. After unexpected detours via law, magazine
nalism, and even musical theatre, she began
ing her first novel in 2006. Holly lives with her
band in London. She still avoids maths. *There
s the Bride* is her fourth book.

Also by Holly McQueen

The Glamorous (Double) Life of Isabel Bookbinder
The Fabulously Fashionable Life of Isabel Bookbinder
Confetti Confidential

There goes the bride

Holly McQueen

arrow books

Published by Arrow Books in 2011

2 4 6 8 10 9 7 5 3 1

First published in Great Britain in 2011 by
Arrow Books
Random House, 20 Vauxhall Bridge Road,
London SW1V 2SA

www.rbooks.co.uk

Addresses for companies within The Random House Group Limited can be found at: www.randomhouse.co.uk

The Random House Group Limited Reg. No. 954009

A CIP catalogue record for this book is available from the British Library

ISBN 9780099545767

The Random House Group Limited supports The Forest Stewardship Council (FSC), the leading international forest certification organisation. All our titles that are printed on Greenpeace approved FSC certified paper carry the FSC logo. Our paper procurement policy can be found at www.rbooks.co.uk/environment

Mixed Sources
Product group from well-managed forests and other controlled sources
www.fsc.org Cert no. TT-COC-2139
© 1996 Forest Stewardship Council

Typeset by SX Composing DTP, Rayleigh, Essex
Printed and bound in Great Britain by
CPI Cox & Wyman, Reading, RG1 8EX

For Laura

Acknowledgements

Thanks even more than usual to Kate Elton and Gillian Holmes for their patience, for steering me in the right direction, and for their excellent taste in romantic heroes.

And thank you to Clare Alexander, not only the best agent but also the best co-conspirator on the cake front.

From: PollyWollyDoodle@hotmail.com
To: Julia247@yahoo.com
Date: 24 December 2011
Subject: Help

Dear Julia

I know it's Christmas Eve. And I know you're halfway up a mountain in Colorado right now, wowing your half-million nephews and nieces with your snowboarding prowess. It's almost ten at night here, so you're probably right in the middle of your afternoon ski. So I'm really, really sorry to disturb you.

I'm only emailing because you said I should always get in touch when things are not good. And things are not good just now. They're not good at all.

I've just run out on my sister's Christmas party. I know, I know – I'm getting good at running out on things, aren't I? And you're probably thinking, *Oh, that doesn't sound too big a deal. Polly's told me all about her sister, Bella, and I can't say I'm surprised she's done a runner from a*

Christmas party of hers. Especially if Bella's annoying boyfriend was there (he was) *and especially if her mum was getting tipsy* (she was) *and especially if Bella and her dad were engaging in competitive one-upmanship over the best way to heat up sausage rolls* (they were). *Anybody would make a sharp exit from a party like that!*

But none of those things was the reason I left.

The surprise guest was the reason I left. Bella invited Dev.

That's right. Dev.

I've no idea what she was thinking. Actually, what am I saying? This is Bella we're talking about. I know exactly what she was thinking. That one look at Dev and I'd realise the error of my ways, and the wedding would be back on before you could say, 'Canapés, champagne, and a sit-down buffet for a hundred and thirty!' This is the way my sister's mind works. Something goes wrong, you just pull your sleeves up and fix it. I call off my wedding to the love of my life, she just pulls up her sleeves and fixes it.

But there isn't any fixing this, Julia. There isn't any fixing me. There isn't any fixing the things I've done.

Oh shit, Dev is calling me. He's calling me RIGHT NOW.

I'm not going to answer. I've not answered his calls in six weeks. I don't need to start now.

Oh, thank God, it's stopped.

Look, if you do happen to get this, maybe you could give me a call? Drop me an email, even, with some of your much-needed pearls of wisdom? Either way, I'd be so gratef

OK, now Dev is calling me again.

This time he's doing our code: two rings, hang up. Two rings, hang up. He used to do it when he was calling me from work and his landline number would come up Withheld. I have a habit of screening calls, you see – too many years spent owing people money or forgetting to pay my bills – but I'd always want to pick up if it was him.

I suppose, if I'm being honest, I want to pick up right now.

Maybe it's because he did our code. Maybe it's because it's Christmas. Maybe it's because he looked so lovely, standing on Bella's doorstep, wearing the coat I picked out for him in the sale last January, and the checked scarf we bought to keep out the unseasonable cold when we spent this past Easter in Vermont. Maybe it's because I feel so bad about running away from him earlier. About running away from him at all.

And there are things – you know, Julia, what things – that I owe it to him to explain. Seeing him tonight, even just for a couple of moments, seeing him all Dev-like and cosy in his coat and his scarf . . . it made me wonder if he just might understand after all.

Two rings again, now silence.

Right, here's what I'm going to do. If he rings again, I'll take it as a sign. And I'll pick up. Even though you're not here to advise me what to do, I'll pick up. Just to talk to him. And maybe I won't explain anything. Maybe I'll just listen to his v

OK, it's ringing again. Got to go.

Love
Polly x

Bella

Tuesday 17 November
It's going to be a busy few weeks, one way or another. Tonight my sister, Polly, is finally coming home, for good, after six years living in New York. She's getting married on New Year's Eve, barely six weeks from now, and as her official chief bridesmaid and unofficial wedding co-ordinator – not to mention the only person in my family with an ability to Get Things Done – I'm up to the eyeballs with plans and to-do lists, trying to settle everything from the exact shade of the roses in Polly's bouquet to the first draft of the inevitably fraught seating plan.

Oh, and it looks like I'm one step closer to getting a baby.

These two momentous events – Polly's long-awaited return, and my baby news – aren't actually *linked*, by the way. I realise that I've made it sound as though my sister might be bringing back a baby for me all the way from New York, along with the cheap Kiehl's products I've requested. Slinging the poor thing into the overhead luggage compartment on the plane, perhaps, or checking it in with her suitcases and waving it away as it trundles off along the conveyor belt.

I know. You may well frown. But it's the kind of thing Polly might do with a baby.

Anyway, that's irrelevant, because she isn't bringing back a baby. (At least I hope she's not; dear God, I hope she's not.) It's just that it so happens that earlier today I received a phone call from a woman named Samantha. She is an adoption social worker. And though we've not met before, from the moment she comes round for her initial visit later on this week, she's the person who starts the process of deciding whether or not I am suitable to be given somebody else's unwanted child.

On Samantha's say-so, I could be judged to be either a) a kind, generous person who just wants to give a child a good home, or b) a sadistic monster planning to adopt a whole brood of needy children with the sole purpose of turning them out to work in the streets as beggars and underage prostitutes.

And convincing the social service that you're in category a) rather than b) is a tough act to pull off, let me tell you.

Which is why, ever since the call from Samantha a couple of hours ago, my mind has wandered, for the first time in weeks, off Polly's wedding preparations and onto all the preparations I'll need to make to get myself and the flat ready for this visit. Food, mainly, is what I've been thinking about. What to serve up to Samantha, with her tea or coffee, that will send out the signals that I'm kind/generous/keen to give a child a good home and not sadistic/monstrous/an exploiter of the vulnerable. A Sicilian lemon drizzle loaf, perhaps, sharp with citrus and moist with butter, and the pleasingly retro coffee-and-walnut cake that my step-dad, Brian, always likes to make for visitors. Plus I could get my best friend (and professional *pâtissier*), Anna, to make her fabled chocolate cake. It's made without flour so it's actually more like a mousse than a sponge, turning slightly fudgy with the addition of ground almonds, and will serve me well if Samantha happens to be wheat-intolerant.

I know, it's probably absolutely ludicrous to be thinking about what kind of food I can serve my adoption social worker, but thinking about what food I can serve people is pretty much my go-to state of mind. I own my own catering company, you see. It's a pretty small affair – just me and, for the last year or so, Anna – doing dinner parties, buffet suppers or canapé events in my clients' homes. But I've been building the business for five years now and these days it's doing so well that sooner or later I'm going to have to take on more staff, just to keep up with demand. It's called Bella's Bites – Polly came up with the name; mind you, I went along with it, so I suppose I'm as much to blame for its terminal tweeness as she is.

So this is why planning the right menu for Samantha's visit is really just professional courtesy. Nothing to do with me being an uptight control freak.

Anyway, I'm using up all my uptight control freakery on Polly's wedding.

'Babe?'

This is Jamie, my boyfriend, calling me from the living room.

Even though he's not taken a massive amount of interest in the whole thorny adoption process just yet, I'm kind of hoping that – along with the trio of cakes – Jamie might be my secret weapon in impressing Samantha. After all, it's the hardest of hearts that isn't melted by his swoony Cork accent, and let's face it, he's not exactly tough on the eyes. He's six foot four and gloriously chunky, with a handsome face, naughty chocolate-coloured eyes and a year-round outdoorsy tan, thanks to his work as a landscape gardener. Though he hasn't done too much of it lately, so the tan is in danger of fading a little bit. When we first met, he was running his own firm, Keenan Landscapes. It's *how* we met, in fact, when he was working on the garden of one of my dinner-party clients in Maida Vale. But over the past few months, Keenan Landscapes has kind of . . . fallen by the wayside. It's the effects of the recession, mostly. Though I can't really explain why the demand for chichi catered parties would have risen steadily while the demand for a hunky Irishman to come and mow your lawn, pressure-wash your patio and plant you some rhododendrons has plummeted.

I head through to the living room, where he's sitting on the sofa with Wii football playing on the TV, and the upchuckers, or whatever the controls are called, in his hand. He's in his usual scruffy state – ripped jeans, a crumpled T-shirt, and a three-day growth of stubble

– but he gets away with it. If anything, the just-got-out-of-bed look just makes him even more swoony.

And yes, of course I wonder what a man as attractive as him is doing with me. I wonder this on a fairly frequent basis.

'Hang on a moment, Bells,' he says, even though he was the one who called me. He's breathing in very sharply through his lips and teeth, putting every ounce of concentration he can into the game . . . then he falls back onto the plumped-up cushions, whooping with triumph, as his team scores the desired goal. 'United three, Arsenal nil!'

'Fantastic!' I've learned, in the course of our two-year relationship, that Jamie is touchingly excited by any interest I show in his beloved Manchester United, whether it's the real team or the virtual kind. (And, to be honest, whether it's real *interest* or the virtual kind; he's touched either way, even if he must know I'm occasionally faking.) 'Did you want something?'

'I was just wondering if you could drop me at the pub on the way to meet your sister? You're leaving at seven-ish, yeah?'

'The pub?' I try to keep my tone non-judgemental. 'I, um, thought you might be coming to the airport with me.'

'Oh, come on, Bells, United are playing Bayern tonight. I want to watch the game with the boys.'

Ah yes, The Boys. The whole time I've known Jamie, he's come complete with The Boys. They're an ever-shifting group, nomadic in nature, but with a core set of defining characteristics that include: a persuasive Cork accent; a capacity for prodigious quantities of alcohol; and a slavish devotion both to their mothers and to Manchester United (not necessarily in that order). And they're traditionalists, too: though they're always perfectly pleasant to me when we meet, it's pretty clear that girlfriends are not welcome on certain sacred grounds, namely The Pub, The Five-a-Side Pitch, and Old Trafford.

'But, Jamie, you said you'd come to the airport to welcome Polly home.' I don't want to sound like a nag, but he *did* say this. Even if it was, almost certainly, under the influence of alcohol. 'And to help me deal with my mother. You know how good you are with her.'

The flattery is half working, but I'm battling against the unbeatable lure of Manchester United.

'And Grace might be there,' I add, casually. After all, if flattery doesn't work, appealing to his penis might.

I'm right, because his eyes light up. 'Gorgeous Grace? The one you don't like?'

This is unfair. I don't dislike Grace, my sister's lifelong best friend. It's just . . . well, I always feel *she* has a bit of a problem with *me*. She's one of those women – always was, in fact, one of those girls – who a lot of other women find it hard to take to. It's not just that she's extremely beautiful – or *gorgeous*, thank you, Jamie – although she does happen to be exactly that: tall, blonde, and still slender as a reed despite having had two children. It's more that she's just a couple of crucial degrees away from warmth. Not glacial, exactly. And not even – at least not when she's making a real effort – chilly. She's just kind of . . . tepid.

'Yes. Gorgeous Grace.'

Jamie screws up his face, caught in a heart-rending struggle between spending the evening in the company of one stunning woman or twenty-two sweaty footballers.

The sweaty footballers win.

'Yeah, but we're playing *Bayern*, babe. It's a huge game. Besides, you know your sister isn't my biggest fan. You're better off going without me.'

I know, from experience, that there's no point arguing. 'All right. But you have to promise, Jamie, here and now, that you won't have a *huge game* to watch on Saturday.'

'What's on Saturday?'

I swear I've told him this three times already. 'Samantha is coming round.'

'Samantha . . . ?'

'The social worker. Remember, Jamie? I told you earlier? The woman coming to talk about the adoption?'

'Oh, *Samantha*. Well, I remember *that*, babe.' He leans down and kisses the top of my head. It's such a long way down for him that I'm surprised he doesn't put his back out. 'Obviously I remember it! I know how important it is to you.'

'To us.'

'Of course! To us.' He tilts my chin up so he can place a kiss on my lips. And very nice it is, too. He's a truly excellent kisser. A full, soft mouth, he's got; a thing I find knee-tremblingly attractive. Probably because it's the opposite of my Evil Ex, Christian, who amongst his other crimes had the kind of lips that look as though they've been vacuum-packed.

'And there's more where that came from!' he says proudly, when he comes up for air, and the two of us start heading for the hallway. 'I'll wait up for you, babe, to get back from the airport.'

'Oh, there's no need for that.' Flattered though I am, I'd kind of been hoping for an early night. Not much chance of that, though, when Jamie's in the mood for lurve. 'I have to be up early in the morning. I've invoices to be doing, and I've got to start getting the flat shipshape for Samantha's visit, and there are about a million calls I have to make about wedding stuff once I've finally made Polly take a few basic decisions . . .'

'Christ, I'd forgotten about the wedding.' Jamie's face falls. Like most men, he's not a fan of weddings at the best of times. And thanks to the fact that this one is going to be taking place on New Year's Eve – one of Jamie's high holy days because of the opportunity (nay, the necessity) of hanging out with The Boys and drinking his body weight in lager – it's causing him even more distress. 'No chance Polly might change her mind about the date, then?'

'After all the work I've been doing? I tell you something, Jamie. Polly makes changes to her wedding over my dead body.'

Jamie pulls on his hooded top and gives me a salute. 'Aye, aye, Big Sister.'

Polly is my half-sister, actually, not my full sister, but neither of us has ever bothered much with the distinction. It was the kind of thing we'd occasionally use, as children, to attack each other with – *You ruined my Nirvana T-shirt, and you're not even my* real *sister!* – but the reality was, and is, that the 'half' has never mattered. The 'sister' part is all that's ever counted. And even though she has been driving me round the bend recently, with her footloose and fancy-free approach to organising a wedding for a hundred and thirty, even though her footloose and fancy-free approach to life itself has driven me round the bend ever since I can remember . . . God, I can't wait to have her back. I've missed her.

When I get to Heathrow Terminal Five, a little before eight thirty this evening, I can already see that Mum and Brian have beaten me to it.

Well, I can see that Mum has beaten me to it. She's loitering in The Perfume Shop, spritzing one wrist with eau de Jennifer Aniston and the other wrist with whatever Sarah Jessica Parker smells of these days. There's no sign of Brian, my stepdad, but he must have been dispatched on some Mum-centric errand. This is the way things work on Planet Atkins.

'Is Brian here?' I ask as soon as I reach her. 'You haven't left him in the car park, have you?'

'Darling, don't be ridiculous.'

Mum's *darlings* are always theatrical, the kind Laurence Olivier might have doled out backstage at the Old Vic when he couldn't remember the spear carriers' names. But then, my mother is pretty theatrical herself. People often think she's an actress, an impression she cultivates even though she's really just the manageress of a jewellery boutique in Devizes. She's still beautiful, even in her sixties, with the impressive height and olive colouring that Polly (but alas, not I) inherited, and she has a tendency to dress for the occasion. Today she's stylish in navy cigarette pants, a neat beige mac and a little black beret over her (dyed) jet-black hair. It's her Greeting-People-at-the-Airport outfit, inspired by *Brief Encounter* and Ingrid Bergman in *Casablanca*.

She kisses me on both cheeks. 'We had a long drive up, you know, and we're both in need of refreshment. He's gone off with Dev, to find some decent coffee.'

Dev is Polly's fiancé, and I'm really excited to see him. This is only partly because I'm keen to pin him down about which of my large-scale catering contacts he wants to try out to do the food at the wedding. Mostly it's just because I adore Dev. We all do. Not only is he kind and sweet, and head over heels in love with my sister, but he's also a hot-shot plastic surgeon who's forever jetting off to some disaster-ravaged country with one of the many charities he works for, to treat burns victims or earthquake-hit orphans.

No, I'm not kidding. He's pretty much Mr Perfect. Sorry – even better – *Dr* Perfect.

I don't really like to have Jamie spend too much time with him at family events. Because let's face it, *anyone* would look lazy and shiftless – actually, just a bit crap – in comparison.

'And Grace? Has she come?'

'No, she couldn't get a babysitter,' Mum sighs. 'Such a shame. It would have been so nice to have her here. She's such an *asset*. Lovely Grace.' She casts an eye over my own, non-lovely appearance, and clearly finds it wanting. 'Did you have a look at those diet sheets I emailed you?' she asks, none-too-subtly.

Look, it's not that I'm actually *fat*, OK? Well, not if your definition of 'fat' is, like mine, restricted to people who actually, visibly wobble when they walk. People with stomachs like mounds of jelly, and bottoms like overstuffed Chesterfields. I'm what my mother has always called, with ambiguous intent, 'stocky'. It's just that, what with a combination of my foodie job, my dwarfish stature, and the fact that my metabolism has seemed to go into reverse ever since I passed thirty-two (and rapidly haring round the bend towards thirty-three), I'm 'stockier' than ever.

'No. I didn't. I don't diet, Mum. Diets are bad for you.'

She gives a little laugh, as if I've just said oxygen is bad for you, or that the moon is made of Dolcelatte.

'Not the diets I do, Bella. The Zone, for example. I've lost eight pounds since last month on that!'

If she's lost eight pounds since last month, it's because she's a functioning anorexic with a mortal terror of carbohydrates. But I don't point out the obvious.

'And you'll want to look trim in your bridesmaid's dress, won't you? Especially as you'll be standing next to Grace.'

'Don't worry, Mum. I can always put a paper bag over my head.'

Mum tuts at me in the way she does when our limited tolerance of each other has passed its tipping point. 'Look, why don't you go and help Brian and Dev bring the coffee? I'm sure Dev will want to chat to you about the wedding. And you can tell Brian he can come back down here and buy me one of these perfumes.' She reaches for a bottle of Hypnôse and spritzes a toxic cloud of it in my direction. 'Gorgeous, isn't it? Very elegant. Very Mother of the Bride.'

I locate Brian and Dev only a few moments later, on their way out of Costa Coffee. Brian is juggling a paper Costa Coffee bag, a giant and rather sinister teddy bear with a blood-red loveheart on its tummy (certainly Mum's doing; she's a cuddly-toy nut, and almost no occasion is deemed unsuitable to be blighted by the appearance of one of the wretched things) and a huge bunch of shiny pink and silver helium balloons. Beneath them, Brian's face is rather pink and shiny itself. In fact, he's always been pretty balloon-like from head to toe, and he's expanding even further with age.

Beside him, Dev is carrying the polystyrene tray of coffees. He's nice-looking, rather than good-looking, a million miles from the himbos Polly used to have a tendency to date. He's not as big or as tall as Jamie, but he's a good solid six foot, and rather Clark Kent-like behind his glasses. He's obviously come straight from the hospital because he's in a mid-grey suit and blue shirt that work well with his colouring. (He's only thirty-six but he's already going just the smallest bit grey at the temples, probably because of all the hours he works. But it's a good look on him.)

'Bells!' Brian's already broad face broadens still further into a smile. He speeds up to reach me so he can give me a hug.

I hug him back and try to disentangle him from his cargo. 'What are the balloons for?'

'They were your mother's idea. Look – they spell out "WELCOME HOME POLLY".'

They don't, actually. What they spell at the moment is 'HOELOYMLOPLMEWEC'.

'How are you, Bells?' Dev leans down to give me a kiss on the cheek. He's looking slightly greyer than usual; the stress of moving back to Britain, probably, and buying a house, and all the other crap that comes with relocating.

'I'm fine. Though I could murder a coffee myself.'

'And you must be starving!' Brian shoves the Costa Coffee bag at me. 'Have one of these muffins, please,

Bells. Your mother will be cross that I bought them anyway, and the chocolate one is really rather good . . .'

It's no wonder people always assume Brian is my real dad and not my stepdad. Even if it weren't for our slightly unfortunate physical resemblance, there are other critical things we share in common. Our mutual love of – OK, *obsession with* – food being the most important of them. Brian runs his own teeny-tiny independent publishing company, with a staff of two (and a half, if Mrs Clegg from over the road remembers to come to work on a Tuesday and Wednesday), producing the kind of little gifty cookery books you find in National Trust shops: *Jams, Jellies and Pies*, *Wonderful Ways with Wood Pigeon*, that kind of thing.

'Brian, why don't I take Bella off to get a coffee while you take Marilyn's cappuccino down to her?' Dev suggests. 'I'm sure she's gasping.'

'And she wants you to buy her some perfume,' I warn Brian, who shoots off at the double at the thought of Mum waiting for him, in need of refreshment and gifts, leaving me and Dev to head back in the direction of Costa Coffee.

'Right,' I say, as we sit down at a free table a few moments later, with a latte for me. 'There's nowhere to run now. You absolutely *have* to decide whether you want the sit-down dinner or the luxury buffet.'

He blinks at me from behind his glasses. 'I thought we were just sharing this muffin.'

'For your wedding, Dev! I have two of my caterer

friends on hold, waiting for your answer! And New Year's Eve is an incredibly busy time, you know. You and Polly can't take for ever to make every single decision.'

'Oh. Sorry. Yes, of course.' He breaks off a bit of the muffin and chews it. For a moment he looks so serious that he reminds me of Elvis, our long-deceased Labrador, the only dog in the known universe to suffer an existential crisis every time you threw him a stick. 'Actually, Bella, I wanted to have a bit of a word with you about that.'

'About the caterers?'

'No, about the wedding. In general.'

'Oh?' This doesn't sound good.

'Well, you don't think . . .' he clears his throat, '. . . you don't think Polly is getting cold feet, do you?'

'Why would I think that?'

'Because *I've* been thinking it. Well, I've been wondering. I mean, it's nothing she's *said*, so much as . . . I don't know. She's been so iffy about buying a house. Would hardly even look at any of the details I emailed her, let alone take a weekend to fly over here and look at any of them. I know she's been driving you bananas about not committing to any of the wedding plans. She turned down Grace's offer to come over to New York and help her shop for a wedding dress a few weeks ago . . .'

Irrelevantly – irrationally – I feel a familiar stab of jealousy that Grace was the one who might have ended up helping Polly find her dress, rather than me.

'. . . and every time I've tried to talk about anything that might happen *after* the wedding – you know,' he adds, with the smallest hint of embarrassment, 'starting a family, or anything like that – she doesn't seem to want to talk about it. I mean, I'm probably just being totally ridiculous . . .'

Actually, he's not being *totally* ridiculous. Polly has always had the capacity for faffiness where her personal life is concerned. What about her long-term teenage sweetheart, Olly, dropped like a hot brick the morning of her eighteenth birthday party? Or that intense Swedish boyfriend she had for a while at university – Erik? Yorick? – with whom she was supposed to be travelling round the Far East at the end of her second year? Poor Erik/Yorick, abandoned literally three hours before their flight to Jakarta, on the Piccadilly Line to Heathrow. And seeing as Polly's men seem never to get over being dumped by her, he might still be there, for all I know. Shuttling back and forth for all eternity in self-imposed purgatory between Hammersmith and Hounslow Central.

But this is Dev we're talking about. *Dev*. A man most women would chop off their right arms for. (The fact that Dev would probably be able to reattach the arm, with the minimum of scarring, is an unexpected bonus.) A man who worships the ground Polly walks on. A man she worships right back.

'Dev.' I reach over the muffin crumbs and pat his hand. 'Honestly. There's nothing for you to worry about. You know what Polly's like – planning anything just freaks her out. That's why I offered to take on most of the burden of sorting out the wedding for her.' Well, that, and the fact that, as I've already mentioned, I'm an uptight control freak. 'It's not cold feet, or second thoughts, or anything like that.'

Dev considers this for a moment, head on one side, in his most doctorly manner. 'Well, you do know her better than anyone.'

'Exactly.' I glance down at my watch. 'And I know her flight has just landed, too. We'd better go and wait with Mum and Brian. God forbid there's no one there to witness Mum's performance when Polly comes through the arrivals gate.'

We head for the shops, where Mum has stopped dousing herself in celebrity scent and irritating the staff at The Perfume Shop. She's daubing on nail polish in Boots and irritating the staff there instead. Once she's got the polish she wants, we all head for the arrivals gate and set ourselves up like some kind of battalion of Greenham Common protestors, pressed up against the barrier with the balloons and the sinister teddy bear.

This is where we are when the passengers of BA0178 from Newark to London start disgorging themselves through the swing doors.

And this is where we still are, almost an hour later, when we finally accept that one particular passenger of BA0178 from Newark to London – namely, my sister, Polly – was never on the plane after all.

*

By the time I pull up the van outside my flat, it's long past midnight. There's been a lot of noisy hysteria (Mum), quite a lot more growing anxiety (me, Dev and Brian), and a frankly rather dismissive attitude from Terminal Five's police force, whose main advice – seriously – was to keep trying Polly's mobile phone. As if we hadn't just spent the last hour doing exactly this, and hearing it go straight to voicemail.

I tried a couple of Polly's friends over in New York, who assured me that she'd been alive and apparently well when they'd met her for farewell drinks last night. Dev tried the neighbours in her apartment block, who assured him that they'd seen her getting into a cab with her suitcase, still alive and apparently well, very early this morning. Which of course sent Mum into a fresh paroxysm of hysteria that the cab driver could have raped and murdered her, or that *one of these very neighbours* could have raped and murdered her, and be trying to establish themselves a false alibi.

What with all these hysterics, both Dev and I finally decided it was best to take the second piece of advice from the police and all go back to our respective homes to see if Polly had just made a mistake about where we were meeting her, and headed straight there.

I have to say, I had my doubts. And even though I didn't hold any truck with Mum's hysteria, the chilling rape-and-murder scenario did keep creeping into my head on the drive back into London. Even more so after I'd taken Dev all the way to the new house in Wimbledon (no sign of Polly waiting there) and driven the lonely few miles back to Shepherd's Bush by myself.

Which is why the last person I expect to see, huddled against the cold as she sits on my doorstep, is Polly.

I get out of the van, slam the door with surprising vigour, seeing as my hands have suddenly started to shake with relief, and stride across the pavement towards her.

'Polly Abigail Atkins! Have you *any* idea . . .?'

But then I stop. She's getting up to greet me. And she looks *terrible*.

Let me just assure you that Polly is, under normal circumstances, a knockout. Tall, unlike me, with abundant va-va-voom curves that land her just on the cuddly side of slim enough. Her skin is dusky, her hair falls in enviably shiny waves past her shoulders, and she has the kind of features, irregular and just a little bit too big for her face, that shouldn't make her anywhere near as attractive as they in fact do. She may not have the perfect figure or the cool, serene beauty of her best friend (Gorgeous) Grace, but almost every man I've ever known has gone absolutely ga-ga about Polly. Throw in her penchant for sexy clothing – bum-hugging jeans, little skirts, off-the-shoulder sweaters – and well, you can just take my word for it. A total knockout.

But right now, she's not so much knockout as washout. Her hair is pulled back in a scruffy ponytail, she's wearing the kind of rumpled chinos that are beloved of a certain kind of American traveller, with a baggy grey hoodie and Converse, and even by the streetlight I can see that she's pale, with bags under her eyes.

'I changed my flight,' she's saying. 'I landed at Terminal Three. I'm so sorry, Bella, if you were worried.'

'We were worried sick. But that's not the point.' I stare at her. I would give her a hug, but I'm too angry. 'Why did you get a different flight? Why didn't you let anyone know? Me, or Dev.'

She takes a deep breath, and rests her hand on the handle of the suitcase that's sitting on the step beside her. 'I didn't want to see Dev, Bella. And I don't want to go to the new house. Can I stay here, just for the night, with you?'

'Well, of course you can, but . . . Polly, what's going on? Why don't you want to see Dev? You're marrying the guy in six weeks' time!'

'No, I'm not.' Her voice is wobbly, but clear and determined. 'The wedding isn't going to happen, Bella. I'm calling it off. I'm not going to marry Dev in six weeks' time. I'm not going to marry Dev at all.'

Grace

Wednesday 18 November

As usual, Charlie is up at six. I feel my side of the bed rise a couple of inches as he hauls himself out from under the duvet, and then I hear, through a fog of sleep, that he's started his customary twenty minutes on the elliptical machine. But I must doze off again completely, because the next thing I know, it's almost six thirty, and I can hear him calling to me from our bathroom, above the noise of the shower.

Which is a lot, by the way. The noise of the shower, I mean. Being American, Charlie can't tolerate the weak and weedy water pressure of the average British shower. Or the cramped size. It's just one of those things where they make our efforts look pitiful; that, and fridges. And steaks. Oh, and winning track and field medals at the Olympics.

Sometimes, to hear Charlie go on about all the things that are wrong with this country, you can't help but wonder why he chooses to live and raise his children here at all.

Still, I suppose I can't really complain, because Charlie's hard line on the shower front at least means that I start each day with a truly terrific bathing experience. The plumber's bill might have been frightening, but it's hard to begrudge when you stand in our glorious new walk-in shower, perfectly pressurised jets of steaming water tumbling down onto you, and wonder whether today you might use the space to perform a few yoga stretches, or some slippery jumping-jacks. It's even more super-sized than our American fridge. And that's saying something.

'Grace? Honey? You hear me?'

I push open the bathroom door – it was only half shut – and pull my dressing gown down from the hook on the back of it. 'Sorry?'

'I said, we're almost out of shower gel!'

'Oh, right.' I pull the dressing gown on. It's a skimpy kimono one that I wear as a direct challenge to the huge white towelling monstrosity that also hangs on the back of the door. This (the monstrosity) is the one Charlie's mother gave me three birthdays ago, when I was very pregnant with Hector. It was far too big for me even then, and I think my mother-in-law was secretly disappointed that I didn't balloon to the size of . . . well, the size of an American shower, I suppose. 'It's on the Ocado order for tomorrow.'

'Honey, I don't think that's going to cut it!' Charlie yells through the swirling steam. Ever since he started his new job he has a tendency to speak this way – as though he's trying to offload a million BP shares before the close of the Nikkei, rather than discussing the ins and outs of the weekly Ocado order. 'Can't you stop by the supermarket and pick some more up today? And get the yellow kind, OK? I think it's lemon, something like that!'

'Yes. I'll get the yellow kind.'

'The green one gives me a rash, remember?'

'I remember.'

'It's still pretty sore, actually. It chafes every time I go for a run.'

Charlie's new fitness campaign is another thing that's roughly coincided with the start of his new job. Or maybe just with his turning forty-five before Christmas. It seems that practically everyone at MMA Capital, his new office, is either working out with an expensive personal trainer, or puffing their way miserably towards the London Marathon, and Charlie Costello will not be left behind. Anyway, I suppose I can't really blame Charlie for his desire to join the marathon-running herd. I know how good it is to feel you're fitting in. And how miserable it can be when you don't.

'Yeah, still pretty sore . . .' he carries on, scrubbing under his armpits with the last of the current bottle of shower gel. 'Actually, hon, maybe you could stop by the pharmacy this morning, get me some of that soothing dermatological cream? The one in the white box?'

One time, just once, I'd like Charlie to be the one who trudges round – sorry, *stops by* – the supermarket and the chemist and dry cleaner's and the deli, identifying his prospective purchases solely on the basis of their colour. 'Cereal, yeah, we need cereal, I usually have the cereal in the purple box . . . shirts, yeah, I'm here to pick up shirts, I think they were blue last time I looked at them . . . cheese, yeah, I'd like some cheese, I think we usually have the yellow kind . . .'

'Could you pass me my towel, hon?' Charlie taps on the shower glass to get my attention. 'No, sweetie, not the white one. The white one leaves lint all over my skin. Pass me the blue one next to it.'

Wordlessly, I pass him the correctly colour-coded towel, and then I head back into the bedroom to start making the bed.

I don't need to look over my shoulder to know what Charlie's doing now: sucking in his stomach and then perusing his form in the mirror from various angles, as though he's conducting some kind of alternative police line-up, with himself as both the officer in charge and the only suspect.

'Can you get me a shirt from the closet, hon?' he calls. 'I'm running late.'

'But it's barely six forty . . .'

'I have a breakfast meeting with Saad Amar at seven thirty. And I can hardly be late for the boss, Grace. Let's wait until he at least makes me a partner before I start pissing him off, shall we?'

It's the patronising tone that really gets under my skin, but it's not the time or the place to start up a quarrel about it. Not, let's face it, that it would get me anywhere. Charlie can no more see that he's being patronising than a leopard can see he's looking a bit spotty.

'I know you can't be late for the boss, Charlie,' I say sunnily. 'After all, I may not have a career, but I have *responsibilities*. I have things I can't be late for too!'

'Sure you do, hon.' His tone of voice is the exact same one he used on Hector the other morning at breakfast, when he announced that he thought he might like to be a chicken when he grew up. 'Oh, hey, have you booked the babysitter for tomorrow evening? You haven't forgotten it's the drinks do at work?'

'I haven't forgotten.' How could I possibly forget? He's reminded me almost every day for the past week. MMA will be celebrating some big deal they've just negotiated (to buy a hedge fund, or take over a hedge fund, or maybe *invade* a hedge fund for all I know . . . I'm sketchy on the details because Charlie never really talks to me about his work). 'I've booked Kitty-next-door to babysit.'

'Well done, honey.' He gets down on the floor to add a few dozen sit-ups to his earlier abs routine. 'Oh, by the way, when you make my packed lunch, can you put in some of that low-fat taramasalata for my vegetable sticks? The white kind, not the pink kind,' he calls after me as I head out of the bedroom. 'Thanks, hon. You're a star!'

On days like this, it's a total mystery to me how I ended up here.

The next hour is filled with a blur of hummus, eggs

Benedict (the only thing my newly gastronome older son, Robbie, will eat for breakfast at the moment) and an apparent explosion inside my younger son, Hector's, nappy. Then, before we can leave for school and nursery, there's a good fifteen minutes of chasing Hector around the living room trying to get a fresh nappy on him, followed by a further ten minutes spent turning Robbie's bedroom upside down to try and find his prized Chicago Bulls sticker book. As usual, as we hurtle out of the house at twenty past eight, I feel less like the boys' mother and more like a well-meaning, but essentially clueless au pair.

That said, at least I look the part. You won't find a yummier mummy than me anywhere in West London. I am blonde. I am slim. I religiously wear the designated uniform of designer jeans, Breton-striped tops, and smart-but-practical flat riding boots. I carry a Mulberry Bayswater. I could have stepped off the pages of the latest Boden catalogue – in fact, I can just picture it. Me in a Drapey Jersey Dress and Colourblock Wedges, strolling jauntily along a sunny beach, with that little side-box of cosy personal info printed a few inches above my head. 'Grace: Favourite Hallowe'en outfit – a sexy witch. Best way to spend a Sunday morning – tea and toast in bed with the supplements; Childhood ambition – artist.'

Childhood ambition absolutely, categorically *not* 'stay-at-home mother of such poor quality that actually more like well-meaning, but essentially clueless au pair'.

Look, it's not that I don't realise how lucky I am. I know plenty of people who would kill for my life; at least the way it looks on the outside. Certainly I know people who'd kill for my two beautiful children. And obviously I adore my boys with every fibre and sinew of my being. I mean, look at them: a couple of blond angels (well, one angel and Hector) that somehow I've managed to bring into the world and keep breathing ever since. How I've achieved this miracle is a mystery to me, but the proof of the pudding is in the eating, I suppose. I *do* have two healthy, happy boys, who aren't (yet, at least) showing any signs of maternal neglect or deep-rooted dysfunction. Accidentally, it appears, I must be doing something right.

But when I take my eyes off Robbie and Hector, and just think for a moment about the rest of my life, it's very, very far from the childhood ambitions I entertained.

And it's starting to show, because I'm just plain *wrong* in the world I'm living in. I mean, I'm twenty-eight years old with a social circle entirely limited to over-forties. I'm a stay-at-home mother who still can't make a proper shepherd's pie. I'm not so much *I Don't Know How She Does It* as *Why Does She Even Bother?*

It's all very well doing the school run in my Breton-striped finest, but at the end of the day, I'm not really fooling anyone.

It's a fifteen-minute brisk walk – very brisk, through the biting November wind – to Hector's nursery, Tiny

Tots, and then a further couple of minutes along the Fulham Road to St Martin's, Robbie's school.

We're amongst the last to arrive, as we are pretty much every morning, the on-duty teacher flapping frantic arms at us to get a move on, otherwise the main gates will be closed, and we'll have to ring the side bell and get the caretaker to let us in. Unlike me, the other stragglers tend to be the working mothers, who have my unending, uncomprehending admiration for the way they can get themselves and their children out of the front door every morning at all. Especially since the St Martin's working mothers tend to have such impressively high-powered careers, the kind that require them to dress up in whip-smart suits and stalky-about heels, with neat, groomed hair and the kind of 'minimal' makeup that takes a good twenty minutes, and a full set of Shu Uemura brushes, to apply.

There's one working mother in particular who always catches my eye, though, and as usual she's here this morning, depositing her daughter before jumping, at speed, into the nearest passing taxi. Louboutin Lexie, I call her, because I know her name is Lexie, and because she's always, but *always*, wearing the most incredible Louboutin heels. Though she's just as minutely groomed as the other working mothers, this is where the similarity ends. Because Louboutin Lexie doesn't pair her Louboutins with a power suit, no matter how elegant. Louboutin Lexie is rock 'n' roll. Louboutin Lexie wears skintight cigarette pants and fabulous cropped jackets, cool printed tees and leather miniskirts. She spurns Mulberry's entire handbag output in favour of absurdly impractical oversized clutches, or animal-print totes. She works – and this is only my imaginings, you understand – in some chic little art gallery somewhere in Soho or Shoreditch, selling incomprehensible art installations by Young British Artists, and pieces of graffiti by Banksy. And at the weekends, she hangs out with her equally fabulous friends – in hip little bars on Saturday nights, and in great big noisy family groups at the River Café on Sundays.

I know I sound just a little bit obsessed. But I want . . . I sort of want to *be* this woman. I actually think I *should* have been this woman. Louboutin Lexie is who I was supposed to be, I'm quite sure, from the art gallery career and the multitude of friends to the stunning wardrobe with the covetable accessories. I mean, I went to art school to do a Fine Art degree, and I was good at it too, until I dropped out at the start of my third year to marry Charlie. I used to have a multitude of friends, until they all began to fall by the wayside when I skipped ahead an entire generation and got pregnant with Robbie only a month after my twenty-first birthday. As for the stunning wardrobe and the covetable accessories . . . well, OK, I'm not sure I was ever anywhere close to Louboutin Lexie's exalted level.

But maybe I *would* have been, if I hadn't married a man who practically has a heart attack every time I attempt to deviate from middle-aged yummy-mummy-style territory. Who made a fuss when I turned up to a colleague's promotion dinner in a pair of bright red patent platforms. Who split his sides laughing the (admittedly ill-fated) day I attempted to rock a pair of harem pants (I'd seen Jessica Biel looking fabulous in a pair in *Grazia* magazine, and as it happens, she's one year older and a full dress size larger than I am).

I give Robbie his usual hug and kiss-on-the-tip-of-the-nose, and after he's gone through the gates, I turn round and start heading back along Fulham Road.

I'm not quite brave enough to venture to a table-for-one at Café on the Green, where all the other (non-working) mothers hang out, but I'm damned if I'm not going to at least get a takeaway coffee before *stopping by* the supermarket in search of Charlie's yellow shower gel. Pathetic but true – a smile and a friendly word with the nice Croatian girl who makes the café's delicious cappuccino is probably going to be the highlight of my week.

Actually, that's a bit unfair. Though usually that would be true, this week I do have another, much better highlight. My best friend, Polly, is getting back from New York, where she's been living for the last six years.

Actually, she'll have got back last night – I wanted to go to the airport to meet her, but I couldn't get a babysitter and Charlie had to work late. Anyway, she's getting married on New Year's Eve – Christ, that reminds me, I really have to speak to her scary sister,

Bella, about picking out our bridesmaids' dresses – and moving into a lovely house in leafy Wimbledon with her even lovelier fiancé, Dev, so the next few weeks will hopefully be a happy blur of picking out her wedding dress and helping her with trips to John Lewis to choose carpets and curtains . . . Though to be honest, I don't even need to do those things with Polly. Just having her back home again, being able to meet for a coffee in her lunch-hour, have a bit of a mooch around Selfridges, or just hang out and do nothing together . . . well, it's the thing that's been keeping my head above water for the last few months.

I mean, even if I hadn't missed Polly as much as I actually have, having her home again is going to be a massive improvement on my current lonely situation.

Two minutes from Café on the Green, I'm surprised by the sight of someone waving at me from a row of parked Range Rovers. I realise with a sinking heart that it's a Miranda.

Miranda, by the way, is the catch-all name for the kind of professional mummy I'm impersonating. It was a (rare) joke of Charlie's to begin with: a year ago, when we first attended a St Martin's open day, we were descended upon by, it seemed, no fewer than a dozen mothers called Miranda. They all had children called ridiculous things like Artemis and Ophelia, and they all wanted to know which other schools we were applying to, and whether or not our son was already reading chapter books, and were we thinking of having him join the after-school French club or was he more of a pottery and painting kind of boy . . . ?

Even though it's pretty obvious now that not all of them are called Miranda, Charlie's joke has stuck.

Though actually, this one – the one climbing out of her Range Rover, over-excited Labradoodle in tow – really *is* called Miranda. *Chief* Miranda, I call her in my head, because she's one of those queen-bee, Alpha women, rather like Charlie's ex-wife, Vanessa. In fact, she happens to be close friends with Charlie's ex-wife, Vanessa, as they live next door to each other in one of the swankiest streets in this area.

It doesn't make for the easiest of relations between us, that's for certain. But still – and rather pathetically – I want her to approve of me. Chief Miranda is one of the linchpins of society at St Martin's, whereas my role in said society is . . . well, I'm just not exactly the prom queen round here, that's all. While being a leggy twenty-something blonde might stand me in pretty good stead if I had a fabulous job like Louboutin Lexie's, or if I fancied hanging out at some kind of mechanics' garage all day, like the woman in the 'Uptown Girl' video, it's a definite drawback in terms of getting 'in' with the Mirandas. While they all look totally fabulous for women in their early forties, they are, unavoidably, women in their early forties. And even though it's not like I'm stupid enough to come and stand at the school gates in a micro-mini with a sign painted on my unlined forehead saying 'And All This Without Botox!', I'm still practically a gymslip mother around here. It's not winning me too many allies.

Then, of course, there's the fact that I'm a lot more shy than anyone ever gives me credit for. Bad at small talk. Nervous with chat.

Oh, and then there's the third thing, probably the most important thing, that's working against me: I'm She Who Must Not Be Named. I'm a second, younger wife.

The thing is that even though everyone who matters knows that Charlie's marriage to Vanessa was over before he made a move on me, I'm not stupid. I can see how it looks. I was their son's babysitter, for goodness' sake. It was a great way to make extra money when Polly and I first came to London together – me to art school, she to university – and even though I was scared witless of Vanessa, she and Charlie quickly became my most frequent clients. But – as I was forced to swear to my extremely old-fashioned, uptight parents before they'd even agree to meet Charlie – he and Vanessa had been sleeping in separate rooms for months before he went to kiss me, as he drove me home after babysitting one night. And he'd moved out and hired a divorce lawyer before I finally reciprocated.

I suppose I'm pretty old-fashioned too. And I'm certainly not a home-wrecker. But like I say, I can see how it looks.

'Grace Costello! Just the woman I wanted to see!' Chief Miranda says. She nods in the direction of Café on the Green. 'On your way for a coffee with some of the others?'

'Um . . .'

'Excellent. I'll come with you. Would you take Jasper for a moment, please, while I get my bag?'

'Jasper?'

She shoves the Labradoodle's lead at me, which I take, only for Jasper immediately to bury his nose deep into my crotch and start whimpering excitedly.

Well, it's nice to know *someone* round here likes me.

'Actually, I've been meaning to have a word with you for a little while,' Miranda says, taking back Jasper's lead as we start on our way towards the café. 'Your husband . . . Charlie, isn't it?'

She knows full well that it's Charlie. She knew him when he and Vanessa were still married, long before I, Shameless Grace the Husband-Snatcher, came onto the scene.

'Yes, it's Charlie.'

'He works for the Amar family, doesn't he? The owners of MMA Capital? Since he was made redundant from Farrell Christie Dench, I mean. Or maybe I shouldn't say "made redundant". I mean, it was more like being managed out, wasn't it? Because he was pushing forty-five, and they were never going to make him a partner?'

Amazing that, despite being apparently unable to remember Charlie's name, Miranda nevertheless has an extensive – and scarily accurate – knowledge of his recent employment history. Thanks, I have no doubt, to Vanessa.

'Anyway,' she carries on, 'we on the fund-raising committee have recently got wind of a very interesting rumour about Saad Amar – you know, the eldest son, the one in charge at MMA – and I thought you might be just the person to help us out.' She starts tying Jasper up outside the café, an agonisingly long process. 'Louisa McCormack – do you know her? – she's my vice-chair on the fund-raising committee, and she works with a family friend of the Amars at Goldman Sachs . . .'

I have the time, briefly, to feel deeply inadequate in comparison with Louisa McCormack – a top-ranked Miranda who manages to hold down a high-flying job *and* take a leading role in the all-important St Martin's fund-raising committee. Oh, and no doubt make a cracking shepherd's pie, too.

'. . . and she's heard that this Saad guy is looking at schools in London for his youngest brother. Ahmed? Mohammed?' She flaps a hand, as if dismissing silent accusations of institutional racial prejudice that might be coming from either myself or, perhaps, from Jasper. 'I don't remember the details. But Louisa says that St Martin's is absolutely *definitely* in the frame!'

I really have no idea how I'm supposed to react to this. 'Right. Um. Well, that's. Um. Great?'

'Grace, don't be thick!' She pulls the door to the café open, and marches through without holding it open for me. 'Don't you realise what an amazing coup it would be for St Martin's to have little Ahmed Amar as a pupil? When you *think* of the kind of welly the Amars could put into the fund-raising for the new science block, or the expansion to the art department . . . I mean, they're *billionaires*, you know!'

I cringe inwardly as my nice Croatian waitress comes up to lead us to a table, and gives Chief Miranda an astonished stare.

You know, it's a pity I can't come and sit at a table here every morning, because it's one of the nicest café's I've ever known, with squashy sofas and the newspapers all along one wall, for people who are just having coffee, and cute little wrought-iron tables for people who are having their delicious-looking brunch dishes. At this time of the morning, though, the wrought-iron tables are full to bursting with mere coffee-drinkers – the Mirandas, who are regarding me now with their usual polite but frosty suspicion as I take my seat amongst them. There's a lot of chat about upcoming Christmas holiday plans that I don't feel quite able to join in with – most of their kids seem to have been enrolled in judo camp, or performing arts courses, so I think it's unlikely the Mirandas will be impressed with my intentions to build a den in the spare room and keep the boys supplied up there with a constant stream of sugary snacks – until Chief Miranda finally turns back to restart her conversation with me.

'Honestly, the last thing we want is the Amars deciding to send little Mohammed to St Thomas's, or

Arnold House. As if either of those needs the kind of financial boost we do! So if there's any way you could get your husband to bring any influence to bear . . . well, it goes without saying how grateful we'd be. And there'd certainly be a place on the fund-raising committee in it for you, if you wanted?'

I realise, in this instant, that yes, I *do* want a place on the fund-raising committee. I want the Mirandas to include me. I'm being allowed to peek through this tiny chink in the doorway into their world, and the sight of it is whetting my appetite for more. Not just a position on the fund-raising committee, but inclusion in one of the Mirandas' book groups, or an invitation to the Sports Day committee lunch . . .

And Charlie would like it if I were more involved at St Martin's. He's told me so often enough.

I furnish Chief Miranda with my brightest, most can-do smile. 'Well, of course I'll ask Charlie to see what he can do. Or maybe I could approach Mr Amar himself. We do have a company drinks party at MMA tomorrow evening,' I add, only slightly inwardly cringing at how Stepford Wife-y this makes me sound, and secretly hoping Chief Miranda will be rather impressed.

'Oh God, no, Grace, don't do that.' Miranda either doesn't realise, or doesn't care, about her astonishing bluntness. 'You don't know how to talk to these kind of people. I mean, you've never *worked* with people like that. Or am I wrong? I thought Vanessa told me you'd never really had a proper job.'

I can feel my cheeks start to tingle with embarrassment. 'Right. Of course.'

'Golly, Grace, don't take offence! It's not a *criticism*. I'm sure you *would* have had a terribly interesting career, if you hadn't married and had children so young.' She sips her coffee, enjoying this. And, I'm sure, taking as many mental pictures as possible so she can re-enjoy it with Vanessa on a later occasion.

Only a few minutes into my excursion into Miranda-land, and I'm already starting to wonder if I should return my visa and flee for the border. But I'm not going to let her put me off that easily.

I plaster a pleasant smile over my burning face. 'Well, it's been really nice having coffee with you, Miranda,' I say, starting to gather my things and get to my feet. 'I'll get Charlie to do what he can.'

'Oh, you're leaving already?'

'I'm afraid so. My best friend has just got back from New York, and she's getting married at New Year, so I've tons of arrangements to help her with. And I've a million things to do in the house,' I say, brilliantly making it sound as though I'm due to spend all day gainfully employed at the organic vegetable patch and Rayburn stove, rustling up tasty shepherd's pies by the half-dozen.

Well, maybe not that brilliantly. Miranda doesn't look all that convinced.

'So you'll get back to me about the Abdel Amar matter?'

'I'll get back to you about the . . . er . . . Amar matter. Bye, Miranda!'

As I leave, I can see through the side window that she's already upped and joined the Mirandas at the table next to ours, and I can tell from the angle of their heads and the light in their eyes that they're talking about me. No matter how hard I try, I know I'll always be a tourist in Miranda-land.

Ten minutes later and I'm on my way to the supermarket, in pursuit of yellow shower gel, when my mobile rings.

BELLA, the screen flashes at me.

It's Polly's sister. The one I'm supposed to have called about the bridesmaids' dresses.

'Bella!' I say, with as much jollity in my voice as I can possibly muster.

Look, it's not that I don't *like* Bella. It's just that she's incredibly hard work. And that no matter how much hard work I do put in with her, she never really seems to give anything back. I think she's always been jealous of my closeness to Polly. Either that or she's just one of those people who mistake my particular brand of shyness for stand-offishness instead.

'I'm so sorry,' I carry on, 'I've been meaning to call you for the past couple of weeks! But I've been so busy . . .'

'Right. With the school run and stuff.'

After Charlie's casual dismissal of me already this morning, not to mention Chief Miranda's open disdain, I can feel myself bristle for the third time today. This is one of my other problems with Bella. Rather, one of the other problems I think Bella has with me. She's concluded (entirely inaccurately, as it happens) that Charlie is loaded, therefore I must exist in a world of manicures, blow-dries, and sprees at Harvey Nichols. As if I'd actually *want* to live in a world of manicures, blow-dries and sprees at Harvey Nichols. Because to be honest, from where I'm standing, Bella is the one with the great-looking life. She runs her own small catering business, which is something I'd give my eyeteeth to do. I mean, not the catering part, obviously, not with my failings in the shepherd's pie department. But running my own small business. A little art shop, actually, is what I sometimes dream of, selling artists' supplies, and gifty prints and cards . . . and maybe bits and bobs of pretty jewellery, if I could find a local designer . . . even the occasional watercolour by yours truly, if I could pluck up the courage to start painting again . . .

Bella doesn't know how lucky she is, that's all.

'Actually, Bella, I have a little bit more to do with my day than the school run!' I say; and promptly panic that she's going to ask me exactly what this is. I do realise how unimpressive my day of coffee shop, supermarket, and ironing in front of *This Morning* will sound to her. 'Now, we need to have a chat, don't we, about these bridesmaids' dresses?'

'Yes, well, it's too late for that now.'

This is typical Bella Atkins. She could be making a

joke. She could be having a dig. You're just not quite sure.

I give a weak laugh, to cover my bases. 'Well, anyway, I really am sorry. Perhaps we could find time for a coffee, have a chat about colours and things? I mean, obviously we might want rather different styles, because we're such different shapes . . .' I realise, too late, that this sounds as though I'm saying that Bella is fat. Which she isn't, as it happens. She's just an entirely different shape from me. 'I've seen some pretty dove-grey ones in Coast,' I go on hastily, 'that I'm sure Polly would like. Actually, I'm sure she'd be pretty relaxed about whatever we choose.'

Bella lets out a snort. 'Oh, yes. *Really* relaxed.'

There we are again. A joke? A dig? Who can tell? 'Um, I could give her a call later, maybe, to see what she thinks? I assume she got in OK to Heathrow last night? I just wanted to give her a chance to sleep off the jet-l –'

'So she hasn't said anything to you, then?'

'Anything about what?'

'About calling off the wedding. About leaving Dev.'

I stop dead, right outside the swing doors of Sainsbury's. 'You're kidding me.'

'I'm not.'

'But . . . I don't understand . . .' I step out of the way of an irate woman with a pushchair, into the path of an even more irate man on a mobility scooter. 'This is kind of out of the blue, isn't it?' I carry on, when I've stopped apologising. 'I was talking to her about her wedding dress only a few weeks ago! I mean, not that she seemed all that keen to discuss it, but . . . I thought that was just Polly. Being Polly.'

'Well, it isn't.'

'Oh my God, I should phone her. Try to find out what's happened . . .'

'She won't tell you.' Bella's tone is defensive. 'She told me last night that she won't talk about it. I just wondered if she'd given you any hints that anything was wrong.'

'No, nothing . . .'

'All right. Well, that was all I wanted to know. I won't keep you, then. Bye, Grace. I'll tell Polly you'll call her.'

'But wait! Where is she?'

'She's with me, of course.'

And Bella hangs up.

Bella

Wednesday 18 November

I shouldn't have bothered phoning Grace just now. I should have known she'd only find a way to get right up my nose. This time it was the tiniest but most ruthless of comments about my weight, and how I'd never manage to wear the same style of bridesmaid's dress as her. To be entirely fair to her, I'm not absolutely certain she meant it to be quite as brutal as it sounds. But then that's Grace all over. Inadvertently, but quite definitely, making me feel like the knockabout Labrador puppy to her sleek Italian greyhound.

The thing is, I'm not a jealous person in general, but there's just something about Grace that makes my stomach lurch with envy. And it's always something new. When she first befriended Polly, it was her closeness to my precious little sister that made me a bit green. As she got older and blossomed into a perfect blonde princess . . . well, I'm only human. Grace's looks would get anybody's goat. The rich husband never really bothered me – not after the deeply unflattering things I've heard from Polly about him – but because of putting up with him, of course, she got the top prize. The treasure at the end of the rainbow. She got children.

Anyway, there's no earthly point in being jealous. Jealousy is counterproductive. And it saps energy, which is something I'm going to need a lot of in the coming days. I mean, if Polly really is serious about cancelling this wedding, there are a hell of a lot of phone calls to make: to the marquee hire place, to the jazz trio, to the on-hold caterers, to tell them they needn't be on hold any more . . . to a hundred and thirty guests . . .

To Dev. Who, I assume, she hasn't told yet. And who, I also assume, is going to be devastated.

Bloody *hell*, Polly. What on earth are you playing at?

You know, maybe it's a good idea for me to cook her up a nice fortifying breakfast. And then take it into the guest room, perch on the edge of her bed, and, what with the distraction of the food and a nice cup of tea, just ask one or two oh-so-casual questions about what's been going on . . . not *pry*, or anything . . .

A few minutes later, I'm already starting to feel less agitated. Because I absolutely love my kitchen. I love it at all times, but especially at this hour of the morning, with the late autumn sunlight streaming in through the big windows, and my ancient Roberts radio burbling away in the background (and before Jamie's had a chance to go in and muck the place up).

It's not just *my* kitchen, to be fair. It's any kitchen. Cooking – any time, anywhere – always calms me down, whether it's a simple breakfast like the one I'm rustling up at the moment, or a full-blown dinner party for sixteen I'm preparing in the kitchen of one of my clients. I know there are some cooks – chefs, mostly; men, practically always – who feel compelled to do a lot of pan-banging and swearing. But for me, there's nothing more soothing than calmly, quietly, preparing a meal. It's Brian's doing. He's the most unruffled cook in the world, and he's the one who taught me, pretty much from the day Mum married him, when I was three years old. Until then, the only foods I could even identify were either breadcrumbed in violent shades of orange or deep-frozen (or both), so it was both a shock and a pleasure to realise that there were other things to eat out there too. Deep-dish lasagnes, made in the traditional (British) way with heaps of dried oregano and sweet tomato purée. Thick, comforting stews of beef and lamb, served with dreamy mashed potatoes and buttery peas from Brian's own vegetable garden. More soups than you could shake a stick at, from recipes that I've never bettered and still use myself to this day, from a velvety Jerusalem artichoke to a truly moreish minestrone.

But this morning, it's Brian's patented perfect scrambled eggs I'm re-creating, adding just a dash of double cream and a smidgen of Tabasco to the mix. Then I pile the fluffy, barely set eggs onto a piece of crunchy toast, load up a tray with the food and a pot of properly made Darjeeling, and take it to the guest bedroom.

Thanks to the tray, I've no hands free, so I 'knock' on the door with the toe of my shoe; then, when there's no answer, I decide to go in anyway. Well, it's gone half-past nine, and Polly will want to get onto British time as soon as possible, won't she? Besides, it's my flat, my rules.

But when I go in, she's already awake and sitting up in bed. Her mile-long legs are crossed beneath her, her computer balanced on her knees.

She slams her laptop shut as though we're both characters in a spy movie and I've just caught her hacking into the Pentagon's mainframe.

'Bel-la! Privacy!'

'I knocked,' I say briskly. 'Anyway, I've brought you breakfast.'

'I can see that.' She eyes the tray with the expression of someone who's about to say something annoying like, *Couldn't I just have a piece of toast, or something*? 'Couldn't I just have a piece of toast, or something?'

'You need to keep your strength up.'

'Bella, I've called off a wedding, not been stricken with a major illness.'

'Oh, you have, have you?' I say, trying not to hop for joy that she was the first one to mention the wedding, not me, and so that therefore I can legitimately mention it without being accused of *prying*. 'You've called off all the arrangements, and told Mum and Brian, and contacted all the guests?'

'Well, no, not yet, but I was hoping you –'

'And you've told Dev, have you, that you're safely back in England, but that you have no intention of marrying him?'

Polly says nothing. Then, wordlessly, she reaches out her hands for the tray. She starts shovelling down the scrambled eggs as if she hasn't eaten for a week.

'As a matter of fact, I called Dev last night,' I tell her. 'Just to tell him you'd made a mistake with your flight and you were safe with me. I didn't mention anything about . . . well, anything else. But I'm pretty sure he'll work it out,' I add, as her phone suddenly starts to trill on the bedside table, 'when you keep ignoring his calls.'

'That wasn't Dev,' Polly mumbles, glancing at her phone. 'Not that time, anyway. That was Grace.'

I can't help the tiny stab of triumph I feel that Polly doesn't seem to want to talk to Grace at the moment.

'Of course,' I say craftily, 'you wouldn't have to make any of these awkward calls, least of all the one to Dev, if you'd just rethink this whole notion of calling off the wedding.'

'It's not a notion.'

'But it just seems so sudden!' It's a rerun of the conversation we had – or rather, I *tried* to have – last night. 'And so unnecessary! I mean, unless Dev's been cheating on you, or been cruel to you . . .'

'He hasn't. Of course he hasn't.'

' . . . then there's no earthly reason why you need to make such a dramatic decision. I mean, he loves you so much, Polly!'

'Well, I don't love him.'

What? Well, this is further than we got last night.

'You . . . don't love him?'

'No.'

'But you used to love him.'

'Yes.'

'So, what, you just . . . stopped?'

'Yes.' She isn't meeting my eye. She's fiddling with the vintage gold locket she always wears around her neck. She calls it her 'Bella locket', in the same way that I call the one I always wear my 'Polly locket'; they're a matching pair that belonged to Brian's mother and aunt. 'I just stopped.'

'But you can't just –'

'And I don't want to hear about how perfect he is, OK? About how kind and clever and funny and handsome and generous he is. Or what a perfect couple we make,' she adds, rather more venomously. 'In fact, I don't want to hear anything about any of it. I mean, it, Bella. All I want to do is get on with my life. Find a new job, and somewhere to live.'

'But you *have* somewhere to live,' I say, unable to keep the despairing note out of my voice. 'You have a beautiful new house in Wimbledon!'

'Bella, stop it!' she snaps.

Which sounds quite peculiar. Because Polly doesn't snap. Polly is good humour personified, in pretty much any given circumstance. Polly was the one who, when I was stuck in a dismal hospital ward for weeks after I had a horrible car accident ten years ago, used to breeze in with a bright, broad smile and, after only a few minutes, have me (multiple crush injuries) and my ward-mates (ruptured spleens, punctured lungs, acute kidney failure) laughing at her jokes and feeling – temporarily – fabulous again.

She takes a deep breath. 'Look. I'm sorry. But I'm not going to marry Dev. So I'm not going to live in the house in Wimbledon.'

'Well, where *are* you going to live, then?' I demand. I'm sort of hoping that once she starts having to figure out this kind of practical concern, not just about cancelling the wedding but about what she's going to do with the rest of her life, her essential faffiness might kick in and she'll change her mind. 'I mean, obviously you can stay here as long as you need, but nice flats are hard to come by –'

'I've already sorted a flat, actually. Well, I know one that's available. My friend Lauren, back in New York, her cousin is staying with her over there while he does some kind of internship, and he's leaving his flat in Clapham completely empty for three months. I just need to call Lauren and ask if I can rent it from him.'

Wait, this isn't faffiness. This sounds positively single-minded.

'But you'll need a job, a.s.a.p., to pay the rent, and good jobs are hard to come by.' I'm hoping I'll have more success with the 'hard to come by' line this time. Besides, good jobs in Polly's field – she's worked in PR for the past few years, mostly for publishing companies – *are* hard to come by.

'I'll find something. Even if it's just on reception somewhere.'

I'm about to point out that this is not only a massively retrograde step, but that actually, she'll have a hard time getting something on any decent reception if she doesn't start brushing her hair again, and putting on decent clothes, when suddenly there's a knock at the open door.

'Morning, ladies,' says Jamie.

Well, talking of not brushing your hair, or putting on decent clothes . . .

It's not exactly surprising that he looks such a mess, given that he didn't get in from the pub until almost three this morning, and that he's only just woken up. Still, he grins his devastating grin, and waves in Polly's direction.

'Welcome home, Dood,' he says, using the childhood nickname (short for Polly-Wolly-*Dood*le), which I still occasionally call her.

'Don't call me that,' Polly says, grumpily resistant, as ever, to his charm. It's nothing personal. It's just her way of protecting me. Besides, compared to the special hatred she still reserves for my Evil Ex, Christian, she's positively giddy about Jamie. 'Late night?' she adds pointedly.

'Just a bit.' Jamie looks sheepishly in my direction. 'I'm really sorry, Bells. Did I wake you when I came in?'

'No. I was out like a light.' It's a tiny fib. Actually, a hearing-impaired sloth couldn't have slept through

Jamie's clattering and banging. Or the mumbled choruses of 'Glory Glory Man United'. 'There are still some scrambled eggs in the pan, if you want some,' I tell him, keen to get him to move along so I can finish this conversation with Polly.

But he waves a hand at me. 'Thanks, babe. But I'm getting dressed and heading straight out.'

'To work?' Polly asks, even more pointedly than before.

'No, to East Sheen. Or was it West Hampstead? Or South Norwood?' Jamie scratches his head, thinking. 'I met a guy in the pub last night who can get me a ticket for the United–Chelsea game on Saturday afternoon. I've got to go round to his place and pick it up.'

'OK, but don't forget we have that meeting with Samantha on Saturday morning,' I say, lightly. 'Still, you probably won't need to leave here until about one thirty, will you?'

'No, no, babe, the game's in Manchester. I'll have to leave here at nine in the morning. Latest.'

OK. I know Polly's opinion of Jamie is shaky at the best of times, so I really shouldn't have her privy to this conversation, but I can't help myself.

'Jamie, you can't. I mean, you just can't. Samantha is coming at eleven.'

'Remind me again who Samantha is?'

I take a very, very deep breath. Count very, very slowly to five. 'The . . . adoption . . . social . . . worker.'

'Ohhhhhh. Course.' Jamie grimaces. 'Well, I'm

really sorry, babe, but it's a huge game. Can you hold the fort by yourself for this one? And I'll make absolutely dead certain I'm there for the next one.'

I don't say anything. I can feel Polly eyeballing me.

'Anyway, it's probably better, isn't it, if you handle her yourself at first? Do all the impressing without me there to muck things up!'

What can I say? I don't want to kick up any more of a fuss about this, not with Polly here to witness it. 'You're probably right. OK. Go to the game.'

'You're the best, Bells!' He leans through the door and drops a kiss on the top of my head. 'Isn't she the best, Dood?'

'Yes, Jamie. She is.'

'Right. Well, I'm off to South Norwood. Or – Christ – was it East Finchley? Shit. I'd better call this guy and find out. I'll see you ladies later.'

'Don't look at me like that,' I tell Polly, as Jamie slopes away.

'I'm not looking at you like anything.' Polly puts the empty breakfast tray on the bedside table, then gets out of bed and starts to rummage in her still-packed suitcase for her washbag. Then after a moment or two of rummaging, she says, 'I don't know, Bella. I don't understand.'

I don't ask her what she means – I'm just assuming it's not washbag-related – but as she starts making her way to the bathroom, she turns back to tell me anyway.

'I mean, you won't take even the slightest amount of

shit from anyone else in your life. But you seem perfectly happy to stand under an entire torrent of it when it comes to Jamie.'

Jamie has gone (to South Kensington, it eventually turned out) and Polly is still in the shower when my front doorbell rings.

It's my friend Anna. We have work to do, finalising the menu for a regular client's anniversary dinner party on Saturday, so I've been expecting her.

But I'm not expecting her to be red-eyed and sniffly when I open the door.

'Vile Debbie just phoned,' is all she says. 'She's pregnant. Again.'

'Oh, *Anna*.'

'I hate her, by the way,' she adds, and bursts into tears.

Vile Debbie is Anna's sister-in-law, and to be entirely fair to her, there's no independent, peer-reviewed evidence to confirm that she's *actually* vile. I've never met the woman. She may well be a delight. But there's one thing she certainly is, and that's super-fertile. She has three – three! – children already, and now, apparently, another on the way. Whilst Anna, who's been trying to conceive, with ever-increasing zeal, since the day she got married ten months ago, is still showing no signs of managing to cobble together so much as one.

'I hung the phone up when she told me.' She's sobbing now, as I lead her gently towards the kitchen, making as many different soothing noises as I know how. 'I couldn't help it, Bella! So now Pete's *furious* with me, of course.'

'Of course,' I say, even though I can't imagine Anna's husband, Pete (or Poor Pete, as we both often call him), being furious with her about anything. Mild disapproval is all I think he's capable of. And certainly all that Anna permits.

'And it's not even like we can *afford* to have a big row about it, because my cervical mucus is thick and stretchy and we need to have truckloads of sex for the next few days.'

There aren't many things I won't do for Anna, but I'm afraid I draw the line at an in-depth discussion of her cervical mucus. Besides, it's a slippery slope (no pun intended, I *swear*). Anna has lost any boundaries she might once have had on such matters, so give her an inch (of chat about cervical mucus), and before you know it, she's taken a mile (of endless agonising about the quality and quantity of Poor Pete's sperm). She pulled this particular trick over the birthday supper I hosted for her back in October, and in the end her mother had to take her gently aside and tell her that she was putting everyone off their vanilla-bean pannacotta.

'You know,' I say, sitting her down at the table and popping the kettle on, 'you just have to try to relax about all this, Anna. You know what the doctor told you. That chilling out and having proper, relaxed, *passionate* sex is the best way to conceive.'

'Yes, well. I don't feel very passionate right now,' she sniffs. 'I'm too angry. With Debbie. With Pete. With myself. With *everything*.'

'OK, so why not try to turn some of that anger into passion!' I say, and then regret it as soon as I realise it made me sound exactly like one of those bouffy-haired, rictus-grinning 'doctors' who pop up to plug their self-help books on American daily talk shows. Because the point is that I know – I really know – how Anna feels. It may be ten years since my car accident, but I can still remember the particular taste of the toxic bile that would well in my mouth every time I'd hear the pregnancy news of an old friend, or a former colleague, or even, for God's sake, a Hollywood celebrity. There's a branch of WH Smith in Victoria Station that I can never go into again, thanks to the meltdown I had at seeing Angelina Jolie's face beaming smugly out at me from the cover of *Grazia* after the accidental announcement that she was expecting not just one genetically blessed baby, but two. I mean, for heaven's sake, doesn't the woman already have enough good fortune? Would it kill the powers that be to share some of it around a little bit more?

Anyway, WH Smith meltdowns aside, at least I've long had the luxury, strange though it may seem, of certainty. Poor Anna has her hopes raised and her dreams shattered every single month.

'Look,' I go on, sitting down opposite her and passing her a piece of kitchen paper to blow her nose on, 'what I mean is, there's honestly nothing to be gained from sitting around hating Vile Debbie, and everything to be gained from remembering why it is you want to have a baby in the first place.'

Anna blows her nose. 'Why is it?'

'Because you love Poor Pete,' I tell her. 'You fancy Poor Pete. You married Poor Pete because you didn't want to spend a day of your life without him, or a single night apart. Now, if you can't go home tonight and have proper, recently married, rattling-the-headboard sex with your husband, then –'

'Polly!' Anna interrupts me, jumping to her feet to greet my sister, who's just come into the kitchen.

Well. It's nice that Anna is fond of Polly, but I wouldn't have minded a *fraction* more appreciative consideration of my words of wisdom.

It makes me a bit envious, watching them hug and laugh, that I can't find that kind of ease with Polly's friends. It's not only Grace I feel intimidated by. Polly's friends have always managed to make me feel like the last prize in the jumble sale tombola.

'How was your flight? Do you miss New York already? How's Dev?' Anna is demanding, in her usual scattergun way.

'Oh, I'm sure Bella will fill you in on all that.' Polly expertly dodges the awkward questions. 'Anyway, I'd love to stay and chat, but I've got a lot of important stuff to sort out . . .'

'Yes. A lot.' I shoot her a Look. 'Are you going to go and see Dev this morning?'

She avoids the Look. Like awkward-question-dodging, it's a technique she's perfected over the years. 'No. But I'll call him and tell him I'll meet him for dinner.'

This, at least, is something. And maybe they'll go to a cosy, romantic restaurant, and their eyes will lock over a candlelit table, and Polly will realise what a silly mistake she's making . . .

'I'll hold off making those calls for the day, then, shall I?' I say.

Polly shoots me a Look of her own as she turns to leave the kitchen. She bangs the front door slightly too loudly behind her.

'What was all *that* about?' Anna hisses. 'Bride drama?'

'In a manner of speaking. Seeing as the most dramatic thing of all is when the bride doesn't actually show up to her own wedding.'

She blinks at me.

'Polly's breaking up with Dev.'

Anna actually laughs. 'What do you mean, she's breaking up with Dev? She can't break up with Dev! He's the perfect man. They're the perfect couple!'

'Yes, well, that's not a popular view in Polly-land this morning. And apparently things aren't so perfect. Not when she doesn't love him any more.'

'Come on, Bella, you don't just fall out of love with someone a month before you marry them! There must be more to it than that. Ooooh, you know what you should do?' she suddenly adds, banging her fist down on the table. 'You should check her phone. That's how I found out *my* sister was having an affair with a married man, remember?'

'I do remember. And I remember the screaming row that took place when she caught you, and the fact that she didn't speak to you for six months afterwards.'

'Or you could check her emails instead. That's a great way to find out what's been going on!' Anna carries on as though I haven't even spoken. 'You know, if you know her password you can do it from any computer, so you won't get caught. And even if you do get caught . . . well, the end justifies the means, doesn't it? I mean, what if Perfect Dr Dev is secretly a woman-beater, or he's got a ruinous coke habit . . . or *she's* got a ruinous coke habit?'

'Anna, nobody has a ruinous coke habit. And if Dev's a secret woman-beater, I'll eat my hat.'

'Yes, but that's the *point*, isn't it?' she says triumphantly. 'The *secret* part. The part you'd only find out from spying on her.'

For a moment, I think about the way Polly slammed her laptop shut when I went into her room with breakfast this morning, with that furtive, guilty look on her face. OK, so maybe Anna is right. Not about the coke habits or the domestic violence, please God. But maybe there is something else going on. Still . . .

'Anna, I'm not going to *spy* on my own sister.'

'Don't think of it as spying, then! Think of it as . . . as covert surveillance!'

I hold up a hand. 'OK. Hold it right there, Miss

Moneypenny. I am not going to *covertly survey* my own sister, either. Anyway, with any luck, this is all just going to turn out to be one of Polly's typical attacks of indecision and faffiness.'

'Faffiness?'

'Precisely.' I put the fact of Lauren's cousin's Clapham flat out of my mind. 'OK, that's quite enough about Polly's wedding for now.'

'Her non-wedding, you mean.'

I ignore this. 'You and me have to talk about the Macfarlanes' anniversary dinner party on Saturday night. Now, I'll want to get as much preparation done in advance as possible, because I've got the adoption social worker coming that morning, so if you could –'

'Bella! You didn't tell me! That's so exciting!'

'Yes, well, I only found out yesterday. Besides, it's not a big deal, Anna, just a preliminary chat. The first stage of many. And not even an important stage, really, just the opportunity for her to take a few details. Stuff she could probably do over the phone, in fact.'

There's a bit of a silence.

'Jamie's wriggled out of it,' she says flatly. 'Hasn't he?'

'No! Not wriggled out! He has something else to do, that's all. And anyway, it's better if it's just me, this first time, without Jamie around to make a mess of it!'

'Bella, you can't keep making excuses for –'

I silence her by banging down the teapot so hard that for a moment I think the spout has fallen off.

Which would be a *real* catastrophe. This teapot is one of the first things I bought when I moved to London eight years ago, and I'm oddly sentimental about stuff like that. Plus, it makes a really excellent cup of tea, keeps it nice and hot, and never once has it leaked or dribbled. Sometimes I think this teapot is just about the only reliable thing I've got in my life.

'Anna, I am not making excuses,' I tell her, in a weird, tight voice that doesn't sound anything at all like my own. 'I know what you and Polly think about Jamie. But you're both wrong. He wants this adoption as much as I do. He's just not quite as focused as I am, yet. That's all.'

Anna doesn't say anything.

'Now, back to the Macfarlanes. Charlotte Macfarlane is asking for individual beef Wellingtons, but I've been trying to tell her there's no way we can cook them medium-rare for thirty-five people . . .'

See, this is what I mean about cooking. Even talking about it makes me feel better, more in control. Even *thinking* about it. If Anna stays for lunch, I might even whiz up a nice fresh pesto sauce to slather over delicate ribbons of tagliatelle, possibly even blanch a few crunchy green beans to go in with it, and toast some pine nuts to sprinkle over the top . . .

OK, so things might be a bit wobbly right now. With Jamie. With Polly. With the non-wedding. But in all these situations, you just have to stay in control. That way everything works itself out. Eventually.

Grace

Thursday 19 November

It's the usual six a.m. start for Charlie, throwing back his side of the duvet and leaping out of bed for his workout.

'Hey, honey,' he puffs, as I get out of bed myself a few minutes later. His legs and arms are splaying forwards and backwards in an unnatural way that makes him look faintly like a puppet. 'Did you pick up that shower gel I asked you about yesterday? The yellow kind?'

'Yes. The yellow kind.'

'Did you put it in the shower?'

'No. It's in the bathroom cabinet.'

'Well, I'll never find it in there!' he says, as though the bathroom cabinet leads to a Narnia-like other world, complete with Shuddering Wood and Wild Lands of the North. 'Can't you get it out and put it in the shower for me?'

'I was just about to go and start the boys' breakfast.'

'It'll take you five seconds!'

'It'd take *you* five seconds.'

'Not when I don't know exactly where to find it.

And don't be so unreasonable, Grace. I have a job to get to, you know.'

It's the trump card. His favourite one, in fact.

I go into the bathroom, grab the shower gel from where it's sitting, in full visibility, on the second shelf down, and put it just inside the shower door.

'Done,' I tell Charlie, as I head back out into the bedroom.

'Good job, honey,' he says, giving me an encouraging thumbs up. 'Oh, and you know the function starts at seven o'clock tonight, don't you?'

'You told me it was at eight.'

'Honey! I *said* seven.'

'Fine. I'll be there at seven.'

'Please, hon, don't be late. And don't forget, it's a very select private members' club, so don't wear anything too, you know, flamboyant.'

'I won't waste time picking my Mata Hari costume up from the dry cleaner's, then.'

'Great.' He's too distracted to realise I'm joking. 'You'll look terrific. Oh, hey, talking of looking terrific, how's Lady Muck been since she got home to Blighty?'

He's talking about Polly. He always calls her Lady Muck, usually with a bit of a sneer. He's not a huge fan of Polly. Or maybe he's just not a huge fan of my friendship with her. It's not something I've ever particularly cared to sit down and talk to him about, resulting as I'm sure it would in a character assassination of my best friend, and all the things she does to irritate him. Still, on the rare occasions when he does ask about her, he always manages to slip in a little comment about her looks, which (of course, he's a man) he seems to appreciate a lot more than her personality. Sometimes I think it's just one of his attempts to keep me on my toes.

'She's fine. I mean, I haven't actually managed to speak to her yet. Oh, and the wedding's off,' I announce, as casually as I can. I mean, I have to let Charlie know we won't be attending a wedding in Wiltshire on New Year's Eve. I'm just hoping he won't use it as an opportunity to bitch about Polly.

'The wedding's *off*?'

'Yes.'

'Well, lo and behold. Isn't that just *typical* of Lady Muck?'

'Actually, Charlie, it's absurd to say that it's typical. It's not like Polly has ever run out on a wedding before.'

'Potato, pot-ah-to,' he says. 'She may not have run out on a wedding, but she ran off to New York, didn't she? And you've always implied the only reason she came with you to university in London rather than sticking closer to home in Bristol was because she was running away from something back home.'

'I don't think I ever implied that.' At least, not deliberately, I didn't. It's a secret of ours – mine and Polly's – and I don't divulge those to Charlie. I don't divulge them to anyone.

'Well, she's a flake. Dan is well shot of her.'

I'm confused, for a moment, about the identity of this Dan. Then I realise that Charlie is talking about Dev, whose name he can never be bothered to remember. Not that it makes what he's just said any less offensive.

'Actually, Charlie, Polly is still my best friend, and I happen to be extremely concerned about her.' My voice is high, and slightly wobbly. 'You don't have to be so rude.'

'Oh, sure, honey!' He switches up a level on his cross-trainer, which also ups his level of puffs. 'Of course. Didn't mean to upset you.'

Which mollifies my anger somewhat.

It's only as I'm starting to poach the eggs for Robbie's eggs Benedict that it occurs to me that what Charlie said, and the tone in which he said it, wasn't so much an apology as a pacifier. Kind of the same thing as me buying chocolate buttons for Hector when he's having a bit of a whinge about his beanie hat being too tight and scratchy. Or having to wear his robot pyjamas because his favourite dinosaur ones are in the wash. Or anything else that a three-year-old gets upset about.

One of the major problems in our marriage – and believe me, there are too many to list right now – is that we have almost no social life. In fact, we have nothing resembling a social life at all. I suppose it's nothing new, really. When we first got together, most of his and Vanessa's friends (not having death wishes) chose her over him, and Charlie never really got along with my friends, thanks to the yawning generation gap. So all we ever really do – and even these are rare – are deal-celebrating dinners or drinks parties with Charlie's work colleagues where I've had to drink my own body weight in booze just to get through the evening without developing a nasty case of narcolepsy.

Tonight is just such an event.

At twenty-five to seven, dressed MMA-appropriately in boring black, I'm kicking my heels outside the private members' club where this evening's drinks party is going to take place. I was so worried about being late, knowing what a flap Charlie would get into, that I flew out of the house three minutes after Kitty-next-door arrived to babysit, guiltily placating Robbie and Hector as I went with handouts of chocolate.

Anyway, now I'm ridiculously early, and I'm too scared to barge up the steps of the club and talk my way in there by myself. So I have a choice – slowly freeze to death on Berkeley Square, with the whipping wind mucking up my hair for my own imminent funeral; or track down a branch of Starbucks to warm my cockles over a soothing caramel macchiato and a sneaky banana muffin.

Starbucks wins. And there's a cosy-looking one just the other side of the square.

I know there are people who live by the tenet that nothing bad can possibly happen in John Lewis, but for me, nothing bad could ever happen at Starbucks. Sometimes I think it's because Starbucks is where I used to drag myself out to, daily, in those blurry, sepia-tinged weeks after I had each of the boys. Where the baristas would help me as I struggled in through the doors with the pushchair or the Maxi-Cosi, kindly suggest that I take a seat so they could bring over my coffee, then take a couple of minutes out of their day to express an interest in my views on the weather or my plans for the morning.

Or maybe it's just because I really, really like the caramel macchiatos and the banana muffins. There is a danger of reading far too much into these things.

While I'm waiting for said macchiato and muffin, I get my phone out of my clutch bag and start composing a text to send to Polly.

I'm trying not to feel offended by the fact that she's been back for two full days now and we've still not managed to speak, let alone fix up a time and place to meet. I've called a few times, and left her one message: I didn't want to seem too needy, or hassle her too much. And to be fair to her, she has called back, it's just that it happened to be while I was talking to Hector's nursery teacher about his interaction with the other children (I think they're getting concerned that he's establishing a cult of personality) and I couldn't get to the phone. She didn't leave a message. But then I suppose she doesn't know Bella's already blabbed her big news, and she might be struggling to work out what to say. Calling off a wedding is a big deal, after all. And I'm desperate to find out what it is that's made her do it.

How r u holding up? I text her now, as the friendly barista steams my milk in the background and pours it into my cardboard cup. *Bella told me abt wedding. Want to meet 4 a drink 2 talk abt it?*

'Excuse me?' There's a voice right behind me. 'I think you've stolen my coffee.'

It's the man behind me in the queue. He's probably about thirty-five, and he's – I notice with a jolt – quite extraordinarily good-looking. He's tall and lean, with dark hair and eyes, and he's wearing a fine wool charcoal suit with an open-necked white shirt that sets off his lightly tanned skin to perfection. He looks amused and, contrary to most of the men you see around here, unhurried. He nods down at the coffee cup in my hand.

'I'm afraid I'm going to have to ask you to hand that over,' he says. 'Unless you want me to call the police.'

Stupidly, I just blink at him.

'They take cappuccino theft very seriously around these parts, I gather. I expect you'll get five years. Though you might be out in three for good behaviour.'

There's something about the way he's just said 'good behaviour' that makes my insides do a backflip.

'God, I'm joking!' he says, stepping forward solicitously. Can it be that he's so unaware of the effect he has on women that he thought my pathetic lust was some kind of attack of the vapours? 'If you want my extra-shot cappuccino that badly, it's all yours.'

'But this isn't your extra-shot cappuccino.' I find my voice. 'It's my caramel macchiato. With vanilla syrup.'

'It's my cappuccino.'

'It's my macchiato.'

'No, it isn't.'

'Yes,' I say with heartfelt conviction, 'it is.'

'One caramel macchiato!' calls the friendly barista, putting down a new cup of coffee on the counter next to the other one. 'With vanilla syrup!'

The man's grin spreads from ear to ear, and he holds out his hand for the coffee I'm holding. 'I think this is what the legal profession would call "bang to rights".'

'I'm really sorry . . .' Flustered, I turn round to get the correct coffee, just as he steps past me to reach for it so he can pass it to me himself. Our arms collide, and my banana muffin tumbles to the floor.

'This isn't going well, is it?' he observes, as we both stare down at the muffin. 'Still, at least now we're even. You stole my coffee, I destroyed your muffin. It's a pity,' he adds, with a long sigh and a glint in his black eyes, 'because I was rather looking forward to thinking of some way you could make it up to me.'

I'm dumbfounded again, and thank goodness, he's moved away to the tills, jangling in his pocket for the change to buy another muffin. Because I've no idea how to handle this. If I'm right – and I've never been remotely good at telling this kind of thing – this astonishingly attractive man is flirting with me.

I mean, is that what this is? Or is he just taking pity on me because I look so obviously out of place in this sea of busy working people, dashing away from their days of gainful employment with pride and purpose?

'Here you are,' he's saying now, with a mock bow, as he hands me a plate. 'I hope this will make up for my mistake.'

On the plate, piled precariously, are not one, not two, but . . . hang on . . . *six* assorted muffins.

'And if you work your way through those, just pop back to the counter and get the girl to give you some more,' he says. 'Or whatever else takes your fancy. I've bought the lot.'

Before I can say anything, he's shot me that wide, wicked grin again, then turned towards the door and headed outside.

I look round at the friendly barista, who's looking as taken aback as I am. There are three salmony-pink notes in her hand that, though I don't see them too often, I know are fifties.

'Wow. He likes *you*,' she says, opening up her till and putting the money into it. 'He comes in here all the time and I've never seen him hit on a woman quite like *that* before.'

It's only three minutes to seven by the time I hurry back to the door of the club, but Charlie is pacing up and down outside as though it's been six weeks without any news, and hope is fading fast.

'Honey, where've you *been*?'

'I needed a coffee. And something to eat.' A dozen muffins, eight caramel shortbreads, myriad Very Berry scones and Fairtrade chocolate brownies and an entire lemon swirl cheesecake – this is what I *could* have eaten, if I'd wanted to. As it was, I asked the nice barista to pack them all up for me and then I took them to the homeless man I saw earlier when I came out of Green Park tube. Which might have been a really heart-warming moment if he hadn't scowled down at them and asked why I hadn't brought any Marshmallow Twizzles.

'Grace, for crying out loud! There'll be canapés and champagne at the party! There was no need to get refreshments beforehand.'

'I'm not even late, Charlie. I don't see why it matters.'

'Well, everyone else has already arrived! Still, better late than never, I guess. Now, I'm pretty sure Malcolm Morley's wife is already here, so you might like to chat to her. She's a stay-at-home mom too.'

Normally I'd feel insulted – is this how children feel when they're shoved in with a bunch of strangers and told to 'play nicely together'? – but I'm still feeling buoyed up by my flattering encounter with the Muffin Man.

'Actually, Charlie, I was wondering if you'd introduce me to Saad Amar. One of the Mirandas has asked me to have a word with him about sending his little brother to St Martin's.'

Charlie blinks at me, as though I've just said those last couple of sentences in Serbo-Croat. 'What do you mean?'

'What I said! One of the Mirandas has specially commissioned me to do some stealth work on behalf of the fund-raising committee. You know,' I add pointedly, 'one of the school committees you've been telling me I should get involved in.'

Nope; from the expression on his face, apparently I'm still speaking in Serbo-Croat. 'I don't understand. Who are the Mirandas?'

The profound sense of sadness that floods over me almost – but not entirely – washes away my muffin high. 'Charlie, it was you who came up with the nick-name, remember? What we call the mums at Robbie's school?'

'Oh, right . . .' Plainly he doesn't remember. 'But, honey, you can't just accost Saad Amar, you know. He's an important guy. This is an important party. He's not going to want to spend it being press-ganged by the St Martin's fund-raising committee!'

I take a deep breath. 'I wasn't planning to *accost* him, Charlie. I just thought you could introduce me, if he was passing by, and I could drop it into the conversation.'

'Well, best not, I think. Maybe I can find the occasion to mention it to him one day at work, or something.' He's started hustling me up the steps and into the club, where a supercilious doorman directs us towards the private room MMA has hired for the event.

It's not a huge room – MMA Capital employs only thirty or forty people, so there's no need to hire an entire ballroom – but it's grand and high-ceilinged, and already starting to fill up with people. They're obviously MMA colleagues, plus husbands and wives, though it's hard to tell which. Everyone is dressed the same – pinstripes for the men and sharp skirt suits for the women – which means that although I thought I'd got it right with my (boring) black jersey cowl-neck dress and (boring) kitten heels, I now feel simultaneously under- and over-dressed. As well as boring. Which is quite an achievement. There are waiters circulating with trays of the promised canapés, there are other waiters topping up glasses of champagne, and there's a string duo of a cello and violin scraping out light classical melodies in the corner. There is a buzz of light chatter above the sound of the music.

It's all terribly civilised and sophisticated, and perhaps because I'm also, as usual, the youngest person in the room by at least a decade, it makes me want to neck a bottle of champagne and find a table to dance on. Perhaps that Mata Hari costume wouldn't have been such a bad idea after all.

Charlie practically shoves me in the direction of an uptight woman in navy, who it immediately transpires is this Malcolm Morley's wife he was talking about outside. And who also, it immediately transpires, is a fully-fledged Miranda.

One of the particular variety of Miranda (lucky me!) whose special obsession is their children's toilet habits.

Within moments she's demanding to know if Robbie still wets the bed and quizzing me on Hector's success (or lack thereof) in the potty-training department.

'Oh, well, you're obviously getting *something* wrong,' she informs me, when I stupidly confess that the closest he gets to his potty is putting it on his head as a 'motorbike helmet' when he rides his scooter round the garden. 'I had all my three using big-boy toilet within a month of their second birthdays, and do you know how I did it?'

I mumble something about her probably just being a really brilliant mum, when in fact I'm assuming it was through a combination of extremist scheduling and shameless intimidation. Possibly also a burning desire on her kids' part to stop their mother from using the phrase 'big-boy toilet' any more than absolutely necessary.

Anyway, Miranda Morley starts talking me *ad nauseam* through her extensive efforts – getting her sons to personalise their potties with creative finger-painting and alphabet stickers; play-acting entire West End shows with their cuddly toys about the pleasures of using big-boy toilet; placing their favourite books beside the toilet so they could brush up on their Hemingway while squeezing out a Number Two (I exaggerate, but not a lot) – until I feel that I've lived through their every dribble and spurt along with her, and I'm feeling thoroughly nauseous at the very idea of any champagne and canapés.

'I really treated the whole thing as a special project – you know, the way we used to do at work,' she carries on, happily sipping her champagne.

'Mm,' I mumble.

'What did you work at, then, before you had your boys?'

'Oh, you know . . . nothing very exciting . . . I mean, I was very young, of course, when I had them,' I say weakly.

'Yes, I suppose you must have been.' She suddenly seems to notice that I'm well under forty, and shoots me a disapproving look, as if she's just seen through my boring, sober, middle-aged outfit and noticed that I'm wearing a peephole bra and split-crotch panties beneath. (I'm not, needless to say.) 'So how did you meet your husband, then? Were you his secretary, or something?'

'Um, no, not his secretary.' I don't want to alienate her by adding, 'His babysitter, actually.'

'Because you look like you might have been a secretary.'

I'm not sure whether she means this to be a compliment or an insult. But I'm left in no doubt when she carries on, lowering her voice only a fraction.

'You know, I don't like the secretaries at MMA, do you? Silly little things, I always think. Hired for the way they look in a short skirt rather than their organisational abilities.'

'I don't really know any of them, I'm afraid,' I say, which is my way of trying to avoid being dragged into the slagging-off.

But Miranda Morley is having none of it. I think, thanks to the champagne, I may be her New Best Friend. 'Oh, well, there's the legal department secretary right over there. Celia, her name is. Malcolm's a big fan of hers, of course,' she adds, scornfully, pulling me sideways so that I can see across the room at her angle. 'Little blonde thing. Silly-looking. Talking to Saad Amar.'

The girl she's pointing at, with the neat blonde bob and – yes – a rather silly expression – is chattering away to a man I recognise right away.

'Oh God,' I croak. 'The Muffin Man.'

'What?'

'Sorry . . . I mean . . . is that Saad Amar? The man she's talking to, in the white shirt?'

'Sex-on-legs-Saad, you mean?' Miranda Morley lets out a surprisingly dirty cackle that suddenly makes me like her quite a lot more. 'I *know*. Isn't he *gorgeous*?'

I can feel the same hot blush spreading over my face as it did earlier, in Starbucks. Because not only is Miranda Morley's open lust making me more aware of my own than ever, but the Muffin Man's – sorry, Saad Amar's – eyes have met mine, and held them across the crowded room.

He smiles, and raises his glass, and does a kind of watch-tapping mime that I think means he'll come over in a moment.

'I thought you said you didn't know him,' Miranda Morley says accusingly.

'I don't! Well, I thought I didn't . . .'

She gives a loud harrumph. 'I don't think Saad Amar is the kind of man you could forget you knew . . . oh God, look, he's coming over!'

It's true; he is. He's got the most fabulous walk, I notice – a cool, confident stroll, with all the time in the world. It's the same unhurried, stress-free air I noticed about him back in Starbucks. The kind of aura, probably, that comes from having such extreme wealth that you never really need to worry or flap about anything. Maybe that's what makes money so incredibly sexy. As if Saad Amar required any extra help in the incredible sexiness department.

'Ladies.' He's reached us. 'Good to see you again, Jennifer.'

I wonder who he's talking about for a moment, but from the squeak next to me I remember that 'Miranda' Morley isn't her actual name.

'And the Starbucks One,' he adds, turning to me. 'Rather brazen of you to show your face at my party. Are you planning a ram-raid on the crab cakes? Will we next see you squeezed into a Lycra catsuit, attempting to burgle the Bollinger?'

Miranda/Jennifer Morley stares back and forth between us, looking confused, and then, suddenly, desperately disappointed, as her husband, a frowning, squat little man, bustles up as if out of nowhere and tells us he's sorry to interrupt, but his wife really must come and meet Martin and Linda Greenberg.

'It's not funny,' I tell Saad Amar, as we're left alone. 'You're giving me a bad reputation.'

'I'm sure you could do that all by yourself,' he says lightly. 'And anyway, you can hardly blame me for my suspicions. Don't get me wrong: it's a delight to have you here. But why *are* you?'

I take a fortifying sip of champagne. My images of the mini-Morleys' toilet training have, mercifully, faded. 'My husband works for you.'

'Oh?' His left eyebrow hitches upwards. 'Lucky husband.'

I'm not sure whether he means lucky to work for him, or lucky to be married to me. Either way, he's making me flustered. I mean, I was uncertain enough about the flirting when I thought he was just a random hunk back in Starbucks. Now I know he's Charlie's boss, I obviously shouldn't even be on the fringes of flirtation at all.

'Yes, he's Charlie Costello,' I say, in as brisk a voice as possible. 'He's in the legal department. He's been working for you for a few months now.'

'Yeah, I know Charlie.' His eyebrow hitches up slightly further. 'You're married to him?'

I'm not quite sure how to take this question. Or the tone he's asked it in. ('*You're* married to *him*?')

'And we have two lovely boys together,' I add, warming to my happily married woman theme. 'Robbie and Hector . . . actually, that reminds me.' Chief Miranda's mission for the fund-raising committee! Yes, it's the perfect way to forestall any flirting he might be doing. (And any flirting that I might accidentally take part in if I don't watch myself.) 'I gather you're looking for a school for your younger brother.'

'Oh, you've *gathered* that, have you?' He grins that sexy grin again.

'So I was wondering whether or not you'd thought about St Martin's at all? On the Fulham Road? My elder son goes there and he's really ever so happy. I'm sure your little brother would love it . . .'

'Mrs Costello!' His sexy grin has turned into a mock-shocked face. Actually, this is pretty sexy too. 'Are you trying to engineer it so you can jump on me at the Nativity play?'

I want to die. I can feel blood rushing to my head. 'No! I didn't mean . . .'

'Or the school Sports Day, perhaps? Luring me in to be your three-legged race partner, just so you can have your wicked way with me round the back of the bike sheds?'

'There are no bike sheds at St Martin's,' I blurt miserably. I know he might be enjoying this banter, but I'm rubbish at it, and I'm certainly not enjoying it. 'And I'm married.'

He stops smiling. He ducks his head down so he's closer to me, instantly solicitous. 'I'm sorry. I was joking. Or trying to. I'm an idiot.'

I don't say anything.

'Maybe if I'd had the benefit of a fabulous St Martin's education, I wouldn't *be* such an idiot. But that's not something I'm going to deny my little brother.' He reaches into a pocket for a small white card, and then produces a pen from the breast pocket of his suit. 'Here. Write your mobile number down and I can call you to talk some more about the school.' He presses pen and card into my hand. 'Perhaps I could even take you out to lunch to discuss it. If you don't think Charlie would mind, that is.'

I know he's being nice, but he's making me feel ridiculous. 'Why should he mind?'

'Oh, I don't know. If I was married to you, I'm not sure I'd be too thrilled with you going out to lunch with a scoundrel like me.' He smiles, but not the sexy grin this time. Just a friendly smile, to show he's taking the piss out of himself. 'I promise I'll behave myself. If you promise you won't try to fleece me out of my post-lunch cappuccino.'

'I promise,' I say, writing down my name and mobile number on the card and handing it back to him.

'Grace,' he says. 'What a lovely name. And very fitting.' He glances up to give me the merest of smouldering glances, before placing a hand lightly on my shoulder and steering me towards the centre of the room. 'Now. Who else do you know here?'

'Nobody, really.' I say, before realising that I sound like the saddest sack on the planet. 'I mean, I know *of* people. Like, um, Celia . . .'

'Oh, I think I can find you some marginally more entertaining conversation than Celia's. Come and meet George, my right-hand man in HR. In fact, I think he may have been directly responsible for hiring your husband.'

He leaves me with plump, cheerful George, who immediately starts talking at me nineteen to the dozen about how he's just got back from a week in the

Maldives, and how – despite having only just met me – he's sure I'd love it.

Next time I see Saad, he's deep in conversation with Charlie.

Bella

Saturday 21 November
So here we are. D-Day.

It's Saturday morning, and the adoption social worker is on her way. Which is why I've just spent the last few hours doing the following:

1) practising my opening-the-front-door face in the mirror. Too serious (I've discovered) and I look like Mrs Danvers in *Rebecca*; too smiley and I look like Tom Cruise *en route* to the nearest sofa
2) cleaning the bathroom twice, hoovering the living-room three times, and scrubbing the grouting between the worktop tiles in the kitchen
3) artfully creating light toothpaste stains in the bathroom sink, dropping a couple of bits of fluff on the living-room carpet, and scrubbing a few realistic stains back into the grouting between the worktop tiles in the kitchen, just in case Samantha blacklists me on the grounds of suspected OCD
4) sticking photos of my family and friends on the fridge door, to demonstrate closeness to all-important Support Network, plus leaving three messages for Brian to CALL ME during

Samantha's visit so I can casually drop in the fact I have previous experience of a 'blended family'

5) rehearsing statements of my child-rearing views out loud, to be sure that saying 'the most important thing is lots and lots of love' doesn't sound like I've lifted it straight out of a bad Disney movie, and
6) *re*scrubbing the grouting in the kitchen. Because on second thought, my carefully applied stains didn't look like an indicator of a relaxed, child-friendly lifestyle. They looked like the work of a maniac who'd just spent forty minutes artistically daubing the place with freshly made espresso, French onion soup and tomato purée.

Still, at least it's kept me busy. Because I've been up since six thirty – nerves, partly. Also the fact that Jamie hauled himself out of bed at the crack of dawn, finding the incredible ability to skip the usual lie-in when he hears the siren song of Old Trafford. All the more amazing given that he had a big night out last night, celebrating one of The Boys' birthdays at The Pub. I know, I know, I probably should have read him the riot act, given that it's the third Big Night he's had this week. But then he did spend almost all day yesterday helping Polly move into the flat in Clapham, so it was sort of my way of thanking him.

Oh, and I also wanted to thank him for keeping me chilled out about Polly's whole flat-in-Clapham thing. Well, chilled out-*ish*. More openly chilled out than I actually feel about the whole thing, at any rate.

I mean, quite apart from the fact that I'm somewhat offended that Polly stayed at mine for barely three nights, upping and leaving for the Clapham flat the moment she knew for sure it was available (am I *that* much of a nightmare to live with?), the bigger issue is that, having moved to her own flat, doesn't she have even less incentive to get things sorted out with Dev? Come to think of it, isn't moving to her own flat a pretty big sign she's no intention of getting things sorted out with Dev? As if it wasn't a big enough sign that she's come clean to Mum and Brian, and made all those cancellation calls, without me having to do it, to the marquee hire people and the jazz band, *and* sent out a mass apologetic email to all one hundred and thirty wedding guests.

But then all those things could just be a sign she doesn't want a big, formal wedding. Moving into her own flat is a sign she's not up for the actual marriage part after all.

And I've still got no idea what she's said to Dev. Or even how he's coping. I've called him a couple of times, but he's not getting back to me. So I'll just have to keep trying. No matter how much Jamie's encouraged me to chill out about the whole thing, I just can't chill out about poor, abandoned Dev. Because I really do know how that kind of rejection feels.

Anyway, Jamie is long on his way now, bombing up the M1 to Manchester in my van, which (another result of my gratitude) I've let him borrow for the occasion. Well, I don't need it for the Macfarlanes' dinner party – Anna will drive round the supplies we need – and it'll save Jamie spending sixty quid – sixty quid he doesn't have – on the train fare.

The other thing that's kept me busy since six thirty this morning is assembling the symphony of cakes. The lemon drizzle is fresh out of the oven, Brian's coffee-and-walnut is newly iced, and Anna, bless her, dropped off one of her incredible flourless chocolate cakes late last night. So every base (and, I hope, food intolerance) is covered. After all, it's almost eleven already . . .

. . . and I'm still in my pyjamas and dressing gown.

Shit. *How* did I not remember I was still in my pyjamas and dressing gown?

I run for the bathroom, splash some water on my face, then hurry for the wardrobe in my bedroom. I fling it open and am just pulling down my neatly ironed top when my mobile rings.

'Hey, it's me,' says Anna's voice. 'I'm just calling to wish you luck!'

'That's great, Anna, but I can't talk now. I've forgotten to get dressed.'

'Nudity. That's an interesting approach. Are you thinking of adopting a Swedish baby?'

'Child,' I say automatically, because the last thing you must do is let your social worker think you're a baby-obsessed loon. You're supposed to want a *child*, of any age, not just a pink, plump, talc-fresh baby. 'And don't joke, Anna. This is serious. I have five minutes till she gets here.'

'OK, stay calm,' she says bossily, even though if it were her in this position she'd be shrieking from the rafters by now. 'What are you planning to wear?'

'Black trousers,' I pant, hauling them on. 'Tunicy top. My Polly locket. Boots.'

'*Tunicy* top? Oh, *Bella*.'

Anna has this on-going mission to get me out of the clothes I prefer to wear – actually, she doesn't call them clothes, she calls them 'garb' – and into . . . well, I don't know what into. Low-cut tops, I suppose. Tight jeans. Bright colours. All these things Anna wears. And though she's a long way from supermodel proportions, she looks rather fetching in them. But I'm even further away from supermodel proportions than she is. And I don't have one tenth of her chutzpah.

'It's what I've planned, Anna. It's what I've ironed.'

'OK, then, can you belt it around the waist?'

'I don't have a belt.'

'You must have a belt.'

'Well, I don't have a waist.'

'Everyone has a waist.'

'Then mine is missing in action. Presumed dead. And this is not the time to start searching for it. I have to get myself sorted out here!'

'OK. Just remember to keep chucking in all those social-worker buzzwords we've discussed.'

'Diversity,' I parrot, obediently. 'Community. Challenges.'

'And you'll phone me right after? I mean, I know

you're all by yourself, without Jamie, and I just want to know that you're –'

'I'll phone you right after. Thanks again for the cake.'

I hang up, do a quick glance around the bedroom to check it's how it should be, an even quicker glance in the mirror to check *I'm* how I should be – well, it's tough when you've not got great material to be working with in the first place – and then I head out into the hallway just as the front doorbell rings.

She's bang on the dot of eleven. This impresses me.

I open the door with a broad smile (*not* Tom Cruise, Bella, *not* Tom Cruise) and find myself eye-to-eye with Samantha.

Literally eye-to-eye. She's almost exactly the same height as I am; actually, given that she's wearing heels and I'm in my flat boots, she might even be closer to five foot two than my lofty five foot three. Even though I know I shouldn't judge short people (I mean, who am *I*?) I'm a bit thrown by her smallness. An inconsequential little person, she looks, to wield so much power. I'm not exactly sure what I'd been expecting – some kind of hybrid of Hillary Clinton and Xena the Warrior Princess, perhaps – but certainly not this squirrelly woman in a faded black trouser suit and sensible courts. And there's one other worrying thing about her.

'You're ever so *young*,' I blurt before I can stop myself.

'Sorry?' She withdraws the hand she was extending.

'No, I mean . . . I just didn't expect . . .' I breathe deep; start again. 'I'm Bella Atkins! Please, come on in.'

She steps over the threshold, pulling her tote bag up onto her shoulder in a slightly tetchy fashion. 'I'm twenty-eight!' she says, with a bit of an edge. 'I'm head of my department!'

'Well, yes, but my sister Polly is twenty-eight. And I'm not sure she should be put in charge of doling out babies to anyone.'

'We're not *doling out babies* . . .'

'God, I mean *children*, sorry . . .' This is ridiculous. My nerves really are getting the better of me. 'What I'm saying is, compared to other twenty-eight-year-olds, you've obviously done terribly well in such a responsible job . . .' I force myself, through a massive triumph of will, to STOP TALKING.

There's a short silence.

Then she extends the hand again. 'Well. It's nice to meet you, Bella. I'm Samantha Reilly.'

I shake the hand. It's a little bit limp. 'Reilly? Is that an Irish name?'

'On my grandfather's side.'

'How amazing! My boyfriend is Irish!'

'Well, I'm not.'

'No, of course, I just thought maybe with the name . . . and London has such a wonderfully rich and diverse Irish and Irish-origin community . . .' I've got in 'diversity' and 'community' already! 'I just wondered if you might know each other . . .'

It's her turn to take a deep breath. 'What's his name?'

'Jamie Keenan.'

'Then no, I don't know him.' She slips off her jacket. 'Can I hang this up somewhere?'

'Of course. I'm so sorry . . .' I take her jacket, hang it on the pegs by the front door, and usher her through to the kitchen. 'I wondered if you might like a cup of tea? A slice of cake?'

'Just a glass of water is fine.'

'Oh.' I can't hide my disappointment. 'It's really no trouble! The kettle is just boiled, and I have a few homemade cakes for you to try. Or I could rustle you up something toasted.'

'Really, I'm fine with just a glass of water.' Brooking no disagreement – I can see why she's already risen to the top of her department, small, young and squirrelly though she is – she pulls back one of my kitchen chairs and sits down at the little gate-leg table, taking files and pens from her shoulder bag as she does so.

I get a glass and pour her some water from my filter jug. I'm longing for a piece of cake myself – Anna's chocolate one would really hit the spot right now – but I don't think I can sit and gorge myself alone.

'So,' she says, nibbling the tip of her pen (well, if she'll nibble that, why won't she nibble my delicious cakes?), 'this is just a preliminary meeting, you understand? I just want to go through some basic details, give you a chance to ask any questions you may have. And if we're both happy at the end of the meeting, the next stage is for us to invite you on a Preparation for Adoption course. That's before the series of official home visits will even begin. Nothing is decided at this stage, OK?'

'Of course.'

'Because I see a lot of people who over-think this initial chat. Get themselves all worked up. As though it's make or break from the moment I walk in the door.'

I give a little laugh. 'How extraordinary!'

'So. I'll just confirm your basic details. Your name is Bella Atkins. You're thirty-two. You're self-employed . . .'

'As a caterer, yes.' I hazard a smile. 'Hence these delicious cakes I've made! Are you quite sure you won't –'

' . . . and you live with your . . .' She casts her eye over my tunicy top, '. . . civil partner?'

OK. So Anna's right. I need a new wardrobe. 'No, no, my boyfriend! Remember, the one I told you about?'

'Oh, yes. Mr Keenan.' She makes a note in her file. 'So he isn't applying for adoption with you?'

'Yes. I mean, yes, he *is* applying for adoption with me.'

'But he couldn't be here for this meeting?'

Do I hear a note of judgement in her voice already?

'Oh, well, he'd have loved to have been here, of course, but unfortunately he had a prior engagement.' No, that doesn't sound good enough. '*Work*, I mean.

He had to work. He's a landscape gardener. Runs his own firm, in fact. And there are never enough hours in the day to work, not when you're self-employed! Not that he's a workaholic,' I add hastily, as she makes yet another note in her file. 'Nor me, as it happens. I mean, I *enjoy* my work, obviously . . .'

Oh God. What the hell is she writing? And is it counting against us already that Jamie isn't even here? Does it look bad that he hasn't made it a priority?

'And you've been together how long?'

'Two years. Which I know is the absolute minimum you guys expect, for couples who are trying to adopt, but I thought that by the time the whole process really gets going, it'll be a lot closer to three!'

She notes this down. She doesn't say anything. I'm feeling a wave of judgement heading my way again.

It's a wave I've got to try to surf.

'Or do you prefer it if couples are actually *married*? Because I'm quite sure that's something that will happen very soon, for me and Jamie. I mean, weddings are a bit of a dirty word around here just at the moment, unfortunately, because my sister has just run out on a wedding of her own . . . well, not *run out*, as such . . . we're usually an extremely reliable family! . . . but I'm sure that as soon as the dust has settled, and she's back with her fiancé again, Jamie and I will think about tying the knot ourselves . . .'

She holds up her pen to stop me, which is good, because I was just about to launch into my favourite fantasy, where Jamie and I not only get married (in a simple registry office ceremony, me in ivory trousers and a floaty top – though not a tunicy one, if Samantha's reaction to today's outfit is anything to go by), but go on to grow old together in a cottage on the North Devon coast, surrounded by a whole brood of our adopted children's children, with me in the kitchen making Sunday roasts, and Jamie in the garden teaching the little ones to plant geraniums.

'Bella, it's up to you what you do with your life. Unmarried couples are perfectly *able* to adopt. That said, our latest guidance from the Department of Health does mean that we will be *prioritising* married couples.'

Damn. Damn damn *damn*. 'Look, Samantha, would it help my application if we were to get engaged, say?'

'I think we shouldn't be jumping too far ahead,' she says. 'Like I said, Bella, this is only a preliminary conversation.'

'Right,' I say miserably. 'Of course.'

Silence descends while she scribbles for a little bit more.

God, I wish I knew what she was writing about me. I'm allowed to know, aren't I? Under . . . what's it called . . . oh, yes, Freedom of Information! Do I have to apply for special permission? Or can I just . . . reach over and grab it?

'Anyway, Bella, let's forget about your marital status for a moment. Tell me a bit about your own family background. Your reasons for wanting to adopt. I assume,' she carries on, without the smallest change in tone, 'that you've had long-running experience of infertility. Perhaps recently come to the end of your own IVF journey?'

'What? I . . . no. I mean, there hasn't been a journey.'

'There's no shame in it. Most of the prospective adopters I see have just failed a final cycle of IVF.'

'I haven't done IVF! It's . . . it's different, with me.'

'Well, can you have children or can't you?' She takes a sip of her water. 'Because obviously there is a bit of a *trend* for people to adopt children just because all the Hollywood stars are doing it. If you've not even *tried* to have your own children, obviously that might make us concerned that –'

'Look, it's not a matter of trying! I can't have children, OK?' I snap, before remembering that it probably isn't a good idea to snap at the woman who holds all my hopes and dreams in the palms of her squirrelly little hands. I force a smile onto my face. 'Samantha, I'm not doing this because Angelina Jolie makes it look so pretty, or Sandra Bullock bangs on about it being the ultimate fulfilment in every magazine interview she gives! All I want – actually, all I've ever wanted, ever since they brought my little sister home from the hospital – is to have a child of my own. I just want to bring someone into my home, and make them feel wanted, and special, and safe –'

I break off.

Because there's a naked, and very, very hairy man coming through my kitchen doorway.

My first instinct, despite the fact he could be an escaped mental patient or opportunistic on-the-loose rapist and we could be in really *serious* trouble, is to flap my hands at him to go away, like he's a stray cat.

His response is to hold up his own hands and just kind of . . . *gibber* at me (though maybe I'm being swayed by the fact that he seems to be half-man, half-gorilla). He looks as astonished by my presence as I am by his.

The most astonished of us all, though, is Samantha. Despite the fact that, as a social worker, you'd have thought she's seen pretty much everything there is to see, she lets out a shriek that could pierce eardrums, reaches for her glass of water, and chucks the contents vaguely in Gorilla-Man's direction.

'Is this your boyfriend?' she gasps, as she jumps to her feet and clutches her files to her chest. 'You let him just . . . just *wander* like this?'

'No! He's not Jamie! I've no idea who he is, how he got in . . .'

At the word 'Jamie', Gorilla-Man begins to gibber a bit more frenetically, recognition in his eyes. It's this that turns the light bulb on for me. He has to be one of The Boys. It's happened before, that a stray one has ended up back in my spare room after one of Jamie's big nights out, like last night's evidently was. But they're never usually naked. And never usually at quite such a disastrously inconvenient moment. Still, the gibberish is making more sense now, if only because I can now recognise it as the familiar sound of a hungover Cork-man.

Taking pity on him despite myself, and keen to prevent Samantha hyperventilating, I throw him a tea towel. 'Please, sir, cover yourself up,' I say authoritatively.

He garbles a few words – I can make out 'jeans', 'spare room', 'no idea' – then turns and lumbers from the kitchen, giving us a flash of (improbably smooth) backside as he goes.

I turn to a white-faced Samantha. There's no way of making this sound anything other than the catastrophe it is. All I can do to mitigate matters is to imply that he's not a total stranger. Naked *strangers* strolling round your home is – probably? – more off-putting than the idea of a naked person you actually know.

'Samantha, I'm so sorry. He's a friend of Jamie's. And it's never happened before, I promise you.'

'It was extraordinarily unpleasant.'

'I know, maybe you need a piece of cake, to settle your nerves . . .'

'I do *not* need a piece of cake!' She reaches for her bag and shoves her files into it. 'Look, I think it's best if I leave you to deal with . . . well, with *that* . . . and we can reschedule this appointment for another time. When we can have more privacy, perhaps.'

'But when will that be?' I follow her out into the hall, making sure the door to the spare room is firmly shut so that she doesn't accidentally catch a glimpse of a still-naked Gorilla-Man bending over to pull his socks on, or some other equally distressing scenario.

'You'll have to phone my office. It should be some time before Christmas,' she says, shrugging on her jacket and reaching for the front-door handle herself.

'Samantha.' I stop her just before she steps out of the door and starts making her way down the three floors to the bottom. 'This won't have any impact on my application, will it? This . . . um . . . incident? I mean, you said there was nothing decided at this stage . . .'

She turns to look at me. For a moment I think I can see pity, or at least some form of discernible human emotion, in her eyes. But then she goes into automaton mode again. 'Just make sure this kind of thing doesn't happen again. No amount of good intentions in the world can make up for a repeat of *that*.'

When I close the door, I turn round to see Gorilla-Man behind me.

He's dressed now, thank God, in jeans and a T-shirt that looks recently ironed but with neat creases from packing. It's a huge improvement, and not just because they mean I don't have to avert my eyes from anything that might be . . . you know . . . dangling. Clothed, he looks relatively normal. Decent-looking, even. Certainly a lot less like an Early Man exhibit from the Natural History Museum.

Which just makes it even worse, frankly, that Samantha had to see him parading about in all his naked hairiness. If he'd just had the decency to throw something on, it wouldn't have mattered so much that he was a stranger in my flat. He'd have looked respectable enough not to scare her off.

'Thank you *very* much!' I spit at him. 'Do you have any idea what you've just done?'

'I'm really, really sorry.' His accent is less of a problem for me now that I'm tuned into it. 'I didn't know anyone was in. I mean, I knew you lived here – you're Bella, right? – but Jamie said he thought you'd be out working this morning, or something.'

This makes sense. Well, it makes sense given that I do bang on to Jamie quite a lot about my near-constant working hours. Mostly – and fruitlessly – just to try to get him to realise that it's not easy being the only one in this relationship who brings in any money.

'Well, who the hell are you, anyway?' I demand. 'A schoolfriend? A cousin?' This might make the most sense; the hairiness aside, there's a vague resemblance to Jamie about him, mostly in the size department. His height and build, I mean! Not *that* size department. I wasn't looking!

'No, no, I'm not a cousin. Just a mate, from back home. 'My name's Liam. Liam Dempsey. I was at school with Jamie. And I'm . . . just . . . well, I'm sort of visiting.'

'*Sort of* visiting?'

'No, I mean, I *am* visiting, obviously. I'm just not, you know, on holiday, or anything. I'm over here to look for a job. And Jamie said it was OK if I stayed here.'

'He did, did he?' I feel my fury ratchet up a few

notches. Who does Jamie think he is, telling his friends they can stay at my place without telling *me* about it? 'And did he let you know how long I can expect to run this impromptu B and B for? Days? Weeks? And are there more, where you've come from? Am I to expect coachloads from Cork, fresh off Ryanair?'

'Look, maybe it's better if I just leave,' Liam Dempsey says, rather more gruffly than I take kindly to, given the circumstances. 'I don't want to cause you any trouble, or inconvenience.'

'Trouble or inconvenience!' I repeat, letting out a strange cackle of laughter. It isn't anything like my usual, sane-sounding laugh. 'Well, as far as trouble and inconvenience go, how about the trouble and inconvenience of fucking up any chance I have of adopting a child?'

Liam Dempsey blinks at me. 'You're kidding.'

'Is it the kind of thing people normally kid you about?'

'No, of course not . . . Christ . . .' He runs a hand through his hair. It's dark and plentiful. Like the hair everywhere else on his body. 'I'm really, really sorry.'

'The social worker could quite happily stick me on a blacklist and never even answer my calls again!'

He actually thinks about this for a moment, before saying, in an infuriatingly calm tone, 'Ah, well, now you're just panicking. I mean, that would just be plain unprofessional.'

I clench my fists. 'She can be as unprofessional as she likes! She's the one with all the power.' I can feel my chest starting to heave, and I know I'm going to start crying any minute. 'Look, there's cakes in the kitchen,' I mumble, unable to flee to the bedroom without expressing my reflex to be hospitable. 'Help yourself to them, and tea. I'm going to have a lie-down.'

'You mean, it's OK for me to stay after all? I honestly don't want to tread on any toes.'

'Treading on toes isn't the problem. Treading on toes is the least I have to worry about, after what you've just done.' I wrench the bedroom door open and slam it shut behind me.

Grace

Monday 23 November

I'm meeting Polly for brunch this morning at Café on the Green, and I don't think I've been more pitifully excited about an event since my fifteenth birthday party, when I'd just started Properly Going Out with the gorgeous Jacob Mercer from the sixth form college, and I knew he was going to turn up looking mean and moody and pouty of lip, and turn everyone else green with envy.

And today is even better! Because my excitement is going to culminate in a sophisticated brunch with Polly instead of a bit of a sweaty grope with Jacob. (Gorgeous, yes, but as it turned out, not so hot in the romance department.) I was imagining it all day yesterday (the sophisticated brunch, not the sweaty groping) after Polly and I – finally! – had the chance to have a talk on the phone. Ever since she got back, we've not managed to do more than leave each other messages – or 'play voicemail tag', as Polly put it; I immediately fell in love with this expression and have vowed to use it as often as possible – but last night we actually settled down for a proper Grace-and-Polly chat.

Or rather, it would have been a proper Grace-and-Polly chat if Charlie hadn't come in after five minutes, demanding to know if I'd ironed him a shirt for the morning and whether I'd put the *Sunday Times* crossword in the recycling yet or not. Recognising defeat when I saw it (Charlie has never liked me spending long stretches of time on the phone to Polly), I suggested that we pick up our conversation again in person, in the morning, unencumbered by the ironing and the irritable husband.

Though I didn't say anything about the irritable husband to Polly, of course.

I haven't ever talked much to her about Charlie, as it happens. I suppose I used to think it might be disloyal, and now I can't break the habit. And, anyway, it might have been insensitive to talk about my husband when Polly is still in the throes of her breakup from her own almost-husband. A subject we didn't quite get round to before Charlie interrupted yesterday, but which I intend to pin her down on today. In the context of a fun, girlie brunch, of course. Because I want today to be the full *Sex and the City* experience I've been so desperate for: great clothes, swingy hair, a good friend, and a proper conversation.

Well, the swingy hair has got off to a good start, at least. I found the time to pop in some heated rollers this morning, after asking Charlie to do the school run for a change. Actually, let me rephrase that: after *begging Charlie to do the school run for the first time in eighteen months*. And what a song and dance he made about it, too. You'd have thought he'd never even met his children before – never met *any* child before – from the way he was trying irritably to cram Robbie into Hector's anorak, and leaving the lunchboxes on the hall table so that I had to dash out after them still in my pyjamas. It didn't help that Robbie was practically apoplectic with excitement about this one-off event, running around like a demented bumper car from the moment he'd finished his eggs Benedict, announcing every stage of his getting-ready protocol to Charlie ('This is my back-pack, Daddy, have you seen my back-pack, Daddy?'; 'These are my new school shoes, Daddy, have you seen my new school shoes, Daddy?'). While Hector, who's never been taken to nursery by Charlie before, so has no dim and distant memory to get overexcited by, suddenly went inexplicably quiet and coy, staring at Charlie with big eyes and completely forgetting to have a last-minute nappy accident.

It was a little bit heart-breaking, actually.

Anyway, broken heart or not, at least I had the chance to get my hair into decent shape, and now I'm proudly sitting at a prime window table in Café on the Green! Outfit-wise, I was torn between wearing my usual yummy-mummy stripes or sporting something insanely stylish and avant-garde that even SJP might approve of: an outfit consisting entirely, say, of fisherman's netting, rubber fetish-wear and a dash of vintage Dior. But when I realised I don't actually own anything of the sort, I reached a happy compromise by pulling on a silk Issa dress that I bought in a fit of optimism at the January sales after reading in a magazine that it was 'perfect for brunch with the girls'. It's navy and ivory, dotted with a beautiful star pattern, and I'm wearing it with the coolest footwear I currently own – ash-coloured high-heel knee boots from Topshop that I love with all my heart, mostly because Charlie thinks they're 'unsuitable for a wife and mother' – and a dash of the 'Russian Red' Lipglass I ordered from the Mac website. Equally unsuitable for a wife and mother, I have no doubt. I feel thrillingly like Louboutin Lexie, and as if I could be tripping off to my very own fabulous creative career just as soon as I've finished my girlie, gossipy brunch!

Now all I need is a large mug of caffè latte so I have something to do with my hands.

Not that I'm nervous, or anything, you understand. Polly's my best friend; she couldn't make me nervous if she tried. It's just that I'd kind of like to . . . well, impress her, I suppose. With the quality of the brunch – tough, with someone who's just left Manhattan. With my swingy hair and my Issa dress. With me. Trying to impress Polly is just a default mode for me, from the very first days of our friendship, formed when she kept rescuing me from mean older girls in the school playground. This is typical Polly, by the way. She may be a bit of a ditz in many ways, but she's always been ferociously loyal when it comes to people she cares about.

Well, almost always.

Oooh, my phone has just started ringing, hurray! Answering it will be even better than keeping busy with a mug of coffee.

As I grab it from my bag, I allow myself the split-second hope that it might be Saad Amar calling, to carry on our discussion about St Martin's. He didn't call over the weekend, which I know is hardly surprising. I mean, he was probably busy doing international billionaire playboy kind of things like . . . actually, like what? Gambling in Monte-Carlo? Purchasing an entire hotel complex in Abu Dhabi with a bit of the loose change he found down the back of the seats of his Ferrari? Snorting a mixture of cocaine and powdered gold from the perfect nipples of Victoria's Secret models?

But it isn't him calling, of course. It's Polly, calling from the tube station to ask for directions to 'this green café place'. I give them to her – as carefully as possible; I'd forgotten that Polly has no sense of direction and couldn't find her way out of a paper bag – and then manage to get hold of the nice waitress for that caffè latte.

It arrives five minutes later, at exactly the same time as Polly.

My first feeling is disappointment. And not in my caffè latte, which is perfect and creamy-looking. But in Polly.

I suppose, given all my efforts, I thought she'd show up looking fabulously brunch-worthy. In an Issa-type dress herself, perhaps, accessorised Polly-style with oodles of jewellery and a sexy strut. But she's wearing ancient-looking jeans and a baggy sweater, her hair in a lank ponytail and her face entirely untouched by makeup. Possibly also by soap. It makes me, in my Russian Red Lipglass, feel like a cross between Katie Price and a Barbie doll.

But then, she has just cancelled her dream wedding to her dream man. I suppose it was unrealistic of me to think she'd turn up looking her usual fabulous self.

'Oh, Gracie,' she says, the moment she sees me. 'I'm so sorry! I thought we were just meeting in a caff.' She gazes around, taking in our surroundings. 'I didn't realise it was posh!'

'Polly, don't be silly!' I give her a huge hug. 'You look great!'

'No, *you* look great. I look like I've been pulled through a hedge backwards. Repeatedly. By an escaped lunatic. On an out-of-control tractor mower.' She sits down opposite me and reaches for my coffee to take a sip. 'God, I need one of these.'

'Well, let's get you one!' I say, in an insanely bright-and-breezy voice that reminds me, for a frightening moment, of Chief Miranda. 'And we should probably have a look at the menu too. The French toast is fabulous . . .' I stop myself, but too late to erase the sheer ghastliness of what I've just said. (I mean, *the French toast is fabulous*? Who do I think I am, Blair Waldorf?) 'Or,' I mumble, as the waitress comes to the table to take our order, 'you could just get a fruit salad or something. I'm sure that's nice too.'

'Actually, I'll just have a coffee,' Polly tells the waitress. 'Black, no sugar, please.'

'Good idea.' I disguise my disappointment that our girlie brunch is now merely a girlie coffee. 'So!' I try again, perkily, just as Polly says, 'So . . .' herself. 'Sorry,' I carry on. 'You go ahead.'

'No, no, you go ahead.'

'Well, I was only going to ask about you, actually. I mean, how you're doing, and everything.'

'I'm OK.'

I bite back the words, *You don't look OK.* 'No one expects you to be OK, Poll. Calling off a wedding is a huge deal.'

She lets out an odd laugh. 'Make me feel even more shit about it, why don't you?'

'I don't mean to. I just want to know how it all happened. I mean, what made you decide to suddenly –'

'Gracie, please. I've had quite enough of this from Bella.'

This I can certainly imagine. Bella is one of life's natural big sisters – a haranguer and a poker-of-nose. It can't have been much fun for Polly, staying with Bella these past few days.

'Hey, I've got an idea!' I say, as something suddenly occurs to me. Something actually practically helpful that I could do for Polly. 'Why don't you come and stay with me for a bit? I mean, stay with us.' Charlie's at home so infrequently, I do sometimes forget that I actually live with him. 'Just to get a break from Bella's questions, I mean. You could spend a bit of time with the boys, and you and me would have the chance to hang out . . .'

'Oh, Gracie, I'm grateful. But I've already got somewhere else to stay. It's a friend's flat. In Clapham.'

'Are you sure?' I don't want to let this chance go. 'I mean, living by yourself isn't the easiest thing in the world, especially when you've just split up with someone –'

'Which I don't want to talk about.'

'I didn't say you had to talk about it!' I have to admit, this isn't going quite as well as I hoped. Polly seems prickly, and uptight, and not at all like anyone ever behaves in an episode of *Sex and the City*. Not even prissy old Charlotte. 'I'm just trying to help.'

'I know. I'm sorry.' Polly breaks off as the coffee arrives. 'But, look,' she says, picking up her mug, and looking pretty grateful for something to do with her hands herself, 'we're not just here to talk about me, for heaven's sake! I want to hear all about you. And my lovely godsons, of course. How are they?'

'They're great. Knackering, but great.'

'And Charlie?'

'And Charlie's . . . well, Charlie is Charlie.'

'Oh. Right.' She sips her coffee. 'Well, I'm glad he's OK.'

'No, that's not the point! I mean, it's *not* OK. Charlie being Charlie isn't a good thing.' I know I said I don't usually talk to Polly about my marriage, but it's been such a long time since I spoke to her properly at all – such a long time since I spoke to anyone, properly – that I can feel it all simmering up under the surface. 'Charlie being Charlie is Charlie being distant, and patronising. And never making it home from the office earlier than nine o'clock at night. And banging on at me about low-fat hummus, and yellow shower gel.'

'Wait. Hold on a minute.' Polly's face is creased with confusion, but at least she's starting to listen. 'He's *eating* shower gel?'

'No, he's not eating shower gel! Shower gel is just one of his many little obsessions! Shower gel is just a . . . a metaphor for the disaster zone that is my marriage.'

Polly puts down her mug. 'Since when is your marriage a disaster zone?'

'Since he started working at MMA Capital. No, since he lost his job at Farrell Christie Dench. No . . .' Now I'm actually thinking about it, it probably goes further back still. 'Since Hector was born. Or Robbie, perhaps. I don't know.' I can feel my words starting to come in a rush. 'Since he stopped talking to me, and since he stopped listening to me, and since he stopped fancying me. I mean, for Christ's sake, Polly, do you know we haven't had sex in six and a half months?' I add, just at the moment that a shadow falls across our table.

It's a shadow that belongs to Chief Miranda.

'Well!' she says, barely managing to hide the smile that flickers across her face. 'I do hope I'm not interrupting anything, ladies.'

'Miranda! How lovely to see you!' Miserably, I plaster on a smile. 'Um, this is my friend Polly. She's just got back from New York,' I feel the need to add, because I don't want Chief Miranda judging Polly on her current state of shabbiness, and 'just got back' could mean she stepped right off the plane an hour ago.

'How wonderful. I adore New York.' But Chief Miranda barely gives her even a second glance, which is a sign of how far from her usual knock-out self Polly is at the moment. 'So, I didn't see you at the school today, Grace. What's the news on the Amar family? Have you managed to speak to your husband about it?'

'Actually, Miranda, I spoke to Saad Amar myself.'

'*Oh?*'

'Yes.' Do *not* blush, Grace. 'I met him at the company party I told you about. We had a quick chat about St Martin's, and he's going to give me a call to talk further some time soon.'

'Soon?'

'Yes.'

'And how soon, Grace, is soon?'

'Well . . . I suppose . . . soon?' The word 'soon' is starting to sound ridiculous.

'You'll have to call him yourself, then. This is too important to wait.'

'Look, I don't know if I *can* actually call him myself, Miranda. I mean, he's a very busy man . . .'

'Yes. That's precisely why I wanted to ask you to ask your husband to do it.' She rolls her eyes. 'You know what, don't worry about it, Grace. I probably shouldn't have even asked you in the first place. It's too important a job to leave it up to you.'

Before I can say anything – before I've even worked out *what* to say in the face of such astonishing rudeness – Polly has leaned forward.

'Sorry,' she's saying to Miranda, 'I'm not trying to eavesdrop. But this is a phone call to a man about a school, yes?'

'Yes, but –'

'Well, I'm not a mother, unfortunately.' She makes 'unfortunately' sound like 'thank Christ for that'. 'So for all I know, the sheer complexity of making a phone call to a man about a school is right up there with brokering peace in Gaza or discovering a cure for male-pattern baldness. But either way, don't you think it might be sensible for Grace to finish the job she's already started, and that she's already put considerable time and effort into?'

Miranda's eyebrows have shot up so far they've practically disappeared into her hairline. 'Excuse me?'

'It's just that it seems like Grace already has an "in" with this man, and I'm sure if he's said he'll call, he'll call. I don't think there's any need for anyone to go getting their panties in a bunch about whether he calls today, tomorrow, or the day after that.'

Polly finishes her statement with a pleasant – indeed, a rather dazzling – smile. But her eyes are fixed on Chief Miranda like a mother lioness's on a prowling hyena.

And for me, it's twenty years ago in the playground all over again, and Polly is hurtling to my defence when one of the older girls is trying to pull my skirt up so her friends can all laugh at my strawberry-print knickers.

'Well!' says Miranda, after a long moment, during which I'm quite sure global warming has been reversed and several ice-caps have refrozen. 'Far be it from me to stand in your way, Grace, if you really want to see this project through.'

I mumble a string of vaguely appropriate words, like 'yes', and 'absolutely', and 'get back to you a.s.a.p.', and then, thank God, Chief Miranda's Miranda cohorts arrive and start shrieking at her from across the café, and she walks away to rejoin her species.

'Oh, Gracie, I'm really sorry.' As soon as she's gone Polly reaches over the table and grabs one of my hands. 'But she was just *such* a bitch, I couldn't help it!'

'No, it's all right. And she is. Such a bitch, I mean.' I take a deep breath. 'Look, Polly, I'm sorry I brought you here. It's not . . . it's not *us*, is it? Can we just go and get a crappy Starbucks or something?'

'Oh, thank God, Gracie. Yes, let's escape to Starbucks! Though I'm not sure if their French toast will be quite so fabulous.'

I laugh, which makes her laugh, and when the bill has been paid and we're on our way to Starbucks, we're still faintly chuckling. Polly links her arm through mine as we march along the street, and I feel an instant warm glow inside. *This* is what I had in mind when I planned my morning with Polly.

'So, Gracie,' she says, after a moment or two. 'Tell me again what you were saying earlier. About things not being great with Charlie.'

Out in the cold, crisp air, freshly triumphant from The Great Defeat of Chief Miranda, it suddenly seems a lot less important to talk about Charlie. 'Oh, I don't know. I'm just being silly, really. We're just going through a bit of a bad patch right now.'

'It sounds like more than that. It sounds like you've been going through a bad patch for the last seven years.'

I don't answer.

'Gracie, if you're really unhappy with Charlie, you can leave him, you know.'

I let out a snort of laughter. 'Yeah, right.'

'People do leave their husbands, Grace! It's not the fifties any more.'

'It's not because of that! It's . . . well, it's because of the boys. I don't want them to grow up without their father. You know, Percy has all kinds of problems, and I'm quite sure they're because Charlie left when he was so young.'

'Percy has all kinds of problems because his mother is Vanessa.'

I can't argue too hard with this.

'Anyway, don't you deserve to be happy, Grace? Don't the boys deserve a mother who's happy?'

I can't argue too hard with this either. 'Polly, please. I'm not even thinking about leaving Charlie. It's a rocky patch. I should never even have said anything. And that's an end to it . . . hang on, I'd better get this,' I say, as my phone starts to ring. I fumble for it in my bag, fail to recognise the mobile number that's flashing on the screen, and answer. 'Hello, Grace Costello's phone?'

'Hello, Grace Costello's phone. This is Saad Amar's phone.'

My heart does a little backflip. I take a deep breath. 'Oh, hello, Mr Amar. Thank you for calling.'

'It's Saad, please. Look, I meant to try you over the weekend, but I assumed you'd be busy.'

'Yes, absolutely.' After all, he doesn't have to know that in my world, *busy* means endless cooking of eggs Benedict, watching the same *Fireman Sam* DVD fourteen times in one day, and running around the garden with Hector looking for giants. 'Very busy indeed.'

'Ah. Then maybe it's the wrong time to ask if you could spare an hour or so for a quick lunch today?'

'Lunch? Today? With you?'

'*With who?*' Polly is mouthing at me.

'Yes,' says Saad. 'With me. I've been thinking up all the questions I wanted to ask you about St Martin's, and I think it's most efficient if we do it while we eat, don't you?'

Of course. St Martin's. I'd completely forgotten. 'Um, yes. I think that would be . . . efficient.'

'Excellent. I'll have my secretary make reservations at Locanda Locatelli. Is one o'clock too late for you?'

'No, no. One at Locanda Locatelli is perfect.'

'Good. See you there, Grace Costello's phone. Oh, and don't forget to bring Grace with you.'

I'm mid-tinkling laugh when he hangs up.

Polly's mouth has fallen open. 'Were you *flirting*?'

'That wasn't flirting! Well, OK. It was . . . attempted flirting.'

'Well, who was it?'

I can't help the smile that I can feel spreading like sunshine across my lips. 'Saad Amar. He's Charlie's boss. And the guy Miranda was haranguing me about.'

'Wait. St Martin's Dad Guy is also Charlie's boss?'

'Yes. But he's not a dad. He's an older brother.'

'And he's incredibly sexy, obviously.'

'How do you know he's incredibly sexy?'

'*Oh, hello, Mr Amar . . . Thank you for calling!*' Polly breathes, in what I presume is supposed to be an impression of me. Even though I highly doubt I was using quite so sultry a voice as that. '*That's* how I know he's incredibly sexy.'

'Well, it's totally irrelevant, anyway, how sexy he is. I'm just meeting him for a quick lunch and a chat about St Martin's. I'm not planning to rip off all his clothes and jump into bed with him.'

'More's the pity.'

'Polly!'

'But don't you see how perfect this is, Grace?' She

grabs one of my hands. 'I mean, OK, I accept that it might be difficult for you to leave Charlie. But if you were thinking, by any chance, of taking a lover . . .'

I can't help laughing out loud.

'I'm serious! It might be just the thing, to keep you happy enough to stay in your marriage!'

I'm starting to see why Polly might not be all that cut out for marriage herself after all.

'Polly. I'm not going to take a lover, as you so eloquently put it. And even if I were, it wouldn't be Saad Amar. The man's a billionaire, for God's sake! An international playboy. He probably goes after models and actresses. Not stay-at-home mums from Parsons Green.'

'He's not interested in you that way at all, then?' Polly folds her arms. 'So is he going to tell Charlie that he's taking you for lunch to one of the most romantic restaurants in London?'

'How can I possibly know what he's going to tell Charlie?'

'Are *you* going to tell Charlie that he's taking you for lunch to one of the most romantic restaurants in London?'

It's my turn to fall silent. After a couple of moments, I say, 'I bet it's not one of the most romantic restaurants in London *at lunchtime*. I bet it's full of men in suits talking about their giant bonuses.'

'Grace, all I'm trying to say is that it sounds as though he likes you. It sounds as though you like him. And I just can't . . .' Her voice wobbles. I think it takes her by surprise as much as it does me. 'I can't stand to hear that you're unhappy with Charlie. And if this Saad guy could make you happier, even if only a little bit . . .'

'It's kind of a dangerous way of making myself happier, though. I mean, having an affair –' I break off. 'Look, Poll, I really need to get going, OK? I feel bad that we've not managed to talk about any of your stuff, but maybe we can –'

'I've told you. I don't want to talk about it.'

'But we'll see each other later this week? I can come to see the new flat in Clapham!'

'Sure,' she says, though without a huge amount of enthusiasm, before giving me a quick hug. 'Call me, Gracie, won't you? Let me know how your lunch goes.'

I nod, and give her a hug back before hurrying for the tube station.

Grace

Monday 23 November
I've half a hour to kill before I'm due at Locanda Locatelli, so I've decided to use up the time in Selfridges, where I've somehow found my way to the lingerie department.

This is where I've just done a very silly thing.

Before stopping to think, I've picked out a pretty new bra and knickers from the Elle Macpherson Intimates range, tried them on in the changing room, and now I'm just waiting for the salesgirl to come back with a pair of scissors so she can cut the labels off and I can buy them and wear them right now, underneath my Issa dress, instead of the slightly saggy M&S knickers and the navy bra I bought in a French hypermarket three . . . no, four years ago.

'It's so important, I always think,' I say to the salesgirl as she returns, 'to have the right underwear on beneath your clothes. No matter what you're doing, I mean! It's . . . it's just a good foundation, isn't it? For external poise and confidence.'

'Mm, absolutely,' she agrees, snipping the label off the knickers (lacy, white) then turning her attention to the bra (matching, with light padding – believe me, I need it – and a plunge front) before handing them both back to me. 'Makes you feel better about yourself, top to toe.'

'Yes! Precisely! Feel better about yourself! It's important – *as a woman*, I mean – to have enough self-esteem to wear pretty lingerie just for the hell of it. Isn't it?' I'm aware that I'm clattering out the words at the rate of a champion typist, and that the salesgirl is looking at me as though she thinks I might have a serious coke habit, or something. 'I mean, they say so in the magazines all the time. So I'm sure loads of your customers do it for that reason. Just so that *we* know we're wearing it. We're not doing it because we're thinking we might end up having sex with someone we're just going out for lunch with.'

There's a bit of a silence.

'I'll just go and put these through on the till, shall I?' the salesgirl says, after a moment. 'Leave you to get dressed and see you there in a couple of minutes?'

Actually, it takes me a bit longer than a couple of minutes, because I use the opportunity not only to put on my new underwear, but also to zhuzh up my hair a bit and touch up my makeup with the bits and bobs I've just bought in the cosmetics hall downstairs. The Russian Red Lipglass was Just Too Much, I decided. Or maybe Just Not Me. Either way, I'm replacing it with a pretty flesh-coloured Givenchy lipstick and subtle shady-cheekbony-effects with a shamefully expensive NARS Multiple.

Pretty, pretty, pretty. Confidence-building. Not

sexy. Or available. Just like my brand-new pretty white underwear. That only I'm going to know I'm wearing.

Because obviously Polly was way off base to get all excited about the possibility that I might end up in bed with Saad. Sorry – take him as my lover. Like I tried to tell her, just because he's happy to flirt with me, doesn't mean he's got the faintest intention of actually making a move on me. And more importantly, even if he did, I really do have absolutely no intention of reciprocating. If it came up (in a manner of speaking) I'd politely decline. Courteously – but firmly – say no to the prospect of his strong body pressing itself against mine, his muscular arms entwining themselves around me, his soft, probing lips working their way from my neck s-l-o-w-l-y down to the hollow of my collarbone, before pausing only to lift me off my feet, throw me down onto a bed, rip open my Issa dress, and . . .

Look, I never said I wasn't *imagining* what it might be like to end up in bed with Saad. I mean, we can all *imagine*, can't we?

I'm five minutes late when I eventually hurry through the doors of Locanda Locatelli, and I can see Saad waiting for me at the (quiet, corner) table.

He's looking better even than I remembered him, comfortable in his smooth, light brown skin and a perfectly tailored grey suit. He's also wearing a pristine white shirt, discreet cufflinks, and a beautiful silk tie in a vibrant shade of burnt orange that looks great with his dark hair and molten black eyes.

I actually have to catch my breath.

He stands up to greet me, putting down his BlackBerry and extending a formal hand. I've barely time to register disappointment that he didn't move in for a continental-style double-cheek kiss when he says, with the smallest of frowns, 'You're late.'

'Only five minutes!' I say, as the waiter shuffles me into my seat.

'Well, I was early. So for me it was more like ten.' He doesn't seem at all concerned about the unfairness of this statement. 'I took the liberty of going ahead and ordering for both of us, if you don't mind. I hope you like rabbit.'

'Um, yes . . . rabbit is lovely . . .' What I really mean by this, of course, is that *rabbits are lovely*; that I kept them as pets as a child and that the last thing I want to put in my mouth and chew is a cuddly, fluffy, pancetta-wrapped bunnikins. But I'm scared that if I object to his choice, he'll just be irritable about me being 'late' again. Because so far – and for the second time today – the meal really isn't going the way I imagined it.

'I would have ordered a glass of wine,' he carries on, 'but it's lunchtime, and we've got rather a lot to be getting through, so I thought it'd be more sensible to stick to sparkling water.'

'Yes, of course.' Thank God, in fact. I mean, wine would have been nice, and everything, just to give me that extra little boost of confidence that even my new knickers can't provide, but obviously it might have sent entirely the wrong signals. Boozing, at lunch, with a man who's not my husband. 'Sparkling water is just what I'd have ordered.'

'Good.' His black eyes meet – and hold – mine for a moment, then move away as he reaches for a spiral-bound notebook that's sitting between us on the table. 'So! First things first. I suppose one aspect I'm most interested in is extracurricular activities.'

I swallow. 'What – er – what kind of extra-curricular activities?'

'Drama. Judo. Other sports. Adnan – that's my little brother, by the way – is a very keen junior cricketer. So I'd be really interested to hear about your son's experience of the added extras St Martin's has to offer.'

Of course. Extracurricular activities *at St Martin's*. That's what we're here to talk about. Damn and blast Polly for putting other ideas into my head.

I take a sip of my San Pellegrino, grateful for its cool, refreshing bubbles. 'Well, yes, the school really has some wonderful added extras. There is drama. There is cricket. There is judo.' I sound like a total imbecile, and from the way Saad is looking at me, not writing a word down in his spiral notebook, he pretty much thinks I'm an imbecile too. Gone is the amused, flirty gaze of the other evening at the party. Now he just looks faintly cross, and harassed, and not all that pleased to be here. 'Um, I'm afraid my son doesn't do an awful lot of those kind of activities, though . . .'

'Oh? Why not?'

'Well, I'm a big believer in not pushing kids to *do* things all the time,' I explain, which is my attempt at making my *laissez-faire* style sound like an actual child-rearing philosophy that even a fully-fledged Miranda would approve of. 'You know, just giving them space and time to grow, finding out their interests for themselves . . .'

I witter on like the most boring and over-involved mother in the universe until the arrival of the pancetta-wrapped bunnikins, for which I'm suddenly absurdly grateful. I mean, at least the act of trying to get it down my neck shuts me up for a few minutes, so that Saad can ask a few different questions – about the quality of the science and maths teaching, and how the children get along with the staff – and actually get the opportunity to write something concrete down in his notebook. He barely touches his rabbit himself, and his manner is brisk and businesslike. When the waiters come to clear our plates away I'm desperate for him to ask for the bill so this meal can end and I can crawl away to my normal, humdrum life, where I don't get my hopes up about flirtation with gorgeous billionaires. My heart actually sinks when he asks for a slice of the lemon tart and two double espressos.

'My peace offering,' he says, as the waiter heads off with the order, 'if you'll accept it.'

Peace offering? I blink at him. 'I wasn't aware there'd been a war.'

'I was cranky when you arrived. And I've carried on being cranky throughout lunch. I apologise.' He runs a hand through his hair in an exasperated fashion that just so happens to make him even more devastatingly attractive than before. Not that I'm letting myself think about that any more. Not now he's made it so obvious that the purpose of this lunch really *was* just business after all. 'It's just that I had a piece of rather bad news a couple of minutes before you got here.'

'Oh, no! Is everything OK?'

'I'm afraid it's not. Not really.' He lets out a sigh, long and weary. 'I had a call from my art buyer. He was bidding for me in an auction at Sotheby's this morning. And I'm afraid I lost out on a Van Gogh I was very keen on.'

I almost splutter a mouth of San Pellegrino over the tablecloth. 'That's your kind of bad news?'

A half-smile flickers across his face for just a moment, then it's gone again. 'Believe me, I'm aware how ludicrous it sounds. But I was really keen on getting my hands on this painting, Grace. I don't know if you care about art at all, but –'

'No, I do! Very much so, in fact. I adore art!' I realise that this might sound almost as silly and pretentious as my *fabulous French toast* earlier, so I carry on, hastily. 'I went to art school after my A levels, actually. Well, until I dropped out at the beginning of my third year to marry Charlie . . .' I tail off, aware that Saad might not be all that interested in my academic disappointments.

But actually, he's still listening, with an engaged expression on his face that looks entirely genuine.

Either that, or he's learned the world's most impeccable manners at some kind of International Playboy training academy.

'Um, so, yes, I really do like art,' I finish lamely. 'I'd be interested to hear about the Van Gogh you wanted to buy.'

'Lying cow.'

I stare at him. 'What did you say?'

'*Lying Cow*,' he repeats, that half-smile crossing his face again. 'It's the name of the painting I wanted to buy.'

'Oh! I . . . I haven't heard of it.'

'No, it isn't exactly a major work of his.' He reaches into his inside jacket pocket, pulls out a slim, folded-back Sotheby's catalogue, and hands it over to me. It shows, indeed, a picture of a cow, lying down and looking forwards, in Van Gogh's swirly brushstrokes. 'What do you think?'

I glance up. He's watching me, intently, as though what I say about it really matters to him. Suddenly – incredibly – I feel inspired to give my real opinion for a change. 'Honestly?'

'Honestly.'

'I don't love it.'

'You don't?'

'No, I mean, it's a Van Gogh, so of course it's not like there's anything *wrong* with it. A Van Gogh painting of a cow is always going to be a million times better than anyone else's painting of a cow. But it's still . . . well, it's just a painting of a cow.'

'That's very true, Grace. Very true,' he says, nodding as if I've just given him the benefit of Ph.D.-level expertise in Van Gogh's pastoral period. 'So what do you think I should have been bidding for instead?' He points at a couple more items in the well-thumbed catalogue. '*Peasants Burning Weeds*? *Still Life with Cabbages and Clogs*?'

'Well, let me think . . .' The rare and exotic feeling that someone – most of all, a wildly attractive, powerful man like Saad Amar – is actually interested in what I have to say is making me feel rather heady and reckless. I've already taken a risk and given him my actual, instinctive opinion about something. Now I'm going to take it one step further. I'm going to do something I haven't done in years. I'm going to attempt a bit of banter. 'The world of art would be a poorer place without weed-burning peasants. But then, there's always room in any good collection for a picture of some wooden shoes and a cabbage.'

My teasing works. He laughs. Out loud.

It's the nicest sound I've heard in months.

'Well, poor old Vincent obviously doesn't have your vote today,' he says, as the coffees and lemon tart arrive. He nods to the waiter to put the lemon tart down in front of me, and then summons the bill with just a suggestive kind of scribble in the air with one hand.

It makes me wonder what other suggestive things Saad Amar might be able to do with that hand.

'So how do you feel about the other grand masters?'

he carries on. 'Picasso, for example?'

'I did my A level dissertation on him!' Well, on Picasso and his mistresses, to be exact, with the rather splendidly portentous title '*Goddesses and Doormats: Dora Maar, Marie-Thérèse Walter and Pablo Picasso, 1927–1943*. It's funny, though, I can remember the title, and I can remember doing all the research, but I have no recollection whatsoever which one was the goddess and which one the doormat.

Saad doesn't say anything for a moment, as the waiter has come up with the bill and the credit card machine. He hands over his card (it's platinum-coloured, or perhaps made from solid platinum, for all I know), taps in his PIN, then takes a hefty wad of cash for a tip out of his pocket and leaves it on the silver salver. Then he clears his throat, fixes his eyes right on mine and says, 'So, Grace. How would you like to come back to my place and have a look at my grand master?'

I'm quite literally lost for words.

'My Picasso,' he adds, before I can say anything stupid.

Ohhhhh . . . *that* kind of grand master.

Because just for a moment there, when he was staring right at me, he had this . . . *look* about him. The same look he had at the MMA Capital party. A look that implied, albeit briefly, that he wasn't talking about showing me a work of art at all.

'It's from his early Cubist period,' he's saying, 'which I don't know if you're a fan of at all. But it's a very striking piece. Well-regarded by art historians. It's really not far to my place, just a few minutes away in Mayfair.'

'I'd love to,' I say.

Look, I don't really have an option. He's already getting up, chivalrously coming round to my side of the table to pull my chair out for me. And actually, I'd give anything to see a real-life Picasso – not in a museum, I mean, or an art gallery, but hanging on the wall of someone's home, like an ordinary person might have a black-and-white Robert Doisneau print or a montage of family photographs.

'Great. My car is parked right outside,' he says, placing one hand in the small of my back as we head out of the restaurant.

Indeed, his car is parked right outside – not a flashy, splashy, bright red Ferrari, as I'd imagined, but a beautiful dark green Aston Martin. Saad opens the door for me himself and I sink into the leather seat before he goes round to his side and climbs in.

It certainly beats jostling on the tube, or even standing in the cold and rain, which has now started, looking for a taxi.

He's a fast driver, but a good one, moving smoothly through the traffic which – maybe this is just the Aston Martin effect – seems to part for him. And there isn't even much chance for us to talk as we drive, because a work call comes through on his phone a moment or two after we get in the car (not from Charlie, thank *Christ*) and this occupies him for most of the four or five minutes it takes to reach our destination, a tall, red-brick town house a short distance from Berkeley Square.

Saad gets out and comes round to open my door for me, while I try to look like climbing out of posh sports cars is the kind of thing I do all the time. I don't think I'm doing a terrible job of it, but even I can't stop my mouth from falling open when the front door to the town house opens (*is* opened, in fact, from the inside, by a very tall, very upright ex-military-looking man who I assume is some kind of . . . what's the technical term? Valet? Aide-de-camp?) and Saad directs me through it.

Jesus Christ.

So this is his 'place'.

I don't know why – because I'm an idiot, I suppose – but I somehow imagined that, because of the swankiness of the location, plus the fact that he's a single guy in his thirties, his 'place' would be some kind of apartment within this building. A bachelor pad, albeit a large and expensive one. But now I can see that I got this utterly wrong.

I'm standing in the entrance hall of what is very obviously a whole house. A very large and exceptionally beautiful whole house. Either Saad himself or an extremely discerning interior designer has gone for the stunning effect you get when you mix old and new. The airy lobby has a classic chequered marble floor and antique console tables, contrasted with graphic contemporary light-fittings and several huge and very modern-looking oil paintings on the walls (though no Picasso here, at least). There's an oak staircase, polished to an almost ridiculous sheen, leading both downwards – to what I suspect, from the delicious food aromas floating from the general direction, is a basement kitchen – and upwards, to what must be a large number of bedrooms. Four doors lead off the hallway, through which I catch glimpses of other equally astonishing-looking reception rooms (oak panelling, Eames chairs, pale grey leather Chesterfields) before Saad lightly touches my shoulder and I realise I should stop gawping like a schoolgirl.

'Would you mind, Grace, if I just go and put in a call to the office? My housekeeper can bring you something to drink while you wait, if you like. Some water? Another coffee?'

'Oh, yes, some water would be lovely, thank you.'

'Sure.' He starts through one of the doors, saying to the upright ex-military man as he passes him, 'Thomas, would you show Mrs Costello through to the drawing room and then get her some chilled water?'

Wait – *he's* the housekeeper? Maybe I've read too many Agatha Christies, but I thought housekeepers had to be sturdy, robust women in their mid-sixties, wearing flowery pinnies, armed with feather dusters and prone to saying things like, 'Lawks a'mercy' and 'I'm a good, God-fearing Christian woman, sir.' But Thomas, quite apart from very much *not* being a sturdy, robust woman, and probably in his mid-fifties rather than sixties, is wearing a dark three-piece suit and carrying an iPad, of all things. And he doesn't say 'Lawks a'mercy' or anything about being God-fearing; he just holds open the door to a room with a pale grey Chesterfield and says, in a clipped, discreet tone, 'Do go on through, madam. I'll bring you that water in just a moment.'

And he's as good as his word. I've barely had time to perch on the edge of the sofa when Thomas reappears, bearing a wide tray with a tall, frosted glass, a bottle of mineral water, a dish of ice-cubes and another of fresh lime slices.

'Ice and lime in your sparkling water, madam?'

'Oh, yes, thank you! But I can sort it out myself, honestly . . .'

He ignores me, but somehow does so with grave politeness. 'Allow me, Mrs Costello.'

Is it just me, or is there something a bit snide about the way he's just said 'Mrs Costello'? An oh-so-subtle emphasis on the *Mrs* that implies some kind of disapproval?

It must be this that makes me blurt out what I say next. 'I'm only here to look at the Picasso!'

'Of course, Mrs Costello. I'm sure you're quite the art lover.'

OK. There was nothing ambiguous about the snideness that time. I can feel myself bristling and getting flustered in equal measure. 'I am, actually! I've written a dissertation about Picasso, as it happens. Well, about Picasso and his mistresses.'

'How interesting. He had a lot of those, I gather.'

'A lot of what?'

Thomas glances up and meets my eye. 'Mistresses,' he says.

There's a meaningful silence.

Then Thomas starts for the door. 'So, I'll leave you until Mr Amar is finished,' he says. 'Unless there's anything else I can get for you?'

'No. Thank you.'

'Very good, Mrs Costello.'

'Thomas,' I find myself saying, before I can stop, 'I really *am* here to look at the Picasso, you know.'

His left eyebrow barely flickers. 'As I said, of course, Mrs Costello. But – and this is just so you're not under any illusions – you should know that the Picasso is extremely popular with the ladies of Mr Amar's acquaintance. A lot of them come here to look at it. Some of them come to look at it two or three times a week.'

He pulls the door silently shut behind him.

Shit. I mean, seriously, seriously, *shit*.

I've really, royally fucked this one up, haven't I?

What was I thinking, coming back to Saad's place like this? All right, I may not be up to the supermodel standards he's accustomed to, but I'm still a woman, aren't I? And as Thomas's warning (I *think* kindly meant, though obviously it would be easier to tell if he removed the poker from up his bum) has just made crystal clear, men like Saad Amar are used to getting any woman they want.

Jesus, there probably isn't even a Picasso here at all! And Saad probably isn't on the phone to the office, he's probably on the phone to his drug dealer, ordering up a nifty little batch of his usual gold-laced cocaine so he can get his kicks snorting it from a pair of distinctly ordinary breasts for a change rather than a pair belonging to a Victoria's Secret model.

OK. Staggeringly sexy though he is, this isn't something I'm going to get mixed up in. I'll say I've just had an urgent phone call from Hector's nursery . . . God, no, I can't use my son to get me out of a sordid situation like this. I'll say I've had an urgent phone call from a friend, and I really can't stick around.

'Sorry about that, Grace,' Saad is saying now, as he comes into the drawing room. 'I didn't mean to keep you waiting so long . . . Oh, are you going somewhere?'

'I have just had an urgent call from a friend,' I say, robotically. 'I really can't stick around.'

'Oh, now, come on! Just another five minutes!' He heads across the room towards me, that sexy walk that's a cross between a confident stride and a panther-like prowl, and makes both my legs and my resolve weaken. 'After all, Grace,' he adds, in a low voice, his eyes boring into mine with that by-now-familiar naughty glint, 'I think that's the very least you owe me.'

'I think there's been a big misunderstanding,' I croak. 'I can't . . . I mean, I'd love to, God knows, I'd love to . . . but I'm married, Saad. And Charlie works for you. Not that it'd make it any less wrong if he didn't! Work for you, I mean . . . but . . . look, obviously I'm very flattered and all that . . . it's just . . .'

'There most certainly has been a big misunderstanding.' He presses his lips together in a thin, flat line. 'Didn't Thomas explain to you that I was planning to try you out to be one of my wives?'

'No,' I whisper.

'Well!' he tuts. 'This is disappointing! I mean, I'm sure you understand that in my culture, a man is entitled to take up to four wives – a kind of harem, if you will – and I'm currently auditioning a select group for the role of number three. I had very high hopes for you, Grace, very high hopes indeed. And frankly, I think you're being rather short-sighted. I can pay Charlie off with a big cheque, no problem, and your children will be very comfortable at the Swiss boarding school we'll pack them off to . . .'

It's at this point that I realise.

He's taking the piss.

'Ha,' I manage to say, 'ha.'

Saad explodes with laughter. 'Grace, you kill me! What were you thinking – that you were trapped in some Middle Eastern vice den? Were you expecting to be taken off to have your feet washed and drink mint tea before I summon you to my chamber?'

More than I've ever wanted anything in my life, I want the polished oak floor to open up and swallow me whole.

And almost more than this, I want Saad Amar to say

the words 'summon you to my chamber' again. Only this time, for him not to be joking.

'No, I didn't think that, actually,' I say, with as much icy hauteur as I can summon under the circumstances (i.e., not much).

'All I meant, Grace, when I said that you owed me, was that you owed me *five minutes*. Because of the five minutes you kept me waiting at Locatelli.' He lets out a couple of shouts of laughter again before noticing my discomfort and calming himself down. 'I'm sorry, Grace. That was very wicked of me. How about a second peace offering for the day?' He puts his hands on my shoulders, turns me to face away from him, and points towards the far wall. 'As promised.'

It's the Picasso. And it's very wonderful and amazing, and all that – muddy terracotta colours and bold, graphic shapes, which I think, though it's tricky to tell, depict a female nude – but I'm still far too embarrassed really to take it in. So I just make the appropriate noises, and agree with him that yes, it's a terrific example of early Cubism, and that yes, this is far more my kind of thing than Van Gogh's weed-killing peasants, or whatever they were.

And I'm weak with relief when, a few minutes later, he finally says, 'So, Grace, will you let Thomas take you home? I'm not heading back to the office, so he's at your disposal.'

'God, no. I mean, thank you, but there's no need. I can just jump on a bus.'

He frowns, as if the very concept of public transport

is alien to him. 'There's no need for anything like that. Besides, it's miserable out there. Won't you at least allow me to put you in a taxi?'

I agree to this, because at least it avoids the Thomas issue. Nevertheless, I still have to run the Thomas gauntlet as Saad ushers me out into the hallway and towards the front door. He's looking rather taken aback at this early end to my visit; probably he was expecting me to stay for longer, doing whatever it is Saad's merry parade of women do behind closed doors. He looks so astonished, in fact, that I almost want to apologise for letting him down.

Between the pair of them, they rustle up a passing taxi and, with Thomas holding an umbrella over both of us, we all three make a dash for it.

Saad places two polite, chaste kisses on either cheek, just the way I was desperate for him to do earlier, but now it feels flat and pointless. Then he opens my door, shuts me inside, and gives a cheery wave as the taxi pulls away from the kerb.

It's the cheery wave that puts the tin lid on it. It's sexless and, though I know it shouldn't be, deeply humiliating.

What was it that Thomas said? That a lot of Mr Amar's lady friends come to 'look at the Picasso'? That some of them come to look at it two or three times a week? But not in my case.

In my case, he really *did* just want to show me his grand master.

And somehow I don't get the impression that Saad

was holding off because I'm married, to one of his employees or otherwise. Saad Amar does not strike me as the kind of man who'd hesitate to take a woman he wanted, married or single.

So it's clear, then: I'm not good enough. No surprises there. That night of the MMA party, I must have mistaken simple friendliness for what I, in my utterly lonely, attention-deprived state, took to be flirtation.

It's a huge relief, really. Not to have to fight off his inappropriate advances, I mean.

But still. I'm almost all the way back home before I stop physically cringing in my ridiculous new Elle Macpherson knickers.

Bella

Thursday 26 November

According to Catherine Zeta-Jones, in a magazine interview I read once at the dentist's, the secret to a happy relationship is twofold: separate bathrooms and a once-a-week date night.

Of course, in Catherine Zeta-Jones's case, choosing to have a relationship with a multimillionaire member of Hollywood royalty probably doesn't do all that much harm either.

But I suppose we could all stand to take a leaf or two out of the divine Catherine's book. And seeing as I don't own a property big enough to boast two bathrooms (though I would, after eighteen months of living with Jamie, *kill* for a separate loo), the least I think we can do is go for regular date nights.

Dates have fallen by the wayside in the past few months, though. A combination of me working three or four evenings a week, and Jamie being too skint to pay for anything.

Which is why I almost fell off my chair when, at breakfast this morning, he announced that he was taking me out for dinner tonight. (Not strictly accurate, I suspect, as I'll no doubt end up actually paying the bill, or, because Jamie can be a bit old-fashioned about wanting to appear to pay, slipping him a handful of cash beforehand.) But it was his *suggestion*, which counts for something. I think it's meant as a combined apology, both for the whole Naked Gorilla-Man episode on Saturday, and for the fact that, five days on, the Naked Gorilla-Man is still staying in my spare bedroom.

I'll be honest, it's the principle I object to, rather than the reality. Now that he's not naked any more, and blowing my chances of impressing social workers, Gorilla-Man – sorry, *Liam* – isn't actually a *bad* houseguest. He's neat, and tidy, which counts for a lot. And anyway, he's practically invisible most of the time. He's pretty much always out, either with Jamie and The Boys, or, I gather, going for job interviews. (I've no idea what kind of job interviews, any more than I've any idea why he's planning on moving to London, or how long it's going to be before he finds a place of his own. Jamie's not hot on having those kinds of conversations, and I don't want to make him feel as though his friends aren't welcome.) But still, it's not ideal to be playing host so indefinitely.

Which is something that, to my astonishment, Jamie seems to have realised. And which I think is the reason behind his invitation to dinner, tonight, at my favourite Italian restaurant. And I'm meeting him there a couple of hours from now, so it's really time to get myself tarted up.

It's been a busy day, catering a lunch for sixteen in

Ravenscourt Park, so I urgently need to have a shower and wash the smell of cooking oil out of my hair. Plus there's the fact that I should have Jolen'd my upper lip three days ago, and I don't want Jamie to turn up for his date only to find a Salvador Dali lookalike waiting for him. Anyway, while Gorilla-Man is staying, I suppose I should make a little bit more effort with the basics of my appearance. Even though he might be pretty lax in the hair-removal department himself.

I've just smeared the thick bleach over my top lip and sat down on the edge of the bath to have a little flick through this month's *Waitrose Food Illustrated* while I wait, when my phone rings in my trouser pocket.

I'm genuinely taken aback to see that it's Dev calling.

I've tried him – three or four times, in fact – over the last week or so, though I haven't taken offence that he hasn't returned my calls. Dev's an erratic caller at the best of times, which I suppose is pretty normal for a hospital surgeon. And I can hardly blame him for taking his time to call me back under these particular circumstances. I know what it's like to be the one who's been dumped, when you feel like you'd rather do anything – hide under the duvet; crawl into a hole in the ground; stick a red-hot knitting needle in your eye – than have to talk to anybody who might want to talk about your pain and humiliation, and remind you of it all over again.

Not that I want to remind him of it. Or talk about

it at all, unless he wants to. I just want to know that he's OK. That my little sister hasn't broken him, irreparably, by calling off their wedding.

'Dev! Hi!'

'Bella.' He sounds tired. Actually, he sounds terrible. 'I'm sorry I haven't got back to you. It's been hectic.'

'Don't apologise. I understand completely. How are you? Are you doing OK?' My plan not to remind him of his pain and humiliation seems to have gone out of the window the moment I've heard how bad he sounds.

'I'm OK. I've been better.'

'Of course. God, Dev, I'm so sorry. I know what it's like to have someone tell you they don't love you any more, and –'

'Wait – who doesn't love who any more?' A note of panic enters his voice. 'Has Polly told you that? That she doesn't love me any more?'

Oh, *shit*. 'I . . . no, no, nothing like that. I'm just . . .' What's that word, the one psychologists use to mean that you're assuming somebody else thinks something just because you think it? '. . . projecting! I'm projecting.'

I'm also, I notice as I glance in the mirror, in danger of sweating off my layer of Jolen bleach. Obviously there are more important concerns than that at the moment.

'But is that it, Bella?' The panic in Dev's voice is mounting. '*Has* she actually stopped loving me?

Because she didn't say anything about that when she phoned last week to tell me she was calling off the wedding. She just kept going round and round in circles, saying all this peculiar stuff about how she didn't deserve to be married.'

'Didn't *deserve* it?'

'Yes! Married to anyone at all, I got the impression. She never said anything about it being specific to marrying me . . . Oh God.' He lets out a sudden, extremely bitter laugh. 'I've been taken in by the *it's not you, it's me* excuse, haven't I?'

'No, Dev, no!' I say, nowhere near as convincingly as I'd like to.

But I'm distracted. I'm bothered by the reason Polly has given Dev for calling off the wedding.

I mean, I suppose it's pretty obvious, now that I come to think of it, that she was never going to come right out and tell him she'd just stopped loving him. I've known people who are capable of that level of brutal honesty – my Evil Ex amongst them – and Polly just isn't one of them. But still. *Not deserving* to be married is a weirdly specific reason to give. It's absolutely not the bland, catch-all, *it's not you, it's me* line that Dev now thinks it is: the line that, I happen to know, Polly has been perfectly happy to trot out to her boyfriends in the past when she's suddenly balked at the idea of settling down.

Actually, come to think of it, why didn't she just tell him she was reluctant to settle down? Run with the 'cold feet' thing that Dev, if our conversation at the airport is anything to go by, was already primed to accept? If you want to let someone down kindly, those are the kind of well-trodden paths you head down.

But Polly didn't tell Dev she was getting cold feet. She didn't say, *It's not you, it's me*. She told him she didn't deserve to be married.

'Bella? Are you still there? You've gone silent.'

'Yes, sorry, I'm still here. Look, honestly, Dev, I don't think you've been taken in by any excuse. I think Polly is . . . I think she's in a very strange place right now. And I don't just mean Clapham!'

'Clapham?' Dev sounds confused by my joke. 'Why would she be in Clapham? She's staying with you, isn't she?'

'No, Dev, she's not staying with me. She's moved into a flat. I assumed you knew.'

'How would I know, Bella? She won't return a single one of my calls. She doesn't reply to any of my texts. I've emailed and emailed again and again, but I get nothing back.' His voice rises. He's sounding less and less like the calm Dev I know. 'What in God's name makes you think she'd have told me she was moving into her own flat? Setting up on her own, permanently. Starting to build a life without me –' He breaks off. There's silence for a moment. Then he says, in a tone that's calmer but so deeply weary that it exhausts me just to listen to it, 'I'm sorry. I didn't mean to take it out on you.'

'You're not. It's fine. And if it helps at all, I don't

think she *is* setting up anything permanent. It's just a rental. Some friend-of-a-friend's place.'

'Oh? Do you know which friend?'

'Um, hang on . . . it might have been a Laura . . .'

'Not a Julia?'

'No. Definitely not a Julia. Why?'

'She's this new friend of Polly's. Well, I assume she's a new friend. Polly was always pretty cagey about her. I wouldn't even know she existed, actually, if it weren't for the fact that she called Polly's mobile one day when Poll had dashed out for a bottle of milk. She got off the phone really fast when I answered it.'

'Well, I've never heard of a Julia. But then Polly has a tendency to be cagey about some of her close friends.' I feel myself bristle, though it shouldn't really matter any more after all these years, about the number of times Polly would clam up if I so much as asked a question about Grace – what she might like to eat when she came over, or whether she was enjoying a particular GCSE subject. Banal stuff, for God's sake. I was hardly asking if she'd slept with her new boyfriend, or whether she was a week late with her period. 'Anyway, I'm pretty sure it was a Laura. Maybe a Lauren. Either way, it's just a temporary rental. I wouldn't worry too much about it.'

'That's good. I don't want the list of stuff I'm worrying about to get all that much longer.' He lets out a laugh that turns, halfway through, into a sigh. 'Look, I should get going, Bella. I have tons of work to be getting on with.'

'Sure.' I should get going too, let's face it, before my Jolen bleach turns my upper lip orange. Even worse than Jamie turning up to find a Salvador Dali lookalike at dinner would be if he turned up to find some kind of mutant Bozo the Clown. 'But I'm so glad you called, Dev. It was really great to talk to you. And I promise, I'll do everything I possibly can to sort out this blip with you and Polly.'

He laughs again, sounding a tiny bit more like himself this time. 'You're calling it a blip?'

'Yes. A big blip, admittedly. But nothing that can't be . . . de-blipped.'

'Oh, Bella. That's what I've always loved about you. You make Moses demanding the parting of the Red Sea look a bit wishy-washy and in need of some willpower.'

Odd, then, that I feel like I wield absolutely no influence whatsoever over my boyfriend.

'Look, I'll try to talk to Polly,' I tell him. 'Find out anything I can about what's really going on, OK?'

'I suppose if she'll talk to anyone, she'll talk to you,' he says. 'Or Grace, I suppose. Maybe you could get her to try?'

'Oh, I'm sure I can get somewhere without needing Grace's input! I'll call you soon, Dev, as soon as I've had a proper chance to talk to Polly.'

'Thanks, Bells. You're a good friend.'

'Don't be silly. That's what future sisters-in-law are for.'

I have a moment of panic, as I end the call and put

my phone down, that maybe I've just given Dev far too much hope.

And then I have another moment of far, far worse panic when the (unlocked) bathroom door suddenly opens, and Gorilla-Man takes a step through it.

I still have a thick layer of white creme bleach above my upper lip.

I'm too shocked to yelp, and he's too shocked – or appalled? – to speak.

We just stare at each other in a horrible freeze-frame for what feels like about three and a half years but which I suppose is only about three and a half seconds. Then he kind of croaks for air and backs out of the door, shutting it firmly and deliberately behind him.

This, perhaps, is another reason why Catherine Zeta-Jones feels so strongly about the separate bathrooms.

I spend a moment or so contemplating suicide, but my razor-blade is too dull and I don't think you get very far poisoning yourself with the dregs of a bottle of Aussie Three-Minute Miracle Conditioner. So there's nothing for it but to wash off my Jolen, clamber into the shower, shampoo and condition my hair, pull on my dressing gown again and head out of the bathroom, hoping and praying that Gorilla-Man has at least had the sense to sneak back to the living room while I make my Walk of Shame back to the bedroom.

He hasn't. He's standing right here, in the hallway, in what looks like the start of an orderly queue.

'Sorry 'bout that,' he mumbles, not quite looking me in the eye.

'It's all right. My fault.' I'm not looking him in the eye, either. 'I forgot to lock it. I didn't know you were even in. Or that you wanted to use the bathroom.'

'Sorry. Still,' he says, just as I start to shuffle sideways past him towards my bedroom, 'it makes us even, at least.'

'What?'

'Well, you've seen me naked. I've seen you defuzzing.'

'I was not defuzzing!' How hairy, exactly, does he think I am? And anyway, who's *he* to judge? 'That was bleach, as a matter of fact . . . look, you just go ahead and use the bathroom. There should still be hot water, if it's a shower you were after. Or maybe it's something else you were planning to do.' Christ, woman, what's *wrong* with you? Haven't the last fifteen minutes been mortifying enough? Do you have to discuss the reason for his bathroom visit as well? 'Well, anyway, um, good luck!' I say, which is the only thing that springs to mind right now.

I dart for the bedroom, shut the door, and consider bracing myself against it for a moment. Then I realise that this is probably unnecessary.

I mean, he's not going to be angling for any *more* sneak peeks of me, for crying out loud. The vision of me in all my Jolen'd glory will probably haunt him for many months to come.

Grace

Thursday 26 November

I'm just trying to talk Hector into his pyjamas – a task that requires the patience of Job, the grit of the Spartans, and the negotiating skills of the entire diplomatic corps of the United Nations – when Charlie calls on my mobile.

He must want to tell me he'll be late (again) tonight.

'Hon? It's me,' he barks at me the moment I pick up. 'What are you doing?'

'Getting the boys into bed. Or rather, trying to get them into bed. Hector's having a bit of a moment on the pyjama front, but I think we're –'

'I need you to do something important,' he interrupts, in the tone of a man who doesn't think putting his sons to bed, pyjama-clad or otherwise, is of any importance in the slightest. 'I've left a flash drive somewhere at home, and it has some documents on it that I need to send to New York. Can you find it and bring it into the office?'

'Now? But I'm –'

'Getting the boys into bed. Yes, you've said. But it's too late for me to have a courier come and pick it up. And I need it urgently. You'll have to get Kitty to come over and babysit for an hour.'

I sigh. There's just no point in arguing. 'All right. If it's urgent, it's urgent. Now, a flash drive . . . do you mean one of those little stick things?'

'No, Grace, *I* mean a flash drive. *You* may mean one of those little stick things. I left it on the kitchen table. Or maybe on the shelf by the front door. Look, you'll just have to find it as fast as you can, then jump on the tube and bring it to me at the office, OK? Just ask the security guard to call up to me when you get here and I'll come down.'

'All right, but you need to give me time to get Kitty over here, if she's even available –'

But I'm talking to dead air. He's already gone.

Kitty, thank God, is not only available but comes over from next door within three minutes of me calling her. She flaps away my promises of generous tips and settles down to read *Mr Gum* books to the boys while I run around like a headless chicken trying to find Charlie's bloody stick thing. Sorry – his bloody flash drive. It appears, eventually, next to the coffee mug he left on the console table this morning, and I sling it into my handbag, pull my coat on and head for the tube station.

I suppose, given that I'm going to Charlie's office, that it's a golden opportunity to do this . . . well, this *thing* I've planned.

Back when I was an impoverished art student – actually, it was all the way back when I was a teenager that I first started doing this – I always used to save money on birthday, Christmas, and thank-you cards by making them for people. Drawing them for people, in fact. It's honestly a lot less crappy than it sounds. I'd make them really personal, you see, with all kinds of little details or in-jokes that meant something to whoever I was giving them to. So for Polly, I'd always draw a card featuring her in a clinch with whichever indie rocker or movie star she was wildly in love with at the time. For my parents, cards picturing them brandishing rakes or secateurs in whatever stately-home garden they'd been to visit most recently. And everyone always loved them. Well, almost always. I did one for Bella, just once (on her engagement to her awful ex-fiancé, Christian), and because I was a bit stumped about the kind of thing either of them was really interested in, I just took the safe route and drew a little cartoon of both of them surrounded by all different kinds of wedding cake. I thought it was a nice little nod to Bella's foodie-ism. Bella thought, I'm fairly sure, that I was calling her a big fat glutton.

Anyway, I haven't done any cards this way for years, ever since I was drawing one to send to Charlie's parents for Thanksgiving (them chasing a comedy turkey around their kitchen with the big electric carving knife we'd bought them the previous Christmas) and Charlie pulled a face and said, 'Do you have some ethical objection against spending money at Hallmark, hon? I mean, we can afford to *buy* greeting cards, you know!'

Which is why I couldn't really explain to you what

made me sit down yesterday morning and start making one of my cards for Saad Amar.

I wanted to thank him for the lunch, you see, and every time I started composing a text message it just came out sounding really stilted and uptight. And after the mortification of earlier in the week, when I misconstrued ordinary friendliness for a terrifying sexual come-on, I don't want him to think I'm any more uptight than he already does.

And . . . I don't know. After our conversation at Locanda Locatelli, and him taking such a polite interest in my opinions about art, I suppose I've been thinking more about my long-dormant artistic skills than I have in a while. And maybe I might be just a little bit keen to show a powerful, successful man like Saad that I'm more than just a boring stay-at-home mother. That I'm not just a St Martin's Miranda.

Whatever the reason, anyway, I spent a very pleasant couple of hours yesterday morning sketching away with an ancient charcoal pencil I unearthed from the back of a desk drawer in the spare bedroom. And I'm really chuffed with the result. After a bit of a hunt on Google Image, I've managed to do a recognisable approximation of the Van Gogh picture Saad was so tragically beaten out for at auction. What I've drawn, in Van Gogh-esque swirly lines on the front of a blank folded card, is the lying-down cow, slurping from a Starbucks coffee cup and brandishing, in one hoof, a huge banana muffin. (This is meant to be a reference to our first, Starbucks-based, meeting; I hope to God that Saad understands the joke, otherwise he'll just think I have an extremely poor understanding of Van Gogh and a really bonkers idea of what goes on in the average farmyard.)

Inside I've written, 'Dear Mr Amar, Thanks for lunch on Monday. Best wishes, Grace Costello'.

I know. And even this anodyne message took me *ages*, and several dry runs on scraps of paper. I'm not half as adept with words, it turns out, as I am with my charcoal pencil. But I wanted to keep it cool and impersonal.

As cool and impersonal as a cute, in-jokey home-made card can be, that is.

On second thoughts, maybe I won't send it to him. I mean, now that I'm looking at it again, I realise how silly and OTT it looks. I mean, it was just a lunch, for God's sake. I've already thanked him in person.

On the other hand, there's a part of me – a new, reckless part of me – that *wants* to let him have the card. Wants to show off, perhaps, what a decent job I can still do on the drawing front. And then there's my first impulse, the thing that made me sit down to start the card in the first place, my burning desire to let him know I'm more than just a (not very good) housewife.

On the other hand, I don't want him to think that what I am is a crazy stalker.

On the other hand . . .

I'm still hotly locked in debate with myself when I reach the glass doors of MMA Capital's smart Berkeley Square office building.

It's a big, modern structure, home to several other companies as well as MMA. There must be a thousand people working here, at least. But as it's long after normal work hours by now, the place has an emptied-out feel. A couple of cleaners pushing vacuum cleaners around the pale beige lobby floor. A security guard rather than a glam receptionist sitting at the long desk in front of the escalators. A few suited-up men and even fewer women coming down the escalators, looking keen to get the evening commute out of the way and get home. Or even keener, perhaps, seeing as it's a Thursday night, to get to the pub, or out to dinner with their friends. Even though it's been years since I had a job – and not even a proper job, just badly paid holiday temp jobs to supplement my student loan – I fondly remember the buzz of Thursday nights. Half of the working population of London out and about, it seemed, especially on hot summer evenings or, like now, in the run-up to Christmas. Everyone determined to have their hangover on the boss's time on Friday, rather than ruin their precious Saturday morning at home.

It makes me miss work. Even boring, creativity-sapping temp work.

I approach the guard, who is overweight and irritable-looking, and making me nervous before I've even opened my mouth. 'Hi, sorry to bother you.' I venture a smile. He doesn't. 'Um, my husband works here, and he's just asked me to bring him a computer stick thi . . . a flash drive. Could you possibly call up to his office and let him know I'm here?'

The guard picks up his phone. 'Name?'

'Grace Costello.'

'*His* name.'

'Oh, sorry, yes. Charlie Costello. He works at MMA Capital.'

'Extension number?'

'God, sorry, I've no idea. I don't disturb him at work very often.'

With much sighing and rolling of eyes, he eventually procures the right number, then bashes the digits into his phone with a heavy finger. We wait, what must be ten or eleven rings.

The guard hangs up. 'He's not there.'

'Oh. But he must be. I mean, he's waiting for me. He needs the flash drive urgently.'

The guard shrugs with a none-of-my-concern look.

'Well, maybe he's just gone to the loo, or something. Could you try again in a minute?'

We wait a long, rather painful minute, at the end of which the guard picks up the phone and dials Charlie's extension again. This time we wait fifteen, sixteen rings. Still no answer.

'I'd better try his mobile,' I say, already reaching for it in my bag. 'He's probably just away from his desk.'

But Charlie's mobile rings and rings, then clicks onto his answerphone.

With the security guard watching me, I'm feeling flustered and embarrassed. I'm more aware than ever that I look a bit of a frazzled mess, with the distinct aura of children's tea and bedtime wafting around me, and violently at odds with the sleek, glossy glamour of this office building.

My embarrassment is only intensified when I unsuccessfully try Charlie's mobile again, and then a third time.

I mean, if the flash drive was that bloody urgent that I had to drop everything in the middle of the boys' bedtime to schlep across town and bring it to him, isn't answering his phone the least he could do?

'Look, why don't you take a seat and I'll try him again in a few minutes?' I'm clearly pitiful enough that even the granite façade of the guard has softened a fraction. He nods towards an area of low, cream-coloured sofas, to the left of the escalators. 'Or you could just leave the flash drive with me, to give to him.'

I don't want to risk Charlie's wrath by handing what could be super-confidential information over to a third party. 'No, thank you, I'd better wait.'

'Fine. I just thought you might have somewhere more important to be.'

I almost laugh at how wide of the mark he is. Obviously I don't have anywhere important to be. The only important place I *did* have to be – at home, putting the boys to bed – is redundant now. Robbie and Hector will be fast asleep.

It's then that, as I'm putting my phone back into my bag, I feel the outline of the envelope that contains my hand-drawn card.

Fuck it. I'm tired of being the timid little mouse. Sick to death of being the one who can be left waiting in an empty office lobby, because obviously I've got nothing better to do with my Thursday evening.

'Actually, there is something else I'd like to leave with you. But it's not for my husband. It's for a Mr Amar.' I slide the envelope across the guard's counter-top towards him. 'Also at MMA Capital.'

'Fine.' The guard takes the envelope. 'This urgent too? You need it to go up now?'

'Oh God, no. I mean, no. It can wait until he comes in tomorrow morning.' And when I'm far, far away from the building, so I don't have to witness whatever reaction it provokes. I mean, I'm not feeling *that* much less timid. 'Thank you. I'll just go and wait over there.'

I sit down on one of the low sofas and pick up a copy of today's *Financial Times* from the neat spread on the glass coffee table. I wish there were a couple of magazines, but the FT is all there is. Well, Charlie has often banged on at me about how he'd like it if I were better informed, so this seems as good a place to start as any. I open up the paper and start to skim-read an article on the Chilean government's new austerity budget. I won't say I'm exactly gripped, but I'm concentrating quite hard on trying to make sense of it all, and so I'm not paying attention to any more of the dwindling comings and goings in the lobby.

Which is why I don't see Saad Amar until he's only three feet away from me.

'Grace? What a nice surprise!'

I blink at him. I don't stand up, or even put down my newspaper. All I can think about is that I left the house without putting on a scrap of makeup, brushing my hair, or bothering to check for the food stains that, after teatime with Hector, are very likely to be somewhere on my clothing.

And that Saad – predictably enough – looks completely, totally, just-kill-me-now *gorgeous*.

'Sorry, Grace, had you come here to see me, or something?' he carries on, with a smile that's just a smidgen more uncertain than usual. 'Kenneth on the desk over there just told me you'd left this for me.' He holds out the envelope.

Oh *God*. Now this really is a just-kill-me-now moment.

'No, no, it's nothing!' I get to my feet. 'A mistake, really. I'm here to drop something off for Charlie, that's all.' I wonder, can I swipe the card from his hand? More to the point, can I swipe the card from his hand *without looking a bit unhinged*? 'The security man . . . Kenneth . . . must have got muddled.'

'But the envelope has my name on it,' Saad points out.

Not a lot I can say to that, really. 'Er . . .'

'Kenneth said you wanted to deliver some kind of a flash drive to Charlie,' Saad carries on, 'but apparently he's gone AWOL?'

I shoot Kenneth – so *now* he gets all chatty – a dirty look over Saad's shoulder.

'Do you want me to see if I can track him down?

Head back up to the office and have a look for him?' Saad's smooth forehead is gently creased with puzzlement and – I think – a little bit of concern. 'I mean, I'm sure he didn't intend to leave you waiting like this, especially if you've brought something all the way in to give to him.'

'No, really, it's absolutely fine. He'll be here any minute, I'm sure. Anyway, it gives me a few precious minutes to catch up on my reading!'

Saad's inky eyes flicker towards the copy of the *FT*, which I've abandoned on the sofa. 'Right.'

'And I wouldn't want to keep you, anyway. You're obviously on your way out.' My own eyes are flickering rather desperately towards the envelope. If I can't wrest it from his grip, the least I can hope for is that he shoves it into a pocket and opens it later, when I'm a long way away. Mexico City, perhaps, might just about be far enough for me to flee to, in order to properly escape the embarrassment of it all. I could hide out there for a few weeks, couldn't I, offer Kitty my entire meagre savings account to look after the boys . . .

'Yes, but I'm still waiting for my date for the evening . . . oh, here she is now.'

I've barely time to feel (stupidly and pointlessly) crestfallen at the mere fact that he's got a date for the evening. Because there are far more important things to feel crestfallen about. Mostly the fact that the girl walking through the glass doors and sashaying her way towards us is the very embodiment of the kind of

Victoria's Secret model that I've been assuming Saad hangs out with (and possibly snorts gold-plated cocaine from the naked nipples of, although I have to admit that the more I've seen of Saad, the less likely I think it is that he has a cocaine habit, gold-plated and nipple-mounted or otherwise).

In fact, I think I may very well have seen this girl strutting her stuff on the catwalk at one of the Victoria's Secret fashion shows I sometimes watch on the E! channel. Her breasts, which are huge, and attached to a stick-like body, and teetering tantalisingly over the edge of her plunging cocktail dress, look exactly like a pair I couldn't take my eyes off on E!, and she's also sporting the big, swingy mane of hair that's a prerequisite for a Victoria's Secret model. The only thing she isn't doing, unlike the models for Victoria's Secret, is smiling.

Still, with a body like that, I suppose she doesn't really need to.

My stomach coils with jealousy. For her eye-popping body, for her astonishing confidence. For her date with Saad.

'It's raining,' she announces to Saad, in an unplaceable accent that's a little bit Scandinavia, a little bit New York. She scowls. 'You said you'd be waiting for me outside with your driver.'

'Yes, I apologise, Britta, I've been slightly delayed.' Saad puts a hand on her elbow – not a kiss on her lips, I can't help noting – and nods towards the glass doors at the pavement outside, where a large, dark car is waiting with its lights on and its windscreen wipers going. 'The car is right there. You can go and get in, get warmed up, while I just finish up with Grace here.'

Britta's scowl intensifies. 'Get the driver to meet me at the door with an umbrella,' she says, not bothering to acknowledge either my existence or the fact that Saad's car is parked a mere one and a half supermodel strides from the building's exit.

Saad proffers her a pleasant smile and hands her the rolled-up umbrella that he's actually carrying under one arm. 'Take mine.'

Her perfectly shaped eyebrows shoot upwards. She's unimpressed. 'Well, how long will you *be*?'

'He'll be no time at all,' I interject, seeing my golden opportunity to get rid of Saad, and that bloody homemade card. 'You really don't need to wait, or anything,' I add to Saad himself. 'Charlie is on his way down right now, I'm sure.'

Britta stares at me as though I'm something she'd like to scrape off her Gina platforms. And Saad shoots me an odd look of his own before turning back to Britta.

'I'll be just one minute,' he tells her, giving her the gentlest of nudges in the direction of the exit. 'You'll be more comfortable in the car.'

She spins on a heel and does that supermodel stride back across the lobby. I watch her, fascinated by how anyone that skinny can have a bottom that plump. Kenneth watches her, probably fascinated by pretty much the same thing. But Saad isn't watching her. He's already turned back to me.

'I'm sorry. Where were we?'

'We weren't anywhere. I'm perfectly happy just waiting for Charlie. You have an evening out to enjoy.'

He pulls a bit of a face. 'I'd hardly say that. Not now that I've angered Her Highness.'

It's a slightly odd way to talk about your girlfriend. I mean, I'm assuming that Britta *is* his girlfriend.

'She's a friend of my brother Wael,' Saad says, as though he's read my mind and – why? – feels the need to offer an explanation. 'I'm attending a party hosted by *Vogue* magazine tonight and Britta is keen to put herself about amongst the movers and shakers.'

Oh, so she's not a fully fledged supermodel yet, then.

Nor, apparently, his girlfriend.

Not that it matters, of course. And anyway, even if he isn't going home with Britta tonight, he'll just be substituting her with some other voluptuous, leggy beauty from the ranks of the *Vogue* party invitees.

Not that *that* matters, either.

'But look, I am running a little late, I'm afraid. So if you don't mind me being rather quick . . .' Saad starts to run his thumb across the top of the envelope.

'Honestly, you don't need to open it now! In fact, I'd rather . . .'

Too late. He's got it open and pulled out the card.

I'm squirming, almost physically, as I watch him

stare at it. From the back, it looks so silly and pathetic: a little folded rectangle of slightly floppy white card. And not even, now that I look at it more closely, folded quite accurately enough. If he stood it up, it would topple over. Although from the expression on his face, standing it up is the last thing he's going to do. Chuck it straight in the nearest bin, more like.

'It's a thank-you,' I croak, 'for lunch the other day.'

'Oh! Oh, right . . .' His usual impeccable manners appear to have deserted him.

'That's the Van Gogh cow you were trying to buy,' I go on miserably. 'And it's drinking a Starbucks coffee, because . . . well . . .'

It's too embarrassing to go on. Mexico City, here I come.

But, thank God, Saad seems to have recovered those manners in the nick of time. 'No, no, I get it! Because of you stealing my Starbucks coffee when we first met. Well!' He stares back down at the card for a moment. 'Well!'

'Look, it was just a silly little thing . . . a hobby I used to have.'

'Well!' is all he manages to say, again, to this, before adding, in a careful tone of voice, 'You know, I don't think anybody has ever made me a homemade thank-you card before. In fact, I'm not sure I've even *had* a thank-you card before.'

'I know. Nobody sends thank-you cards. Even my

son emails his grandparents, these days, to say thank you for his Christmas and birthday presents. I should have just emailed. Texted, or something.'

'Not at all!' He stops staring at the card and almost – but not quite – meets my eye. He's embarrassed for me, I can tell. 'It's a very . . . sweet gesture.'

'Right.'

'And a very, er, a very amusing picture.'

Not for the first time in the last ten minutes, I wish fervently that someone – Kenneth, perhaps – would just kill me now.

'Thank you, Grace,' Saad carries on, stuffing the card back into its envelope and then into his trouser pocket. 'You didn't need to thank me for the lunch. But thank you anyway. To take all that time to do the drawing.'

'Oh God, no, it only took me about three minutes! No time at all. Really, it's just a silly scribble, and . . . oh, here's Charlie!' I never thought I'd say this, but thank God for my husband, who is just making his way through the glass doors into the building. He's looking pink-cheeked from cold and, I immediately realise, a beer or two.

'Obviously popped out for a post-work drink,' says Saad, in a tone I can't quite identify. 'Well, I'd better leave you to it. Can't keep Britta waiting any longer than I already have. Evening, Charlie,' he says, as he heads for the exit himself and the two of them cross paths. 'See you in the morning.'

Charlie does a bit of brown-nosy and jocular

ho-ho-ho-ing, even though Saad hasn't said anything funny, and then the moment Saad is out of the doors, he turns to me. 'Grace?' I'm expecting him to ask if I've been waiting long, but what he actually asks is, 'You were talking to Saad Amar?'

'Yes. We met at the party.'

'But what on earth were you talking *about*?' He looks astonished, as though the idea that I could possibly have anything to say to Saad Amar is as absurd as suggesting that Robbie could make stimulating small-talk with Barack Obama.

'Plenty! The . . . the austerity budget in Chile, for one thing.'

Charlie lets out a laugh. I can smell the faint trace of his recent pint on his breath.

'And, for another thing, why my husband made me hurtle out of the house to bring him a terribly urgent flash drive, only to vanish to the pub for half an hour.'

Now Charlie stops laughing. 'Hey, I hope you didn't talk about me to my boss, Grace. That would be seriously inappropriate if you did. And anyway, almost everyone but me has left for the night. It's not a problem that I went for a quick drink with the rest of the team.'

'I'm sure it's not a problem for Saad Amar. But what about whether it was a problem for me?'

'Oh, come on, hon, I've only kept you waiting a couple of minutes!'

'Try fifteen. I could have finished putting the boys to

bed, if I'd known you were just going to slip out for a post-work drink.'

'OK, OK, I'm sorry, OK!' Charlie holds up his hands in an exaggerated display of apology that he doesn't remotely mean. 'Anyway, did you bring the flash drive?'

I dig in my bag and hand it to him. He pockets it without actually saying thank you.

'So look, I would take you out for a bite to eat or something, now that you're over here, but I'm going to be at least another couple hours finishing up with this stuff from the flash drive. Anyway, you haven't exactly dressed for dinner.'

'No, Charlie. I haven't.'

'OK, well, I'd better let you get back to the tube, then.' He leans down and places a brief peck on my forehead. Even this lukewarm show of affection is, I think, done for Kenneth's benefit. Outward appearances are very important to Charlie. 'Unless you were going to hitch a lift in my boss's Bentley, or something. Now that you're on such cordial terms with him, I mean!'

I don't join in his laughter. 'Are you going to walk me to the tube?'

'Honey, it's only five minutes away. And it's hardly the depths of night. And like I told you –'

'Your work is really urgent. I know. I'll see you later, Charlie.'

Outside, it's really bucketing down. I set off for Green Park tube station, hoping that maybe the pouring rain will flood away not only my anger with Charlie, but – more importantly – my embarrassment about my silly Starbucks cow card.

Though I'm not sure there's enough rain in all the heavens for that.

Bella

Thursday 26 November
Jamie texts, just before I leave the flat, to say he's running late for our dinner date, but I get to the restaurant just after eight anyway. There's no reason to hang about the flat. After my Jolen moment with Liam, let's face it, I'm desperate to get out of the flat. And anyway, it's a nice opportunity to have a chat with the restaurant owner.

This isn't, by the way, because I'm one of those insufferable people – usually middle-aged men with large BMWs and even larger God complexes – who like to have their egos plumped up by some fawning maître d'. It's because this particular restaurant owner, Vito, happens to be an actual friend of mine. He's the owner of two restaurants, in fact: this one, the eponymous Vito's on Chiswick High Road, and Vito e Angelina in Shepherd's Bush, which is where I worked for eighteen months when I first came to London and I was saving up the money to start my own catering firm. Neither is exactly a fancy place: the likes of Grace Costello would probably feel the need to decontaminate themselves and flee to Locanda Locatelli the moment they walked through the door.

But that isn't the point. Vito and his sister, Angelina, took me under their wings in the kindest, most genuine way imaginable, and though I tried to return the favour (by attempting to teach them to cook properly, amongst other things; they may be only second-generation immigrants, but the things they do to Italian food have to be seen to be disbelieved) I never feel there's anything I can do to repay them for the way they took care of me back then.

As soon as I walk into Vito's tonight, see the cheery green tablecloths and smell the familiar smell of ever-so-slightly singed garlic, I feel the knot of tension in my stomach ease. Vito himself practically self-combusts with excitement when he sees I'm here, and has me sat at the best table in the house with an extremely large (and not terribly Italian) Bacardi and Coke within two minutes of my arrival.

'You look beautiful, Bella,' he proclaims, returning after a brief disappearance with a plate of what he'd call bruschetta. I'd call it *chopped tinned tomatoes on barely toasted Mother's Pride*. 'So, what are you doing here tonight? Are you celebrating something?'

'No, no, Vito. Just having a nice meal with Jamie.'

'This is the same Jamie you were with last time?' Vito looks unimpressed. 'He asked you to marry him yet?'

'No. But anyway, who's even saying I want to get married?'

'All women want to get married,' he says, with touching certainty. He disappears behind the bar for a moment to get the bottle of Bacardi and refills my glass. 'Hey, you know, Bella, it's funny you should come in tonight, because I was talking about you just the other day.'

'Oh?' This sounds ominous.

'Yeah, I was chatting to a regular of ours – her daughter just recently found out she can't have babies, poor thing – so I was telling her all about my beautiful friend Bella, and how you had that nasty car smash and damaged all your insides, but that even though you can't have babies, you're still planning to adopt a few.'

I take a long drink of my Bacardi and Coke. It's sickly sweet. 'Well. I'm sure you made her feel much better, Vito.' Another syrupy sip. 'But next time she's in, you should probably just let her know that it doesn't happen quite as fast as that. I mean, her daughter probably needs a bit of time to grieve before she starts filling in the adoption applications and stuff.'

'But still, Bella, she should know about success stories, shouldn't she? Brave ladies like you whose world doesn't just stop turning because they can't have a biological baby of their own. Hang on a sec, I've got to get that phone . . .'

Off he goes to answer it, leaving me alone with my drink and the 'bruschetta'.

Oh, and my thoughts, of course.

The thing about Vito is, he honestly doesn't mean to be insensitive. I think because he's known me for so long, and because he knew me back when I was still struggling to come to terms with the fall-out from the accident, he doesn't tiptoe around the topic like some people do. But he does have a unique way of making it all sound a bit flippant. A bit glib. I mean, 'that nasty car smash'. And how I 'damaged all my insides'. That kind of thing.

For the record, and the sake of accuracy, this is what actually happened.

One night, ten years ago this past summer, my Evil Ex, Christian, came home to our flat in Bristol and told me he was leaving. That our wedding, planned for that coming September, was all off, as far as he was concerned, because he didn't love me any more.

I know I've already said that this takes a certain kind of brutal honesty. But actually, when I think back to that moment, to the chill in Christian's voice and the ice in his eyes, I don't think there's anything honest about it at all. I think it's just plain brutal.

There was a huge and terrible row, obviously, and at some point I decided to get in the car and drive the forty-five miles home to my parents, where at least I could weep into Elvis the dog's comforting fur and I wouldn't have to look at Christian's face another moment longer.

Of course, with hindsight I now know that it's not terribly wise to drive along winding country lanes at dusk while sobbing so hard you can barely see the bonnet of your own car, let alone any cars that might be coming towards you.

I don't remember very much about the actual moment of the accident, but the police thought I must have drifted to the right of the white line just as a Ford Fiesta was coming round a blind corner in my direction. The Ford Fiesta slammed on its brakes. I made the decision to yank my steering wheel sideways, swerving my car off the road to slam, at fifty miles per hour, into a large and rather beautiful oak tree.

Unsurprisingly, the final score was Oak Tree, one; Bella, nil.

I shattered three ribs. I broke my left femur. There were lots of extremely nasty cuts and lacerations from all the flying glass. But all those things were just cosmetic, really. The main problem was the fact that I slammed with such force into the lower half of the steering wheel that I suffered some extreme pelvic fractures, which did a very nasty thing to my uterus. If you're a doctor, you'd call it 'a massive haemoperitoneum due to avulsion of the uterus at the colpocervical junction'. If you're not a doctor, you'd say that I had an extremely scary amount of blood in an extremely important part of my body. Either way, the end result was that the doctors whipped out most of my uterus within an hour of me arriving at the hospital, in order to stop me bleeding to death.

And you certainly don't need to be a doctor to know that you can't very well have a baby if you don't have a uterus to store it in.

Still, Vito is right about one thing. You do get over it. Eventually. And there were some upsides, even if I didn't realise it at the time. That's when I first met Dev, for one thing (he was one of the junior doctors treating me, taking an interest in my horrible skin abrasions before he actually became the kind of top plastic surgeon who could treat them), and so of course that's when he first met Polly, even though it took another five years before they finally left the Friend Zone and actually became an item.

And if one upside was that it led Polly to the love of her life (supposed to be, anyway), the other, even bigger upside was that it led me to fall pretty swiftly out of love with the man who was supposed to be the love of mine. Christian.

Funny, really, that he's named that when he isn't. Christian, that is. I don't mean in the religious sense. I just mean that he's probably about the most *un*-Christian person I think I've ever known. Not because he dumped me, which of course was entirely his prerogative. But because of the way he behaved after my accident. He didn't come and see me once – not *one single time* – while I was in the hospital. Nor, in fact, when I was out of the hospital. He never sent flowers, fruit or a measly box of chocolates. Oh, there *was* a cheap, floppy get-well card, which Polly ripped up and threw in the bin for me: 'Sorry to hear about the accident, get well soon, Christian'.

But nothing else. Nothing, throughout months and months of painful recovery. He just packed up his things, dropped off the keys to our flat, and went away.

I think he's living in Nottingham now, where he was originally from. At least, that's where I heard he moved not long after our breakup. His sister and I exchanged Christmas and birthday cards for a couple of years, dwindling to just Christmas cards for a couple of years after that. It's been at least five years since either of us has sent anything at all.

The door to the restaurant is opening now, and Jamie is walking in.

I practically fall off my chair. And it's nothing to do with my Bacardi and Coke.

Jamie is washed. He is shaved. He's combed his hair and he's wearing proper clothes – clean(ish) blue jeans and an ironed(ish) shirt – in place of his normal khaki cargo trousers and Manchester United T-shirt. Plus, he's carrying a bunch of flowers. All right, they're the kind of tired-looking tulips you get from the stall outside the tube station, and not three dozen red roses that he's had trimmed and hand-tied by an expert florist at Jane Packer. But *still*. They're *flowers*. And this is Jamie we're talking about. The last time he bought me flowers was . . . actually, come to think of it, it was never.

My God, I wish Anna and Polly were here to witness this.

And my God, doesn't my boyfriend scrub up well when he wants to? I can see a gang of women sitting near the front door openly gawping at him. They're not going to believe it when he comes and sits down opposite me.

Vito has got his hopes up at the sight of the flowers, and now he's ushering Jamie over to the table, jigging with excitement as he does so.

'You said it wasn't a special occasion, Bella!' he accuses me, before turning to Jamie and wagging his finger at him. 'What have you got planned, mister?'

'I'm sure he doesn't have anything *planned*,' I say hastily. If I don't kill this notion stone-dead, it'll only be a matter of moments before Vito has brought champagne, dug out a box of confetti and summoned a violin player to stand by our table and scrape out 'Some Enchanted Evening'. 'You don't have anything planned, do you?' I whisper at Jamie, as Vito trips away to fetch us menus.

'Depends what you mean by planned.' Jamie shoves the flowers in my direction. 'These are for you.'

'They're really beautiful. And they smell gorgeous,' I fib, because if anything they smell of exhaust fumes and Glade PlugIn.

Now Vito is back, like a bad penny, with the promised menus and more 'bruschetta', running through the daily specials (chicken tikka linguine; Hawaiian ravioli with ham and pineapple; did I teach him *nothing*?) until finally he goes away to eavesdrop shamelessly from behind the bar, just a few metres away.

'You look nice tonight, Bells,' Jamie says.

'Thanks.' I do feel like I look nice, for a change, in my tummy-flattering black trousers and cleavage-revealing (*not* tunicy) top. 'So do you.'

'So now I'm here,' he swallows, hard, so that his

Adam's apple visibly lifts and lowers, 'I have a couple of things I wanted to talk to you about.'

OK. Now he's making me really nervous.

'J, it's all right. It's forgotten. The trouble with Goril – with Liam and the social worker, I mean.'

'Yeah, I'm really sorry about that. And you're an angel, babe, to let Liam stay like this.'

'Oh, that's fine, Jamie. You know your friends are always welcome.' I take a sip of my drink. 'Any idea how much longer it'll be before he gets a place of his own?' I add casually.

'Christ, I'm not sure. Just as soon as he gets back on his feet.'

Wait – this doesn't sound promising. I was hoping for an answer like *a few more days* or *only a week longer*. 'Um. Back on his feet? I thought he was just looking for a job.'

'Yeah, course, but there's a bit more to it than that. He'll have to find somewhere that's big enough so that he can bring his kids over here.'

'He has *kids*?' This is astonishing news. Liam doesn't strike me as a man who could bring up anything more than last night's curry, let alone children.

'Two of them. Girls. And a wife. Well, an ex-wife. Well, a *former* wife. What do you say, when someone's died?'

'A late wife.' I put down my drink. 'Liam has a *late wife*?'

'Yeah. Kerry. I didn't know her well. She died a few years ago.'

'But . . .' Now I feel terrible, for thinking the slightest of bad thoughts about Liam and his ability to bring up his children. And terrible for Liam too. 'Jamie, that's . . . oh, it's awful. How did she die?'

'Hit-and-run. No, wait – a climbing accident. No, wait – it might have been water-skiing . . . Well, it was definitely an accident. I don't actually remember what kind.'

'Jamie!'

'Babe, you know I'm never big on detail.'

This much is certainly true. Though whether he's *worse* at detail than any other man on the planet, I can't be sure. The only details most of The Boys ever seem to be certain on, when pressed, are their mothers' birthdays and the precise timing of the goal Ryan Giggs scored against Arsenal in the FA Cup semi-final in the treble-winning season of 1999. Other details – their job descriptions; their girlfriends' names; what a young wife and mother might have tragically died of – don't seem to register.

'Anyway, that's not what I came here to talk to you about tonight,' he carries on, frustrated, I think, that his big topic has been sidelined by talk of horrible misfortune. 'Though I suppose in some ways, it is. I mean, things like that get you thinking, don't they? About what's really important in your life.'

'And what *is* really important in your life?' I ask warily. Because honestly, this is just as likely as not to turn out to be about Manchester United's summer signing strategy. Or the state of his mum's sciatica.

'Well, *you* are, Bella.' He looks surprised that I'm even asking, then takes my hands across the table and looks deep into my eyes.

I'm dimly aware that behind the bar, Vito is about to spontaneously combust.

'Look, I know I've taken you for granted a lot recently, Bells. And I suppose I feel like I've let you down. You know, with this whole adoption thing and all. I haven't shown the interest I should have done. No, no, it's true,' he adds, holding up a hand as though I were about to jump in to protest. 'But I want you to know that all that is going to change from here on in. I mean, a man reaches a point in his life, you know? A point where he realises that he has to step up. Take responsibility.'

'And that point is . . . er . . . now?'

'It is.'

'But it wasn't the point, say, Wednesday last week?'

Solemnly he shakes his head. 'It was not. See, the thing is, Bells, I feel bad. I feel bad about you begging me to show some proper signs of commitment . . .'

'I don't think I ever actually begged.'

' . . . and going on at me to work harder. And show more interest in this whole adoption thingie.'

'Jamie, it isn't a *thingie*. It's something I passionately want to do with my life. Something you once told me you wanted to do with your life, too.'

Vito chooses this moment to sidle up with – oh God – two glasses of sparkling wine and a hopeful expression. He pops the glasses down on the table, ostentatiously discreet, before announcing that he'll just bring us two daily specials – oh *God* – and sidling off again.

Jamie picks up his glass and takes an expansive swig that empties the contents immediately. 'Look, Bella, I'm trying to give you what you want, here. I'm promising to get on board with the adoption. I'm going to get Keenan Landscapes back up and running. Fuck it, we can even get engaged, if you want us to.'

'Engaged?' I'm gripping the stem of my own wine glass, in the hope that this might stop me from collapsing in a shocked heap under the table. 'To be married?'

'Yes, Bella. That is what people intend, when they get engaged, don't they? I mean, apart from your crazy sister, that is.' He lets out a loud and ringing laugh, pleased with his joke. 'I mean, obviously I don't want to go setting any dates or anything. Or doing anything mushy like . . . I don't know . . . any of the girlie stuff people do when they get engaged.'

'Like buying a ring? Throwing a party?'

He pulls a face. 'Yeah, that's not really me, is it, babe? But come on, let's say we're engaged anyway. I mean, why the fuck not?'

I'll be honest, it's not exactly a dream proposal.

I mean, even my Evil Ex Christian did a lot better than this. A romantic gondola-ride round Venice; a vintage sapphire on bended knee, with tears in his eyes, outside the Salute . . . But then, Christian turned out to be a cold, unfeeling bastard. And who wants a dream proposal, gondolas, sapphires and all, when it's coming from a cold, unfeeling bastard? Wouldn't everyone prefer a . . . well, OK, a slightly rubbish proposal, as long as it's coming from someone who actually seems to care about you?

Because the thing is this. I'm not an idiot. I know why Anna and Polly have their reservations about Jamie. He's not perfect. But life isn't perfect. If anyone knows that, it's me. And if he really is turning over a new leaf, if he really does want to start making a life with me, a proper life, with a proper job, and maybe a nice little house, with separate bathrooms for us, and room for our very own child – maybe even more than one – well, I'm not going to look a gift horse in the mouth.

Let's face it, I'm pretty damaged goods. And I'm not all that sure there's anyone else who'd have me.

'OK. Let's do it.' I beam at him, feeling my eyes fill up with happy tears. Then I lean across the table and kiss him.

I don't even care that Vito is watching with bated breath. Or that any minute now, I'm going to have to work my way through an entire plateful of Hawaiian ravioli.

Even though we didn't tell Vito anything about the sort-of-engagement (there wasn't really all that much to tell, after all) he still plied us with oodles of free booze in the desperate hope that we might suddenly feel a burning desire just to announce *something*. So

I'm one (refilled) Bacardi and Coke, two glasses of sparkling wine, and just over an entire bottle of dubious Calabrian red down by the time Jamie and I finally stagger home a couple of hours later.

Jamie heads straight for bed, barely even making it under the duvet before he's asleep and snoring. It's a pity, because I was kind of hoping we might round off the evening with a kiss and a cuddle, see where it might take us. After all, if you can't have sex on the night you get sort-of-engaged, when *can* you?

Mind you, I suppose this is just a trial run for the night of our sort-of wedding. When – I can pretty much guarantee – Jamie will get absolutely trolleyed on champagne and Guinness, half-arsedly attempt to consummate the marriage in the back of the taxi home, *throw up* in the back of the taxi home, and then pass out on top of the duvet without consummating anything.

Still – and I do know that this is a bit pathetic – it doesn't stop me from getting excited about arranging our wedding. All the more of a challenge, in many ways, to create a special day without any of the usual girlie frills and extras that Jamie is so vehemently anti.

Because I'm still wide awake – that'll be the Coke part of the Bacardi and Coke, then – I think I might just go and make myself a cup of warm cocoa; maybe, while the milk is heating, spend a couple of minutes on the internet having a look around for possible venues. I mean, I know Jamie said he didn't want to set any dates or anything, but decent places do get booked up, so it's just good organisation to see what kind of thing might be available. A small, non-flashy venue, preferably within the M25 for minimum hassle, and minimum driving distance from the airport for whichever of Jamie's relatives he wants to come over from Ireland . . . or we could always *do* it in Ireland, I suppose, if that wouldn't count as too much fuss. Actually, that's a great idea! There are some lovely venues, the food is good, it would win me much-needed brownie points with his mother, who's otherwise going to blow a gasket when she finds out Barren Bella is going to become her daughter-in-law . . .

Ten minutes later and I've got out my laptop and already got myself a hit list for phone calls tomorrow morning. Googling 'wedding venues Cork' has led me to a few stunning-looking places, only some of which are a bit obviously OTT for Jamie's taste. My first choice is this sweet little hotel a few miles out of Cork, with incredible views overlooking the ocean. The ceremonies are held in a nice simple-looking room, big enough to seat only about forty or fifty guests, and there are pictures on the website of all kinds of brides, not necessarily all done up in the kind of pouffy white dress that would make me look like a corpulent Christmas-tree fairy and give Jamie a heart attack.

And, that's another thing I'll need to start investigating: where to find a nice, wedding-appropriate outfit that's special enough to make me feel just a *little* bit bridal, but not the kind of thing that Jamie would think of as 'mushy'. That floaty top and ivory trousers option I've always seen myself in on my wedding day.

I'm Googling 'non-bridal bride outfits trousers floaty top not tunic' when I remember Polly.

For fuck's sake, how could I have forgotten Polly?

How can I possibly think about making wedding plans when she's only just gone and cancelled her own wedding? When both of us are still getting calls (I endured three of them only this morning, in fact) from our nosiest relatives (a.k.a. pretty much all of Mum's side), asking what's happened and why it's such late notice, and whether this means they won't be setting up a wedding list, then. I can't ask Polly to stand beside me in some kind of bridesmaid confection, however low-key it would have to be to match my floaty top and trousers, and endure the pitying stares and whispered comments that would ensue. Even if I only invited the relatives that really *have* to be invited.

And then there's the pain I'd be worried about causing her, so soon after she's started coming to terms with cancelling her own big wedding, so soon after falling out of love with Dev.

Sorry – so soon after she's *allegedly* fallen out of love with Dev, that is.

It's been gnawing at the back of my mind all evening, actually: my conversation with Dev, and what he told me about Polly saying she *didn't deserve* to be married.

Hmm.

Look, I know I told Anna that I wasn't going to spy

on my sister, but maybe it wouldn't hurt just to have a fleeting glance at Polly's email. While I've got my laptop open, that is. I mean, it's not just so I can satisfy my feelings of guilt about planning my own wedding. At the end of the day, this is my sister we're talking about. And poor, poor Dev, of course, who sounded so devastated and confused when we spoke earlier.

In one sense, it would actually be seriously remiss of me *not* to investigate further.

Anyway, probably I won't even be able to access her email. Because even though I can load up her email log-in page easily enough – PollyWollyDoodle@hotmail.com – her password could literally be anything, couldn't it? Though they do say you can narrow most people's passwords down to things like old pets, or favourite holiday destinations, or childhood nicknames . . . I type in 'Elvis', the name of our old Labrador – no luck. All right, then: 'Woolacombe', where we used to go for whole summers as children . . . nope, nothing. OK, how about a nickname: 'Dood.'

Bloody hell. 'Dood' worked.

Really, Polly ought to be a little bit more vigilant about her security. Not that I'm going to be able to say anything to her, but a four-year-old could hack this.

I stare at the screen, as the emails come up. They're the usual selection of obvious junk ('Perfect Rolex C1one'; 'Get Cheaper V1agra'), e-vites, and status alerts from Facebook, with a few 'real'-sounding emails from friends thrown into the mix. A couple of emails I sent her, before she left New York, haranguing her about choosing her hymns and getting in contact with the vicar to arrange the order of service.

There's one particular name that crops up again and again – ten or twelve emails in the space of the past week, for example – and that belongs to a Julia247@yahoo.com.

Wait – Julia? Wasn't that the friend Dev mentioned, the one that Polly was being cagey about?

'I thought you were supposed to be a professional cook.'

The voice takes me by surprise. I spin round – shutting the laptop guiltily as I do so – to see that Liam is standing at the kitchen door.

'Sorry?'

'I thought you were supposed to be a professional cook,' he repeats. He's unwinding a scarf from his neck, and starting to take his coat off. Evidently he's been out for the evening; I was too tipsy even to notice that the front door had been double-locked.

'I *am* a professional cook.'

'Ah, right. So that's the professional way to boil milk, is it?' He nods over at the hob, where my pan of milk is doing a worthy impression of a witch's cauldron, bubbling over with frothy white stuff and emitting a foul, sickly burned smell.

OK, I'm definitely even tipsier than I thought.

'Shit!'

'It's all right. I'll get it.' Liam strides past me while I'm still struggling to get to my feet, takes the pan off the hob, throws it into the sink and starts the cold tap over it. There's a long, hissing release of steam. 'And is this something a keen amateur cook can try?' he goes on, as we both stare at the ruined pan, 'or is it something you'd say was best left to those who really know what they're doing?'

'Very funny.' I glare at him, until I suddenly remember the awful tragedy Jamie told me about earlier this evening. This wipes the glare off my face at once. 'Thanks,' I say instead. 'I'm not sure I would have noticed that until the smoke alarms started going off.'

'No big deal. I'm used to that kind of thing. My elder daughter decided she'd make me breakfast the morning I left for London, turned the toaster setting up too high and almost burned the house down. Not that I'm saying you cook like a seven-year-old,' he adds, hastily. 'I mean, Jamie's always saying what an ace you are in the kitchen.'

I'm not too drunk to feel a mild sensation of astonishment that Jamie's mentioned me in conversation with a friend. And to say something unequivocally nice. On the other hand, I'm far, far too drunk to stop myself saying what I say next.

'I'm really sorry, Liam, to hear about your wife.'

The unusually chatty, pleasant atmosphere between us vanishes as he flinches, visibly.

'Oh. Right. Thanks for saying so.'

'I mean, Jamie told me, of course, but he didn't say, you know, *how* it happened.'

'Hit by a car.'

'Oh God.' I can feel all the usual, obvious sympathetic platitudes deserting me, at the sheer awfulness of this. 'God, Liam, I . . . that's terrible.'

I think he's about to bark something at me about it obviously being terrible – after the way I snapped at him for mucking things up with Samantha, I wouldn't really begrudge him a sarky comment – but all he does is stay silent for a moment or two. A long moment or two.

Then he shrugs, with a twist of his lips that I recognise only too well. It's the way people smile when they know the basics (curve lips upwards, display appropriate amount of teeth) but have temporarily forgotten that when you smile, you're supposed to be happy about something.

'Yes, it was. Terrible, that is. Still is terrible, actually. When I think about it. Which I don't, any more. I mean, not as much as I used to.'

'I completely understand! I had a terrible car accident myself, ten years ago. It's the reason I can't have kids, as it happens . . .' I don't know what's got into me. Can it really be simply the booze? I never talk to strangers about what Vito would call 'my insides'. For God's sake, I barely talk to my friends about it. Or Jamie, even. '. . . and it took me years before I'd totally come to terms with it. Before I stopped thinking about it every single minute of every single day. And that was nowhere *near* as tragic as what's happened to you! I mean, widowed! At your age! With two daughters –'

'Yes.' Thank God, Liam interrupts me before I can

paint any more horrific a picture of his life. 'Look, don't ever think about going into PR or anything, will you?' he goes on, with the ghost of a smile – but a proper one this time – forming on his lips. 'You seem to have a unique gift for . . . what's the opposite of sugar-coating?'

'Er – savoury-coating?' I venture.

'That'll do. You seem to have a unique gift for savoury-coating. Making things sound even worse than they really are.'

'I'm sorry! I didn't mean –'

'It's OK!' He holds out a paw-like hand. 'I know you weren't trying to make it sound bad. I was joking.'

My panic subsides. 'Oh. You have a very strange sense of humour.'

'I never used to,' he says, suddenly looking so sad that my heart breaks for him.

We stand in silence for a moment while I frantically try to think of something to say that isn't – what was it? – *savoury-coating* his troubles.

'Well, it was nice talking to you,' Liam suddenly says, breaking the silence, and nodding at the computer. 'I'd better leave you to your work.'

'Oh, no, it isn't work, it's . . .' *Hacking into my sister's email account.* '. . . nothing, really.'

'Still. It's late.' He's already moving for the kitchen door. 'Good night, then.'

Oh, no. I blew it, didn't I? Just when we were having a pleasant-ish bit of banter about the burned milk, and the awful episodes of nakedness and upper-lip-bleaching were fading into the past, I had to go and start bleating on at him about his tragically dead wife, and my mutilated sex organs.

I knew I wasn't remotely cut out for the role of landlady.

Well, I'll write him an apology note, shove it under his door before I have to have the awkwardness of facing him on the way out of the bathroom tomorrow morning. Write it after I've returned to Polly's emails, that is.

Though I should probably just stop for a minute and think it through before I go any further. Talking to – OK, talking *at* – Liam has made me doubt whether or not spying on my sister really is excusable after all. Heaven knows, at the end of the day there are more important things than people cancelling their weddings. There are tragic deaths, and horrible accidents . . .

Still, I've already got into her email account now. And I'd be lying if I said I wasn't wondering who this Julia247 person is, whom Dev seemed a bit suspicious about. The Julia that Polly seems to have so very many emails from.

I reopen my laptop, wait for her email page to appear again, and then click on the most recent of the mails from Julia247.

All it says is this: *I'm here right now. Call me. Julia.*

The other two say almost exactly the same thing.

Call me whenever. Julia.

Got your email. In office until 5.30 NY time. Call me? Julia.

Well, I'm obviously not going to find out much from Julia herself. Whoever she is, she's evidently a woman of few words.

I let the cursor wander over to the Sent folder and click on it. Then I click on the most recent email Polly sent to this Julia woman – the day after she got back from New York – and I start to read.

From: PollyWollyDoodle@hotmail.com
To: Julia247@yahoo.com
Date: 18 November 2011
Subject: Home

Hi Julia. And greetings from sunny London!

Actually, that's not strictly accurate. It's pouring here, just for a change; this particular kind of relentless, uncompromising drizzle that seems to strike the moment I ever hit town. And yes, I *know* it's not as if it's always sunny in New York, but for some reason even the rain never feels quite as oppressive over there as it does here. All in the mind, no doubt. But still, right now I think I'd take torrential downpours, freak snowstorms and devastating tornados in New York over balmy blue skies in London.

I'm already starting to think I should never have come home at all.

You're bound to say – in fact, I can almost hear your voice saying it now – that I've barely been back twelve hours, that I need to give it a lot more time before I can start declaring that I don't want to be here. But things just feel . . . I don't know. Off-centre. Tilting. Like one of those haunted houses you'd go to at theme parks as a child where the floor would suddenly just fall away from underneath your feet, usually accompanied by hollow demonic laughter from a clapped-out speaker system just above your head. (I'm talking about crappy English theme parks, of course, so probably you Americans with your swanky Disneylands and your ritzy Universal Studios would have no idea of the kind of rubbish experience I'm talking about.)

Maybe, though, the scary tilting feeling is nothing to do with coming back to London. Maybe my world just feels as though it's off its axis because Dev was my anchor, and because I'm not anchored any more.

Honestly, though, I think at least part of the scary tilting feeling is London's fault. Well, if not London's *fault*, then certainly triggered by coming back here. I don't think I'd thought through the stress of it all – coming back and telling people the wedding is off. I don't think, actually, that I'd thought about the practicalities of having to tell people the wedding is off at all. Naturally, my sister pointed it out to me first thing this morning, before I'd even had time to digest my breakfast. I know she means well, but I really didn't need to hear about all the phone calls I'm going to have to make, all the arrangements I'm going to have to cancel, all the people I'm going to be letting down.

And I certainly hadn't properly thought through the practicalities of telling Bella. Yes, with hindsight, of *course* I should have known she'd nose around the matter like a bloodhound on the scent. Of course I should have known that she wouldn't just leave me in peace until she'd challenged every last little shred of my reasoning. Which is why I ended up spinning her, this morning, some line about not loving Dev any more. It was the only way I could think to get her to back off. After all, not even Bella would think I should marry a man I don't love, just for the sake of going through with the wedding she's been so carefully planning. At the end of the day, she has nothing but my best interests at heart. I just wish I'd always been so good a sister.

Anyway, hopefully my little white lie will keep her at bay for a bit, until I can work up the courage to explain to her the real reason I'm not marrying him. *If* I can work up the courage to explain to her the real reason I'm not marrying him. All that will seem easier – I hope – when I'm a bit more settled. When I'm not living in such close proximity with her (and the annoying boyfriend) any more. I should be in a temporary apartment in a few days' time, and then I'm going to start looking for something more permanent. Assuming I don't decide to jump back on a plane to New York again any time soon.

This was a joke.
Sort of.

I know you already think I'm just running away from my problems, breaking up with Dev. I know you think I can't run away from things for ever.

Right now, though, I'm honestly not running. I mean, I'm here, aren't I? Back in rainy old Britain.

I'll call you on Friday, shall I, or whenever you're next available? Any time you're able to talk, to be honest, would suit me.

P x

Grace

Tuesday 1 December

Much excitement in the ranks today, because Polly is meeting me and the boys up at Selfridges after school. It was her suggestion, to fulfil a godmotherly duty she's not been able to exercise before: taking them to Santa's grotto. Hector was so apoplectic with anticipation when I told them where we were going that he was almost sick on the bus, while Robbie managed to remain laid-back and older-brother blasé about it all until we actually arrived at Selfridges, when the realisation of the joint thrill of Santa and Auntie Polly kicked in. He's been jittery and over-emotional ever since.

And seeing as Auntie Polly was due to meet us half an hour ago, that's been quite a lot of 'ever since'.

I wait to chase her up until exactly the thirty-minute mark, which is enough of a compromise between the fact that I don't want to hassle Polly and the fact that if I stand in the packed, overheated basement Christmas department with a nauseous Hector and a jittery Robbie for very much longer, somebody is going to throw a tantrum of epic proportions. And that person might very well be me.

I'm just about to ring her mobile when there's a sudden flurry of activity on the escalator closest to us, and Polly appears halfway down it.

She looks even less kempt than she did the last time I saw her, at Café on the Green, wild-haired and pale-faced, though obviously still managing to attract lustful stares from every passing male in the place.

I can tell right away, from her guilty expression, that she's late because she totally forgot about the outing.

'Oh, *fuck*,' she says, the moment she sees us, before clapping a hand over her mouth, too late, to prevent the bad language in front of the boys. 'You've been waiting. I'm so sorry I'm late! The tube . . . delays on the Northern Line . . .'

'It's OK.' I can't entirely hide my irritation. 'You're here now. That's the important thing.'

And obviously I've pretty much forgiven her about three minutes later, when she's lavished praise and attention on both Robbie, who remembers her, and Hector, who doesn't but who instantly falls passionately in love. She puts an immense amount of effort into their whole grotto experience, telling them all kinds of exaggerated stories about the Christmases Mummy and Auntie Polly had when they were little, and making them laugh by putting silly reindeer antlers on her head, and flirting with Santa just enough that he not only gives the boys extra time but also slips additional presents – colouring books and crayons – in our direction.

It's all so full-on that I'm totally exhausted just

being in the vicinity of it. So I'm grateful when she offers, in her final bid for the title of Godmother of the Year, hot chocolate and cupcakes in the nearby in-store café.

'I'm really sorry, again,' she says, when Robbie and Hector have settled down to their colouring books at the table next to ours. 'It did kind of slip my mind, I'm afraid. But I've been so busy, with job-hunting, and trying to find a flat I can move to permanently . . . plus it seems like every time I pick up my phone there's a message from one of my cousins, or one of my aunties, or one of Mum's friends, and I have to be polite and return their call and spend an hour convincing them that I haven't gone mental, I've only cancelled a wedding.'

'You can't blame people for being concerned, Poll.'

'No, but there's no *need* for any of them to be concerned! How many more times do I have to say it?' She gives a brisk, brittle laugh that sounds nothing at all like her usual chirpy giggle. 'So, what's news with you?' she asks, deftly deferring the subject to me instead of her. 'I've been dying to ask you more about your lunch with this sexy St Martin's dad bloke.'

'More? You want *more* details of my hideous embarrassment?'

'Oh, come on, Gracie, I'm sure it wasn't half as embarrassing as you made it sound.'

'So you don't think it's embarrassing that I thought he was about to declare his desire to make . . .' I lower my voice, conscious that Robbie and Hector are within earshot, '. . . violent love to me? And then that I *told* him so?'

Or that I showed up at his office three days later with a lovingly hand-drawn thank-you card? Something I'm still too utterly humiliated to mention even to Polly. I mean, I can barely bring myself to acknowledge to myself that I did it.

'Not embarrassing at all! I bet he loved it! Come on, Grace, there's no need to go so red!'

I don't tell Polly that the reason I'm turning roughly the colour of a freshly boiled beetroot is not because I'm reliving the embarrassment again. It's because I'm thinking, for about the hundredth time already today, about what might have happened if he *had* declared his desire to make violent love to me.

And what might have happened if I'd been foolish enough to agree . . .

'So you *do* fancy him,' says Polly, with the satisfaction of someone who can read me like an open book.

'*Polly!*' I jerk my head towards the boys. Though thankfully they're more engrossed in their search for the perfect shade of red pencil for Rudolf's nose than their mother's crush on a man who isn't their father. 'Look, I never said I didn't fancy him!' I hiss. 'Whether or not I fancy him is hardly the point. And anyway, why are you playing matchmaker all of a sudden? Isn't that the kind of interference you usually leave to Bella?'

'I'm not playing matchmaker.'

'You're trying to! And if you don't want people poking their noses into *your* love life, I don't think you've got any right to go around sticking your nose into anybody else's.'

'I'm not poking my nose!' Her own face is flooding with colour now, and she looks so genuinely upset that I regret what I've just said. 'It's just . . . look, your face lights up, Grace, when you talk about this guy . . .'

'It doesn't light up. It flares up. It's a biological indicator of total mortification.'

'. . . and it never does when you talk about Charlie.'

I take a deep breath. 'Polly, I've been married to Charlie for seven and a half years. We have two children and a very large mortgage. We have neither the time nor the funds to go for impromptu lunches at Locanda Locatelli, or swish around town in an Aston Martin. Maybe that's the reason I don't light up when I talk about him.'

'I'm not sure you *ever* lit up when you talked about him,' she mutters.

'Hey! I lit up! When we were first together, I lit up all the time!'

She pulls off another morsel of cupcake and doesn't say anything.

'It's just *marriage*, Polly.'

'Which old runaway bride here would know nothing about, right?'

'I didn't say that.'

'You didn't have to.' She pushes back her chair, and I think she's about to stalk off, but actually she's getting up to go and look at the boys' colouring, back in Manic Godmother mode again. 'You know, I may not have actually *been* married, Gracie,' she adds, before she turns to crouch down at their table, 'and I know it's not all about cosy lunches and Aston Martins, but surely there's room for the occasional bit of romance? The odd hint of passion? Oh, Hector, your Christmas tree looks *beautiful*! How clever of you to colour it in that lovely purple colour . . .'

Charlie is out at a client dinner – is Saad with him, I can't help wondering? – so it's a more relaxed evening routine than usual, knowing I don't have to get the boys fast asleep before he walks through the door. After supper we watch *Fireman Sam* for almost an hour before I finally persuade them into the bath, tuck them up in bed, and read *You're a Bad Man, Mr Gum!* (once) for Robbie, and *The Smartest Giant in Town* (three times) for Hector. It's almost nine by the time they're both asleep.

As I go to the fridge and pour myself a large glass of wine, which will constitute tonight's dinner, I finally have time to think about what Polly was saying this afternoon.

The thing is that, even though I think she's incredibly unrealistic about marriage, she does have a minor point. It *is* wrong that things have got so . . . stale, I suppose, between me and Charlie. And though I seriously doubt that there's a married-couple-with-kids in the whole of London – OK, the whole of Britain – OK, the whole *world* – who are finding new and exotic ways to pleasure each other – to *light each other up* – I do agree that it's important to put in a bit of effort.

Even when you don't feel like it in the slightest.

It's the grown-up thing to do, isn't it?

Not that I haven't tried at *all*, by the way. Even though things have been rocky between us for a long time, his being made redundant did seem to make everything much worse. So I made repeated attempts, throughout his redundancy, to make him Feel Like a Man (I read an article on 'Redundancy and Your Sex Life' in *You* magazine. All right, I obsessively Googled the subject until I found an old article on 'Redundancy and Your Sex Life' in *You* magazine). You can probably imagine the kind of thing it recommended: flimsy nighties, come-hither glances, casual comments about how hunky/manly/powerful he still looks. But when none of that worked, I didn't search around for an alternative. I suppose I just thought things would magically improve one day, somehow.

Well, maybe it's time not to be so passive any more. Come to think of it, I'm bored rigid with being passive. Let's face it, probably that's the only reason I developed that teeny-tiny little crush on Saad Amar. That was just the subconscious of a grown woman, in what's supposed to be the prime of her sexual life, gently reminding herself that she has needs too. I mean, it's all very well trying (and failing) to get

Charlie to Feel Like a Man, but what about me Feeling Like a Woman?

And I might never stop thinking about violent lovemaking with Saad Amar if I don't make an effort to do a bit of violent lovemaking with my own husband.

Charlie will be back from dinner pretty soon, so I take my glass of wine upstairs. I double-, then triple-check the boys are asleep before going into my own bedroom. Wait – *our* bedroom. Maybe I've been thinking about it as *my* bedroom for too long. A place to make idle sketches of the boys that no one will ever see. A place to watch reruns of *Keeping Up with the Kardashians*. A place to drop off to sleep, while Charlie sits over paperwork and his emails in the living room before dozing off in front of the *News at Ten*. Well, no more! I'm going to banish all thoughts of sleep, paperwork, the entire Kardashian clan, and Saad Amar, by welcoming Charlie home to the best sex of his life.

And as for that sex, I'm suddenly pondering the idea of indulging in a little bit of dressing-up. Partly because I haven't quite been able to shake this fantasy of . . . well, a sheikh fantasy – me in ivory chiffon and dangly gold jewellery, *summoned to the chamber* of a cruel-but-tender Arabian prince – and partly because role play is precisely what all the magazines tell you to do when you're trying to rediscover the – what did Polly say? – oh, yes, the romance. And the passion. I mean, I'm not the most experienced lover in the world

– even thinking the word 'lover' makes me cringe, to be honest with you – so perhaps this could be the start of a whole new chapter for me. A bit of cheeky role play: putting on a totally different character from boring old Grace Costello, Parsons Green mother-of-two, might just prove the ideal way for me to shake off some of my usual inhibitions.

OK, then. Let's get this show on the road.

The sticking point, I realise pretty swiftly, is going to be Wardrobe. As far as ivory chiffon and dangly gold jewellery go, the very best I think I'd be able to come up with is the floaty Whistles dress I wore for our registry-office wedding, and some hoop earrings I ill-advisedly bought after seeing Eva Mendes looking smouldering in a pair in the 'You, the Fashion Jury' pages of *Grazia*. So the sheikh fantasy is out, I think. Besides, this is supposed to be an evening that brings me closer to Charlie, which is hardly likely to happen if I keep accidentally substituting him with an image of Saad. Who, naturally, has a big advantage in the whole sexy sheikh department, one that I don't think pale, Dutch-Irish, native Chicagoan Charlie is going to be able to compete with.

All right, then, what would play to Charlie's strengths, as it were? Could he pull off a stern-but-tender headmaster? Well, he'd certainly do a sterling job of the *stern* part. Even if he has one or two issues with the *tender*. But that begs the question, can I pull off a naughty schoolgirl? Dig out that flippy tartan skirt I wore last winter, when they were all the rage with the Mirandas, roll it up until it's eye-wateringly mini, knot a shirt Britney-style at the navel, put my hair into bunches . . .

No. I can't do it. I'll die. Women, as far as I can tell, pretty much divide into those who can pull off Sexy Schoolgirl, and those who have more chance of pulling off a million-dollar diamond heist. I don't think I need to risk trying it out to know that I'm one of the latter.

So. What does that leave us with? Naughty Nurse? Again, I'm not sure how to cobble together an outfit. Slutty Secretary? Well, the get-up is easy enough – pencil skirt, possibly my new Elle Macpherson lingerie, sinfully high heels – but I don't know. It feels a bit bogus, for someone like myself who's never joined the world of office work. Besides, the script possibilities make my toes curl. I suppose I'd have to say things like, 'I think the team meeting went well, sir, but you might want to debrief me,' and Charlie would have to say, 'Maybe later, but first I want you to take some dictation,' and I'd have to say, 'Absolutely, sir, I'll bend over backwards to help . . .'

No. Oh Lord, no. Slutty Secretary is out too. Very, very out.

I'm just starting to think that maybe I just don't have a romantic or passionate bone in my body when it occurs to me. Cheerleader! It's the one and only fancy-dress costume I ever enjoyed, for a Fourth of July barbecue at Charlie's parents' several years ago. All right, it was before the boys came along, not that long after Charlie and I first got together, in fact, and when we still had something resembling a sex life. But I can remember what a huge hit it was with him. It's an American thing, I imagine: all to do with those frustrating high-school years, when you're all bubbling testosterone and oozing pimples, and the perky, popular cheerleaders won't even look at you.

And back then I wasn't even doing it *slutty* cheerleader-style, like I could do it tonight, the cute shorts rolled up as high as they'll go on my thighs and the letterman sweater slipping sexily off one naked shoulder rather than layered over a long-sleeve cotton T-shirt. And Charlie can be the gruff-but-tender sports coach! Yes! This could just about work. Now, if I can just dig out the costume, from where I suspect it still is, languishing in a packing case at the very back of the wardrobe . . .

Fifteen minutes and quite a lot of dust later, and I'm ready to roll. The red-and-white cheerleader uniform still fits perfectly – no mean feat after seven years and two children – and I think I can get away with a bouncy, shiny ponytail instead of the dreaded bunches. I'm just putting the finishing touches to the ponytail, in fact, when I hear Charlie opening and then locking the front door.

Now, how do I kick-start this whole role-play thing, so as to get Charlie on board the moment he walks into the bedroom? Should I be bending over saucily to tie up my plimsolls? Performing a cheeky X-rated cheer? Something to do with . . . with getting balls over the line . . . or scoring in the penalty area?

There's no time to decide, because the bedroom door is opening, and Charlie is walking in.

He looks tired, and his suit is crumpled. Great. He'll want me to press the trousers for him before work tomorrow. Though I banish this thought as soon as I remember that now is not the time to be thinking about ironing.

'Grace!' he says, his eyebrows shooting up. 'Honey! Wow. I'm impressed.'

'Really? It looks OK?' No, that's not right. Desperate attempts to fish for compliments are not conducive to convincing role play. 'Well,' I carry on, in a sultrier tone, 'I've been waiting for you to get back all evening. Because I was hoping you could . . . help me get some exercise?'

'Absolutely!' He starts pulling off his tie and undoes the top button on his shirt. 'Now, what were you thinking of, honey? Because I tell you, the elliptical machine has really worked wonders for me. Twenty minutes on that and you'll feel it in your thighs tomorrow morning, I promise you!' He crosses to the elliptical machine and starts pressing buttons with enthusiasm.

Wait a minute. Those aren't the buttons he's meant to be pressing with enthusiasm.

'Charlie, this isn't what I meant . . .'

'Oh, come on, honey, I know it looks a little scary, but it's pretty easy once you're up on it.' He ushers me up onto the treads, not taking No for an answer. 'Now, you can just do a manual programme to begin with, but maybe if you like it we could try starting you on one of the more targeted programmes. Fat loss, I figure, is what you're after? . . . Honey, there's no need to look so offended! I didn't say you were in *bad* shape! Just that you could stand to lose a couple of pounds.'

'I weigh *exactly* the same,' I tell him stiffly, 'as I did when you first met me.'

'Really?'

'Yes. Really.'

'Still, it doesn't hurt to do some regular exercise. And you've taken the first step. Now, tell you what, why don't I head downstairs and leave you to do your workout in peace? I have a ton of emails and paperwork to catch up on.'

'Charlie!' I hold up my hands. All right, my pride is massively dented, but I've come this far. I'm not going to let this go. 'Look, can't you just forget about the emails? And I'll just forget about the . . . workout. I thought we might get into bed together for a change. You know – have a cuddle, dim the lights. Do something romantic and passionate for once?'

He steps about a foot back from me, such an expression of dismay crossing his face that you'd think I'd just suggested playing Hungry Hippo with his dangly bits.

'Oh Christ, honey, no. I mean, not tonight. I'm exhausted, for one thing. And I have emails to catch up on, for another.'

'Yes. You mentioned that.'

'And I really don't want to interrupt your workout.'

Quite suddenly, I feel as if all resistance has deserted me. I can't fight the tide of Charlie's disinterest any longer. I suppose, in true All-American style, the only thing to do is to work my frustrations off on the sports field. Or in this case, on the elliptical machine.

I start pedalling, moving my arms in synchronicity with my feet. 'There's wine open in the fridge, if you want a nightcap. Don't forget to turn the lights off when you come up.'

When I glance over my shoulder a moment or so later, he's already gone.

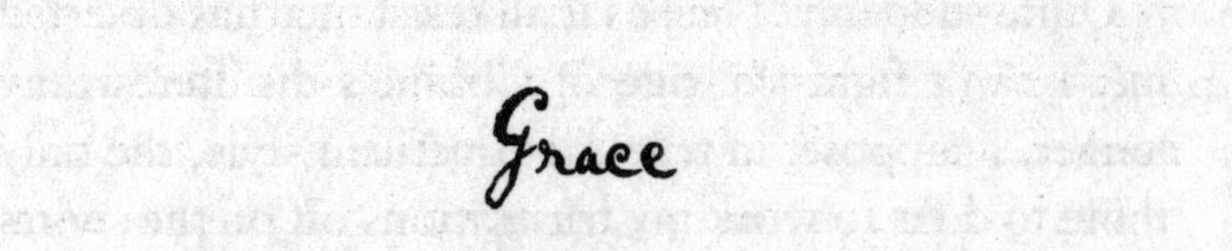

Wednesday 2 December

Next morning, and I realise Charlie was right about one thing: I really can feel the elliptical machine workout in my thighs. And then some.

It's all I need, quite frankly, as today I'm due to meet Vanessa, Charlie's ex-wife, for what she calls 'diary co-ordination' and I call 'the seventh circle of hell'.

We do this three times a year, always in advance of the school holidays, so that we can agree on where Percy, her and Charlie's son, will be spending what proportion of his time. Well, I say *we* agree: mostly it's Vanessa telling me what arrangement she will find acceptable, and me agreeing. You'd think today's meeting, in early December, would be to discuss the Christmas holidays. But no. Vanessa's far more organised than that. We sorted out the Christmas holidays back in early September. Today it's the turn of the Easter holidays, three full months from now.

My whole body usually aches with dread about these occasions, and now I've got properly aching legs to add to the misery. So it's a slow and wincing walk to take the boys to school (not improved by the sight of Louboutin Lexie springing into her cab like a particularly sprightly young deer, her own still-mobile legs encased in knee-high tan suede Louboutin boots) followed by a bandy-legged hobble round the supermarket, and finally a reluctant shuffle to Vanessa's.

Vanessa lives in the *really* posh part of Fulham with her second husband, Alasdair, her baby twin girls, Esme and Freya, and a constantly changing cast of ill-treated foreign nannies, most of whom stick it out for less than two months before fleeing the country. Charlie once joked that if they weren't asylum seekers before they arrived to work for Vanessa, they certainly would be when they left. But when I tried to repeat the joke back to him, after a Bosnian nanny left Vanessa's employ a few months ago, Charlie just frowned and said, 'That's not funny, Grace. There really was a terrible war in the former Yugoslavia, you know. You should brush up on your general knowledge before you start making jokes about that kind of thing.'

Anyway, my first thought is that there's a fresh nanny crisis today, because Vanessa opens her front door looking furious, with bits of rice cake in her hair and what looks like spit-up milk on her grey silk blouse. Despite this, she's supremely elegant, as ever, in head-to-toe Armani, her chic dark crop freshly blow-dried and her mouth its usual cerise slash. Nature intended Vanessa to be a comfy size fourteen, but through sheer force of will she's a whippet-like size ten, an impressive testimony to her daily workouts and a ban on puddings that's worthy of the Taliban.

'Oh, it's you,' she says, by way of greeting.

'Good morning, Vanessa!'

'No. It isn't a good morning, as it happens.' She ushers me indoors. 'For one thing, the new nanny has just left. With *zero* notice.'

'Oh dear, I am sorry.'

'And for another thing . . .' Her face darkens still further, as we're both suddenly distracted by a noise on the stairs behind us.

When I turn round I can see that it's Percy. He's wearing absurdly baggy jeans, a David Bowie T-shirt, and an extremely sheepish expression.

'I've been suspended,' he mutters, before I can ask what he's doing home from boarding school at ten o'clock on a Wednesday.

'Oh, Perce,' I say, in a tone carefully calculated to offer him support as well as (please God) not to further enrage Vanessa. If it were just me and him, I'd go and give him a hug, but I've always been careful about how demonstrative I am with Percy when Vanessa is around. I don't want her to think I'm treading on any toes. Still, he looks much in need of a hug. His body, a scrawny boy's when I last saw him back in mid-October, seems to have transformed practically overnight into the wiry awkwardness of a teenager, and he needs a haircut. 'What happened?'

'*Drugs* happened,' Vanessa says, more gorgonesque than ever as she shoots both of us – hey, why is this *my* fault? – looks that could quite conceivably turn us into stone.

'Mum! *Please* stop calling it drugs! It was just a

spliff. Everyone at school smokes them. I was the only one who got caught.'

'Then you're an idiot as well as a criminal,' she snaps.

'But it *isn't* criminal! It was just for my own personal use, Mum. Which means it isn't any worse than having a glass of wine.' Percy has clearly spent most of last night up on this rather tired teenage soapbox, but I can't help admiring him for trying again. Something about his tenacity reminds me of Hector's continuing and consistent refusal to abandon his beloved nappies. 'I mean, you and Alasdair drink wine, don't you? And that has mind-altering affects just as much as a spliff does. *And* it's safer to smoke weed than go out and get drunk. Nobody has ever killed anybody over a spliff.'

'There might be a first time,' Vanessa says.

'You're not going to tell Dad, are you?' Percy asks me.

'Er . . .'

'Most certainly she *is* going to tell your father. I'd have told him myself if he'd returned my call – my *two* calls – yesterday afternoon. Not that I imagine he'll take too much interest,' Vanessa adds archly. 'I'm sure he's spending far too much time at the office as usual.'

I feel the need to leap to Charlie's defence, though less of a need than I might have felt before last night, I have to admit. 'He's got a lot on his plate, Vanessa.'

'Mm. Well, are you just going to stand on the stairs all morning,' she suddenly demands of Percy, 'or are you going to go to your room and get on with your maths coursework?'

'I'll get on with my maths coursework,' Percy mutters, after shooting me a look that suggests he's contemplated saying, *Oh, I thought I'd stand on the stairs all morning, actually*. 'Nice to see you, Grace.'

'Lovely to see you too! Your mum and I are going to sit down and sort out all the plans for the Easter holidays!' I say, loading my voice with an insane amount of enthusiasm, because I always feel so guilty about the part I've played, however unwittingly, in Percy's parents' divorce. It's a feeling of guilt that Vanessa is happy to exploit.

'Yes, well, not if we don't get a move on. I have a conference call at eleven, so we'll need to be finished by no less than three minutes to the hour. Go on through to the kitchen, Grace, and help yourself to coffee and biscuits. I just need to get the girls down for their nap. I'll only be a minute and a half.'

She will, as well. Vanessa's to-the-split-second childcare routine makes Gina Ford look slack and sloppy. To be entirely fair to her (and I've no idea why I feel the need to be fair to her, because she's certainly never been remotely fair to me), her high-powered career means it's pretty essential to keep some measure of control. It just seems a little unfair on her twins that they're the ones who end up on the receiving end of it. Vanessa is a top ENT surgeon at one of the best London teaching hospitals, specialising in fitting cochlear implants that restore hearing to deaf people. Though as Charlie once said, probably she just *frightens* deaf people into getting their hearing back.

I haven't tried to repeat this joke to him any time recently.

The thing is, actually, that in another life Vanessa and I might not get on too badly. Yes, she's spent the past seven years guilting me for their divorce, despite the fact that she seems far happier with Alasdair, her wealthy, almost-invisible, hedge-fund-manager husband than she ever was with Charlie; yes, she bad-mouthed me to Chief Miranda before Robbie even started at St Martin's, so I never had a hope of making friends with anyone there. But honestly, I don't think she's *all* bad. I admire her career, for one thing, because I wish I could be just one-twentieth as successful as she is. I admire her determination, at forty-six, to go through several gruelling rounds of IVF so she could end up with the extra children she wanted (though she never would have shown it) so badly. Most of all, I'm incredibly fond of Percy, and it's difficult to dislike Vanessa entirely when I see parts of her in someone I care about so much.

It's just a pity, really, that I got in her firing line by marrying her first husband.

And that she doesn't seem to be able to find anything at all to like or admire in me.

'Miranda's here, by the way,' she tells me now, as she starts up the stairs and I head for the kitchen. 'She popped in for a coffee this morning and when I told her you were coming she said she'd stick around to say hello.'

Oh shit. Creaking thighs, Vanessa, *and* Chief Miranda. It's a terrible triumvirate I'm not sure I have the energy to cope with.

Miranda is sitting at the French country-style scrubbed oak table, sipping an Emma Bridgewater mug of coffee and avoiding a plate of Duchy Originals shortbread. She stands up when I come in and greets me, unconvincingly, with a kiss on each cheek.

'Lovely to see you,' she says, equally unconvincingly. 'I haven't managed to catch up with you at the school gates for a while.'

I don't want to admit that this is because we've been getting there later than ever. 'We've been getting in very early the past few days.'

'Right, well, I really just wanted to find out where you were with Saad Amar.'

Nowhere. I am nowhere with Saad Amar.

'I mean, I know you were saying you'd have a chat with him *soon*,' she carries on snittily. 'And I remember your friend was rather defensive about that. But the deadline for new-pupil applications is coming up fast now, Grace, and the fund-raising committee are getting really concerned that we're going to lose out on this big fish –'

'I've spoken to him. Yes,' I continue as Miranda looks surprised. 'We had lunch together last week, actually.'

'*Oh*.'

'It was only a quick bite. Just, you know, for him to ask me more questions about St Martin's.'

'And . . . ?'

'And nothing! It was just a quick bite, I said already!'

'I *meant*, and how did it go?' She leans across the table. 'Did he say he'd be going ahead with the application? Did he mention any other schools that are still on their radar?'

'Ohhhh. Um, no, he didn't. I mean, he didn't mention any other schools. I'm pretty sure he'll be going ahead with the application to St Martin's.'

Chief Miranda's clenched fist bangs on the French oak table. 'Get in!' she bellows triumphantly, and just for a moment there's the strongest hint of Geordie in her usually plummy accent.

'Oh, Vanessa,' she says, as the woman herself strides into the kitchen, sits down at the table and starts to pour herself coffee from the cafetière. 'Grace has brought some excellent news. Something to interest you too, if you're going to be sending your girls to St Martin's one day in the future. It looks like the Amar family are intending to send little Hassan to St Martin's after all!'

'Adnan,' I say.

'Sorry?'

'Well, it's just that his name isn't Hassan. Or Ahmed. Or Abdul, for that matter. It's Adnan.'

Miranda's eyes narrow. 'Oh, well, of course, I'm not the one who's been for a cosy lunch with his older brother Saad, so I don't have the precise details at my fingertips.'

'Cosy lunch?' Vanessa's eyes have lit up. For someone so no-nonsense, she's certainly a surprisingly big fan of idle gossip. 'Who have you been having cosy lunches with, Grace?'

'There was nothing cosy about it at all!' I give a little laugh and help myself oh-so-casually to a biscuit. 'Purely a business lunch, I'm afraid!'

Vanessa lets out a snort. 'Where have I heard *that* before?'

'What do you mean?'

'Come on, Grace, isn't that exactly the type of thing a man would say if he was boffing his secretary or something?' She shoots Miranda (who is *loving* this, incidentally) a sly little smile.

I'm feeling more picked-on-by-the-mean-girls than ever; any minute now I fully expect the pair of them to try to reveal to the world that I'm wearing strawberry-print knickers. Where's Polly when I need her?

'Precisely the type of thing,' Vanessa continues, 'that I'm pretty sure Charlie told me when he was off boffing you, in fact!'

'Vanessa,' I hate having to stand up to her, but I don't want to be bullied. Well, not any more than I have to be, 'you know Charlie wasn't bof . . . wasn't doing anything with me when he was still trying to make things work with you.'

She lets out a little laugh of her own, a high-pitched,

edgy one. 'Oh, well, who can remember that far back? If it wasn't you it was someone else!'

Christ, she really is pissed off about Percy's suspension, isn't she? She only ever drops snide little hints about Charlie's repeated infidelity – infidelity he totally denies, by the way – when she's in a truly terrible mood.

'Vanessa . . .' I begin, just as I feel my phone buzz in my bag beside me. I glance down, and when I see who the text message is from, I quickly press the View option.

Don't suppose u r free this am? Need to talk to you about something.

It's from Saad Amar.

'You know, I'd love to have a proper *chat* with Charlie one day,' Miranda is saying, archly. 'We've not really caught up in years, and I always think what an amazing man he must be to have had two such *stunning* wives.'

Vanessa's reply is cut short by the yowling of one of the twins on the baby monitor, and while she stamps ominously upstairs to 'put a stop to this', and Miranda nips off to the loo, I take the opportunity to reply to Saad's text.

Sure. Where and when is good to meet? I can come to the office?

Which I think is the right thing to say. Letting him know I'm happy to come to the office, with Charlie around the place, will communicate the fact that I'm not wrongly assuming he's up for some funny business. That I absolutely understand, this time, that all he wants to discuss is school applications. On the other hand, last time I saw him it *was* at his office, and I was waiting there stalker-style with a cutesy homemade card. But before I can think up a fresh suggestion for a totally neutral place to meet, and text him again, he's texted back.

Am not at office. Can u come 2 mine?

I'm just texting back in the affirmative when Vanessa comes back into the kitchen, the Great Twin Rebellion of SW6 successfully quelled.

'Who's that you're texting so furiously?' she demands, as she slides back into her seat, shooting longing glances in the direction of the plate of Duchy Originals.

'Nobody.' I just want to get out of here now, and set off for Saad's. 'Sorry, Vanessa, we should really get on with that chat about the Easter holidays.'

'Oh, yes, well, I was thinking you could take Percy for two whole weeks this time. Give him a chance to spend some time with his little half-brothers.'

Vanessa isn't, I know, interested in Percy spending some time with 'his little half-brothers'. She's interested in palming him off on me because in the last year he's morphed – in her eyes, at least – from a nice little boy doing his Latin vocab into a terrible teenage tearaway doing banned substances. I mean, anyone with eyes can see that he's just reacting to being shoved away to boarding school while his mother pours every ounce of her spare time and effort into the twins (whom, I notice, Vanessa never calls 'his little *half*-sisters').

I take a deep breath. 'Vanessa, you know we love having Percy, but we are having him for Christmas. And he came out to my parents' in Normandy for pretty much the whole summer. Don't you think he might like to spend some time with you? I mean, you don't see him much during the term-time, and . . .'

I falter in the face of Vanessa's icy stare.

'I didn't *want* him to go away to school, you know. I preferred the idea of a day school in London. *Your husband* was the one who insisted on boarding school.'

'Well, I think Charlie just thought, with you working such long hours –'

'Oh, yes, shove him away to boarding school, with all the other kids from broken homes, whose fathers would rather stump up the school fees than face up to the fact they've done wrong by them.'

'Fine.' I know when I'm beaten. Vanessa has brought out the big guns. 'We'll have him for two weeks at Easter. We'll be glad to.'

'Well, if you're sure,' she says, all sweetness (ish) and light now that she's got what she wants.

'I'm positive,' I say, as Miranda walks back into the room. She starts exclaiming rapturously on the new hand towels Vanessa has in the downstairs loo, and the two of them fall into a frankly horrifying game of one-upmanship over their interior fixtures and fittings for the remainder of the coffee morning. By the time

I'm eventually released, at precisely fifteen minutes before eleven, I've heard enough about why Cath Kidston is *so* much superior to Oka to last a lifetime.

I suppose I'm expecting Saad's front door to be opened by Thomas, the formidable housekeeper, but as my taxi drives away, it's Saad himself who appears on the front step.

He's looking unusually uncertain, as well as predictably gorgeous, dressed in casual clothes – jeans, battered brown shoes, a light blue shirt – rather than a business suit, for the first time since I've got to know him. Maybe it's the casual clothes that have taken away his usual air of smooth invincibility.

'Grace.' The lightest peck on each cheek. He smells of pine forests, and mountain air. 'I hope I haven't dragged you away from anything enjoyable.'

'Just coffee with Charlie's ex-wife.'

'Ah. Then, as my little brother would say, yay for me.'

He ushers me through the front door, then, after a moment's hesitation, into the drawing room, the one with the Picasso.

'I've already told Thomas to bring us in some tea . . . do you like tea?' he asks, graciously handing me into the pale grey leather sofa, then sitting down beside me. 'I can have him bring coffee if you'd prefer? Or . . .' he glances at his watch, '. . . is it too early for something stronger?'

'Oh, I think a little too early, yes.' I'm not falling

into the trap again of thinking that this is anything other than a get-together to talk about St Martin's. 'Tea is perfect.'

'Good, good. This is probably a conversation we should be sober for, after all.'

Oh shit, this sounds serious.

He's decided to enrol his brother at another school, hasn't he? And right after I've gone and told Chief Miranda he was a dead cert for St Martin's. Bloody brilliant.

But I don't want Saad to realise the immense pile of crap he's just landed me in, so I plaster a smile over my face. 'Saad, look, I understand completely. You've had to make the right decision for Adnan. Anyway, between you and me, I don't have all that high an opinion of St Martin's. The teachers are ever so pushy, and the parents are even worse, and –'

'Grace, this isn't about St Martin's.' A glimmer of a smile crosses his face. 'But thanks for the late show of honesty on that front. Maybe I'll have another look at St Thomas's after all.'

I really should have just kept my mouth shut, shouldn't I?

'Look.' He moves a fraction closer on the sofa, then seems to think better of it. 'It's not been an easy few days for me, I'm afraid, Grace . . .'

'Of course. I mean, it didn't seem as if that client dinner went very well last night.'

'What?'

'The client dinner. Charlie . . . well, he wasn't in the

most relaxed of moods when he got home from it, that's all. I assumed it hadn't gone very well.'

His eyes darken. 'No,' he says, after a moment. 'No, it didn't go well. At all.'

'I'm really sorry. I know it must be really stressful, running an entire company. Well, actually, I *don't* know how stressful it must be to run an entire company, but I can imagine, obviously . . .'

'Grace.' Now he does move closer on the sofa, but it's only to place a finger on my lips. 'Please. Stop talking about work.'

Well, the touch of his finger on my lips has pretty much done for me talking about work. There's a good chance, in order to keep it there for ever, that I may never feel the need to speak again.

'The reason I've had a difficult few days,' he carries on, 'is nothing to do with work. I've been spending a lot of time thinking, as it happens. Complicated thoughts. Thoughts about . . . well, about you.'

'Me?' I say. Actually, seeing as his finger is still over my mouth, it comes out more of a *mmngh*.

'Yes. About you, and that lunch we had the other day, and Charlie.'

OK, now I'm really stressed. Did Saad say something about our lunch to Charlie when they went for the client dinner last night? And did Charlie go uncharacteristically mental on him? And – oh my God – has Saad been forced to fire him as a result?

But if this is the case, why didn't Charlie say anything to me about it when he got back last night? And why hasn't Saad got a black eye, or anything, instead of looking just as perfect as always? Not that I think Charlie's capable of giving anyone a black eye. His temper tends to come in the form of monstrous sulks rather than open aggression.

'And then when I saw you at the office the other evening . . .' He removes his finger from my lips, which is my opportunity to start frantically apologising for the homemade thank-you card. But before I can begin, he carries on, 'Anyway, I've decided, Grace, that I can't just do nothing about this.'

'About what?'

He seems to be searching for the right words before he simply says, 'About *you*.'

'What about me?' I'm aware that I sound like a total half-wit, by the way. But I've suddenly got this weird roaring noise in my ears that's making it difficult for me to form complete sentences.

'Grace, I can't stop thinking about you, OK? I was doing pretty well, after that lunch of ours, at not thinking too much about . . . well, about how attractive I found you.' Now that he's found the right words, they're tumbling out in a rush. 'But then you turned up at the office with that card, and . . . look, there is nobody in my life, Grace – *nobody* – who's ever done anything like that for me before.'

'Drawn you,' I just about manage to utter, 'a stupid picture of a cow?'

'No. Taken ten minutes out of their day to do something that would make me smile.' His inky eyes fix onto mine. 'I'm not used to it, Grace. I'm used to women like . . . well, like Britta.'

Wait. He saw me in the same space-time continuum as supermodel-on-the-verge Britta, and *I'm* the one he was attracted to?

'And ever since that, I *really* haven't been able to stop thinking about you.' His words are coming in a rush again. 'About making you smile the way you made me smile. About your smile, full stop. About your beautiful hair, and your incredible body. About touching you. About you touching me. And I can't stop thinking about you being with Charlie instead, and honestly, Grace, it's driving me absolutely nuts.'

At this moment, two things happen simultaneously. The door to the drawing-room opens, and Thomas walks in carrying a tray laden with tea things. And out of absolutely nowhere, my nose starts to bleed.

This has only ever happened to me twice before: first, strangely enough, when I got the call from Polly telling me her sister had been in a terrible car crash; and second, when I found out I was pregnant with Robbie. But at least on both those occasions I wasn't sitting on a pale leather sofa, with an absurdly attractive billionaire mopping at the streaming blood with his shirtsleeves, and his housekeeper handing me fresh linen napkins with an expression on his face that was part utter disdain, part anxiety for the soft furnishings.

'Wait, I'm going to go and get some ice,' Saad says, after a couple of sticky and stressful minutes. 'No, no,

Thomas, let me,' he adds, getting to his feet as Thomas starts to move for the door. 'You've got more first-aid training than me. It's better if you stay with Grace.'

'I don't need anyone with first-aid training,' I croak. But it's too late. He's gone. 'Honestly, it'll stop in a moment,' I tell Thomas.

He hands me another napkin, which I accept with shaking hands and wodge up my nose. 'I gather that this happens frequently, then, Mrs Costello?'

'No, God, no, only twice in the past decade. I think it usually coincides with a bit of a shock.'

Because that's what this has been. The most God-almighty shock, I think, that I've ever had.

OK, let's just try to press a pause button here. Followed by a rewind. What did Saad just say to me? That he can't stop thinking about me. Specifically, about my smile and – did I mishear this? – about my body. I think the word 'incredible' might have been bandied about in there somewhere. Certainly the word 'touch'.

'Shock?' Thomas is repeating, his eyebrows raised in – what? – interest? Concern? Sticky-beakiness? 'I do apologise, Mrs Costello, if Mr Amar has said something to offend you.'

'No, no. I mean, I'm not offended. It was just something . . . it was a bit out of the blue, that's all.' I know I'm blabbering, but it feels like my entire world has just been upended. And po-faced and poker-bummed though Thomas may be – and a virtual stranger at that – he is at least some kind of anchor.

Something constant. He was sniffy with me before Saad turned my life upside down, and he's being equally sniffy afterwards. 'I thought I was just here to talk about school admissions. I wasn't expecting anything else. Though I'm sure he's probably changing his mind about it all right now. I mean, I'm quite sure his usual – what did you call them? – the *ladies of Mr Amar's acquaintance* – don't bleed all over his living room.'

'That is correct, Mrs Costello.'

I stare up at him. I'm aware that I've got a blood-soaked linen napkin wodged up inside each nostril, which must make me look like a demented walrus after a vicious killing spree, but I'm past caring. 'Then what am I doing here, Thomas? I mean, even without the bleeding nose, you and I both know I'm hardly the type I'm sure he usually goes after.'

'I wouldn't say that, Mrs Costello.' He's doing a rather terrifically impressive job of not *quite* looking me in the eye, fixing his gaze approximately half a centimetre north of my eyebrows. 'You're clearly a very attractive woman. Mr Amar is always partial to an elegant blonde. And if you'll forgive me, Mrs Costello, I think you may be reading just a little too much into what – I presume – have been his advances.'

'What do you mean?'

'Mr Amar is a handsome, vigorous and extremely wealthy young man,' he says, in a tone of voice that makes me wonder, suddenly, if he hasn't got a bit of a hopeless crush on Saad himself. 'If I may be frank, this means he can have almost any woman he wants, when he wants. Today, that woman is you. Tomorrow it will be someone different. It is, as people say –', he clears his throat – 'no biggie.'

'No biggie?'

'Yes, Mrs Costello. I don't see that there is any cause for –' he makes the smallest of gestures in the direction of my bloody nose and all the soaked napkins – 'any kind of overreaction.'

He falls silent, immediately, as Saad comes back into the room with a decanter full of ice, a large bottle of brandy and two tumblers. Thank God, though, the ice is a bit redundant, as my nose seems to have finally shut itself down. He sits down next to me again and pours me a glass of brandy. By the time he hands it over, Thomas has discreetly and tactfully vanished from the room.

I remember, only a moment or so too late, that it's probably time to discreetly and tactfully remove the bits of napkin from my nostrils. I haven't had much opportunity to sit down with a magazine for a while, but I'm fairly sure the Psycho Walrus look isn't in this season.

'Thank you,' I say to Saad, taking a couple of very large sips from the glass. 'And I'm sorry.'

'No, *I'm* sorry.' He pours himself a glass too and knocks the contents back in one unrestrained gulp. 'I shouldn't have said anything. It was unforgivable of me. I hope you can just forget about it and we can go back to being friends.'

'No. I can't.'

He pulls a regretful face and gets sharply to his feet. 'Of course. I understand. Well, let me get Thomas to take you home, and –'

'That's not what I meant.' I reach up and touch his hand. I can feel my own hand shaking, but I'm doing a reasonably good job of controlling it. 'I mean, I don't want to just forget about it.'

He doesn't say anything for a moment. He just sits back down on the sofa next to me. Then he takes my glass out of my hand and puts it on the coffee table before using the same hand to turn my face towards him, fixing his eyes onto mine.

'You know, if I was with you,' he says, in a near-whisper, 'I'd count myself one of the luckiest men in the world.'

Even though I appreciate his efforts, they're sort of immaterial. Because he doesn't need to sweet-talk me into this decision. And even though, as decisions go, it's probably up there with the *worst* I've ever made, it's not the *biggest* I've ever made.

It's like Thomas was just trying to tell me – and Polly has already made clear – this could be purely transactional. *Taking a lover*, that is. I mean, I have a husband who can't even bear to touch me. Saad Amar is a man who, temporarily at least, would very much like to touch me. So he gets another notch on his bedpost and I, before he moves on to the next willing female, get a few moments of kindness and appreciation.

Oh, and some of that touching that I just can't stop thinking about.

Saad leans his head down to mine and breathes in, sharply. 'Oh, *Grace*,' he says, before he starts to kiss me.

I've just got the presence of mind, before I start reaching for his shirt buttons the way he's reaching for mine, to check over his shoulder that Thomas isn't hovering in the doorway with yet another tray of something.

When I realise he isn't, I start returning Saad's kisses with total and utter abandon.

Bella

Tuesday 8 December
Later today, Samantha the social worker is coming for her second attempt at the preliminary visit, so Anna has popped round to offer me moral support.

She arrives only a moment or so after Liam has left. He's off for another job interview, I assume. We've barely spoken since that night in the kitchen, the night with the burned milk pan and the awkward conversation about his late wife, but I gather from Jamie that he hasn't had much luck yet. Anyway, Anna has evidently run into him on the stairs or something, because the first thing she says when she comes in is, 'Your unwanted lodger is *gorgeous*.'

'*Gorilla-Man?*'

'I thought you said he was called Liam.' She puts down the carrier bags that suggest she's already found the time to nip into town for a quick shopping spree, and sits down at the table. 'Well, whatever he's called, he's tall, dark and handsome.'

'You mean high, wide and hairy.'

'I didn't see any excess hair.'

'You weren't looking in the right places. And, Anna, *really*? You think he's gorgeous? Even with that whole . . . Neolithic thing he's got going on?'

'*Especially* with that whole Neolithic thing he's got going on.' Anna wets her lips. 'I mean, doesn't he just look like the kind of man who can go out and hunt a wild boar, bring it back and roast it over an open fire, then sling you over his shoulder, carry you into his cave and have his way with you?'

'I'm not sure he looks *quite* like that kind of man,' I say, rather faintly. 'I think he works in computers . . .'

'Well, he can show me his hard drive any time. And on that note,' she goes on, starting to fish in one of her carrier bags, 'have a look at what I've just bought.'

'Some computer equipment?'

She snorts and shakes her head. 'Not exactly. I've been thinking about what you said the other day, you know, about how me and Pete are so much more likely to conceive if we get some real passion back into our sex life.'

'I didn't say *so much more likely*.' Instinctively, I want to distance myself from this. 'I said I thought it might help.'

'Yes, well, you're completely right, Bells. Sex has become nothing but a chore for the both of us. I mean, quite honestly, I think I'd rather stack the dishwasher. And I know Pete would rather be pressure-washing the patio. Well, that can't be sending very positive messages to either of our bodies, can it? What embryo is going to choose to be born to a couple of parents who'd rather do household chores than take the time to make love to one another?'

'Anna, honestly, I'm not sure it works like that.'

'So, what do you reckon to this lot?' She shoots me a wicked grin as she upends a posh paper carrier onto the table. 'I went to this amazing little erotic boutique in Covent Garden this morning, and I got chatting to the woman there about all the kind of things Pete and I *used* to enjoy – and a few things I've always wanted to do that I'm quite sure Pete *would* enjoy, if he'd just man up and go along with it – and this is what we came up with!' She picks up a frankly terrifying-looking black leathery item from the clutch of black leathery items she's just poured over my kitchen table, and waggles it at me. 'So, this is what's known as a bondage belt . . .'

'I can see that.'

' . . . which I thought would appeal to Pete because it's just like his tool belt, with all these bits and bobs dangling from it – look! Now, this is a paddle, and this is a blindfold, and this . . . oooh, now what do you think this is for?'

'Heavens, Anna, I don't know, some sort of manacle? Look, I'm really thrilled you're taking positive steps, but –'

'And here we've got some PVC body wrap; and look at this divine little feather duster! The woman in the shop said lots of her clients make it double up as a whip for the second half of a French Maid fantasy. And you know I've always had a French Maid fantasy, Bells.'

'Who plays the maid?' I hear myself croak, horribly fascinated all of a sudden. 'You or Pete?'

Anna doesn't answer. Instead, she opts for a swift change of subject. 'And I bought a couple of books too: some erotic Victorian lithographs, because we're just *swamped* with boring old twenty-first-century porn everywhere nowadays, aren't we? Much more fun to leave something to the imagination! And this one on the seductive art of Japanese bondage. I'm not sure what makes this particular kind of bondage Japanese, to be honest with you,' she adds, starting to flick through the pages with a mildly curious air, as though she's thumbing a dictionary for a tricky definition. 'I mean, do you think there's sushi involved? Because I'm perfectly happy to snack while we're doing it, but I can't quite see where you're supposed to put the raw fish –'

'Anna,' I silence her with a firmly raised finger, 'I have a social worker arriving in precisely two hours, to evaluate the safety and suitability of my home, and I'd really rather you took all this . . .' I wave a hand at the assembled kinkery, '. . . safely back to the privacy of your own.'

'Well, she isn't going to *know* about it. I mean, it's not like it's going to leave behind a lingering *smell* or anything,' Anna grumbles, but she starts clearing her wares back into her tote bag. 'Anyway,' she adds, as if the word 'smell' has suddenly reminded her of something, 'I thought you said that Jamie was going to be here for the social worker's visit this time.'

'He is. I mean, he will be. He's just got some work to do first.'

'*Work?*' Her eyebrows shoot upwards. '*Jamie?*'

'Yes, Anna, Jamie. He's putting leaflets through doors, getting his gardening business started up properly again. I told you what happened at Vito's, didn't I?'

Actually, I haven't. Well, not everything.

I mean, I've told her all about the astonishing new leaf Jamie is planning to turn over, and the promises he made about getting more involved in the adoption. But I haven't mentioned the whole sort-of-engagement. For one thing, I know I'm going to struggle to lie to her about the details of it, and I don't think Anna's anti-Jamie position will be reversed if she finds out about his non-proposal proposal ('let's say we're engaged anyway. I mean, why the fuck not?'). And for another, I don't want to say anything to Anna until I'm ready to tell Polly and the rest of my family.

And I'm still hoping that Polly will be back with Dev, and getting ready for their own postponed wedding, before I have to do that. I mean, these emails she's been writing to this Julia friend of hers make it perfectly clear that, just as I was starting to suspect, this whole 'not loving Dev any more' thing is just total bollocks. Something to distract me from – what did she call it, in her email to Julia? – the 'real reason' she didn't want to go ahead with the wedding.

Whatever that 'real reason' may be, that is. Because that's something I'm still none the wiser about. I mean, even if what she told Dev was exactly that 'real reason' – that she feels like she doesn't deserve to be married – that still only solves half the problem. There's still no explanation *why* she's suddenly started feeling that way.

However, the important thing to focus on is that she quite plainly *does* still love Dev. Which means there's plenty of reason for optimism. Which means, fingers crossed, that their wedding will be back on before I need to mention anything about my own.

'Yes, but I wasn't sure how much I could *believe* that,' Anna is saying, toying with one of the Unidentified Flogging Objects on the bondage belt. 'I mean, he's said that kind of thing before, hasn't he?'

'Yes, well, it's different this time,' I say, staunchly. I'm quite accustomed to having to leap to Jamie's defence where Anna is concerned, but today I do really mean it for a change.

Because Jamie has been incredible ever since that dinner at Vito's. He's cut down on his pub time to stay up late into the night with me talking about the adoption, and all the really important little details of it too, like where we might take our first family holiday, and where we'll spend our first family Christmas (his suggestion: at his mother's; my unspoken suggestion: anywhere *but* his mother's). He's printed up those flyers he's just gone out with, and he's started looking at second-hand vans he might be able to afford (if I lend him the money) that he can use for his gardening jobs. He's even started to make more effort around the flat, tidying up after himself in the kitchen, and working out the incredible mysteries of the toilet brush.

'Anyway, I thought you were supposed to be here to give me moral support about the adoption visit,' I carry on. 'Not covering my kitchen table with bondage accessories and slagging off my boyfriend.'

As usual, once you've pointed out that she's being difficult and a little bit selfish, Anna is overcome with remorse. She spends the rest of the time she's here trying to big me up – everything from my dormant mothering skills to the genius way I make an omelette – so that by the time I walk with her back in the direction of hers (I have to go to the corner shop and pick up fresh milk for the tea that Samantha almost certainly won't drink) I'm feeling utterly dependent on her and don't want to let her out of my sight.

'You'll be fine,' she tells me, with the kind of total conviction that I love her for, as she gives me a hug outside the corner shop. 'Honestly, Bella, there's a child already waiting for you somewhere out there. And they might have been pretty unlucky up until now, but they'll be the luckiest kid in Christendom if they get to have you as their mother.'

Which is, I think, just about the nicest thing anyone's ever said to me.

So I'm feeling OK as I head into the corner shop and make my way to the chiller cabinet for the pint of milk. I mean, I'm still nervous about Samantha's visit, obviously. But at least this time there isn't going to be a naked man roaming my hallway (lightning can't possibly strike twice, can it?). Plus I've got a wonderful addition to my Samantha-impressing arsenal – Jamie. Jamie, who can charm the birds from the trees when he wants to. Jamie, who now that he's sharpened up his act a bit, is going to be able to convince even the most dubious of doubters that he and I would make great adoptive parents. Jamie, whose name, in bold black print on emerald-green paper, is staring me right in the face from the flyer he dropped off here earlier, now on the notice board right behind the counter, as I approach it to pay for my milk.

JAMIE KEENAN LANDSCAPES
NO JOB TOO SMALL OR LARGE FOR OUR CHEERFUL, HARD-WORKING GARDEN TEAM

That was my idea, by the way – 'Garden Team'. Even if it is just going to be Jamie working on his own. It just sounds more official, doesn't it, and professional? I'm about to proudly announce to the young man behind the counter that it was my boyfriend who came in here earlier and put that up when the middle-aged woman in front of me, who's just paid for her *Good Housekeeping* magazine and bottle of orange juice, says to him, 'Hard-working? Lazy sod, more like.'

The young man looks confused. 'Sorry?'

'Up there.' The woman jabs her orange juice bottle in the direction of Jamie's flyer. 'Keenan Landscapes. I'm not trying to be funny, but I really don't think you should be giving him advertising space. He did some work for us last summer, and he just wreaked utter havoc. He was always late, he trod mud all over the house and didn't clear it up, and as for the mess he made of the garden . . .'

'You know, you're the second person come in today who's said something similar about him.' The young man is looking worried that he's going to get in trouble for allowing the flyer to be put up in the first place.

'Yes, well, I'm not surprised. Do you know, he caused fertiliser burn on my camellias and destroyed six French lavender bushes with water-logging! My husband wanted to report him to Trading Standards, but in the end we decided it was more hassle than it was worth.'

I clear my throat – not deliberately, but because it suddenly feels like there's something very sharp and dry stuck in there – and the woman makes an apologetic gesture as she pockets the change from her twenty.

'Sorry, sorry!' she says. 'Holding up the queue! But I'd take that flyer down, if I were you. Either that, or stick a great big warning sign on the front saying Khan's Convenience Stores don't authorise it. Word of mouth, you know, that's the thing that will scupper someone like him. There's not a person on our street that would let him near their garden after they saw what he did to ours.'

My hands are wobbling, a moment or so later, as I hand over the seventy pence for the milk. 'Have you really had someone else in complaining about that guy?' I ask, nodding up at the flyer.

'Oh, yeah, only an hour or so ago. Some woman who said this Keenan guy had ruined her lawn with too much weedkiller. Cost her a grand to get it fixed, apparently.' He hands me my five pence change before turning round to the notice board and unceremoniously pulling down the emerald-green piece of paper. 'Anything else I can get for you?'

'No, no, just the milk, thanks,' I mumble. Whatever that sharp, dry thing is, the one that I noticed in my throat a few moments ago, it's getting worse. I need to get home and wash it away with an ice-cold glass of water before Samantha arrives.

When I get back to my flat, I think for a horrible moment that Samantha's pulled a surprise early arrival on me – trying to catch me out smoking my crack pipe, or entertaining deviant chief executives in a Nazi-themed orgy? – because when I slot my key into the lock, I realise it's not double-locked.

But obviously that's stupid, because Samantha doesn't have a key.

And I'm not sure why I assumed that, when the obvious explanation is that Jamie must be here. As he said he would be. I haven't been doubting that he'll show up, or anything. If he said he'd be here, then he'll be here.

But he isn't. Here, I mean. When I open the front door into the hallway, Liam is the sight that greets me.

Actually, he's half in the hallway and half in the kitchen, kind of backing out of the kitchen door into the hall with an extremely disconcerted expression on his face. When he sees it's me coming through the front door, he looks even more disconcerted.

'I was just popping in for a glass of water,' he mumbles hastily, as though I've caught him in the act of fiddling the gas meter, or something.

'No, no, that's fine. But weren't you out at a job interview?'

'No. That's later this afternoon.'

'Right. OK.' We both just stand there, staring awkwardly at each other. Then, because it's been on my mind for the last week or so, I say, 'Actually, Liam, while I've got you here, I just wanted to say sorry about the other night.'

He blinks at me.

'Blithering on about my accident, and your – um – late wife's.'

'Kerry.'

'Yes. Kerry. I'm sorry, Liam, if I said anything that upset or offended you.'

'Oh, sure, whatever.' He seems distracted. Actually, he seems as if he just wants to get out of my way. 'Honestly, no offence taken.'

'OK, good. I'm glad.' I clear my throat. I'm not a

skilled conversationalist at the best of times, and Liam is making me feel like I'm dragging my words out of toffee and black treacle. Whatever brief camaraderie we might have found the other night is long gone. 'Um, so, I really don't want to be rude or anything, but my social worker is arriving any minute now.'

'And you don't want me scaring her off again,' he says, sounding – why? – mildly astonished.

'Well . . .'

'Of course. It's your home. 'Sup to you.' He shrugs and starts towards me, and the front door. It's only as he passes me that I see the flash of green paper in his back pocket.

'Liam,' I suddenly blurt, 'are you . . . are those some of Jamie's gardening flyers?'

'Oh, yeah.' He reaches up past me to grab his jacket from the coat-stand. 'I offered to help him out. He's got a lot to deliver. Two sets of feet are better than one.'

There's something about the way he's not meeting my eyes that makes me say the next thing.

'He's in the pub. Isn't he?'

Liam doesn't say anything for a moment. Then he says, 'Look, I don't know exactly where he is. Might be the pub. Might have gone for a kickabout with some of The Boys.'

'Oh, for Christ's sake, Liam, does it really matter?' I snap. 'Either way, he's getting you to deliver his flyers instead of him?'

He says nothing and just gives the briefest of nods.

'And either way, he's not going to be here for the social worker visit?'

'Did he tell you he would be?' Liam looks surprised for a moment, before covering it up and carrying on. 'Well, I couldn't honestly say if he's going to make it back here in time . . .'

'Right. Fine.' I'm pulling off my own coat and scarf, which isn't easy to do when your hands are shaking with barely repressed fury. 'You don't need to say anything of the sort, Liam, thank you.'

'Hey,' he says, after a moment. 'You don't need to take it out on me, you know. If you're stressed about this adoption visit –'

'I'm *stressed*,' I begin, in a high-pitched, Valkyrie screech, 'because Jamie promised he was going to be here, and he isn't. I'm stressed because he promised he was going to work his arse off to get his business back up and running, and at the first opportunity, he's talked his mate into carrying out the easiest fucking job of the lot, wandering the streets for a few hours pushing flyers through letter boxes. I'm stressed because he wrecks lawns, and poisons innocent French lavender bushes, and treads mud all over carpets . . .'

The doorbell rings. I can see Samantha's squirrelly form on the other side of the stained glass, so I stop screeching at once. I just have time for a glance in the mirror – red cheeks, but hey, I could have just been for a jog; slightly frizzed hair, but ditto – before I take a deep breath and prepare to let Samantha in.

It's only as I pull open the front door that I realise

Liam has darted back into the kitchen.

Well, fuck him. As long as he's not gone in there to take his clothes off – he *wouldn't*, would he? – I'm beyond caring. I just want to get this visit over and done with, impress Samantha as best I can (all by myself), then open a bottle of wine, drink the lot (all by myself), and work out what in God's name I'm going to do about my sort-of-fiancé. And the father of my future adoptive child.

'Samantha! Great to see you!' I sing, fixing that well-practised beam to my face and hoping, once again, that it hasn't got a Sofa-Leaping Scientologist glint to it. 'Won't you come on in? I've just popped out for milk, so if you come through to the kitchen I'll get the kettle on for a nice cup of tea.'

'There's no need to go to any trouble,' she says, in her flat monotone. Then, 'Oh!' she suddenly says, in much less of a monotone. Actually more of a squeak. '*Him* again.'

I spin round, fearing the worst, but thank *God*, Liam is fully clothed. He's striding purposefully from the kitchen towards us and there's an unusually steely look in his eye, which belies the fact that he's quite clearly, and shiftily, trying to hide something behind his back.

It's Anna's black leather bondage belt. Paddle, blindfold, suspected manacle and all. She must have left it lying on the kitchen table by accident. And Liam must have seen it there, which is why he was looking so thoroughly disconcerted when I walked in on him a few minutes ago.

The first thing I think is how badly I want to curl up and die. I mean, if Naked Hairy Man-gate wasn't embarrassing enough, if Jolen-gate wasn't embarrassing enough, the fact that Liam now thinks I've carelessly left my favourite bondage accessory lying about the place – the fact that Liam now thinks I *have* a favourite bondage accessory – is almost too appalling to stomach.

The second thing I think is how essential it is that Samantha doesn't realise that the bondage belt is a bondage belt. Because though Liam is clearly trying, he's not doing the world's most brilliant job of concealing it behind his person. I mean, it's extremely big, and extremely black, and very, very leathery; not the easiest thing to conceal even when you're built on gorilla proportions. Besides, I can see Samantha's beady, watchful eyes being drawn, as well they might after the sight she saw on their last encounter, in the direction of Liam's crotch area. Unfortunately this means she's also staring directly in the general region of the bondage belt.

'Oh, yes, you two have already met, haven't you?' I say, breezily, as though Samantha and Liam are nodding acquaintances from a rush-hour commuter train or walking their dogs in the park. 'Liam, this is Samantha, from the council. Samantha, this is Liam, my temporary lodger and . . . er . . . odd-job man.'

'Odd-job man?' Liam raises his bushy eyebrows in

confusion.

'Well, I'm sorry if the title offends you, Liam!' I want to reach out to draw Samantha towards the kitchen, but I have a suspicion she's not the kind of person that reacts well to being manhandled by relative strangers. 'Watch out!' I suddenly squeak, as one of the manacles slips into view and I see Samantha crane her neck to peer at it. 'Mind where you're going, Liam, with that . . . that tool belt!'

'Ohhh, it's a *tool belt*,' Samantha says, sounding rather relieved.

'Yes, it's absolutely a tool belt. Now would you mind, Liam, going and fixing that leaky drainpipe, while I go and have a chat and a cup of tea with Samantha here?'

'Sure thing. It probably just needs sealing with a bit of putty,' says Liam, suddenly up for giving an Oscar-worthy performance as Odd-Job Man now that he's cottoned on to what I'm trying to do. 'But it might be a build-up of condensation, of course. I'll have a good old look, see what I can do.'

'Right. Good. Well, thank you, Liam.' I give up on my concerns about manhandling Samantha and start leading her towards the kitchen, babbling all the while about tea and cake in a way that must make her think I've got some kind of snack-related OCD. But I don't care about any of that, because we've dodged the bullet of the bondage belt. And I'd rather she thought I was borderline obsessive compulsive than full-throttle sado-masochistic.

As I shepherd her through the door, I glance back over my shoulder to shoot Liam a look of gratitude, even to mouth a heartfelt *thank you* at him. But he's already disappeared out of the flat, taking Anna's bondage belt and Jamie's emerald-green leaflets with him.

When Samantha leaves, an hour or so later, I open my bottle of wine as planned, take it into the sitting room, slump onto the sofa, drink swiftly from the first glass and then pour myself another.

The thing is, it went well with Samantha. Really well.

Once I'd relaxed about the possibility of her accidentally sitting down on *The Seductive Art of Japanese Bondage*, or spotting a roll of PVC body wrap under the table, we actually had a pretty decent conversation. She didn't ask too many intrusive questions – in fact, I did most of the asking this time – and at the end of it she started writing down the details of the Preparation for Adoption course, where you go and discuss the whole adoption process with other prospective adopters. On top of that, she even started looking for suitable dates in her diary to start the first of the in-depth home-study sessions, a couple of months from now.

But what in God's name am I going to do about Jamie?

It's not just the fact that he didn't show up for Samantha's visit. Or the fact that he isn't even sufficiently motivated to get his own business back up and running to pound the pavements with a few leaflets. Or the fact that it sounds pretty much like getting his own business back up and running is a non-starter anyway, given that he is to gardens, apparently, what Hurricane Katrina was to New Orleans.

It's the fact that he said he was going to change. And the fact that I, like an idiot, believed him.

Maybe it's because I can't do it as easily as other people can, but I happen to believe that becoming a parent is an overwhelming responsibility. You don't get to pick and choose the fun parts, or the easy parts; if you're lucky enough to get the chance to bring up a child of your own, you're in it up to the eyeballs. And if Jamie, before we've even got to the difficult parts, isn't even in it up to the toenails, then it looks like I have a really serious problem.

When my phone rings, just as I'm pouring my fourth glass of wine, I immediately assume it's Jamie, and don't even look at the caller ID before I snatch it up.

'Where the fuck were you?'

'What?' says Polly's voice. 'Was I meant to be seeing you this evening, or something?'

'Oh. It's you. Sorry. I thought it was . . .' I don't want to say 'Jamie'. '. . . someone else.'

'I see.' There's the briefest of silences. 'Look, Bells, I was just calling to see how it went today. You did say the social worker was coming, didn't you?'

'Yes, she did. It went fine. I mean, it went great, actually!' I make the effort to inject more enthusiasm into my voice. It'd be easier if the wine weren't dampening my abilities. 'She's fixing up dates to begin the home study, and she's putting me up for a Preparation for Adoption course, and –'

'And Jamie.'

'Sorry?'

'You said, she's putting *you* up for a course. Don't you mean, you and Jamie?'

'Oh. Yes. Obviously. Me and Jamie.'

It's just occurring to me that I haven't the faintest clue how I'm going to get Jamie to show up for the Preparation for Adoption course – tell him Ryan Giggs might put in a surprise appearance? Drug his food and carry him there, like B. A. Baracus in *The A-Team*? – when I realise that Polly is talking again.

'You sound weird, Bella. Are you OK?'

'Yes.' I let out an inadvertent hiccup. 'Just a little bit drunk.'

'What? You don't get drunk! Why are you drunk?'

'Because that's what happens when you drink half . . . no, wait, two-thirds . . . of a bottle of wine in less than half an hour.'

She takes the kind of give-me-strength breath that I usually use with her. 'That's not what I meant.'

'Yes, all right, I know it isn't what you meant.' I can hear the irritability in my voice, and make a mental note to reserve some of it for where it should really be directed, at Jamie. 'It's been a hard day, that's all. The adoption visit was stressful. And OK, it went well, but I still think Samantha is confused by the fact that

Jamie didn't show up again, and –'

'He didn't *show up*? And it's the second time? *Bella!*'

I'm taken aback by the alarm in her voice. 'Look, it's probably not even that big a deal. It's early days. Anyway, when he *does* show up, I'm sure Samantha will be so charmed by him that she'll forget all about it!'

There's silence.

I finish my glass of wine and pour another.

'You know, Bells,' Polly breaks the silence, 'I've been meaning to say this to you for a little while now. But have you thought, at all, about the possibility that you might be better off doing this on your own?'

'Doing what on my own?'

'Adopting.'

I laugh. I can't help it.

'But isn't that a huge advantage of it, in many ways?' she carries on. 'That you get a child without having to get a man to inseminate you?'

'Polly, please. I am nowhere near drunk enough to talk to you – or anyone else, for that matter – about insemination.'

'But it just sounds as though Jamie can't be relied upon. I mean, I've always suspected so, but now it looks like it's even worse than I thought.' Her words are coming in a desperate rush, the way they do when you've been storing something up for a long time and you suddenly get the chance to say it. 'And you want a child so much, Bella – you deserve a child so much –

that it seems the craziest thing in the world to risk it all for . . . well, for *Jamie*.'

'I love Jamie.'

And even if I didn't, I can't *dump* him. Not when I know what it's like to be dumped, after so much time together. I can't have spent all the hours I spent hating my Evil Ex Christian – even *thinking* of him, still, as my *Evil* Ex – only to go and do to Jamie what Christian did to me.

Not that I think it's likely that Jamie would get in a car, sobbing, and drive into an oak tree, or anything.

I mean, OK, there's a chance (especially if Manchester United were holding steady at the top of the table) that Jamie wouldn't be all that cut up about me dumping him at all.

'I love Jamie,' I repeat, wanting to feel the words in my mouth. Just to be sure.

'Will you love him if he doesn't show up for this course, and the social services decide you're not a suitable couple to go on their list? If he puts a spanner in the works by getting drunk the night before the home visits and sits there with a hangover, oozing beer from every pore?'

'Polly!' I snap. I don't want to hear any more of this. 'This is none of your business.'

'Of course it's my business. I'm your sister.'

'Yes, well, apparently that rule doesn't apply when it comes to me delving into your life. When it's me who's concerned about you, it's OK to fob me off. Spin me a line about not loving Dev any more, just so

I get off your back and don't pry into the *real reason* you're not marrying him.'

'*What do you know about the real reason?*'

I almost drop my wine glass in shock. I've never heard Polly sound like that before. In all honesty, I've never heard *anyone* sound like that before, apart from possibly that creepy Gollum thing in *The Lord of the Rings* movies.

'I mean, I'd be fascinated to learn what this so-called real reason is,' she's carrying on, marginally less Gollum-like, but still in a low, aggressive hiss. 'The one you seem to think you know so much about.'

I'm starting to realise, through the alcoholic haze, that I'm on dangerous ground here. I never should have mentioned the words 'real reason'. Not seeing as it's exactly the phrase she used in her email to Julia.

'Dood, please calm down, OK, I didn't mean anything. I just thought, maybe you had some private reason between you and Dev –'

'For the last time, stop trying to talk to me about Dev! Stop trying to meddle in things between me and Dev.'

'How can I possibly do that,' I ask, 'when according to you, there's never going to be a you-and-Dev any more?'

She hangs up.

I sit for a moment, too stunned to do anything but blink, blankly, at a stain Jamie has made on the carpet. I haven't noticed it before. It could be tea. More likely beer. I'll have to get the carpet shampoo out either way. It really would be nice if he didn't leave such a mess behind him.

Then, wobbly from, by now, my entire bottle of wine, I get to my feet. On autopilot, I go into the kitchen, open up my laptop, and navigate my way back to Polly's email page.

I'm going to check her emails again.

Her overreaction just now – morphing into a creepy nutter from *The Lord of the Rings* – has made me more determined than ever to get to the bottom of this.

Whatever the *real reason* is, I'm not stopping until I find it out.

From: PollyWollyDoodle@hotmail.com
To: Julia247@yahoo.com
Date: Wednesday 2 December 2011
Subject: Thank you

Hi Julia

I know it's been only an hour or so since we spoke, but I just wanted to say thanks for talking to me. I know how busy you are at work, and I know you have plenty of other people in your life that need you too. I'm just not sure any of them need you like I do.

If it helps, at all, talking to you did make me feel a lot better. A LOT. I don't know what it was that got to me earlier – it was just supposed to be a nice trip to Selfridges to hang out with my adorable godsons – but honestly, Julia, if I hadn't got you on the other end of the phone, I might have just gone out into the middle of Oxford Street and howled.

Poor Grace. Poor, poor Grace. I don't know if she knows just how miserable her life looks, trapped as she is on the inside of it. And I don't know if it makes it better or worse that she doesn't know. It's like I said to you earlier – she's just so different from the Grace I used to know. She was always shy, and never exactly self-confident, but Charlie has sucked every last bit of life out of her. She dresses twenty years older than her age, and she's given up any hope of finding anything to do with her life that interests her, or excites her in any way. Like, she always used to talk about being an artist, or maybe even running her own little gallery. But these days her biggest goal seems to be getting in with the witches on school committees, who look like they're only going to bully and belittle her as much as her husband does.

But still, you were right earlier – I shouldn't have started getting excited about the possibility of her taking a lover. (For fuck's sake, who even *uses* the phrase 'taking a lover'?) Affairs are dangerous territory, aren't they, especially with everything I've done in that department? After all the hours I've spent with you, I should know that better than anyone.

God, it was good to hear your voice, Julia, and to feel that you're with me in spirit. I can't tell you how much I miss our Thursday afternoons together.

Thank you again. I'm OK now. I'm sorry I still need you as much as I do.

P x

Grace

Friday 11 December

Hector has succumbed to Tiny Tots' latest outbreak of head lice, which means I've spent much of the last week rubbing tea-tree lotion into his hair and combing it through with an electrified nit-comb. When I'm not doing this, I'm constantly prising his fingers away from his head and telling him that no matter how much it itches, it'll only make it worse if he scratches it.

Though maybe this is only the case with chicken pox? The Mirandas, I'm sure, would all know this kind of thing.

But it's a pretty general rule, isn't it? That the more you scratch an itch, the worse it gets? Because the powerful itch I've had for the past couple of weeks has been the fantasy of having sex with Saad Amar. And now that I've gone ahead and actually scratched the itch, it's become more powerful than ever.

I've seen him six times in the past ten days. And on the days I haven't seen him – and even on the days I have – I literally have not been able to stop thinking about him.

I was thinking about him during our family outing

to the zoo on Saturday (though seeing as Charlie spent the entire two hours that we were there tapping away on his BlackBerry and snapping at Hector when he tried to get his attention at the monkey enclosure, I don't feel quite so bad about my own mental absence). I was thinking about him while I simultaneously folded laundry and watched a feature-length *Fireman Sam* with the boys on Sunday afternoon. I've thought about him on the walk to school in the mornings and on the walk back from school in the afternoons; I've thought about him while I'm making Robbie's eggs Benedict and while I'm putting Charlie's dinner in the oven to keep warm late at night; I've thought about him while I brush my teeth and while I shower.

Oh God, the ways I've thought about him while I shower.

And – obviously – I'm thinking about him now, while I put the finishing touches to the boys' lunch-boxes, and while I steel myself for my first ever fund-raising committee meeting. It's at Café on the Green, at nine o'clock this morning. Though even this isn't making me quite so stressed and miserable as it might otherwise have done. The ripple effect of what I'm doing with Saad is cheering me up enough to be able to face the Mirandas with a bright smile and a spring in my step. Not to mention the positive effect it's having on the boys' lunchboxes. Admittedly this is mostly through sheer guilt. Somehow I like to think that if I bake slightly wonky cupcakes rather than bunging in a Cadbury's Mini Roll, or cut their sandwiches into exciting star shapes rather than humdrum squares, maybe it will lessen the awfulness of the fact that I'm cheating on their father, but the end result is the same.

I mean, Robbie and Hector are still so young, aren't they? Homemade cake is a pretty good trade-off, at this stage, for the fact that their parents' marriage is unhappy and insecure enough for me to be unfaithful.

OK, who am I kidding? I'm not sure that there's any amount of cake in the world that can wipe away the sins I'm currently committing. It's just that right now – and yes, I am ashamed to my very bones to admit this – I'm so happy, for the first time in years, that I don't even care.

Super-dooper lunches packed, the three of us are just on the way out of the door at quarter past eight (see – cheating on my husband also makes me on time for school for a change – another bonus!) when the boys suddenly both stare at the front gate, their eyes going wide.

Thomas, Saad's disapproving housekeeper, is coming up our garden path.

He doesn't look any less disapproving than the last time I saw him, I have to say. If anything, he looks even more so. This could be to do with the smallness of my house, the uncombedness of my hair, the uncombedness of Robbie and Hector's hair, or, just possibly, the presence of Robbie and Hector at all.

He stares right over their heads, pulling his usual

trick of not quite looking me in the eye, and holds out a large, bright yellow Selfridges carrier bag.

'Good morning, Mrs Costello. I do apologise for disturbing you when you seem so busy, but I've been asked to bring you this little gift.'

I blink at him. I'm quite literally lost for words.

'My boss wanted me to let you know that he picked them out himself, and that he'd very much like you to wear them for your . . .' his eyes flicker in the direction of Robbie and Hector, '. . . your *meeting*, later on today.'

Oh my God, it's lingerie, isn't it? 'Them' must refer to some absurdly slutty knickers, the kind of thing I've seen on Agent Provocateur-type websites – OK, the kind of thing I've specifically searched for, these past few days, on the Agent Provocateur website – with ribbony bits to lace up the back, and see-through bits at the front. The kind of thing that makes my Elle Macpherson knickers and bra look like something a particularly uptight nun would wear on a fat day.

And he's having Thomas deliver them to my *home*? At school-run time, when I'm with my *children*? For God's sake, fifteen minutes earlier and Charlie would have still been at home!

Unless Thomas has been parked outside the house for a while, waiting until Charlie left and then until I finally emerged? Just to be sure he wasn't encountering a nanny (ha!) or a cleaner (double-ha!) or something.

Not that this makes the invasion into my home life any more acceptable.

'Thomas, I can't possibly –'

'Turn down such a thoughtful gift? Of course you can't.' Before I can stop him, Thomas has put the carrier in my hand and closed my fingers around the handle. It's not done with affection or pleasure though. More with the air of a man who's going to go and wash his own hands the moment he can. 'I'm sure I'll see you later, Mrs Costello,' he adds, already turning to walk back down the path to the gate.

A moment later he climbs into the biggest, shiniest dark blue car I've ever seen: a Bentley, maybe, or a Rolls. I've not been Saad's latest fancy woman for long enough to learn to distinguish between all the different varieties of luxury cars just yet, but I know it was the same one that was parked outside MMA Capital that time I met Saad in the lobby. The boys watch with saucer eyes as it pulls away from the kerb in a stately fashion.

'Mummy, Mummy, you've been bringed a present!' Hector squeaks, hopping on his feet with glee at this unexpected excitement on a boring school morning. 'Who was that man?' He gasps suddenly. 'Was that *Santa*?'

If I weren't still so discombobulated by what's just happened, I'd actually laugh at the notion that chilly, judgemental Thomas could possibly be an incarnation of Father Christmas. 'No, it wasn't Santa.'

'But he gave you this!' Hector prods at the yellow

Selfridges bag, which I pull away from him like it might burn his fingers. 'It's like the bags when we saw Santa at the grotto with Auntie Polly.'

'Don't be silly, Hector,' Robbie informs him, in his loftiest older-brother tone. 'Of course he wasn't Santa.'

'Exactly, Robs. Look, why don't we all go back inside for a moment, just so Mummy can open her present ever so quickly?' I just can't wait until after the fund-raising committee meeting to see exactly what it is that Saad has endangered my marriage to send.

'He *works* for Santa,' Robbie is carrying on, as I usher them back indoors. 'Isn't that right, Mummy? He said the gift was from his boss.'

Oh God. 'No, no, I think you misunderstood that, darling. Now, why don't the two of you just sit down and finish off the last five minutes of *Fireman Sam* . . .?'

The moment I've got them sitting down on the sofa, and got Fireman Sam performing his traditional rescue of naughty Norman on the TV, I hurry into the kitchen to open up the bag.

It's not knickers at all. It's shoes.

Black crocodile-print, peep-toe, high-heeled Jimmy Choo shoes.

They're the sexiest present I think I've ever received.

I take them out of the box, kick off my right-hand boot and start to slip one of the shoes onto my foot. It fits like a glove. He got the size spot-on. Does that mean he took the time to examine one of my old shoes, kicked off at the foot of his bed, or is the art of knowing a woman's shoe size just another of the many things he learned at International Playboy school? Either way, it makes the whole thing even sexier still . . .

'Mummy?' It's Robbie, peeping round the door. 'Hector is scratching his head again, even though I *told* him it would just make the nits get stronger, with bigger, sharper teeth . . .'

I can hear the howling from the living room as I kick off the shoe and shove it back into its tissue and box.

'Come on, Robs!' I say, with the kind of insanely bright smile a Miranda would be proud of. 'Let's go and cheer Hector up, and get the both of you – and the nits – to school!'

At the Mirandas' usual cluster of tables at Café on the Green, I arrive early enough to slide into a comfy seat by the wall. Then I busy myself checking my phone and pretending to update my diary, to detract attention from the fact that nobody seems to particularly want to talk to me.

I wonder just how much the Mirandas would ostracise me if they knew that not only am I Grace the Evil Husband-Snatcher, but have recently also become Grace the Even More Evil Extra-Marital Cheat.

Well, thank God, none of them will ever need to know this, because it's all going to be over before anyone has a chance to find out about it. My fling with Saad has lasted ten days and I don't need Thomas to tell me that obviously Saad is going to tire of me sooner rather than later. In fact, the more I think about the Jimmy Choos, I decide they're probably a kind of parting gift, the billionaire playboy's way of saying, *It's been fun but it's time to take a hike.* And anyway, even if it takes a little longer for him to tire of me, even if I have another few weeks of sexually acrobatic bliss in store, I can't possibly allow it to continue. Absurd though it might sound that I should be the one breaking things off with a man like Saad, obviously that's what I'd have to do if it came to it.

I'm distracted, suddenly, by the fact that the armchair on my other side is being pushed sideways, and that there's a waft of Chanel perfume coming my way. Someone sits down beside me.

I'm astonished to see that it's Louboutin Lexie.

She's looking effortlessly chic and as out of step with the Mirandas as ever: Charles Worthington'd of hair and Stella McCartney'd of outfit. And, of course, Louboutin'd of foot – gorgeous leopard-print court shoes today, worn with fishnet tights that give an edge to her slim grey pencil skirt and crisp white wraparound blouse.

'Hi!' I blurt, before I can stop myself, and even though she's giving off distinct signals that she's not in the mood for conversation: head down and tapping at her BlackBerry, just like I've been doing. Except for the fact that I get the impression Louboutin Lexie *does* actually have meetings to plan and a diary to schedule. Still, I feel, somehow, that now I own my very own pair of luxe designer shoes, maybe I'm worthy of a few minutes of her consideration. 'Amazing shoes!'

'Sorry?'

'Your shoes. They're amazing.'

'Well, they're Louboutins,' she says, as if – and she's not wrong, to be fair – this alone is enough to explain their amazingness.

'I have a brand-new pair of Jimmy Choos myself.' I want to kick myself – with the utterly *un*amazing Carvela boots I'm wearing – for sounding (at best) like a total country mouse and (more likely) like a total imbecile.

'Oh, right.' She returns to her emailing. Actually, she never stopped her emailing. 'Well, good for you.'

'I didn't know you came to this kind of thing,' I carry on, too embarrassed to abandon the conversation now that I've made the mistake of starting it. 'Committee meetings, I mean. I thought you were too busy dashing between school and your job at the art gallery . . .'

Now she takes her eyes off the BlackBerry and looks at me. Well, I can hardly blame her for wanting to get a proper look at me. It'll help in her description of me to the police, when she reports me for stalking, and takes out a restraining order.

'*If* you work in an art gallery, that is,' I say hastily. 'That's just the impression I got. I mean, you *look* like that might be the kind of job you do. You don't look like you're usually involved in the fund-raising committee, that's all.'

'I'm not,' she says shortly. 'Wild horses wouldn't drag me to this kind of thing, normally. But my daughter has palled up with Miranda's youngest, and I don't want to jeopardise her popularity by refusing to join in the social side of the school every now and then. St Martin's girls can be quite vicious, you know, when they identify an outsider.'

'Do you mean the girls or the mothers?' I joke. But I say it quietly, because Chief Miranda has arrived, taken her rightful place at the head of the cluster of tables, and is calling the meeting to order.

'We start with some *good* news, for once,' she begins, as though the average fund-raising committee meeting is fraught with catastrophic announcements about the state of sterling, or the mobilising of forces on the North Korean border. 'Grace Costello – this is Grace over here, for all those of you who don't know her,' she adds, which makes me feel more of an outsider than ever – 'has spent much of the past couple of weeks in bed with Saad Amar.'

I choke on my sip of cappuccino. Half of it goes the wrong way down my oesophagus. The other half goes all over the crisp white blouse of my new 'friend', Louboutin Lexie.

'Metaphorically, of course!' Chief Miranda carries on, seconds too late, and to much jolly laughter from around the table. 'Still, I'm sure it hasn't been too much of a hardship for you, Grace!'

I mutter a few words – even I couldn't tell you exactly what – and dab ineffectually at Lexie's blouse with an ancient Boots wet wipe I've found in my bag. She's waving me away, irritably grabbing paper napkins from the table, but I'd much rather help if she'd let me. It would be good cover for my flaming cheeks.

'Anyway, the end result is that our head of admissions called me over the weekend to tell me that the office have just received the Amar family's application! This means we will be graced by the presence of little *Adnan* –' she shoots me a triumphant look – 'next September. So congratulations, Grace Costello!'

There's a brief ripple of light applause, and a couple of smiles, albeit chilly and suspicious ones, from the other Mirandas, before Chief Miranda swiftly moves onto the rest of the fund-raising committee business. This mostly seems to centre around the eleven million needed for the new classroom block, and the various upcoming events that will be staged to help raise it, from the far-off – a couples' tennis tournament in the summer term – to the fast-approaching: a silent auction, to be held on the very last Friday of term, on the evening of the end-of-term carol concert.

I've drifted off into a daydream (I won't embarrass you with the details, but if I tell you it featured Saad, the Jimmy Choos and a huge tub of Ben & Jerry's Chunky Monkey, you'll get the general picture) so I don't notice everyone's eyes are on me until Chief Miranda suddenly barks at me: 'Earth to Grace! Is anyone receiving me?'

'Sorry, Miranda.'

'Are you all right?' she demands. 'You look sweaty.'

'Do I?'

'Yes, all around your upper lip.' She's obviously relishing pointing out my unattractiveness for a change. 'Are you feeling sick? Lord, you're not *pregnant*, are you?'

'No!' At least, I hope to God not. The mind boggles about what Charlie's reaction would be if I were to give birth, nine months from now, to a coffee-coloured, dark-haired baby instead of the Celtic-pale blondies Robbie and Hector were. Mind you, given that Charlie and I haven't had sex for months, he'd probably be pretty taken aback no matter what shade the baby was. Though there's always a chance that he'd be too busy checking his emails to notice. 'Sorry, Miranda, what were you asking me?'

'I was asking what you'd like to donate for the silent auction,' she says, with an eye-roll. 'I do like my committee members to lead from the front, Grace, so generosity is very much welcomed. And of course, it is Christmas!'

'Oh, right . . . of course . . . er . . . I've got a really nice unworn towelling dressing gown, and I'm sure I could find the original Bloomingdales bag it came in . . . or I could get my mother-in-law to send over a big boxful of Christmassy goodies from America – Hershey's do really nice little tree decorations that I bought last time we spent the holidays over there . . .' I tail off. There are half a dozen faces staring at me in a hostile fashion. I suddenly panic that I've said quite the wrong thing.

And that saying the wrong thing at one of these meetings is punishable by being beaten to death with a dozen Mulberry handbags.

'Um, is that not the kind of donation you were after?'

Chief Miranda points her Biro at the Miranda beside her. 'Caroline, what did you just pledge?'

'A week in our chalet in Verbiers,' says Caroline.

I've no time to register this before Miranda points her Biro down the table at Louboutin Lexie.

'Lexie, can you tell Grace what you've pledged?'

'Three days' salmon fishing and deer-stalking at my in-laws' estate in Perthshire,' says Lexie, not even bothering to glance up from her BlackBerry.

'And Louisa, you've generously offered . . .' Miranda glances down at her Moleskine pad before turning to the Miranda on her right, '. . . two weeks of wine-making and tasting at your vineyard in Puglia, is that correct?'

I can feel the blood rushing to my cheeks as Louisa confirms that this is, indeed, what she has generously offered.

'So, delightful as a nearly new towelling dressing gown and a box of Christmas-themed American junk food would be,' Miranda is continuing, 'I suggest that you have a bit more of a think, Grace, about what you'd like your donation to consist of.'

While I'm mostly concentrating on not dying from

embarrassment, there's a small part of me that wants to announce to Miranda that I'm terribly sorry, but we don't have a second home, so the best I can offer her is an overnight stay in a badly run household just round the corner, with claggy eggs Benedict for breakfast, and a lice-ridden toddler announcing 'A poo is coming!' while you're trying to enjoy your morning coffee.

But I don't – of course I don't. I agree that I'll give the matter more thought, and concentrate very, very hard, for the duration of the meeting, on not curling up and dying from embarrassment.

Oh, and on the fact that after the meeting, my next stop is Saad's.

I may not be able to boast a family estate in Scotland, or a vineyard in the Italian countryside, but for the next three hours in a bedroom in Mayfair I will be ascending heights of pleasure that I never knew I could reach. There's no amount of deer-stalking or wine-tasting in the world that could top that.

Grace

Friday 11 December

You know, there are a lot of things about spending time with Saad that have taken me by surprise.

First, the fact that I'm nowhere near as shy in the bedroom as I thought I was. I mean, I'd never have thought that the Me who couldn't even bring myself to *imagine* a slutty secretary fantasy ten days ago is the same Me who'd not only think up those sinful ideas about the shoes and the Chunky Monkey but be fully prepared to put them into action.

A second utterly astonishing thing is that, despite his track record with a bevy of desirable-sounding women, Saad seems to think I'm just about the most desirable he's ever had. Not to mention the fact that he seems to actually enjoy *talking* to me. After years with Charlie, the talking part is even more of a novelty than the incredible sex part. And, though the bar is set pretty high by the sex part, the talking part is even more enjoyable.

But by far and away the most surprising thing is how very much I feel like *myself* again, how it feels as if the past seven and a half years of my life have simply fallen away. No shopping lists; no laundry basket; no nits or pending poos or eggs Benedict or disinterested, critical husband.

I feel *young* again. Young, and free, and just like the Grace I used to be.

And the fact that *the Grace I used to be* is, apparently, the type of woman who'll sleep with her husband's boss . . . well, I'm not thinking too closely about stuff like that just now.

Anyway, all I want to think about now is the truly glorious reaction that wearing the new Jimmy Choos has afforded me. Honestly, I don't think I've felt as desirable since Polly and me were the only girls invited to Jacob Mercer's Cornwall beach house the summer after our GCSEs. (Half a dozen teenage boys, all hopped up on Scrumpy Jack and testosterone; no adults; and us.) Saad practically pounced on me the moment I came through the door wearing them, and now, half an hour of *most* pleasurable activity later, the shoes – plus a strategically placed (empty) Chunky Monkey carton – are all I'm wearing.

Saad's bedroom isn't really a bedroom at all. It's more like an entire hotel suite, and it takes up the whole first floor of the house. It's formed of four separate rooms (actually, five if you count the little lobby between the suite itself and the hallway outside, and you probably should count this because it's fully furnished and bigger than most people's bedrooms. Bigger than some people's *houses*). Immediately as you walk in from this lobby, there's a full-sized dressing room lined with sleek wooden wardrobes, where all Saad's clothes are kept (by Thomas, of course) in almost obsessive compulsively pristine condition. After this, there's a sitting-room with a huge wall-mounted plasma TV and slouchy sofas and armchairs. Then there's the actual bedroom, with a super-kingsize bed, a slightly smaller plasma TV and some truly stunning original Art Deco furniture; and finally a colossal ensuite bathroom, made entirely of marble, with a claw-foot bath, and a walk-in shower, approximately the size of a squash court, that would impress even Charlie.

Though obviously I don't want to think too much about Charlie's opinion of the shower. Or about Charlie himself, for that matter.

Me and my Chunky Monkey carton are in the bedroom part of the suite right now, languishing post-coitally amongst the tangled sheets, while Saad is out in his dressing room putting on fresh clothes. And I do mean *fresh* clothes. He discarded his suit and shirt while we were still snogging like a couple of teenagers out in the suite's lobby, which means that at some point after we disappeared into the bedroom, Thomas will have silently emerged, taken the crumpled suit to be pressed and the shirt to be laundered, and hung up something new for Saad to change back into. This isn't just me making up something to sound like it's right out of *Lives of the Rich and Famous*, by the way. This is what's happened every time I've come here. I have two conflicting theories about why this is: 1) that Thomas really is bordering on the obsessive compulsive, and can't see a suit dropped in a heap on the floor without taking immediate practical action; or 2) my old suspicion that Thomas is secretly in love with Saad, and takes pleasure in finding an excuse to lurk nearby while his boss is taking some practical action of his own. I'm getting more and more convinced that it's the latter.

Thing is, even though at first I thought that Thomas disliked me because he's still haunted by the havoc I wrought on his pristine linen napkins, I can't help thinking he's just plain haunted by *me.* I know from what he told me, The Day the Nosebleed Came, that he was assuming I'd be here today, gone tomorrow, just like all the other women he was so keen to inform me about. But now that I've seen through ten whole 'tomorrows', maybe he's getting resentful. I don't think he likes the idea of Saad's conveyor belt of meaningless women being replaced by a solitary, meaningful one.

But that's ridiculous. Because that would have to mean that Saad really *was* getting more serious about me than a mere fling would imply. And I know we're having an amazing time together, but I can't honestly believe – I can't let myself believe – that it's anything more than that.

No, it probably is just the obsessive-compulsive thing, after all. Thomas's desire to keep Saad's clothes spick and span, I'm sure, out-does whatever desire he may have for his handsome employer.

I'm just trying to remember at what point my own

clothes came off – blouse in the bedroom's lobby, if I recall correctly, skirt in the dressing room, and God knows where my underwear landed – when Saad comes back in.

He's in a fresh shirt and a pair of suit trousers I've not seen before, and he sits down on the bed beside me.

'Beautiful,' he says, with a longing groan. 'You're just beautiful, Grace. I knew those shoes would look great on you.'

I had intended to tell him that he absolutely mustn't get such expensive presents for me again, not to mention the fact that he absolutely mustn't get Thomas to deliver them. But somehow that all seems irrelevant now. This is the hypnotic effect that Saad has on me.

'You know,' he continues, 'if I was an artist myself rather than just a collector, I'd paint you like this. Hey, you could do a self-portrait! You've told me you'd like to go back to proper painting one day, haven't you?'

'Yes.' I'm surprised, and thrilled, that he remembers this conversation, seeing as it's one we had in bed the other day, while being distracted by other things. 'But portraits – especially self-portraits – were never my forte.' I nod over at the Starbucks cow card, which, I was astonished to notice the first time I came up to his bedroom, Saad keeps propped up (because it won't stand up) against the clock on his bedside table. 'That's more my sort of level, really.'

'I bet that's not true. Anyway, you could expand your horizons. You could call your self-portrait . . .' he searches the air, as if for inspiration, '. . . *Femme nue avec carton de Chunky Monkey.*'

I laugh. 'And you think it would sell?'

'For millions. And I guarantee I'd see off the highest bidders.' He leans forward to pull on the (freshly-polished, natch) shoes he's carrying. 'You don't know how much I wish I could stay here all afternoon.'

'You have to get back to . . .' I don't like to say 'the office', because it reminds me that Charlie is there, '. . . work. I know.'

'Not today, actually. But I have got an appointment with someone.' He glances at his watch. (It's a Patek Philippe; so not *his* watch, I suppose, but just one he's taking care of for the next generation.) 'Maroun Sawaya.'

'Don't be silly,' I say, because I assume this is an apology in Arabic. Saad often drops into Arabic when he's especially relaxed. 'No *Maroun Sawaya* necessary.'

He grins. 'Maroun Sawaya is a person, Grace. Haven't you heard of him?'

I blush, even though he's not asked this in a patronising way. Saad hasn't – so far – patronised me once during the course of our brief relationship. 'Ohhh, Maroun *Sawaya*. Of course.'

His grin widens. 'Well, as well as being a member of the House of Lords and a close personal friend of the Prime Minister . . .'

I nod knowledgeably. And I'm grateful for the unspoken heads-up.

'. . . he's an old friend of my father. And of course, he's an extremely serious art collector. He's got a Braque and a couple of Cezanne still lifes that he's looking to sell, which my family is quite interested in acquiring. Not to mention the fact that he's extremely interested in getting his hands on a couple of pieces of ours in exchange.'

I nod. That's another of the surprising things about spending time with Saad Amar. That after just a short time in his company, I can hear him talk about 'acquiring' priceless artwork without so much as blinking an eyelid.

'So do you mind if I abandon you now?' he goes on. 'Only Thomas just told me that Maroun and his art buyer are already here, and I shouldn't keep them waiting.'

'No, of course. You go. I'll get ready and then I'll be on my way myself.' I don't want to add that actually, I really *need* to be getting on my way myself, to pick Hector up from nursery in forty minutes' time.

'Good. As soon as you're ready, call Thomas and ask him to help you find a cab.'

'I'll just get one myself.'

Saad puts a hand on my cheek. 'You're not *scared* of Thomas, are you?'

'Scared? Me?' I give a little laugh. 'Don't be ridiculous!'

'Because I know he can be a little bit . . . off-putting.

He comes to trust new people in my life very slowly. But I'll have a word with him, if he's been at all difficult.'

I feel the way I'm sure Robbie felt when, after an older boy called Sebastian emptied his lunchbox over his head on his second day of school, I briefly threatened to call the boy's mother and tell her to stop her son bullying mine. 'No! There's no need, honestly. We get along just fine.'

'Mm. Well, you must let me know. Especially if he starts pulling any of his little tricks.'

Little tricks? That sounds ominous.

Saad gets to his feet, then leans down to place a long, lingering kiss in the hollow of my neck and collarbone. 'So can I see you tomorrow?'

'Tomorrow?'

'Yes. Why? Are you busy, or something?'

'No, not busy at all . . . I just mean . . . well, I've already seen you today, that's all. And the day before that. And the day before that.'

He blinks at me. 'Sorry, is there some kind of Grace-quota I don't know about?'

'No, but –'

'Some kind of regulation –' he places another kiss on my neck, a little further up this time – 'that says that I can only get my fix of you twice a week, or something?'

'No.' I'm distracted for a few moments, drifting off on a wave of nerve-tingling pleasure as he kisses all the way up from my neck to my lips, and then all the way back down again. 'I'm just,' I manage to utter, eventually, 'surprised that you can make so much time for me.'

'Grace, I run the company.'

I take a deep breath. 'OK, then. That you *want* to make so much time for me. I mean, haven't you got other women you want to be . . . um . . . getting your fix of?'

He lets out a loud laugh. 'A bevy of Serbian supermodels, you mean? Or a girl like Britta? The kind of girl my brother thinks I ought to be shagging?'

I'm truly shocked. '*Adnan* thinks you should be shagging Serbian supermodels?'

This time his laugh is even louder. 'Yes, Grace. My six-year-old brother thinks I should be shagging Serbian supermodels. God, you kill me!' He leans down to place a kiss on the top of my head. 'I'm talking about my other brother. Wael. You probably see him in the papers sometimes, falling out of a nightclub with – would you believe it? – a Serbian supermodel on his arm.'

'But don't *you* want to? Fall out of a nightclub with a Serbian supermodel, that is. Or, well, I suppose she doesn't have to be Serbian. There are a lot of very stunning Russian models, aren't there, and some super-hot South American ones. And then there was Britta, of course. Who I assume was Swedish, or something – all that incredible blond hair – or . . .'

'Grace. I can understand why my party-loving coke-head of a brother wants to persuade me to shag supermodels, but it's not clear to me why *you* want me to.'

'I don't want you to! I'm just wondering why you're not, currently.' I swallow, hard. 'I mean, I'm assuming you're not, currently. It's none of my business if you are.'

'I'm not,' he says gently.

I let out a little laugh that's supposed to be an unconcerned giggle but is in fact more a kind of belch of relief.

'And you know something, Grace. Messing around with models can get pretty boring.'

'My heart bleeds for you.'

'It's true! Models don't have great senses of humour. They don't tend to be all that good in bed. They all seem to want to just lie back and have all the work done for them.'

I'm torn between nausea (at the idea of Saad in bed with models), and triumph (at the fact that they are all, allegedly, humourless and lazy).

'That kind of woman has never turned me on like you do, Grace. In fact, I've never slept with anyone like you before. Anyone quite so giving.'

Now I'm torn between embarrassment (at the fact that I'm so obviously an even bigger slut than I realised) and exhilaration (at the idea that I'm better in bed than an entire catwalk of international models!!!!).

Exhilaration wins. Just.

'Hey, don't blush!' Saad tells me, as he gets to his feet and starts heading for the door. 'Actually, forget that,' he adds. 'You look gorgeous when you blush. I must try to find ways to make it happen more often.'

He blows me a final kiss and leaves the bedroom.

Once he's gone, I stop post-coitally languishing right away, jump up out of the bed and start to walk, naked but for my Jimmy Choos, out of the bedroom. I have to find my discarded items of clothing first, then I'll give Thomas a call on the internal phone system and broach that issue of the cab.

The trouble is, I can't find my discarded items of clothing.

My skirt isn't where I left it in the dressing room, my blouse isn't where Saad removed it in the lobby, and as for that underwear I was already uncertain about, well, there's no sign of any of it. There's only one explanation.

Thomas.

I scurry (no mean feat in these teetering heels) to the nearest phone, which is on the Paul Frankl coffee table in front of one of the squashy sofas. I dial 1.

Thomas picks up a couple of rings later. 'Mrs Costello?'

It's not the time to say, *Please, for the love of God, just call me Grace*. This is going to be an awkward enough conversation as it is. 'Thomas, I'm upstairs in S – in Mr Amar's bedroom, and I'm afraid I . . . well, I seem to have misplaced my clothes.'

'I do apologise, Mrs Costello,' he says. 'I picked them up when I was gathering Mr Amar's clothes. I didn't realise you were staying for such a short visit.'

'That's . . .' *even more snide and sneaky than I thought* '. . . really nice of you, Thomas. But I just need them back. That's all.'

'Certainly. Now, what is it you need back, specifically? Your skirt? Your brassiere? Your –'

'All of it!'

'Of course. Would you hold on just one moment, please?' There are a couple of moments of silence, and then he returns. 'I'm terribly sorry, Mrs Costello, but that won't be possible.'

'What do you mean, it won't be possible?'

'Your skirt and blouse were picked up by the dry cleaners when they came to collect Mr Amar's suit half an hour ago. And your *intimate* items have already been put in the washing machine.'

This is one of his *little tricks*, isn't it?

'You . . . put my undies in the washing machine?'

'On a *delicate cycle*,' he says, sounding deliberately offended.

'That's not my point! The point is . . . look, I need them! *And* my skirt and blouse. I have a toddler to collect from nursery in half an hour's time!'

'Well, I'm afraid there isn't very much I can do. I mean, I *could* phone the laundry pickup people, but it'll take them a good half-hour to get back here, even if they haven't already put the clothes through for processing. Remind me, Mrs Costello, did you bring a coat?'

'Oh, no, Thomas, I am not walking out of here in nothing but my coat and my stilettos.' Panic has made me unusually bold. 'So I suggest you think of something else for me to put on. You've made it quite clear that Mr Amar has, um, *entertained* other women here on a pretty regular basis. Hasn't one of them ever left something behind that I can borrow?'

He thinks about this for a moment. 'I'm just not sure I could find you anything that would *fit* –'

'Well, try! And I'm only a bloody size ten, you know!'

'Of course. I'll see what I can find in one of the guest bedrooms. Wait there, Mrs Costello, and I'll bring something along in just a couple of minutes.'

I head for the dressing room again, planning to grab a shirt of Saad's from the wardrobe, to use as a temporary cover-up, when suddenly the door to the lobby starts to open.

Powered by the thought of the humiliation that will ensue if Thomas sees me naked but for my Jimmy Choos, I hurl myself at the door like Usain Bolt on a really, really fast day. But as I reach it, twisting myself sideways so that if Thomas *does* get a glimpse of me, it's a side-on view rather than the full frontal, I realise that the person opening the door isn't Thomas at all.

Not unless Thomas has taken to wearing a slim grey pencil skirt, fishnet tights, and leopard-print Louboutin court shoes.

Oh, sweet Jesus. It's Louboutin Lexie.

I don't know if she's seen that it's me. If I'm lucky, all she's seen is that there's a high-speed, naked woman slamming the door on her foot.

‘Fucking *hell*!’ she shrieks, on the other side of the door. She pulls her foot backwards, so that I can slam the door properly. ‘What the hell are you *doing*? You nearly took my fucking *foot* off, woman!’

‘Woman’. Not *Grace*. Not even *whatsyourname-that-I-spoke-to-for-the-first-time-this-morning*. Maybe I have been lucky after all.

‘Sorry!’ I call back, in a high, quavering voice that’s partly meant to be a disguise, and is partly just the way I sound when I’m this nervous. ‘But this is private!’

‘You don’t say?’ Now I know for sure, from her voice, that it’s definitely Lexie. And she doesn’t sound badly injured. She just sounds extremely pissed off. ‘Look, I’m just trying to find a loo. And I only came up here because Mr Amar said I should go and have a look at the Gauguin on the half-landing.’

Even though I haven’t really had time to process too much information in the past fifteen seconds, I’m still relieved to realise that Lexie must be this Maroun bloke’s art buyer.

And not, as I’ve had at the back of my mind for at least five of those fifteen seconds, one of Saad’s visiting ‘ladies’.

‘There’s a loo on the ground floor!’ I warble.

This is met with silence. Which I assume means that Lexie has limped off in either the direction of the half-landing or the direction of the downstairs lavatory. And which is broken, a couple of moments later, by Thomas’s smooth tones from out in the hallway.

‘Can I help, madam?’ he’s saying.

'I was just on my way back down to the loo,' I hear Lexie say. 'That is, assuming the weird naked girl in there has told me the right place to go.'

'Oh, I'm sure she has.' Thomas's voice is even more mellifluous than usual. 'Mrs Costello knows her way around here.'

I'll kill him. I don't care if he's ex-military. I don't care if he's former Special Ops, for fuck's sake. I will literally *kill him*.

'Costello?' Lexie is saying. 'You don't mean *Grace* Costello, do you?'

OK, I know I've got a memorable surname, but she wasn't even supposed to be paying attention at the bloody meeting this morning! She was only meant to be there to get popularity points for her daughter!

I have to act fast. Thomas hasn't the slightest loyalty to me – I think we've already proven that, if anything, it's quite the opposite – so if I'm going to prevent him from announcing to Louboutin Lexie (and thus to every Miranda in existence) that yes, he does mean Grace Costello, the very Grace Costello, in fact, who's having an affair with Saad Amar, well, I need to come up with something good.

I make a dash for the dressing room, grab the first shirt of Saad's that I see on one of the wardrobe rails, and start pulling it on.

'Thomas?' I yell, as I do so, in my ordinary voice. 'Is that you?'

'Yes, Mrs Costello. I'm just bringing you the clothes you asked for –'

'Excellent!' I cut him off, before he can say anything else. 'If you'd just leave them outside the door, please, Thomas. My model can get them when you've gone.'

There's a brief, confused silence. It's long enough for me to grab a pair of Saad's trousers and start pulling those on too. They're going to be far too loose and far too long, but I'll just have to belt them tightly and roll them up to my ankle. With my sky-high Jimmy Choos, I might even have found myself a brand-new look.

'Your *model*, Mrs Costello?'

I can't find a belt to hold the trousers up, so I pull a silk tie from the special hanging tie rack. It's the bold orange one Saad wore to our lunch at Locanda Locatelli. I wrap it round the trouser waist and tie it, sharply, in a knot. Then I grab my handbag and stride to the lobby door, flinging it open. Thomas is staring at me, his eyes wide as saucers.

'Yes, Thomas, my model. Mr Amar's girlfriend. The one I've been commissioned to paint a nude portrait of!' Shit. Now that I've said it, it sounds more ludicrous than I thought. 'She's rather shaken, I'm afraid,' I force myself to carry on, 'because someone opened the door on her a couple of minutes ago when she was looking for the clothes you were bringing her . . . Oh! Lexie!' I pretend I've just seen her, hovering in the hallway behind Thomas. 'What a lovely surprise! You never said you knew Saad Amar. What are you doing here?'

'I don't know Saad Amar. I didn't even know I was coming here until a couple of hours ago. I'm with my boss, Maroun Sawaya. I buy art for him. And . . . *what* did you say you were doing here, again?'

'Oh, just getting some preliminary sketches for a portrait,' I say, as breezily as I know how. I can feel myself sweating into the fine wool of Saad's suit trousers.

'A portrait?'

'Mm-hmm. I happened to mention to Mr Amar that I trained as an artist – specialising in the female nude, in fact – and he asked me to do one of his girlfriends.' I think I'd better try to make this non-existent nude girlfriend a more convincing presence. 'Britta, her name is. Stunning, blonde, legs to die for –'

'I had no idea you were an artist,' Lexie interrupts.

'Yes, well, it's not something I go around bragging about at the gates of St Martin's. That's where *our children go to school*,' I add, pointedly, to Thomas.

To his credit, he turns rather pale. Judging by the ridiculously small cocktail dress he's holding in one hand, the dress he's brought up for me to put on, I think he was just trying to get in a bit of a dig at my expense. I don't think he knew quite what a fire he was stoking.

'Could you take that dress to Britta, please,' I tell him, 'and tell her not to worry – nobody saw anything? Um, did you, Lexie?'

'No . . .' She's looking at me with a very particular

gaze. I wouldn't call it suspicious, as such. But it's certainly *beady*. 'I didn't see anything.'

'Good! Let's go on downstairs together, shall we?' I link my arm through Lexie's, and start practically hauling her down the stairs, despite her loud protests about wanting to look at the Gauguin. But they're obviously much louder than even I realise, because as we reach the bottom of the stairs, Saad and a rather rotund man in his early sixties emerge from the drawing room to see what the racket is all about.

'Grace?' Saad's eyebrows have vanished up behind his floppy dark fringe, and he's shooting me *what the hell?* looks. When he notices that I'm wearing his clothes, he looks more astonished still. 'I . . . didn't know you were still here . . .'

'Sorry, I should have let you know. But I had just a couple more sketches I wanted to make of Britta before I left. It's going to be a fabulous portrait,' I go on, before he can blow my cover by asking what the hell Britta is doing in the house, and why I'm suddenly claiming to be sketching her. 'Such a wonderful thing, to commission a nude of your girlfriend – don't you agree, Lexie?'

'Do you two know each other?' Saad asks, comprehension beginning to dawn across his face.

'Yeah,' Lexie says. 'Our kids go to the same school. Same place you're sending your brother, so I gather. Thanks to Grace here.'

'Oh, it was nothing.' I hoist my bag up onto my shoulder. 'Well! I really should be going. Leave you to your powwow in peace. It was lovely to meet you, Mr Maroun,' I say to the rotund man, even though we haven't, really, met. And even though I've just remembered his name isn't actually Mr Maroun. 'And great to see you again, Lexie! We should have lunch sometime.'

'Absolutely. We could talk about your . . . art.'

I shoot her a dazzling smile, but I can't quite find the right words to reply to this.

'Can I help you get a taxi?' Saad begins, but I brush him aside as I start heading to the front door.

'No need. Thanks anyway! I'll send you the sketches as soon as I've put the finishing touches to them,' I add. And then with shaking hands, I shut the front door behind me.

Bella

Tuesday 15 December

I'm in a top-of-the-range kitchen in top-of-the-range Fulham, catering a pre-Christmas buffet supper for fifty. Buffets are usually easy jobs, because you can get pretty much everything – terrines and pâtés, savoury tarts and quiches, varied salads – completely ready in advance. But today's buffet isn't proving quite as easy as I'd assumed it would be. Anna is running late, for one thing, which means I'm stressed about getting all the desserts ready in time. For another thing, my mother has called three times already since I arrived at the client's, and isn't taking my no-answer as a hint. And most difficult of all, the client is a Total Nightmare.

I probably should have expected it from the phone calls and email correspondence we've had, but it's far worse than even I could possibly have imagined. Despite the fact she's recently been made nanny-less (I can't say I'm surprised) with baby twins to take care of as well as (I assume, seeing as she's told me this evening's party is for her colleagues) a demanding full-time job, she's still somehow found the time to police the kitchen ever since I arrived, double- and triple-checking everything from the sell-by dates on my cartons of double cream to the consistency of my home-made mayo.

'Actually, this mayonnaise tastes quite good,' she's saying, rather grudgingly, now, as she licks a teeny-tiny amount from the teaspoon she's just stuck into my Magimix. 'A soupçon more lemon juice wouldn't go amiss, though. Correct it, would you, please?'

'I'm sorry, Vanessa,' I'm calling her this even though she's not directed me to call her by her first name – anything to correct her view that she's the lady of the manor and I'm the lowliest scullery maid, 'but my mayonnaise really does work best with that precise amount of lemon juice. Any more than that and it can start to taste just a little bit too sharp for the potato salad.' My phone starts to ring, with the Darth Vader theme ringtone that I've allocated to Mum. 'And I'll be putting lots of herbs in with the potatoes, so that will give the whole thing a lovely fresh taste,' I carry on, speaking louder than before to drown out the noise of tinny Star Wars music. 'I really don't think there's any need for more lemon. A fraction more salt, maybe, will bring out the fragrant lemony flavour a bit more.'

She skewers me with the kind of glower that would terrify me if I were prone to being terrified by these kinds of things. But I've had difficult clients before – although Vanessa is up there with the worst of them – so I hold my nerve and just give her a wide, bright smile.

'You have a great palate, though,' I tell her, as I

pretend to sprinkle a pinch of sea salt into the mayonnaise. I'm working on the basis that compliments might placate her, and thus divert her attentions from my recipes. 'Try this now and see if you're getting more lemon taste in there.'

She tastes the mayo with the kind of concentrated, suspicious expression most of us would reserve for the rare occasions when we're defusing a nuclear bomb, and then pronounces it, 'Much better. I knew there was something wrong with it before.'

'Well, thanks for the assistance.'

'Now, I've had a taste of the game terrine, haven't I? That was decent enough . . . and I've tried the duck liver pâté and the quiche Lorraine. Both fine . . .'

'You've tasted pretty much everything I've cooked, Vanessa!' My smile feels like it's stretched to snapping point. 'And I really don't think your guests are going to be disappointed!'

'No, no, the food is good.' She doles this out more like a warning than a compliment. 'Still, I knew you'd do a decent job after I tasted your *coq au vin* at the Wilsons' twentieth anniversary party.'

'Oh, that's how you knew about me. Harriet Wilson.' Another one of my more difficult clients. I should have known. 'I'm always glad to get business through personal recommendations!'

'Well, if I'm happy with how everything goes tonight, I'll put you in touch with my next-door neighbour. She's just been let down by some caterers she'd booked for an end-of-term charity do at her children's school. It's terribly short notice, of course, but I'm sure you could do with the custom.'

Now the smile has stretched way beyond snapping point. My face feels like the cuff on an old sweater that's been pulled out of shape for so long that it's gone baggy and saggy, never to return to normal.

'Actually, I'm extremely busy at this time of year, Vanessa. But of course, if I have the time to do your neighbour's event, I'd be glad to –'

We're interrupted by the ringing of the doorbell, at the same time as there's a whimper from the baby monitor. Vanessa, with the air of a woman who is happiest when multitasking, instructs me to carry on what I'm doing while she both gets the door and checks on the babies. Then she heads out of the kitchen, muttering dark threats, as she goes, about the vanishing nanny.

This will just about give me time to return Mum's call – sorry, her *four* calls – and give her firm instructions to back off for the evening.

She's called at least twice a day for the past week, ever since she gleaned from Polly that the two of us had what Mum is calling 'a contretemps'. Ostensibly her concerns are about whether or not we'll be speaking by Christmas Day, but I'm pretty sure what she's really angling to find out is what the 'contretemps' was about. After all, there's nothing she loves more than a family drama. And nothing she hates more than feeling excluded from one.

'Mum, hi, it's me,' I say tersely into the phone.

'Look, I'm sorry I couldn't answer, but I'm working at the moment, and –'

'Oh, Bella, you're *always* working. Honestly, darling, there are more important things in life than the constant daily grind, you know.'

'It's not a grind. I love my job.'

'Yes, and don't we all know it! If you spent half as much time nurturing your relationships as you do your career, you might find you're in a much happier place in your life. And talking of relationships, how are things between you and Polly?' Her voice purrs; I think she's proud of her subtlety. 'Are the two of you speaking yet? I only ask because Christmas is going to be ever so miserable if you haven't worked out whatever problem you –'

'We're speaking.'

'Oh!' She sounds surprised, not to say a bit pissed off. 'Polly hasn't said so.'

'No, well, it was only yesterday.'

Yesterday I called Polly to see whether or not she still wanted to come round to mine for Christmas Day; she said she'd love to. Both of us left it at that. It wasn't exactly a huge kiss-and-make-up, but there's no harm in letting Mum think that it was. Besides, I'm not going to give Mum any of the real information – that it looks very much like her younger daughter has opted to become a lesbian with a mystery 'friend' named Julia – until I've had the chance to talk to Polly about it myself. And *that's* a conversation I have no idea how to bring about.

Because right now, assuming that Polly is a lesbian is just about the only thing that makes sense to me any more. I mean, why else is she emailing this Julia woman – the one whom, after all, Dev told me Polly was cagey about – and calling her all the time in New York? She's not emailing any of her other friends over there, not from the look of her email account. More to the point, what about that last email that I read, after Polly turned into Gollum on me? *Affairs are dangerous territory, aren't they . . . After all the hours I've spent with you, I should know that better than anyone*. And just to put the tin lid on it: *I can't tell you how much I miss our Thursday afternoons together*.

But for now, I'm saying nothing to our drama queen of a mother.

'We had a really great talk, actually, Mum, hammered out all our issues –'

'Issues?' Mum squawks, her drama radar flashing so brightly I can practically see it down the phone. 'What issues?'

It's at this point that Anna, whom it must have been ringing Vanessa's doorbell, finally appears in the kitchen. I mouth to her that I'll be off the phone in a minute.

'Oh, you know, Mum, just the usual things sisters disagree about.'

'But what . . . I mean, you two never tell me . . . I'm your *mother*, for heaven's sake.'

'Look, Mum, I'm sorry, but I really do have to go

now. We'll speak later in the week, about exactly when you'll be coming up for Christmas, yes?'

She doesn't reply. She's sulking.

'OK, bye, Mum! Great to talk to you!' I end the call and turn my attention to Anna. She's just back from her usual pre-Christmas Winter Sun break, this year a long weekend in Morocco, and she's looking sunny and smiley, albeit a rather violent orange shade from the Fake Bake she insists on applying before she goes within ten miles of a tankini. 'Thank God you're here,' I tell her, picking up an apron to chuck in her direction. 'You've got to make a start on the mousses before madam can come back down and start quibbling over the cocoa percentage of the chocolate –'

'I think I'm pregnant.'

I drop the apron. '*Anna!*'

This blows my news about Polly's new-found lesbianism out of the water.

'OK, OK, don't go getting all over-excited about it just yet!' she squeals, sounding extremely over-excited herself. 'I didn't say it was definite. But I don't know . . . we had this absolutely incredible sex our first night in Morocco, out on the balcony . . . well, kind of *leaning over the rail* of the balcony . . .'

I go to the kitchen door and shut it firmly closed, just in case Vanessa decides to make a reappearance. If she was worried about the sell-by dates on the double cream, she probably isn't the sort to be happy to have thirty mini chocolate mousses and thirty mini raspberry Pavlovas made by a woman who's recently enjoyed filthy sex on an even filthier hotel balcony.

'. . . in fact, it was just like one of the pictures in my book of erotic Victorian lithographs . . . or wait, was it the Japanese bondage book? Anyway, I'll lend you whichever book it was, because you really should try it some time, Bells. I swear to you, it was the most powerful, intense –'

'Anna, please,' I beg her. 'Just cut to the chase. I'm not interested in the sex part. All I'm interested in is the pregnancy part.'

'OK, then.' She takes a deep breath, turns to me and places both her hands on my shoulders. 'Ever since that night, Bella, I just *feel* pregnant.'

Ah.

It's another Anna Lavery Phantom Pregnancy.

You see, this is the thing with Anna and her pregnancy saga. It goes in cycles: the depths of despair she was plunged into by Vile Debbie's baby news is always eventually followed, as night follows day, by this weird kind of euphoria.

I should have spotted it right from the start, in the intensity of her smile when she arrived. It's happened . . . hang on, let me think . . . at least three times in the past ten months. The first time, she was convinced she was pregnant; the second time, she was not only 'pregnant', but 'pregnant' with twins; the third time, it wasn't just twins, it was a boy and a girl, and she was going to name the girl Ruby, after her great-grandmother, and the boy Ian, after Ian Botham, one of Poor Pete's cricketing heroes. She'd already picked out the perfect pink and blue Farrow & Ball emulsions and started planning her trip to John Lewis to kit out the two separate nurseries when her period started, three days late.

That was a really bad one.

'I even wonder if it might be triplets,' she's saying now, dreamily. 'I just have this *feeling*.'

I make a non-committal noise.

'Of course, if it *is* triplets, I'll really have to think very hard about my work hours. I mean, you know I desperately want to carry on working with you, Bells, but if I'm doing round-the-clock feeds and nappy changes, I won't be in any fit state to come back to work for at least six months. Maybe even a year.'

I start transferring the mayo into a stainless-steel dish and moving the Magimix to the sink. 'Well, let's just cross that bridge if we come to it.'

'I mean, obviously my mum will help out, and Pete's mum too, if she must, but I don't think time with the grandmas is a real substitute for the kind of attention *I'm* going to be able to give them, is it? And obviously I'm going to be desperate for your help with them too, but only if it's not too upsetting for you, Bells.'

'It's not too upsetting.'

'I mean, bloody hell, if it *is* triplets, you might even have to take one of them off my hands for me.' She lets out a breathless laugh. 'Take your pick, I'll probably be saying, five minutes after popping them out! Obviously I won't be able to let you take Ruby, and

Pete might have a thing or two to say about you taking Imran –'

'*Imran?*'

'After Imran Khan.' She pulls a face, the first thing that's wiped away her smile so far this afternoon. 'I know. Imran Lavery. But it's Pete's top choice now. He won't be talked back into Ian, no matter how hard I try. Now, it depends on whether the spare one is a boy or a girl, but for a girl I was wondering about Betsy, and for a boy –'

'Anna. Stop. Just for one moment.' I'm going to have to word this extremely carefully. 'Look. Don't you think it might be wise to just hold off on a few of these . . . well, these extremely fixed-sounding plans? Just until you know for sure that you're absolutely, definitely, no-doubt-about-it pregnant?'

'Oh, but, Bella, if you knew how I *feel*, you know, *inside* . . .' She pats her lower stomach.

'I know. I'm sure. It's just that we've been here a couple of times before, and the last thing I want you to do is get any false hope.'

'It isn't false hope! Ooooh, now I think about it, I had all these weird cravings, on the flight back home, for Marmite and lime marmalade.'

'Together?'

'Separately.' She looks crushed. 'Shit. Do you think that matters? Because I'm sure I *could* manage them together . . . mm, yes, now I think about it, I *do* quite fancy them mixed together. Mingled on a piece of toast, all salty from the Marmite and sweet and sticky from the lime marmalade . . .' Despite her claims that she fancies this revolting combination, she's actually starting to turn a little bit green. 'Actually, Bells,' she suddenly says, 'do you know where the loo is? I'm a bit worried I might . . .'

She gets to the kitchen sink just in time to be sick, noisily and violently, all over my Magimix.

Despite the fact she's practically hopping with delight – 'Pregnancy sickness! It has to be!' – I insist that she goes and splashes her face with some water and then sits down quietly at the table while I clear up the horrific state of the sink. Even though I'm normally rubbish with anything vomity, the thought of Vanessa coming back downstairs before I've bleached away every trace of it is enough to make me roll my sleeves up and get stuck in as fast as possible.

If there's one thing I hate, it's being behind schedule. This evening Anna and Vanessa between them have both contributed to me being almost half an hour behind with my carefully calculated timings. So it's probably no wonder that I'm a little bit snappier than usual as I struggle to get the salads made. Or that I'm in such a stress-zone that I only just get the trestle tables loaded up with the food by the time the first guests start to arrive at eight o'clock.

Vanessa has hired a couple of friends' gap-year teenagers to help out with the handing round and the clearing of plates, so luckily I can get on with heating the hot canapés in the oven while I leave Anna to direct things in the living room above. Under normal circumstances, being below stairs and cooking away as though my life depends on it is great for my mood. But today, for some reason, I'm feeling seriously grouchy and under-appreciated.

It couldn't be anything to do with all the baby talk, could it?

I mean, it would be absurd if it were. Anna *isn't* pregnant, for God's sake. She's fantasy-pregnant. And even if she *were* pregnant, my overwhelming emotion would be happiness, obviously. Happiness for my best friend who'd be finally getting something she's dreamed about for so long. I mean, I'm not a mean-spirited person. I love Anna, and I desperately want for Anna what Anna desperately wants for herself.

So why is my head filled, right now, with the image of Anna floating beatifically round a nursery filled with three plump, pink, sleeping babies? And why is this image causing a sharp, stabbing pain deep down in my gut? And for goodness' sake, why can't I tear my mind off it? Why do I keep returning to this image – a fantasy image at that – and niggling away at every nook and cranny of it, as though it's an old wound that I really, really want to reopen?

I mean, I must be going a little bit mad here, or something. Because now that I think of it, I can almost *hear* a baby crying.

Shit. I'm cracking up, aren't I? Properly, totally, cracking up. It must be the strain of the whole adoption – worrying about Jamie's attitude, and whether he's ever going to put his money where his mouth is – and worrying about how Anna's going to fall to pieces when she works out that actually, she's not pregnant after all, and . . .

Oh. Wait a minute. Maybe I'm not cracking up after all. Because the sound is coming from behind my vast mound of fresh potato salad. Which is where Vanessa left her baby monitor earlier.

A couple of moments later, I hear the crying come to a temporary halt, and then the rather brisk tones of Vanessa herself, demanding of her baby exactly why it is that she's crying, and what she would like her, Vanessa, to do about it. I'm half-expecting the baby to reply – for all I know, children from Fulham are reciting poetry and doing their times tables long before they hit their first birthdays – but actually all that happens is that the howling starts up again, even louder than before. I hear the clunky sounds of a cot being leaned into, and a baby being picked up, and then the crying fades out for a moment or so before fading back in again – only this time, off the monitor and in real life.

Vanessa is bringing the baby down the stairs and into the kitchen.

'Esme is having one of her moments. I need you to heat up some milk, please, Bella,' she says as she stalks through the door. Since I last saw her, lurking around the kitchen complaining about my mayonnaise, she's changed into a black cocktail dress and spiky heels. Neither of these items of clothing makes it look particularly easy to balance a baby on one jutting, silk-clad hip, as she's currently doing.

And, oh my God, what a baby.

Even though her face is screwed up with the wilful energy of a deliberate temper tantrum, and turning roughly the colour of the ripened vine tomatoes I've just used for my bruschetta, she's just *gorgeous*. A plump little body and a cherubic little face, topped off with wispy blond hair that only just covers her head and makes her look beautifully comical rather than a fraction too angelic. She's wearing – of course she is – some totally fabulous kiddie-designer night-wear creation, all white smocking and sorbet-pink embroidery, but she's wearing it in a manner that suggests she'd be much happier and more at ease in a pair of *Thomas the Tank Engine* pyjamas.

I don't usually go all gooey over babies. Not any more. It's a habit I've rigorously trained myself out of. But looking at Esme, my heart is melting and breaking all at the same time.

'Bella, don't just stand there! I asked for some milk to be heated up, please,' Vanessa snaps, above her daughter's roars.

Her rudeness brings me back down to earth. 'Actually, Vanessa, I was just about to get a fresh tray of the Gruyère tarts into the oven.'

'Oh, well, then, *I'll* do it. Of course! Don't I always end up doing everything?' She strides to the fridge, handing the howling Esme to me as she does so. 'Hold her for a moment, will you?'

This sort of entirely misses my point about the Gruyère tarts.

But I'm not going to complain about it. Esme is even more rewarding up close and personal than she was from a small distance. In addition to her enchanting plumpness, I can now feel how heavy and warm and wriggly she is, and most of all I can inhale her perfect baby smell: Johnson's powder, InfaCare bath bubbles and . . . and just *baby*.

Maybe it's just Anna that's put the idea in my head, with her talk about letting me have one of her non-existent triplets and all that. But I can't stop myself from thinking that Vanessa has another one, exactly like Esme, up in a nursery somewhere. And that she's such a busy woman, with such a hectic life, that she might not only barely miss Esme, if I were to take her; that she'd probably *prefer* it, even. Less stress with unreliable nannies, and one less mouth to feed, and Esme is obviously the naughtier one of the pair, ruining Vanessa's sophisticated evening like this –

'. . . what on earth it is you're doing,' Vanessa is saying.

She's also staring at me, I realise, like she's just been reading my every thought.

'I wasn't doing anything!' Shit. She thought she'd just hired a caterer, but now it's dawning on her that she may have inadvertently invited a psycho baby-snatcher into her home. 'I was only holding her . . .'

'Well, whatever it is you're not doing, please keep on doing it.' She gives me a brief flash of a smile and nods at Esme, who – I now notice – has stopped howling and is just gurgling and sighing a bit, and gazing up at me with her huge grey eyes.

Ohhhh. So *that's* what Vanessa meant. That I'm good with babies. Not that I'm a psycho baby-snatcher.

At least, I hope to God I'm not a psycho baby-snatcher. Because you wouldn't *know*, would you, if you actually were? You'd think you were just a normal, kind-hearted, baby-loving person, like me. Someone who isn't able to have a baby of her own, like me.

'Oh Christ, more people,' Vanessa is saying, as we both hear the doorbell ring, for about the twentieth time so far tonight. 'Alasdair will be too busy waffling about house prices to hear the bloody thing. Can I leave Esme with you for a moment, while the milk heats? I know you said something about some Gruyère tarts, but . . .'

'They can wait.' Anything to snatch – fuck, no, sorry, to *get* – a few more minutes alone with the divine Esme. 'You go.'

And Vanessa goes.

Esme is closing her eyes now, making it almost unnecessary for me to rock her gently, and croon at her, but I do it anyway, the way that's come naturally to me all my life. I've always had a bit of a knack for settling them down, even when I was as little as four or five, and Polly was a baby. Needs must, I suppose: Polly was a screamer; Mum was forty per cent useless and sixty per cent disinterested; and Brian meant well but was mostly committed, as a dad, to perfecting the perfect blend of puréed vegetables. So if I wanted to get any peace and quiet, or even if I just wanted to spend time with my exciting new baby sister without being deafened, I had to work out ways of getting her to stop crying. I was too little to hold her much at that point, but silly songs were always a winner, as were the endless hours I spent pushing her in her buggy up and down the back garden . . .

'Bells. Oh, I *knew* it was you.'

I look up to see – I don't believe this – that Dev is standing in the kitchen doorway.

Bella

Tuesday 15 December

'As soon as I tasted the quiche Lorraine, I knew it had to be you doing the food!' Dev is saying. 'Only you and Brian make pastry as light as that. And then I asked that blonde you've got organising things up there, and she confirmed my suspicions. But hang on – you're nannying as well?'

'No, no, just . . .' *thinking up ways to steal one of Vanessa's babies*, '. . . just helping out while Vanessa gets the door.' I wave him over to me so I can go up on tiptoes and give him a kiss on the cheek. 'More to the point, what are *you* doing here?'

'I work with Vanessa at St George's. Well, we're in different departments – she's ENT – but our paths cross a good deal on cleft palate surgeries. Wow,' he says suddenly, reaching to squeeze my shoulder, and in a tone of voice that suggests this has taken him by surprise, 'I can't tell you how great it is to see you, Bella.'

I believe that he's pleased to see me, but he doesn't look it. He looks, in fact, absolutely terrible. There are lines around his eyes that weren't there the last time I saw him, furrows in his forehead, and a brand-new patch of light grey in his brown hair at the left temple. He looks ten years older than he did the last time I saw him. Barely a month ago.

'Dev, look, I'm so sorry I haven't called you back these past couple of weeks. I know I said I would, but I've been trying to work on Polly, find out what it is she's got herself all confused about . . .'

Though now, of course, that it looks like she's a lesbian, it's fairly obvious what she's confused about. And if I'm honest, that might be part of the reason that I haven't plucked up the courage to call Dev lately. I'd wanted to call him back with good news, with hope that things were still going to work out between him and Polly. Ringing him to say that his best chance of winning Polly back would be to book himself in for painful and lengthy gender-reassignment treatment isn't exactly the triumph I was after.

'It's OK, Bells.' Dev pulls back his lips in imitation of a smile. It might work, except for the fact that I've never seen anyone look less smiley in my life. 'It was good to talk to you that day anyway. And I thought it would take you some time to make headway on – what did you call the situation with me and Polly? – the blip.'

OK, *big* mistake calling it a blip.

'So . . .' He leans against the wall, deliberately casual. 'How is she?'

'She's OK.' I avoid his eyes. 'I don't really know. She's not talking to me very much at the moment.'

'Oh?'

'We've had words. I don't approve of the way she's handling things with you. She doesn't approve of the way I'm handling things with Jamie. And, you know, the adoption.'

As if on cue, Esme suddenly lets out an extremely loud and satisfied burp. I laugh – I can't help it – but Dev just stares down at her, a weird spasm crossing his face.

'God, she's gorgeous, isn't she?'

'Yes. She is.'

He looks up and stares rather bleakly around the kitchen. 'You know, I was so sure this was where me and Poll were heading.'

I'm confused. 'Fulham?'

'No. *This*.' He nods down at Esme, who – not really caring about her audience – burps once again. 'Babies. Two or three of them. Four, even, if we were lucky. A family. But the more I think about it, the more I think . . . I think that's the thing that's driven Polly away.'

Oh God.

Though in one sense, I suppose, he's absolutely right. If she really is a big old lesbian, then Polly probably *isn't* all that keen on the idea of having babies. Not the old-fashioned way, I mean. Not that she mightn't be up for it with some kind of artificial insemination . . . Shit. That reminds me, now that I think about it, of how Polly spoke about Jamie that night we had our row. The way she seemed to think of him as nothing but a means of insemination. Which would be, wouldn't it, exactly the kind of view of men that a lesbian might take?

'I mean, do you remember what I told you, Bells, at the airport?' Dev continues. 'The first time she started getting all distant was when I began emailing her all the pictures of the houses I was looking at. And I kept pointing out how we needed lots of bedrooms for our kids, whenever they came along, and I kept insisting on a big garden, so they'd have somewhere to play . . .' He stares, bleakly again, into midair, as if seeing the myriad bedrooms and the big garden floating before his eyes. 'I should never have gone on about it. I should never have placed that pressure on her.'

'Dev, I honestly don't think –'

'But I'd give it all up – children, I mean – if it meant that she'd take me back. Honest to God. Having children used to mean the world to me, but having Poll would mean more. You know what it's like, don't you, Bells? Not having kids. It's something you can completely deal with, as long as everything else in your life is happy . . . Oh, Vanessa! Hi there,' he says, putting back on his doctor's face as Vanessa reappears at the kitchen doorway. 'I must apologise for keeping Bella chatting and slowing down the production of her incredible food!'

Vanessa's eyes narrow. Obviously she doesn't like The Staff consorting with The Guests. 'You *know* her?'

'We're old friends,' I say swiftly, because I don't know if Dev has told his colleagues about his messy personal life, and he's looking like he hasn't the faintest clue how to answer Vanessa's question. Not that she seems all that interested in the answer.

'Right. Well, I would appreciate it, Bella, if you could carry on getting the food out,' she says, as though she hasn't just left me babysitting for the past ten minutes. 'And Dev, why don't you go on back to the party? Alasdair has been dying to talk to you about the new place you've bought in Wimbledon. Just, for the love of God, tell him it cost a hundred grand less than it actually did. *I'll* take Esme now, thank you,' she adds, chivvying an obedient Dev out of the door behind her and then stalking over to take Esme from my arms. 'Still, you got her to sleep, I suppose. You must have a knack for infants.' She casts her eyes over my soft, paunchy body, built for child-bearing. 'You obviously have one or two of your own.'

I don't say anything. I can't say anything.

I just turn away and start loading a fresh batch of Gruyère tarts into the oven.

I drop Anna home, still heady with the joys of her attack of 'pregnancy' sickness, at almost one o'clock in the morning, and then I carry on the short distance to my flat and park the van right outside.

I can tell, before I even get my keys out of my bag to put them in the door, that we have company.

There is a cacophony of noise coming from the direction of the living room: ridiculous West Coast rap, excitable male voices and a smidgen of boozy singsong.

The Boys are back in town.

And Jamie appears to have invited a dozen of them over to drink, smoke, and find new ways to trash my flat and annoy my neighbours.

Sure enough, as I open the front door, a wave of testosterone engulfs me. There's whatisname, Sean Something-or-other, propping himself up against my newly polished hallway mirror, and Thingy – is it Mike? – splashing a can of Guinness around my carpet. They both hail me, happily but confusedly (I can't be certain they'd know exactly who I was if they were stone-cold sober; pissed as a pair of newts, there's no chance), but I don't hang about to chat. Jamie is my target, and I suspect he'll be in the living room, engrossed in Wii football.

Jamie is in the living room, engrossed in Wii football.

I'm not exactly dropping dead from shock here.

'Babe!' he greets me, handing his upchuckers to one of The Boys who's next to him on the sofa (Kev? Ken?) and getting up to give me a big, smoochy, proprietorial kiss. 'Talk about a sight for sore eyes.'

As he sits back down, I notice Liam, standing by the fireplace. He's drinking a bottle of Becks. And he's looking at me.

I turn my back to him and talk to Jamie in a low voice. 'J, you didn't tell me you were having people over.'

'Ah, that's because these aren't *people*.' He's talking in a very un-low voice himself, the way he does when he's drunk. OK, the way he does when he's *really* drunk. Jamie has all kinds of stages of drunkenness. I sometimes think of them as ranging from DEFCON 1 (sweetly tipsy) to DEFCON 5 (belligerent and semi-conscious). Right now, I'd say we were holding steady at DEFCON 4. 'It's just The Boys. You don't need me to tell you when it's just The Boys coming over, Bells.'

'Actually, Jamie, I do. I've had a really difficult night, and –'

'*Three-nil!*' comes a sudden yell from Kev/Ken, which is Jamie's cue to throw himself back down on the sofa beside him, wrestle the upchuckers from his grip, and launch himself back into the parallel Wii universe.

I leave the room, forge through the throng of Boys, and go into the kitchen. Though actually, and despite the cries of, 'Any chance of a bacon sandwich, love?' floating after me, the kitchen itself isn't where I'm headed.

There's a huge window, on one side of the tiny utility room, that opens out onto the world's smallest terrace. Actually, let's just call it a balcony. And a cramped one at that. It's one of the things that made me practically bankrupt myself to buy this flat when I first saw it five years ago, but in reality it's not something I use very often. There's barely room for the ancient cast-iron garden chair I keep out here, and even in the height of summer it manages to be chilly, positioned as it seems to be in its own unique microclimate that gets very little sun and an awful lot of wind.

But it's private, and nobody will know I'm out here. And I can sit on my freezing cast-iron chair and mop away the dampness in my eyes without any of my unexpected guests noticing and assuming I'm tearful about the result of last week's shock loss to Arsenal.

And maybe the icy wind will blow away the sticky, toxic debris of my evening at Vanessa's house. Anna, Dev, Esme and all.

Please, God, especially Esme.

But I only get about thirty seconds of cleansing air before I hear the kitchen window creak further open behind me, and turn to see a huge shape looming out of it. It's like something out of a bad horror movie.

It's Liam.

'You all right out here?' he asks.

'What? Yes.' *Go away*.

There's a brief silence. 'It's pretty cold.'

'You don't say.'

There's a longer silence. 'Might get snow for Christmas.'

For fuck's *sake*. The last thing I want right now – apart from a posse of sweaty, sozzled men trashing my flat – is festive meteorological discussion with my unwanted lodger.

'Course, I won't be here for Christmas, you'll probably be thrilled to hear. I'll be headed back to Cork to spend it with my girls. Spoil them with presents in the morning, big roast turkey for lunch, drag them out for the traditional Dempsey walk along a freezing, rainy beach in the afternoon . . .' He can't hide the pleasure in his voice. 'Anyway, I'll be out of your hair, for a change.'

I surreptitiously dab away a stray, blobby tear. 'Mm. Look, Liam, I don't want to be rude, but I actually wanted a moment or two alone.'

'Yeah, I know.'

But he doesn't move. In fact, he settles himself down half in-half out of the window, resting on the ledge, with an air of a man who isn't planning on going anywhere. Whether this is because he's concerned about me or because he's an oblivious ignoramus, it's impossible to tell. And I'm not exactly sure how to respond. So we sit in silence for a moment or two until he lets out a long, slow breath. I can see it condense in the icy night air.

'It's nice, out here.'

'Yes. It is.'

'I really hope I'm not keeping you from doing anything you were planning to do out here. Anything, you know, personal and embarrassing.'

'What the hell are you talking about?'

'Oh, I don't know. Bleaching any part of your anatomy . . . pleasuring yourself with a wide array of sex toys . . .'

I've no idea where my laugh comes from, especially seeing as it comes along with a much less unexpected sob.

'Fuck. You're not all right, are you?'

'No, I am . . . I mean, I'm not, really, but I will be. It was just . . . a difficult night.'

'Like you told Jamie.'

'Like I told Jamie.'

He lets out another of those condensing breaths. 'Anything I can do to help?'

This idea is so absurd that I laugh out loud again, but bitterly this time. 'Well, let me see. Can you do anything about the fact that my best friend is accidentally making me want a baby all over again, when I've spent the past ten years willing myself not to want one? Can you do anything about the fact that I wish actual harm on women who have the audacity to have not just one plump, perfect, snuggly, beautiful baby, but *two*? Can you do anything about the fact that I wish actual harm on my sister, for having that chance, and for throwing it all away – as if those things mean nothing – just because she's decided to pretend to be a lesbian for a bit? Can you do anything about any of that, Liam, because if you can –'

I stop talking as, quite suddenly, he gets up and leans right out through the window towards me. I feel something being placed round my shoulders. It's warm, and it smells oddly, but nicely, of ginger snaps. It's his hooded top.

'Should have offered you this earlier. With the cold, and all that.'

'I don't need it.' I start to shrug it off, but he stops me.

'Just for once in your life, Bella, let somebody else be the judge of what you might need.'

I think it's the first time he's ever called me by my name. It sounds weird, hearing it in a Cork voice that isn't Jamie's. But OK weird. Not . . . *weird* weird.

'And can I just ask,' he's carrying on, 'how your sister is *pretending* to be a lesbian? I mean, it's not like charades. Don't the other lesbians suss you out when – oh, I don't know – you carry on fancying men, or something?'

I can't help smiling. 'Oh God, I don't know. It's just . . . well, there's this woman, Julia, back in New York, who Polly's always emailing. Talking to on the phone a lot as well.'

'So? Maybe she's just a friend.'

'Polly doesn't *talk* to her like a friend. It's always just about her problems, and how much she needs Julia's help, and they obviously used to meet up once a week in New York, in secret it sounds like.'

'Are you sure she's not some kind of counsellor?'

'What?'

'A counsellor. Shrink, maybe, if it's a New York thing. I mean, if all your sister talks about is her problems, and if they used to meet once a week . . .'

It's weird – and *weird* weird this time – but with sudden, blinding clarity, I know that he's right. Now that I think of it, Polly's don't have the tone you'd expect of emails to a friend. No questions about how Julia's life is going, no mention of any ordinary stuff, like films just seen or clothes just bought. Just endless monologues of Polly tortuously trying to work through her problems. And then there are all the weirdly specific scheduling arrangements for times to call . . .

'I mean, I should know,' Liam is continuing. 'It sounds a lot like the kind of relationship I had with the counsellor I saw back home, after Kerry . . . well, you know. I'd go for a session once a week, and talk about my feelings, and I always felt a bit bad that we were only talking about me.' He lets out an awkward chuckle. 'Anyway, I still drop the bloke an email every now and then, just to let him know what's new in my life. That I'm doing OK.'

The question flashes into my head, totally irrationally, whether Liam has mentioned anything to his counsellor about me. Just as something new in his life, that's all.

'But look, Bella, for what it's worth, I don't think your sister is a lesbian. On the other hand, she might well be having a nervous breakdown.'

'But that would be great news!'

He stares at me.

'Nervous breakdowns can be cured, can't they? Unlike being a lesbian. And all these bonkers things she's doing – dumping Dev, cancelling the wedding – they can all be turned around if she just gets better!'

'Well, yeah, maybe, but it's hardly an exact science.'

'Nothing is an *exact* science.'

'True. Oh, apart from nuclear physics. And molecular biology. And inorganic chemistry.'

'I mean *these types of things* are not exact sciences. Relationships. Mental states.' My own mental state is, quite possibly, a little bit altered right now. Because the possibility of getting Polly and Dev back together – of being responsible, in some small way, for their opportunity to have a life and build a proper family together – is making me feel slightly giddy. After all, Polly needs Dev more than ever, right now, doesn't she? And wouldn't she be better off trying to solve her problems from within a happy marriage rather than miserably on her own? Rather than feeling, as well she might if she's in the middle of a nervous breakdown, that she *doesn't deserve* to be married? As Dev said himself, he'll do anything to get her back. And if he's even entertaining the possibility of giving up the idea of children, the mere act of helping Polly recover from whatever emotional crisis she's experiencing will be easy. 'If I could just get her to talk to him, face to face, make her realise that he's the one she needs to lean on, not push away . . .'

'Hmm. I wouldn't meddle in this kind of thing. Leave things to sort themselves out on their own, maybe.'

'Do you have a sister?' I demand.

'I have three brothers.'

'And would you just leave them to sort things out on their own? If you honestly knew what was best for them? And thought they were at risk of making the biggest mistake of their lives?' I don't give him a chance to answer before I'm getting to my feet.

'Thanks for the hoodie, Liam,' I tell him, pulling it off my shoulders and handing it back to him.

'Where are you going?' he asks, as I force him back through the window, climbing inside myself. It would risk being a tangle of arms and legs if I wasn't so short and stubby-limbed. Not to mention determined not to make physical contact.

'Just to bed. And I have an important call to make.'

To Dev, to ask what his plans are for Christmas. And to suggest that, if he hasn't got anything else going on, he comes over to mine.

'But it's half-past one in the morning,' Liam points out.

'Text messages, then. Emails.' Maybe have another sneaky look at Polly's emails too, try to get a sense of exactly why it might be that she's seeing a counsellor. 'It was good to talk to you, Liam. Thanks for everything.'

'Actually, Bella, I've been meaning to thank *you* for everything. Letting me stay, and –'

'You're welcome.' I'm already on my way to my bedroom, where – unless The Boys have got hold of it and started downloading internet porn – I'll be able to shut myself away with my laptop. Start on the road to getting at least one Atkins family fuck-up sorted out, once and for all.

From: PollyWollyDoodle@hotmail.com
To: Julia247@yahoo.com
Date: 8 December 2011
Subject: Phone session

Julia

Any chance at all we could move our call forward by a few hours? I think we'd agreed on four thirty in the afternoon, your time, but if there's any chance at all you could squeeze me in before that, I'd really really seriously appreciate it.

I've just had a bit of a . . . well, a *thing*, with my sister. I don't know if you could call it a row, really. She was pretty drunk, which she almost never is, drowning her sorrows because her wretched boyfriend hadn't bothered to show up for a meeting with their adoption agent. So I started blurting out a ton of stuff about how she should ditch him, and how she'd be better off alone if she ever wanted to have the child she deserves, and she started on at me about Dev, and what she called 'the real reason' I broke up with him . . .

Not that I think she knows the 'real' reason. Obviously we'd have been having quite a different conversation if she did.

But all it did was make me realise how far I am from telling her the truth. And make me think that maybe I *should* just let myself marry Dev – inflict myself on the poor innocent guy, warts and all – if it would mean I never had to tell her.

What I'm saying, I think, is that I'm thinking about the halfway house you suggested. I'm thinking of talking to Dev. Trying to explain why it is, exactly, that I feel so utterly, totally unworthy of marrying him. Seeing if, like you said in our session the day before I left New York, it's just enough for me that he forgives me. So that nobody else has to forgive me. So that I don't have to forgive myself.

Anyway, we can talk about this in our phone session. I'm right here, Julia, whenever you can fit in the call.

Thanks as always.

P x

Grace

Friday 18 December

I could lie here in bed, with Saad's arm wrapped tightly around me, for the rest of my life.

Except that I can't, of course. Because I've got to get up any minute now and start making my way home to Fulham for Robbie's end-of-term carol concert.

Oh, and because I'm married to another man. That's the other reason I can't stay here with Saad for the rest of my life. But it's easier, and much less painful, to concentrate on the small practicalities and inconveniences for the time being.

'Do you have to go?' Saad groans, waking from the half-doze he's been in for the last hour.

'I really do. Duty calls.' And not just the carol concert but, later this evening, after what's bound to be a manic dash getting the boys back from school, fed, bathed and put to bed, back to St Martin's for Chief Miranda's blessed silent auction. For which, by the way, I still haven't come up with an acceptable 'donation'. Chief Miranda has made it quite clear that the offering I've been forced to go with – almost bankrupting myself to buy two tickets for a production of *Così fan tutte* at the Royal Opera House – is very low down on her list of Things To Be Impressed By.

Saad entwines his other arm around me and pulls me, only half-joking, back down onto the bed. 'How do you feel about a bit of voluntary kidnap?'

'How would that work, exactly?'

'Well, seeing as you'd be co-operating ever so nicely, I'd make things really comfortable for you. Set you up in a lovely prison on the top floor. Only chain you to the bedpost if you'd been really, really naughty.'

'Tempting though that sounds –' and it does sound really, *really* tempting – 'I think a few people might have objections. Thomas, for one.'

Saad is nuzzling my neck. 'I'll double his salary. Hush money.'

'My children, for another.' It's the first time I've mentioned Robbie and Hector since this affair started, and I'm not quite sure what makes me do it now. Is it because I'm so relaxed here with Saad – more relaxed, I think, than I've ever been in my life – that I feel like I can say absolutely anything right now? Still, I hold my breath to see if it ruins the flirty, jokey atmosphere.

'See if you can talk them into the voluntary kidnap thing too,' Saad suggests, with a grin. 'Kids are pretty easily bribed, aren't they? Just tell them I'll build them a whole separate prison, with a bowling alley and a sweet shop, and they won't have to go to school ever again. They'll be putty in your hands.'

'Throw in a *Fireman Sam* screening room as well, and you're golden,' I tell him, just as my phone starts to ring in my handbag.

It's Charlie.

I would avoid the call but if I don't pick up, he'll just keep ringing until I do. That's Charlie's usual style; it's OK for him to be out of contact but he doesn't like it if I am. Anyway, I need to know what he's calling about, because I have a horrible suspicion that he's about to tell me he can't make it to Robbie's carol concert. Which will be even worse than it sounds, because Robbie came home from school last night with the excited announcement that the appointed soloist for his class's rendition of 'Little Donkey' has been struck down with illness – hurray for the winter vomiting bug! – and Robbie has been lined up to take his place. I triple-checked this morning with his class teacher and my most up-to-date information is that 'Little Donkey' will be a 'go' at exactly halfway through the carol concert, at three twenty p.m. So Charlie has to leave the office no later than ten to three if he's going to make it in time for the all-important solo.

'It's Charlie,' I say flatly, to Saad. 'I need to get this.'

Silently – tactfully? – he gets out of bed and goes into the bathroom, closing the door behind him.

I pick up the ringing phone. 'Charlie, hi.'

'We have a big problem,' says Charlie.

Shit. Does he know? Has someone at the office realised that Saad must be having an affair? I mean, he's taken so much time off work these past couple of weeks, it wouldn't be difficult to work it out. And even though I think I've been incredibly careful and discreet, I haven't accounted for the possibility of anyone following Saad home from the office, seeing me arrive in a cab, and emerge a couple of hours later looking flushed of cheek and mussed of hair.

Oh God, Charlie is going to kill me. He is literally going to kill me. Or just kick me out of the house and take custody of the boys, which means he might as well just kill me.

'It's about Percy,' he says.

'Percy?'

'Yes, Grace, Percy. My son?' There's a particularly sarky edge to his voice that comes out when he's stressed. 'His term finishes today and Vanessa thought I was meeting him from the train at Paddington, and I thought she was meeting him from the train at Paddington. Did you forget to write it down on the calendar, Grace?'

This is typical. One of the rare things that can bring Charlie and Vanessa closer these days is blaming me for stuff. But I'm so relieved not to have been caught out about Saad – this time – that I don't really care.

'No. I didn't forget to write anything down. Vanessa told me to expect Percy from the weekend onwards. Not this evening.'

He sighs, the way he does when he doesn't like an answer. 'Nevertheless, a mistake has been made. Vanessa is in surgery all afternoon, and I have back-to-back meetings –'

I knew it. 'And what about Robbie's carol concert?'

There's the briefest of pauses. It's all I need to hear to know that he's forgotten.

'Obviously I'm still hoping to make it to that. But Robbie might just have to learn that his dad has bills to pay, school fees to earn. It's a good lesson in life.'

'When you're six years old? And you're singing a solo?'

'Great idea, Grace. Lay a guilt trip on me. Maybe you'd like to be the one to slave away in the office every day, while I get to be the one to go to the carol concert, and drink coffee with my friends, and go shopping.'

This is such an unfair assessment of my average day that I'm too astounded to speak. On the other hand, a good deal of my time lately has been spent in a far more pleasurable way than I imagine Charlie's days are at the office, so I don't really have quite as much of a leg to stand on as I'd like.

'Look, Charlie, I'll just call Percy and tell him to get a taxi at the station. He can come straight to meet me at the school, and I'll take him back to Vanessa's from there . . .'

'Are you crazy? It may have slipped your mind, but Percy was suspended from school recently for getting involved with drugs. I don't need Vanessa on my back about letting him wander the streets of London on his own. No, look, you'll just have to slip out of Robbie's concert early or something. Percy's train gets in at quarter to four. Meet him on the platform, will you, Grace? The last thing I want is him going AWOL.'

And that's it. The call is over. Charlie hangs up.

I stare down at my silent phone.

'Everything OK?' It's Saad, appearing in the bathroom doorway. He's wearing his towelling robe and a concerned expression.

'No, everything isn't OK.' I can feel my throat burning with the effort of holding back furious tears. 'My pig of a husband has decided to fix his own screw-up about forgetting to collect his son by getting me to miss my son's first ever carol concert solo. And I'll do it, too, because I always feel so guilty about Percy growing up without his dad, and because I don't want him to feel he isn't Charlie's top priority, and because I'm too scared of Charlie's ex-wife to risk letting Percy get a taxi, just in case he high-tails it to some opium den or something . . . and because I feel so guilty about everything I'm doing here, with you . . . but the only person that really suffers is poor Robbie.'

The thought hits me of Robbie, proud as a peacock in his freshly pressed school uniform, standing up to sing his solo and searching the rows of parents to see neither me nor Charlie there for his big moment . . .

'Oh, Grace, don't cry. Please don't cry. We can fix this.' Saad walks up and puts his arms around me. 'Look, why don't you call your stepson – Percy, right? – and tell him that a man called Thomas will be meeting him off the train at Paddington. Thomas can drive him right over to meet you at the school. And if you're worried about what Percy might say about it to his dad, I'm sure we can come up with some kind of decent explanation.'

Actually, I'm far more worried about what Thomas might say to Percy. 'I don't know . . .'

'Look, Thomas doesn't even have to mention that he works for me. And Charlie wouldn't have a clue what my driver was called even if the news did get back to him. And you could always just bribe your stepson to keep shtum about who picked him up. OK, it might take a bit more than a sweet shop and a Fireman Sam screening room, but –'

'I can't bribe Percy, Saad. I can't put him in that position.'

'Then just tell him Thomas is a friend of yours. It's kind of true, after all.'

I give him a look. 'It really, really isn't.'

'So it's a white lie. Thomas will be perfectly happy to go along with it. He feels bad, Grace, about that prank with your clothes.'

'So he bloody should!'

'Then this is a chance to let him make up for it. Look, this way you get to see Robbie's solo, and Percy gets to take a ride in a top-of-the-range Bentley, and everybody's happy. Come on.' He slides his arms around my waist and looks into my eyes. 'Let me help, Gracie. Please.'

It's the first time he's ever called me Gracie. In this moment, I realise just how hopelessly I've fallen for him.

I pull away, feeling my face flame. 'OK, if Thomas doesn't mind . . .'

'He won't. I'll tell him now. Oh, by the way,' Saad adds, as he starts towards the bedroom door, 'did Charlie say why he couldn't get out of the office this afternoon? I mean, is there some big crisis going on over there, or something?'

'He didn't say. Back-to-back meetings, apparently.' I start pulling on my clothes, hoping I can make myself look respectable enough in time for the carol concert, and hoping that putting on the uniform of the upstanding yummy mummy will magically obliterate the sudden rush of feeling I've just had for Saad. Back into Breton stripes, back to normality. 'I knew something like this would happen. Charlie's never been much good at time management.'

'No. That's for sure.' Saad is already on his way out. 'I'll go and get things sorted with Thomas.'

Robbie's solo goes beautifully, his clear, high voice floating out over the school hall to the massed mothers and fathers, and even though his own father hasn't actually graced us with his presence, the unexpected appearance of Percy, right at the end of the carol concert, is enough to distract Robbie from too crushing a disappointment.

There's something a little bit downbeat about Percy, though. At first I panicked that Thomas had said something to him about the real reason he knows me. But as I've realised that he isn't being hostile to me –

quite the opposite, in fact – that suspicion has gone.

And been replaced by the suspicion that he's a bit downbeat because he spent most of his journey to London smoking something funny in the train toilets.

Still, he's just been incredibly, sweetly helpful with Robbie and Hector's slightly rushed supper- and bath-time, and a little bit of his general aura of melancholy has lifted with the arrival of Kitty-next-door to baby-sit. Or, as I've told Percy, to *help him* babysit. I could have cancelled her now that he's staying over but I can't just ignore those suspicions about those funny cigarettes on the train. Besides, Kitty is a red-hot eighteen-year-old blonde with a penchant for flimsy vest tops and visible candy-coloured bra straps. So, like I said, her arrival seems to have shaken off a few of Percy's pot-induced doldrums.

He sticks his head out of the living room now, as I stand in the hallway buttoning up my coat over my little black dress, ready to set off for the silent auction.

'Grace, can I have your card for the DVD shop? Kitty's never seen *Saw*, so I thought I'd see if they have it.'

I hand over my DVD card, even though I'm not sure it's the wisest thing in the world to allow my fourteen-year-old stepson to arrange an evening of horrific screen violence with the neighbours' daughter.

'Get a nice romantic comedy too,' I suggest, 'just in case Kitty doesn't like – er – *Saw*.'

'She'll love it. And if they've got *Saw II, III* and *IV* as well, we can do a whole marathon!' He watches me as I pick up my handbag. 'So is Dad meeting you there?'

I bite back the words 'I should be so lucky'. 'Yes. If he finishes work in time.'

'Right.' He stares down at his feet. 'Typical Dad, yeah?'

It would be disloyal to comment. 'OK, well, we shouldn't be back later than midnight, and Kitty knows where everything is if you want a sandwich, and –'

I'm silenced by Percy suddenly launching himself towards me and wrapping his long, gangly arms around my shoulders. 'Thanks, Grace,' he says, his voice muffled by my coat fabric, 'for sending your friend to pick me up, and everything. I know Mum and Dad forgot.'

'Perce, they didn't forget! They're both really busy with work, that's all! And it was no trouble, asking my fr – asking Thomas to come and get you. I thought you might enjoy the ride in the Bentley.'

He steps back, letting go of me. 'It *was* a seriously awesome car.'

'Great! Oh, and by the way, Perce, could you not mention that to your dad? The Bentley, I mean, and Thomas? It's just that . . . well, I was meant to come and get you myself, and your dad would be ever so cross if he knew I hadn't.'

My God, who have I turned into, manipulating and coaxing Percy like this? I feel like the Child-Catcher from *Chitty-Chitty-Bang-Bang*, or some creepy pervert promising rewards to a child as long as he doesn't tell anybody what I'm up to.

'Don't worry about it, Grace. I won't say anything.' Percy is ducking back into the living room, avoiding my eye again. 'You're cool. Thomas was cool. Have a good night.'

I'm still in shock about this – Thomas, *cool*? – when I arrive at St Martin's fifteen minutes later.

Chief Miranda, it's no surprise to see, has done a terrific job transforming the cavernous, slightly chilly school hall into a location worthy of her silent auction. Gone are the rows of grey plastic chairs and hard wooden benches from the afternoon's carol concert. The lights have been dimmed, and there are tables covered with crisp white linen stationed all around the hall. Each table is dedicated to one of the dozen or so different auction lots, where the milling parents – fifty or sixty of them already – are invited to write down their bids for the various treats on offer. The tables featuring the very best lots – the wine-tasting in Puglia, Louboutin Lexie's salmon- and deer-slaughtering fest in Scotland – have been decorated with these themes in mind. Half a Waitrose fruit section, from bunches of grapes to clementines and lemons, has been piled up on the Puglia stall, along with Italian tricolore flags and – bizarrely and stinkily – a huge hunk of Gorgonzola cheese. And Lexie's stall is featuring big swatches of mixed tartan (old curtains?), a CD player blaring out 'Scotland the Brave', and a set of actual deer antlers that make me wonder if Chief Miranda has pulled off a recent stealth raid of Buckingham Palace. Oh, and standing beside the table, being talked at nineteen to the dozen by Chief Miranda herself, is Louboutin Lexie.

Well, I can hardly blame her. Old curtains and random bits of dead animal don't exactly chime with her usual glamour: today a fabulous drapey minidress in chic French navy, and some incredible over-the-knee boots with stalky stiletto heels and, I'm sure, signature red soles. And she looks bored to tears by whatever Chief Miranda is nattering on at her about. Which is probably why she hails me, when she sees me, with quite as much enthusiasm as she does.

'Grace. Hi, there!'

'Hi, Lexie. Hello, Miranda. You've made the place look amazing!'

'Well, it's taken me *hours*. I must say, I did think I'd have a few more offers of help from my fund-raising committee members.' Chief Miranda stares, disapprovingly, at both of us. 'Especially when so many things have gone wrong at the last minute. Two dozen of the wine glasses were broken on delivery, and I had to go to three different Waitroses to get enough grapes for Louisa's stall, *and* the caterers cancelled on me only a week ago, and I'm not at all sure the woman I've got to replace them is any good. Oh, she knows you, apparently, Grace. She saw your name on your table, over there, next to where she's set up all the food. She's called Bella something-or-other.'

'Bella Atkins?' I don't know why I'm even bothering

to ask, because as I look over to where Miranda is pointing, I can see Bella herself. She's standing behind a buffet table laden with huge platters of food, trying to persuade a clutch of reluctant-looking yummy mummies to take bread rolls from a wicker basket.

Oh, *shit*. I really don't have the energy to cope with Bella tonight. Especially not here at St Martin's, where she'll just be radiating disapproval about everything, from the conspicuous wealth of the other parents to the way practically everyone in here is on a low-carb diet.

'What a nice surprise,' I half say, half sigh.

'Talking of nice surprises, another friend of yours has showed up tonight,' Miranda says. An expression of satisfaction replaces her deliberate look of put-upon weariness. 'I must say, I wasn't expecting him, but it's *wonderful* that he's here. And such a good sign, too, that he *already* wants to get involved in St Martin's fund-raising!'

'She's talking about your client,' Lexie tells me, because I must be looking slightly bewildered.

'My client?'

'Saad Amar, of course.'

Saad is here?

Oh God, Saad is here.

'What do you mean, her client?' Miranda demands, as I start casting frantic glances over each shoulder, trying to catch a glimpse of Saad amongst the throng.

'Grace is painting a portrait of his girlfriend. A nude, in fact. Isn't that right, Grace?'

'What? Oh . . . yes . . .'

'You *paint*?' Chief Miranda's eyebrows have shot upwards. 'I didn't know you painted.'

'Um, well, I don't like to talk very much about it . . .' Where *is* he? I can't see him anywhere. '. . . in case it disrupts the creative process, you know.'

'But you must be fairly good,' Miranda is carrying on, in a tone of utter amazement that I could be good – that I could be even competent – at anything at all. 'Or Saad Amar wouldn't have commissioned you. Honestly, Grace, you should have *said* something! I mean, what on earth were you thinking, offering up crappy old opera tickets as your auction donation, when *obviously* you can donate your time to paint a professional portrait instead!'

'Oh God, no, Miranda. I don't want to do that.'

'Don't be ridiculous. This is no time for false modesty. Some of the parents here would kill to have a painting done by an artist who's been commissioned by a renowned art lover like Saad Amar. This could raise us five, six grand! At least! Come with me so we can change the details on your table, Grace.' Miranda actually links her arm through mine, and starts leading me in the direction of the table with a sign on it saying 'GRACE COSTELLO OFFERS . . . AN EVENING AT THE OPERA!' 'What should I change this to?' she asks. '"A professional portrait of you, your children, or all the family"? I don't think we want to mention anything about *nudes*, do we? It might entice some of the fathers, but a lot of the mothers will be rather turned off.'

'Honestly, Miranda, I really don't think this is a good idea. My work is . . .' Absolutely non-existent? '. . . really quite experimental, and I'm not sure the parents will get it.'

'Nonsense.' With a flourish, she finishes writing out the new sign for my table and starts to Blu-Tack it over the old one. 'Now, I'm going to start spreading the word, so wait for some bidders to start coming over. And talk yourself up, for God's sake, Grace! You've hidden your light under a bushel for far too long.'

She hurries away before I can tell her that there isn't a light.

I mean, for crying out loud, there isn't even a bushel.

Grace

Friday 18 December

Peering through the growing mass of people in the school hall, trying to spot Saad turns out to be a mistake when I accidentally meet Bella's eye instead. To be fair, it was always going to happen, seeing as her food table is stationed only a few metres away. But I'm surprised by how enthusiastically she hurries over to me.

'Grace, hi.' She leans in to give me what I assume is meant to be her usual brief hug, so I'm embarrassed when it turns out to be an attempt to kiss me on both cheeks. I think she's pretty embarrassed too, because she has to kind of haul me back in for the second kiss, and we both mistime and fumble, and end up practically snogging each other right on the lips.

'All the food looks amazing, Bella,' I tell her, eager as I always am with her to get in a couple of compliments, to curry favour. Anyway, it's hardly a lie. As ever, all her food *does* look amazing. 'And you look great too!' Still not a lie – she does look great, in her short, scary, dynamic kind of way, and I can't help the pang of jealousy that I always feel whenever I see someone making such a terrific success of themselves.

She ignores this. 'I should have remembered your boys come to this school! Or maybe just your older one at the moment? I'm sorry, I've totally forgotten his name.'

Oddly enough, I have too, for a moment. 'Er . . . Robbie.' Luckily Bella isn't the tallest person in the world, so I can still look over her shoulder for any sign of Saad in the crowd. 'Yes, he's very happy here.'

'I'm not surprised. The place is like a palace.'

I knew she'd get in a dig or two about St Martin's' poshness. 'I know. Ridiculous, isn't it? I'd be happier sending him to the local primary, but my husband has other ideas.'

'You know, I don't think I've ever met your husband. Is he here this evening?'

Oh good grief, I'd completely forgotten about Charlie. This will be the first time that he, Saad and I will all be in the same room at the same time since Saad and I began sleeping with each other.

'No, he's not here. Yet. I mean, there's a very good chance he won't make it at all. He did miss our son's carol concert this afternoon, and he might very well be caught late at the office . . .'

'Right.' Bella doesn't seem all that interested, though she's wearing a deliberately friendly expression that I'm not used to. 'Actually, Grace, it's a really good thing I've run into you this evening, because I wanted to ask you a bit of a favour. What are your Christmas plans, if you don't mind me asking?'

This isn't a question I was expecting. I mean, quite

apart from anything else, I've been so caught up with everything that's been going on with Saad that I haven't given much thought to Christmas at all.

'Er, nothing all that exciting. Just staying in London, having my stepson to stay.'

'Excellent! Then I'd love you to come over on Christmas Eve. Say, around eight? Nothing formal, just some drinks, a bit of food . . .' Her eyes are a little bit too wide and bright. 'It'll be a small gathering: my best friend, Anna, and my parents; Polly too, of course . . . and I thought it might be nice if you joined us.'

'Oh!' This is even more unexpected. I've always known Bella isn't exactly my biggest fan, and now she's inviting me over for a Christmas party? 'Um, well, that sounds very nice . . . I'll have to check with Charlie, of course . . .'

'Yes. Look,' Bella takes a step closer, 'even if Charlie can't make it, I'd really appreciate it if you could definitely come along.'

This is starting to sound less like an invitation and more like a three-line whip. Mind you, that's pretty much the definition of an invitation, Bella Atkins-style.

She's about to carry on when we're interrupted by a small gaggle of parents coming to write down their bids for the marvellous professional portrait (ha!) that I'm going to provide for them. There follow a couple of minutes of them asking me about my stylistic techniques and favoured medium, and me fobbing them off with half-baked replies and trying to persuade them not to consider spending very much before they write down their bids and wander off towards the food table to restock their plates.

I assume Bella is going to ask me at what point I suddenly became a professional portrait painter, but she doesn't seem to have paid all that much attention, and is right back to her Christmas party plans as though we've not even been interrupted.

'The thing is, Grace, I might need you there for a bit of . . . well, a bit of moral support.' She takes a deep breath. 'I'm hoping to use the occasion to get Polly back together with Dev.'

It's the first thing she's said that's got my full attention. I stop craning my neck for a glimpse of Saad and look directly at her. 'What?'

'I thought this might just be too good an opportunity to miss,' she's carrying on, talking rather fast. 'I mean, they got engaged on Christmas Eve last year, so she'll probably be feeling quite emotional about that – swoop when she's vulnerable, and everything! – and besides, she can't cause that much of a fuss at a Christmas party! And she can't exactly *argue* if I've just happened to invite Dev to my Christmas party. I mean, he was a friend of mine before he was her boyfriend.'

Ahhh. I get it now. This hastily convened Christmas party is Bella's smokescreen for some meddling into Polly's life. Some pretty ill-advised meddling, if you ask me. I'm just going to have to be a bit braver than I usually am with her and tell her what I think.

'Bella, honestly, this is a bad idea. I don't like this breakup any more than you do, but Polly must have her own reasons for wanting to leave Dev, and we just have to accept that they're good ones.'

'But they're not. They're not good at all. They're . . . look, I don't know how much you've noticed, but Polly isn't in a very good place right now.'

'People don't tend to be, when they call off their wedding.'

'It's more than that. Anyway, she's not miserable because she's called off the wedding, she's called off the wedding because she's miserable. Because for some reason, she doesn't feel worthy of marrying him.'

Now she's started to lose me. And – hang on a moment – was that Saad I just saw, on the other side of the hall? That flash of grey jacket, that fleeting glimpse of jet-black hair?

'The point is,' Bella continues, 'Polly is in crisis. And I for one don't think it's right to just stand by and let her make the biggest mistake of her life with Dev just because she's having some kind of total nervous breakdown.'

This gets my attention back again. 'Polly's having a nervous breakdown?'

'OK, maybe that's taking it too far. But she's in a bad place, Grace. Seriously depressed, at the very least. Why else would Polly – gorgeous, amazing Polly – feel unworthy of getting married?'

I don't know whether to be confused or very, very worried. Or just to laugh. Hysteria feels like it might be starting to bubble up inside me. 'But how do you know she's depressed? She seems OK – well, OK enough – when I talk to her. Has she said anything about feeling depressed? Because she hasn't said anything to me.'

A fact that I'm trying not to take personally, by the way. But if any of this is true, even if it's not quite the full-on breakdown that Bella is claiming, well, why hasn't Polly told me anything about it? I mean, Polly has always told me everything. I mean, *everything*. Her deepest, darkest, most unpleasant secrets. The kind of things you can't even admit to your own reflection in the mirror. The kind of things that, once admitted, you lock away in a little box and shove down as far as you can inside yourself, and try never to think about, let alone talk about, ever again.

Have I become such a rotten friend, so wrapped up in Saad ever since she got back from New York, that she hasn't felt able to tell me about any of this?

'Look, there's no need to get bogged down in those kind of details,' Bella is saying, impatiently. 'It doesn't really matter *how* I know. The fact is that I *do* know. And I know that if she's depressed, she needs Dev more than ever. And that Christmas Eve is the perfect time to –'

'Ambush her?'

'– do something about it.' She eyes me with her usual expression now: something close to dislike. 'Well, I just thought it was worth intervening before something happens that's totally beyond anyone's control. You know, like Dev meeting someone else, or something. Which obviously would devastate Polly. But obviously it's too much trouble for you to come all the way to Shepherd's Bush for a couple of hours for a Christmas party. I just thought it might be helpful to have you around, you know, as Polly's lifelong best friend.'

Brilliant. Just brilliant. Play a fucking symphony on my overwrought and guilty heartstrings, why don't you?

And anyway, I'm not so stressed about the way this evening is turning out that I don't have room for worrying about my best friend too. After all, if Polly really is in the terrible state that Bella is claiming, I really ought to be doing something to help. Instead of taking every free moment I have to be with Saad, or planning on being with Saad, or thinking about being with Saad . . .

'All right, I'll come. But, Bella –'

'Oh, Grace, thank you. You're a star.' She reaches into her trouser pocket and passes me a business card. 'My address is on there. Eight o'clock, Christmas Eve.'

'I'll look forward to it,' I fib, my ingrained politeness coming to the fore. 'Can I bring anything?'

'God, no.' Bella clearly remembers my non-existent culinary skills from years back, when I almost managed to burn down her kitchen making cheese toasties in her flat in Bristol at three o'clock one morning. Me and Polly had gone to stay there, ostensibly to check out the university, but mostly to get very drunk and go clubbing. Mind you, almost burning down her kitchen was the least of the bad things that happened that weekend. Bella continues, 'I mean, no, thank you. Just bring yourself. And your husband, of course, if you'd like.'

I'm about to give her some fob-off of a reply – because I know the last thing Charlie will agree to do on Christmas Eve is go round to a party in Shepherd's Bush – when the crowd near the entrance doors clears for a moment and I see the man himself.

Charlie.

He must have just arrived, because he hasn't yet taken off his scarf and gloves, and he's heading with great purpose for the middle of the hall. In the direction of Louboutin Lexie's stall, in fact.

Which is where Saad is standing.

I was wrong to think I'd caught a glimpse of his grey suit before, because he's wearing dark jeans and a midnight-blue sweater, looking saturnine, and compelling, and casually, almost absurdly handsome. This isn't a fact that's been lost on Lexie, who has abandoned her usual disinterested body language in favour of peering up at him kittenishly as she attempts to engage him in intense conversation. But it's an intense conversation that's interrupted as Charlie reaches them. He's grinning at Saad, extending a hand to shake, a politely confused *what are you doing here* expression on his face.

'I have to go,' I mumble at Bella. 'Great to see you.'

'Hang on a moment, Grace. You must promise me not to say anything to Poll –'

'Not a word,' I call over my shoulder, already heading for Louboutin Lexie myself.

OK, I have to stop this little gathering in its tracks. It was going to be difficult enough to fudge the issue of my secret career as a portraitist with Charlie without Lexie introducing herself to him and mentioning the piece of work I'm meant to be doing for Saad. Or the fact that she's bumped into me round at his place. I feel sick just thinking about it.

'Grace, where do you think you're going?' My elbow is grabbed, and Chief Miranda's shrill voice sounds in my ear. 'You're supposed to be persuading people to bid huge amounts of money at your stall! Not spend ten minutes nattering to the caterer and then set off to do some more socialising! Louisa has already got a bid for over four thousand pounds from one of the hedge-fund dads, and she looks like the back end of a bus. If she can sweet-talk someone into four grand, I'm expecting twice that amount from you!'

'Miranda, for God's sake . . .' I pull my sleeve out of her grip, then realise I'm not going to get out of her way any faster by pissing her off. 'Look, I was just off to get Saad Amar over to my stall. Persuade him to place a bid. I mean, I know I'm already doing a portrait for him,' I add hastily, 'but he's the biggest fish here, isn't he? If I can get him to put his name down for . . . for ten thousand pounds, say, somebody else is sure to come along and out-bid him. Just for the thrill of beating Saad Amar.'

Miranda's eyes narrow, and for a moment I think she's about to snap at me not to be silly and to get back to flirting with random men in Rolexes. But instead she hisses, '*Go, go, go*,' and shoves me so hard in Saad's direction that I stumble and almost knock over a couple of exceptionally scrummy mummies. There's no time to apologise, though, no matter how outraged they look, because I've lost almost an entire precious minute, a minute during which Louboutin Lexie could have dropped me in the biggest pile of steaming horse manure I've ever been dropped in.

But she can't have done. Because Charlie is laughing. As I reach the three of them, he's not glaring at me, or shouting at me. He's laughing.

'Hi, hon! I've just heard the funniest thing about you!' He draws me towards him, placing an arm around my shoulders in the warm, husbandly way he only does when we're in company, and which now makes me freeze like a shop-window dummy, avoiding Saad's eye. 'Apparently you're a big, famous artist!'

Shit. Shit, shit, *shit*.

'And here was me thinking you were just a stay-at-home mom!' Charlie lets out another loud guffaw. 'Honey, I don't know if you met Saad Amar at the MMA party,' he carries on, 'or if you know . . . I'm sorry, I didn't catch your name,' he tells Lexie.

'Lexie.' She's folded her arms, pursed her mouth, and is staring right at me.

'Well, Lexie here is under the impression that you're an artist – no, wait, specifically a portrait painter – and that you're doing some big commission for Saad here. My boss,' he adds, shooting me a private look that's supposed to indicate that I should shake Saad's hand.

OK. What the fuck do I do now? I can't *pretend* to introduce myself to him, because Lexie will scream blue murder about it. No more than I can announce to Charlie that yes, actually, I am a big, famous portrait painter, it's just something I happen to have forgotten to mention over our hurried breakfasts and silent dinners for the past few years.

'Grace, hello there.' Saad takes my frozen hand in his and shakes it. I think – but I'm probably not the best judge of this kind of detail right now – that he adds a light, meaningful squeeze. 'It's lovely to see you,' he goes on ambiguously, before turning to Charlie. 'Your wife was such an enormously helpful supply of information about St Martin's, while I was deciding where to enrol my brother Adnan. So grateful for her assistance.'

Charlie looks confused for a moment but then he obviously remembers that I did mention this matter to him, before the MMA party. Even if I never actually mentioned that I was going ahead and helping Saad myself.

'Oh, well, I'm glad to hear it. Grace is quite the expert on schools in this area. When she's not dashing off another brilliant portrait, that is,' he adds, with another ringing laugh. 'Is there some artist with a similar name, or something?' he asks Lexie, attaching his most charming smile to his lips. Evidently her obvious attractions, in the drapey minidress, haven't eluded him. 'Is that where you think you've heard of my wife?'

'I haven't *heard* of her, I've seen her. Round at his place –' Lexie nods impatiently at Saad – 'doing her nude sketches.'

'Sketches *of* a nude,' Saad interrupts, with a charming smile of his own. His is a good deal more successful than Charlie's, even though I know he must be rattled. 'Anyway, Charlie, it was good to run into you here, I wanted a quick chat about the Brussels deal, if –'

'So wait – you're saying Grace *is* doing a portrait for you?' Charlie is frowning. 'But that doesn't make any sense. Grace doesn't paint. Grace doesn't do anything.'

'I do plenty!' I hear myself say, before I can stop myself.

'Sure, honey, but not *art*.' Charlie squeezes my shoulder. 'Being an artist isn't just about crayoning with Hector, you know! Even if you are a little better than him at staying inside the lines!'

He guffaws again, looking round at all three of us to join in. But none of us does. I'm too humiliated, Lexie is too suspicious, and Saad . . .

Saad is staring at Charlie as if he'd like to kill him. With his bare hands. Very, very slowly.

'Charlie, why don't you come and get something to eat?' It's my turn to try to break up this horrible little foursome. 'You should come and say hi to Bella Atkins as well – Polly's sister – because she's doing the catering, would you believe it? And we should let Lexie get back to getting in bids for her fantastic Scottish holiday . . . and I'm sure Saad – er, Mr Amar – I'm sure he'd like to circulate a bit, get to meet a few more people.'

'Yes. I'd like to do that.'

'But you wanted to speak to me about Brussels?' Charlie says.

'It can wait.' Saad turns abruptly and walks away.

This is the cue, thank God, for Lexie to turn back to her table, and for me to start trying to hustle Charlie in the direction of the buffet. But he's not all that willing to be hustled. In fact, now that we're on our own, his affability has taken a serious hit.

'What the hell was all that about, Grace?'

'OK, look, I probably should have told you.' I've got to stick to this painting thing now, haven't I, seeing as I've got a bloody sign only a few feet from here declaring that I will paint a portrait for the highest bidder. 'I have been doing a bit of painting . . . on the side, as it were . . .'

'But for Saad Amar?' Charlie's face is like thunder. 'And you didn't think to mention it to me?'

'I'm sorry.'

'Do you have any idea what kind of position you've put me in? Dragging my boss into this silly little new hobby of yours? For Christ's *sake*, Grace, do you have any idea how important a guy he is? How important my working relationship with him is? And you want to screw it up by . . . what? Getting him to pay for some crappy painting you're doing? I mean, how the hell did that even come up in the first place? Was that what you were talking to him about that day in the office lobby?' His face darkens further still. 'And is this Lexie right? Did she see you round at his place? Because I'm not happy about that. Or about the fact that you didn't tell me. I mean, do you have any idea of the kind of womanising he's notorious for?'

'I . . . no, I . . .'

He snorts. 'Come on, Grace, why else would a slutty-looking woman like this Lexie be at his house in the first place?'

'I don't think she looks slutty,' I mumble.

'Yeah, well, apparently you don't *think* at all. Because if you did, you'd never have put me in this embarrassing position. What, I have to hear about my wife's new-found career from a total stranger and my boss? I look like an idiot, Grace. So thanks a fucking bunch.'

'I'm sorry,' I say again, prepared to put up with this temper tantrum because I know exactly what I'm really saying sorry for, and it's a lot more than just springing a surprise career on him.

'Yeah, you're sorry. That's fantastic, honey. I need a drink.' He stalks off towards the buffet table.

I don't think it's the time to introduce him to Bella, even though she's the one who ends up pouring him a large gin and tonic. Nor is it the time to mention that we've been invited round to hers on Christmas Eve.

The safest thing, I think, is just to keep my head down, my nerve up, and try to pretend that the past ten minutes just haven't happened. And avoid Saad, at all costs. Especially after the way he was just looking at Charlie.

It's a strategy that works brilliantly, until he ambushes me just as I'm coming out of the ladies', an hour later.

'Saad, I can't talk to you. Not here.'

'Don't be ridiculous.' He's still fizzing with angry energy. 'We're not shagging up against the wall. We're just having a friendly conversation.'

'But Charlie's already suspicious!'

'No, he isn't. Charlie doesn't think you're capable of having an affair. Charlie doesn't think you're capable of doing anything.'

'OK, he can be incredibly dismissive . . .'

'He treats you like a child. No, worse than a child. Like a pet. A fluffy, silly, insignificant pet.'

This stings. 'The way Charlie treats me is absolutely none of your business.'

'Of course it is. It's the business of anyone who cares about you!' He rakes back his hair irritably. 'Don't your parents object to the way he treats you? Your friends?'

I open my mouth to say that my parents haven't showed all that much interest in me since they retired to France (and not all that much interest before that) and that I haven't really had any friends since I married Charlie, apart from Polly, who for most of that time has been three thousand miles away.

But I don't say any of it, partly because it's just too depressing and pathetic, and partly because Saad suddenly steps forward, leans down, and kisses me, hard, on the lips.

I kiss back for a moment before remembering where we are and pulling away. 'Don't! Honestly, Saad, this might all just be a big game to you – turning up on my territory, kissing me in the corridors – but it's my *life* we're talking about! What do you think will happen to me if I get caught?'

'If Charlie ever laid a hand on you –'

'It's not about that, you idiot!' I can't believe I've just called him an idiot. On the other hand, I can't believe he's being one. 'It's about real, horrible, grown-up things like divorce, and finances, and custody. It's about Charlie abandoning Robbie and Hector the same way he's abandoned his eldest son – at best. At worst, taking them away from me and turning them against me. It's about you deciding you're bored with me, or tired of me, and moving onto the next woman without the slightest concern for the havoc you might have left behind you.'

'Grace, that wouldn't happen. I promise you, that wouldn't happen.'

'And I promised Charlie I'd love him, forsaking all others, until death did us part. I'm the last person in the world to be setting any store by promises.'

I start to go past him, but he stops me, grabbing my hand.

'Grace, listen, you can't waste the rest of your life with him. You can't throw away everything you have to offer, have him keep you in your meek little box.' He takes a deep breath. 'Look, no court in the land is going to take your children away from you. And if it's money you're worried about, well, that's just an absurd reason to stay with someone who makes you miserable!'

'Helpful advice, coming from someone who's got billions in the bank. From someone who never has to work, or worry about bills. From someone who can buy Van Goghs and Picassos and . . . and Jimmy Choos at the drop of a hat!'

'And you think that's all that matters to me, do you?' he shoots back. 'You think I don't need anything in my life except pretty possessions? You think I'm happy having everything else in the entire world, if I can't have you?'

I want to kiss him and kick him at the same time. Kiss him because I can't believe he's just said something so unutterably lovely. And kick him for being so naïve, so blasé about the complications he's brought into my life. Before Saad, I'd never even thought about a life without Charlie, miserable though my existence might have been. But now Saad stands here in front of me, heart-stoppingly gorgeous in his midnight-blue sweater, and gives me mad, desperate visions of an alternative reality. A fantasy reality, the kind that a billionaire playboy can inhabit without so much as a backwards glance, but totally off limits to a mother of two without a single useful qualification or skill to her name.

'Grace Costello . . . could somebody please find me Grace Costello?' The voice – Chief Miranda's, multiplied to roughly ten times its usual grating level by a microphone – is coming from inside the hall. 'I have an announcement to make!'

'I have to go,' I blurt, trying to pull my hand away from Saad's. 'People are looking for me.'

'Oh shit.' Saad has turned rather pale, and he lets me go immediately, though he follows me at a careful distance as I start heading for the hall door. 'Grace, listen, you have to understand, I only did this because I couldn't bear the way he was putting you down about your art. And I told the bloody woman in charge that she should keep quiet about it . . .'

I'm not really listening, because all I can think about is getting back into the hall before Charlie notices I'm not around and starts wondering where I've been. As I hurry through the door, I see that Chief Miranda is up on the stage at the far end, that everyone is turned to look at her, and that her face is beetroot pink with a mixture of triumph and shock.

'Ah, Grace! The woman herself! Would you come up here, please?' She's relishing her new role as MC, so much so that as I walk up to her, on shaky legs, I half expect her to break into a chorus of '*Wilkommen, Bienvenue*, Welcome'. 'Ladies and gentlemen, I'm very pleased to be able to announce some quite astonishing news.' She puts an arm around my waist, as though we're the oldest of friends, and actually hugs me to her side. 'I'm sure you've all heard of Grace Costello, and I'm sure many of you have spent the evening frantically bidding for the chance to have her paint your family's portrait.'

I stare across the crowd, to where Charlie is standing right at the back. He's looking bewildered, and annoyed about being bewildered, in equal measure.

'But I'm afraid that unless some of you have *very* much deeper pockets than you care to admit,' Miranda is carrying on, to a polite round of titters, 'your chance to own an original Grace Costello has been lost. Because, ladies and gentlemen, we have received a *staggeringly* generous bid for this particular auction lot. Now, the bidder in question has asked if he can remain anonymous, though I will just say he's done *a mar*-vellous thing, if you catch my drift . . .'

Across the hall from Charlie, still hovering by the door, I see Saad visibly cringe, but he looks too much like a rabbit caught in the headlights to do very much more than that.

I know what Miranda is about to say. Saad has done something stupid, hasn't he? He's bid an absurd amount for 'an original Grace Costello'. Oh God, it could be fifty, a hundred thousand pounds . . . What the fuck is Charlie going to say when he hears this? Is he honestly going to carry on suspecting nothing, when a well-known art connoisseur bids six figures for a painting by crappy old not-even-remotely-a-proper-artist me? Even if it *is* for the good cause of a science block at the school he's about to send his brother to.

'I'm thrilled to be able to announce that this anonymous bid has taken us closer to our target for the new science block than anyone on my fund-raising committee could possibly have dreamed of.' Miranda takes a deep breath. 'Ladies and gentlemen, please put your hands together to congratulate Grace Costello on raising the incredible amount of *one million pounds*!'

There's an audible, collective gasp. A moment later, the entire hall breaks into noisy applause. Miranda hugs me to her side again, raising a clenched fist, as though I've just won an Olympic gold and she's the inspirational coach it's all down to.

I look first one way, and then another. First, to Saad, who's shaking his head at me like the most penitent man alive and mouthing *I'm sorry*. And second, to Charlie. Who's staring at me like I'm the most disgusting woman alive, and not mouthing anything.

Fifty grand might not have done it. A hundred grand, even, and it might still have been just about OK. But with the bidding standing at one million pounds . . . come on. Charlie isn't an idiot.

He knows.

He catches up with me about four paces before I reach the main school gate that leads out onto Fulham Road.

I fled the hall thirty seconds after Miranda finished her announcement, and right now all I want to do is get home. Get anywhere that isn't here.

'Where the hell do you think you're going?'

'Home, Charlie.'

'*No.*' He stops me, grabbing my elbow so hard that it hurts. For an insane moment (as if anything could be more insane than what's just taken place) I wonder if I was naïve to dismiss Saad's comment about Charlie laying a hand on me. 'It is not your home, Grace, to go back to.'

I open my mouth to ask him what he means, but no words come out.

'Everything you have, Grace, is bought and paid for by me. *Everything*. But it's still not enough for you. You have to go after the big prize. The billionaire prize. My fucking *boss*.'

'Charlie.' I find my voice. 'I . . . I didn't go after him.'

'You're *denying* it? He just dropped a million quid on some non-existent painting of yours, and you're denying that there's anything going on between you?'

I don't know I don't know I don't know. Am I denying it? *Can* I deny it? Will denying it make it any better? Will it turn back the clock thirty critical minutes to the time before Saad decided to do the most stupid, the most reckless, the most dangerous thing he could ever have done to me?

'Or are you telling me he's just that fucking charitable?' Charlie still hasn't let go of my elbow. 'Because

I know the way he spends his money, Grace. And believe me, if he just wanted to give a million pound donation to his kid brother's school, he'd find a significantly smarter way to do it.'

'No, I'm not telling you that. I don't know why he bid a million pounds, Charlie.' This much, at least, is true. I *don't* know why he bid the million pounds. I don't know what in God's name he was thinking. 'Look, can we just go home and talk about –'

'I've told you, Grace, there is no *home. Home* is a place for wives and mothers. Not for women who cheat on their husbands! Not for women who take every penny their husband earns, just so they can adorn themselves with all the latest *trinkets* –' he spits the word, taking his hand off my elbow so he can swing it against my handbag – 'to catch the eye of a sugar daddy who can buy them even more stuff!'

'Charlie, please, stop making this all about money!' I'm astonished to hear my own voice rise. 'Money has nothing to do with it! Money isn't the reason I . . . got involved with Saad.'

'Course not,' Charlie sneers. 'Course it wasn't the money. Might have been the houses. The staff. The private island. The cars.' He gestures rather wildly in the direction of the row of cars that are parked beneath the glaring security lights on the wall nearest us; one of them is a dark Aston Martin that has to be Saad's. 'But it *definitely* wasn't the cold, hard cash. How could I possibly think that of a woman like you, Grace?'

'What do you mean, a woman like me?'

'A woman who's always used her looks to get what she wants, no matter who she hurts. A woman who lured me away from my wife and son,' he carries on, wagging a finger in my face, 'because she thought I might be a good meal ticket. A good safe bet for a nice house, and nice things, and a few babies.'

I'm too appalled by this to say anything for a moment. 'Do you really believe that?' I say, when I can speak. 'Or are you just saying it because you're angry with me? I mean, do you really think I *lured* you away from Vanessa and Percy? So that I could give up the degree I loved and settle down to breed? At the age of twenty-one? With someone seventeen years older than me?'

'Oh, is *that* it, as well as the wads of cash?' Charlie lets out a short bark of laughter. 'My boss's youth and good looks? His undoubted prowess in the sack? Because you should know, Grace, that if he's the expert lover I'm sure he is, then it's pretty much all down to good old-fashioned practice.'

'Stop it.'

'That's what makes me laugh the most,' he carries on, 'the fact that you probably think you're the only one. Well, believe me, hon,' he leans in, very close, 'you're nothing special. Nothing special at all.'

'Charlie –'

'You know what? Come to think of it, you should go home. To *my* home. I'll be the one to spend the night in a hotel.' He pushes past me, towards the gates.

'But what shall I tell the boys?'

'Tell them whatever the hell you like, Grace. I'm sure you've had plenty of time to think it all through, while you lay on your back for Saad Amar. But some of us have been caught a little more on the hoof than that. Still, I can catch up with you pretty fast, you know. I'll be speaking to my lawyer first thing in the morning.'

'Charlie, please . . . look, I'm sorry . . .'

But he's out on the Fulham Road now, raising an arm for a passing black cab. 'Oh, it's way too late for sorry, hon,' he says, before he slams the cab door shut.

I stare after him. I wonder, briefly, if I'm going to be sick. Then another, much better, prospect occurs to me. I stride across the car park to Saad's Aston Martin and start to kick it. Just the wheels, at first. God knows why, after the hand grenade he's just chucked into my life, but I can't quite bring myself to do any real damage to the beautiful car itself. But after a moment or two it starts to feel really, seriously cathartic. If that's the right word to describe the blood that's suddenly pumping through my veins. So I aim a good, hard kick at the bumper. It hurts my foot, when it connects, but I still bring my leg back to kick it again.

'Grace!'

It's Saad, running towards me across the car park.

'Grace, stop!'

'Why?' I turn and push him away. To my surprise, it's enough to send him a couple of steps backwards.

If my new-found super-strength is anything to go by, hell hath no fury like a woman exposed as an adulterer in front of the entire parent population of her son's school. 'Because you don't want the dents in your paintwork? Because you don't want something that's precious to you completely ruined?'

'No. Because it's not my Aston Martin.'

Oh.

Oh Christ, I hope I haven't done it any real damage.

Even though whichever ludicrously overpaid St Martin's parent it belongs to will be able to afford the repairs, and even though it's the last thing I should probably be fixating on right now, I pull my diary out of my handbag, rip out a page and start scribbling down my phone number and insurance details to put under the car's windscreen wiper.

'Grace, for God's sake, don't worry about that right now!' Saad is looking at me as if I've gone mad. In fact, he's looking pretty crazy himself – less smooth than I've ever seen him, with stark eyes and positively wild hair, by his usual sleek standards. 'Look, are you all right? I saw Charlie talking to you . . . shouting at you . . . I wanted to come over but I thought it might just make things worse.'

In my mind's eye I see Charlie and Saad rolling around in a death grip on the concrete while a bevy of St Martin's parents, led by Chief Miranda, whoop and holler and place bets on the likely victor.

'That's the only sensible decision you've made all night,' I tell him, folding my note and sticking it under the mystery Aston Martin's windscreen wiper. My voice is shaking even more than the rest of me.

'I know. Grace, I *know*. Look, I'm an idiot! I don't know what got into me. I didn't think it through, I didn't think about the consequences . . .'

'No. But I'm the one who's got to live with them.' I start to stalk towards the gate, but he blocks me.

'No, Grace, no. You don't have to live with them. Not like you think. I mean, you don't have to let him bully you like this. Look, the worst has happened. He knows about us now! So let him carry out every threat he wants to make. Bring it on, and I'll take care of you!'

'Slip some money my way for the lawyers' fees, you mean? Buy me a place to live so that you don't have to feel so guilty when Charlie chucks me out of my house, and where you can come round for a bit of grateful sex until you get tired of me and move me out for the next incumbent?'

'No!' He looks horrified. 'Grace, we've been through this! There isn't another incumbent! There isn't going to be! It's you I care about. Just you.'

'Yeah, right.' I've had enough scorn poured on me by Charlie this evening. It's about time to start redirecting some of that scorn somewhere else. No matter how crushed it makes Saad look. 'What you've done tonight is a funny way to show how much you actually care about me. Please, Saad, get out of my way.'

'Look, let me take you home. You shouldn't be by yourself.'

'I won't be by myself. I have two children. Whom, thanks to you, I somehow have to inform that their dad is leaving. Which is why I need you to let me go. So I can start thinking about how I might set about that.'

He opens his mouth. Then, wordlessly, he steps aside.

I head for the gates.

'Grace, I'm sorry!' he calls after me. 'I'm so sorry . . .'

I put my head down and keep walking.

Bella

Thursday 24 December

I should have known not to tell Mum and Brian that my Christmas Eve party starts at eight. This pretty much guarantees that they'll turn up at roughly half-past five, Brian because he genuinely wants to help, and Mum because she wants to pretend to help. Actually what Mum wants to do (and you can pick any combination of the following) is: interfere, pass judgement, have a bit of a nose around, disapprove of the high-fat items on the menu and take the credit for everyone else's hard work.

But even I'm surprised when the doorbell to my flat rings at four thirty-six precisely.

'Happy Christmas, darling,' says Mum, barging through the front door as soon as I open it. She's in her 'travelling' outfit of black velour tracksuit and leopard-print ballet pumps, unmade-up and with her hair scraped back. Oh shit. This means she'll be planning on getting ready in my bedroom and bathroom, affording me no time to get properly ready myself, and her more opportunities to sneak around in my private things.

'Mum . . .'

She air-kisses me on both cheeks. 'So you're not zhuzhing up the flat, then? That's a shame. I was hoping you'd have put up some tinsel, at least. Ooooh, what are those you're holding?' she adds, looking down at the tray of homemade sausage rolls I was just about to pop in the oven. 'Oh. Sausage. You know, you can make really delicious little savoury pastries with *healthy* ingredients, darling. Spinach and feta, for example. And if you used margarine instead of butter for the pastry, they'd work out at only seventy-five calories a pop.'

Excellent. So we've ticked off interfering, passing judgement, and disapproving of the high-fat items on the menu. And she's not even been here thirty seconds.

'You're early,' I say, helping Brian through the door behind her. He's carrying large bags of extravagantly wrapped Christmas presents that they could probably have left at their hotel until they come round for lunch tomorrow, and that are now going to take up far too much space during the party. They'll have to be stuck in a cupboard, which will offend Mum, who will want them to be – who in fact has specifically brought them here to be – prominently displayed so that all the other guests can see what a generous gift-giver she is.

I take one of the largest bags from Brian, who looks relieved to be rid of the extra weight. 'Robbie and Hector?' I say, reading the labels attached to two large red-wrapped parcels on the top. 'You've brought presents for Grace to take home to her children?'

'Well, *obviously*. Poor little mites.' Mum pulls her

terribly-upset-and-shocked face, which would have a lot more impact if she weren't trying to catch a glimpse of herself in the mirror as she's doing it.

'Polly told us everything about what's happened with Grace,' Brian says, giving me a hug and then taking my sausage roll tray from me as we head into the kitchen. He's popped them into the oven and taken down a spare apron from the back of the kitchen door before I can even tell him to sit down. 'Isn't it terrible?'

'That awful American husband has just walked out on her, you know!' Mum is always keen to be the bearer of dramatic tidings, even if they're old news by now. 'And barely a week before Christmas!'

So evidently Polly hasn't told them *everything*. Because if she had, she might have mentioned the fact that there's a reason why Grace's 'awful' American husband has walked out on her.

I mean, not that Polly's mentioned the full facts of the case to me either, but I was *there*, I'm pretty sure, when it all came out. It was at this auction event I was catering, only a few days ago, at the school Grace's kid goes to. Anyway, one minute Grace was being her usual superior self, patronising me about my job and making it quite clear she'd rather shoot herself in the Manolo-shod foot than come to a party in the iniquitous wilds of Shepherd's Bush, and the next, she was hauled up on stage for this big announcement about some mystery bidder paying a million quid for a painting of hers. A mystery bidder, incidentally, that she's quite clearly been having an affair with. I'd seen her with this ridiculously good-looking playboy type out in the corridor a few minutes before the big announcement, and I saw her again with him afterwards, having a heated debate next to an Aston Martin, when I went out to get a few bits and bobs from my van. Not to mention the fact that the 'awful' American husband (I don't know why I'm bothering to dispute his awfulness; to be entirely fair to Grace, he does look pretty awful) turned on his heel and stalked out of the event before Grace had even come down off the stage.

'He's already filed for divorce, you know,' Mum is carrying on, taking up pride of place at the table, 'and Polly says Grace is terrified he'll be able to take the children, though I can't believe anything like that would happen to a lovely young mother like her, can you? Ooooh, unless she has a drug problem, or something.' Her eyes light up. 'Could that be it? I mean, she does manage to stay beautifully slim, and they do say that's a side effect of cocaine . . .'

Thank God – for once – for Jamie. He's been last-minute Christmas shopping since lunchtime, but now he's loudly announcing his reappearance from the front door. He comes into the kitchen, laden down with shopping bags (he's done all his Christmas shopping at Niketown? *Really?*) and while Mum is distracted by flirting with him, and Brian is offering to pop on the kettle and make him a nice bacon sandwich to line his stomach before tonight, if he'd like one, I grab the chance to head to my bedroom. This is ostensibly to store away Mum's overflowing gift bags and Jamie's Nike bags, but it's actually to clear away anything that I don't want Mum to see.

The cellulite cream on my bedside table, for example, because otherwise she'll only corner me later, by the nibbles, and suggest that I ease up on the cheesy-puffs rather than rely on lotions to *de*-cheesy-puff my thighs. My mobile phone, with Dev at the top of my most recent call list, to check that he's still coming tonight because the last thing I need is Mum discovering this in advance, and accidentally-on-purpose blurting it out to Polly before anyone else – including Dev – gets here. Anything at all to do with the adoption, like the letter that just came yesterday with the details of the first Preparation for Adoption class, in mid-January, because I don't want to talk about the adoption to my mother at the best of times, let alone when I'm also having to endure her flirting with He-Who-Can-Do-No-Wrong Jamie. Anything at all to do with Liam, like the little bag with Christmas presents he left for me and Jamie late last night, before he caught his hideously early flight this morning to spend Christmas with his daughters in Cork . . .

Oh God, Liam's room. Sorry – I mean the *spare* room, with Liam's stuff in it. I'd planned to erase all trace of Liam from it before Mum showed up.

I don't really know why – I mean, it's not as private as my plans for Dev and Polly tonight, or the adoption, or anything – but I'm not inclined to endure her nosiness on this front. She'll be intrigued if she knows we've got someone staying here, and she'll start circling like some kind of emotional hyena around Liam's private tragedies if anybody (a.k.a. Anna) happens to mention to her that he's single, widowed and extremely attractive.

That *Anna* thinks he's extremely attractive, I mean. I'm not saying *I* think he's extremely attractive. Obviously.

I head out of my bedroom – jolly noises of Jamie holding forth and Mum giggling convince me it's not only OK but actually essential that I stay away for another few minutes – and head for the spare room.

I go in without knocking and immediately head to open the curtains so that I can see what I need to do in here. Strip the bed, probably, unless Liam's continued to be the perfect houseguest and has stripped it himself. Put away any clothes he might have left waiting around to be folded. Open the windows; not that I'm saying he's smelly, or anything, because in actual fact he's supremely fresh, but there is a distinctly masculine scent in here that will only have Mum assuming Jamie has been banished to the spare room if she snoops around and gets a sniff of it. You know the kind of smell I mean: pine-scented shower gel, and zingy deodorant, and that nice ginger-nut smell, and . . . well, right now I'm getting a distinctly beery, boozy aroma as well. Which is odd. And which is *really* going to have Mum thinking that Jamie has been banished to the spare room.

The other thing that's odd, I notice the moment I

open the curtains, is that there isn't only a smell of booze, but actual evidence of recent boozing as well. Eight . . . nine . . . ten . . . almost a dozen empty beer bottles. Plus, lying next to the empties, a small stash of Tesco carriers that, when I look inside them, show the paraphernalia of some kind of Instant Christmas-for-One: a box of Quality Street and another of Celebrations; a thawed-out bag of frozen Brussels sprouts; a mini plum pudding; a single breaded turkey escalope in a plastic packet.

'Hnnggh?'

The noise takes me so much by surprise that I actually let out an embarrassing girlie shriek, and drop the Tesco bag I'm holding. When I spin round I realise that it's come from the bed, and that it's Liam.

'Wha . . . hnnng . . . light . . .' he's saying, covering his eyes as he half-sits up in bed. His chest is bare, and – wait a minute – has he had it *waxed*?

Why would he have had it waxed? Is he seeing a woman, or something? Is there someone in bed with him right now?

No, no, thank God, no. It's just a large lump created by what appears to be, from a set of pink plush ears, a giant toy pig. Though obviously the fact that Liam apparently sleeps with a giant toy pig ought to be far more disturbing than the possibility that he was sleeping with a woman.

'What the hell are you doing here?' I demand, when I realise that I'm not supposed to be staring at the toy pig, or at his newly smooth chest, and find my voice.

'Weren't you supposed to be on a flight to Cork at six fifteen this morning? Because if you've overslept –' I gesture at the alarm clock beside the bed – 'you've managed to break even Jamie's record.'

'What time . . . ?'

'Almost five o'clock. In the *afternoon*.' I throw open the window, because the beery, boozy smell isn't getting any better. Then I stare down at him. Studiously avoiding that smooth, firm expanse of bare chest. 'Liam, what on earth have you done? It's Christmas, for God's sake. Your daughters . . . won't they have been waiting for you? At the airport?'

'No.' He slumps backwards against the cuddly pig. It's hard to tell if it's because of a hangover or misery. 'My mother-in-law phoned me yesterday afternoon. Sally's come down with chicken pox. And I've never had it, and what with the third-round interview I've got at Google on the twenty-ninth, I can't afford to catch it.'

'Oh, Liam. I'm so sorry. I know how much you wanted to be with them.'

'Yeah, well. What can you do? Anyway, I Googled it last night, and apparently Sal won't be contagious any more in five or six days' time. So I can go back for New Year, I guess. It's no biggie.'

I'm not fooled by his faux geniality. If it really were 'no biggie', he wouldn't have got as absurdly drunk as he obviously did last night. And fallen asleep clutching what must be one of the girls' Christmas presents.

'Anyway, I promise I won't get in the way of your

Christmas plans. I'll just keep to myself in here from now onwards. Though if you don't mind me using the kitchen for about half an hour or so tomorrow lunchtime . . .'

'To cook this?' I hold up the Tesco carrier.

Which, now that I realise it, really *is* the paraphernalia of some kind of instant Christmas-for-one, and may well be the most depressing thing I've ever seen in my life. If I didn't have a party to throw tonight, and Polly and Dev to get back together, I might hurl myself out of the window right now.

'Oh.' Liam looks embarrassed. No – mortified. 'Oh, bollocks. I must have forgotten to put that in the fridge. I got a bit . . . well, I got a bit drunk last night.' He takes a very deep breath. He isn't looking at me. 'I'm not very good at Christmas, to be honest with you. Never have been. All the details, I mean. I can just about manage to sort out the presents, and I'm always up for the traditional Dempsey walk on the freezing beach, but all the other stuff – the food, the decorations, the festivity – that was always kind of Kerry's thing.'

'Right. Of course.'

'I mean, I don't really know what the fuck I'm doing, to be honest.'

'That's not completely true. I mean, OK, leaving the frozen Brussels and the turkey out overnight is a bit of a rookie mistake. But you were on the right track with the Quality Street and the Celebrations. And you'll be on even more of the right track if you get up, get dressed, and come and endure my family over a couple of my stepdad's lethal White Christmas cocktails. Trust me, you'll have to develop a taste for them if you're going to survive lunch with my mother tomorrow.'

'Bella, I . . .' He looks at me now, a strangulated kind of expression on his face, '. . . I really don't want to intrude. I mean, I've already massively outstayed my welcome here . . .'

'No, you haven't.'

'. . . and now you're having me lurk about the edges of your family's Christmas.'

'So don't lurk. Throw yourself into it.' I don't know if I should say what I'm about to say next, but I feel like I have to. 'Kerry would kill you if she knew you were hiding away from the real world, with a turkey escalope and a plum pudding for one.'

There's a silence. A long one. Far too long for my liking. Then, just as I'm about to start profusely apologising, he says, 'You're right. You're . . . an angel, Bella.'

I snort. It's not a terribly angelic thing to do. But then, nobody has ever accidentally mistaken me for an angel before. I'm not used to acting like one. 'You won't be saying that after I've made you peel three kilos of chestnuts for the stuffing tomorrow morning.'

'Yes I will.'

'Or after I've made you play Trivial Pursuit for three hours, or sent you off to the supermarket to get fresh stocks of crème de menthe . . .' I'm babbling. It's what

I always do when people stare at me the way Liam is staring at me right now. 'In fact, I'd really appreciate it if you could head down to the supermarket right now, actually. Brian really will want to make his White Christmas cocktails, and I'd forgot we'll need crème de menthe, and single cream.'

'They sound revolting.'

'You've no idea.'

'I'd love to try one.' He pushes back the duvet before letting out an embarrassed yelp and pulling it back over himself again. 'God, sorry.'

'It's nothing I haven't seen before.' I don't know why I'm feeling myself turn pink. I mean, he had a pair of jeans on under there, for heaven's sake.

'No, I meant Peppa.' He pulls the cuddly pig out from under the duvet and shoves her, with a rueful expression, back into a Toys R Us bag he's got squashed up at the other end of the bed. 'Sally's favourite TV character. I don't usually sleep with pigs, I'll have you know.'

'Right.'

'No, wait, that sounded wrong! I didn't mean *sleep with* in *that* sense. I meant, actually sleeping with, not having sex with.' He's turning pretty violently pink himself now. 'Not that I was even thinking about sex, when I said that! I mean, it wasn't supposed to be some sleazy *double entendre* . . . I'm not one of those people who get turned on by the idea of cuddly toys! Don't they call them Plushies, or something? I wouldn't want you to think that, Bella . . .'

I think it's probably best to leave him now, before he can get himself into any more of a pickle.

Besides, I've left Jamie alone with Mum and Brian for far too long. Not to mention the fact that I have half a dozen guests arriving three hours from now, my sister's happiness to salvage, and two trays of high-cholesterol mini sausage rolls cooking in the oven.

Bella

Thursday 24 December

By half-past eight, the party is in full swing. Polly is here, thank God, seeing as she's the whole point of this party in the first place. Anna and Poor Pete have arrived, bearing wholly unnecessary amounts of home-made stollen, a vast Yule log, and enough mince pies to feed every elf at the North Pole. Brian has mixed up a big jug of White Christmases, and even though, if you ask me, his hand accidentally slipped when he was adding the brandy, at least it's taking the edge off Mum a bit. Having spent the last two hours dolling herself up in her full Christmas finery (scarlet cocktail dress and glittery accessories) and the last fifteen minutes trapping Liam in a corner and attempting to break the Guinness World Record for Inappropriate Flirting, she's just now come over all woozy and sleepy, and is currently slumped in blissful peace and quiet in the corner of the sofa. (Come to think of it, maybe Brian's hand slipped *deliberately* . . .)

Grace turned up a few minutes ago, for which I was really grateful, given the tsunami that's just hit her personal life. Though I've been just a tiny bit less grateful ever since, because even in the midst of crisis, she's managing to look just as stunning as ever – more stunning, in fact, in tragic black and with dramatic rings around her weepy eyes. Naturally it's a look that appeals to the protective side in most men, so naturally both Jamie and Liam have been hovering solicitously around her, offering drinks and titbits of food and, probably, shoulders to cry on.

Naturally, I'm a little bit pissed off about this.

I mean, Jamie is not a single man. And it's his own girlfriend's bloody Christmas party, so he really shouldn't be hovering around a newly dumped woman. Offering drinks or shoulders or anything at all.

And Liam . . . well, I suppose it's up to him who he hovers around. Bit disappointed in him, I can't deny, that he's the kind of man to go for so *obvious* a type as Grace. You know: tall, slim, blonde, beautiful. But then, that's entirely up to him, of course. And at least he seems to be enjoying himself. The turkey escalope and the frozen Brussels are long forgotten.

So, the only person we're still waiting for is my surprise guest, Dev. Which isn't exactly surprising, given that I told him it was starting at nine. I wanted to get Polly settled in with a couple of drinks before her big surprise shows up – just enough so that she relaxes, not so much that she starts teetering on the edge of aggression – and so far at least, this part of the plan is working pretty well.

She's a large White Christmas cocktail and a glass of white wine down by the time I finally get the chance to catch up with her, properly, in the kitchen.

'It was so nice of you, Bells, to invite Grace,' she says in a low voice, as she starts to help me fill nibbles bowls with top-ups of my spice-roasted almonds and arrange my cheesy-puffs on a baking tray to go into the oven. 'I really think it's good for her, getting out like this. You know, under the circumstances.'

'Oh, that's OK. I thought it would be good for her too.' I quickly suppress my pang of guilt at the little fib. 'She looks exhausted. How is she coping, do you know?'

Polly shrugs. She's looking pretty exhausted herself, and I can't help wishing she'd made a bit more effort for the party tonight, instead of just turning up in baggy jeans and a cardie. Probably an external symptom of this unworthiness she's feeling. Still, she isn't to know that Dev will be arriving at any minute. And I hardly think he's going to feel any differently about her, even if she is looking a bit ropey.

'I don't know. She won't really talk about it. I think there's . . .' She bites her lip. 'It's complicated.'

'There's someone else, you mean?'

She stares at me. 'What? What do you know?'

'Well, obviously I was there, at the school, the night it all kicked off, wasn't I?' I don't know if it's OK to go down this route, because Polly has always had the tendency to clam up about the secrets she and Grace keep from the rest of the world. But then, I'm getting the impression that maybe I know more about this particular secret of Grace's than she does. 'I mean, maybe I'm wrong, but it looked a lot like there was something going on between Grace and some Middle Eastern-looking guy. He looked like a dad at the school. Inasmuch as he looked like a dad at all, that is.'

Her mouth has fallen open. 'She hasn't said . . . I mean, I knew she *liked* him, but . . .'

OK, this is interesting. 'Look, maybe I'm wrong.'

'No, I don't think you are wrong. I think she's just decided not to say anything to me about it.' Polly is turning pink, the way she always does when she's very upset about something.

No, no, no. I can't have her very upset about something. About *anything*. I need her in a good mood, in a good, festive, Christmassy mood, for the moment when Dev knocks at the front door.

'Look, it's basically great news!' I beam at her brightly, then tone it down a watt or two when I remember that, after all, this is the break-up of a young family we're talking about. 'I mean, obviously it'll be terrible for Grace while she's actually going through a divorce, but when it's over, she'll finally be free of that horrible husband of hers. Which is what you've always wanted, isn't it?'

'What do you mean?'

'Come on, Poll! This is me you're talking to! I know why you ran off to New York in the first place, remember? Because of horrible Charlie coming on to you? Only a couple of months after Grace married him?'

Given that this is absolutely, one hundred per cent

true – I mean, I can even recall the tinny taste of the Merlot we were drinking when Polly told me about it, in the airport bar before she caught the flight that took her away to New York for all these years – I can't really understand why Polly is looking at me as though I've just falsely accused her of some terrible crime. Or why she's looking at me like I'm accusing her of any crime at all, falsely or otherwise. But when she opens her mouth, she's gone a bit Gollum-y again.

'I've told you never to mention that, Bella! Why the fuck would you do it now? With Grace in the other room! When her entire fucking life has just gone up in smoke!'

'Poll, calm down, I didn't mean –'

'Need any help in here, ladies?' comes Anna's sing-song voice, as she sashays into the kitchen. She's gone the Mum route, not the Polly route, on the dressing-up front, and is wearing a rather fabulous silvery dress that clings to every curve because, as she told me gleefully when she arrived earlier, 'in a month or so my bump will start growing, and then it'll be kaftans and trackie bottoms all the way!'

'No, we're fine.' Polly composes herself with startling speed, though she does head straight to the fridge to get out the bottle of white wine, and refill her glass almost all the way to the brim. 'Anna, can I get you a top-up?'

'Oooooh, no, only soft drinks for me, Polly. And a few more of these amazing sausage rolls,' she adds, scooping some up from the plate I've just refilled.

'Now that I'm eating for two! I assume Bella's told you?'

'Told me what?'

The entirely delusional idea that she's pregnant. 'Actually, Anna, I haven't said anything to Polly yet. I didn't know if I was supposed to be saying anything, until you were, you know, *sure*.'

'Bella!' Anna rolls her eyes, pops in a sausage roll, and turns back to Polly. 'Honestly, your sister! She seems to want assurance from the Vatican, the Pentagon, and half a dozen separate spy satellites before she'll believe that I'm pregnant!'

'You're *pregnant*?'

'Mm-hmm. And I know it's a bit too early to be certain of this, but I have the strongest suspicion that it's multiple babies. Twins, at least. I'm hoping even triplets.'

Polly looks from Anna to me, and back again. 'Wow . . . Anna . . . that's . . . it's great news. For you.' She swallows, very hard. 'Are *you* OK about this, Bella?'

'Polly!' Anna's pregnancy may be totally fictional, but until she accepts this herself, we still need to go by the usual rules of polite behaviour. And polite behaviour is not greeting the announcement of a pregnancy with a stricken enquiry as to whether somebody else is OK about it. 'That's rude!'

'I'm sorry.' Now Polly is staring at Anna. 'I'm really pleased for you, Anna, of course. I just . . . you know, with Bella's situation . . .'

'I understand completely.' Anna is more magnanimous than ever now that she's so content. And now that she's on what I think is at least her tenth mini sausage roll of the evening. 'But with any luck, Bells and I will end up being first-time mothers together! I mean, knock on wood about the adoption and all that!'

I don't think this is the time or place to say that I think it might take quite a lot more than knocking on wood to see this adoption through to the bitter end. Like getting a personality transplant for my boyfriend, perhaps.

'Anyway!' Anna carries on super-brightly, as if to try to cut through the weird atmosphere she's inadvertently walked into. 'I won't have you two shutting yourselves away in here, not when it's Christmas Eve! I'm up for a bit of a boogie, if either of you will come and help me shove back the sofa. By the way,' she adds to me, in a low voice, as Polly makes a start towards the living room, and we follow, 'I really came in to tell you that you might want to come and sort out the situation with the Black Widow in there. Grace, I mean. I think you might want to prise your man off her.'

I feel almost winded by a sudden blow of jealousy. 'Liam?'

'*Jamie.*' Anna stares at me. 'Hence the fact I said "*your man*".'

'Oh! Of course. That's who I meant.'

'Right. That's who you meant.'

I ignore her pointed tone as we walk into the living

room, where – oh, for the love of God – Jamie is quite literally all over Grace. He's kind of backed her into a corner, and put an arm around her shoulders, and as I approach I can hear him saying, in a very un-Jamie-like tone of immense gentleness, 'You know, sweetheart, if there's anything at all I can do to help, just say the word.'

'That's so nice of you,' Grace is gulping, 'but I'm honestly OK . . . Oh, Bella! Hi!' She looks relieved, rather than guilty, as I approach, which makes me think Anna has been just the tiniest bit unfair in describing her as a Black Widow. I mean, it's not *her* fault she attracts men, what with those doe eyes and those mile-long legs, and that delicate, porcelain skin . . .

Oh, who am I kidding? I've never really trusted Grace. And that's not about to change just because she's going through a dreadful personal tragedy.

'Hi, Grace. Jamie.' I shoot him a pointed look but I can tell, immediately, that he's already the worse for wear for however many of Brian's White Christmases he's just seen off in that empty glass he's holding. We're probably at around DEFCON 3 right now. 'Everything OK here?'

'Yeah, babe, everything's fine. But I think maybe Grace could do with another drink. Right, sweetheart?'

'No, really, I'm fine.' Grace gives a watery smile and waggles her own full glass at both of us. Drinking to excess really isn't a very Grace-like thing, even on

Christmas Eve. And even in the throes of a fresh divorce. 'Everything's really lovely, Bella. Thank you so much for having me. And – um – is there any sign of anyone else arriving yet?'

'You mean your bastard of an ex-husband?' Jamie demands, before I can subtly indicate to Grace that actually, Dev should be here any minute. 'Bella wouldn't have him through the front door, would you, Bells? Do you know, babe, he's threatened Grace with eviction from their house? Told her she'll end up in a B&B, without the kids.'

'That's terrible,' I say, and mean it.

'Yeah, well, I've already given Grace my lawyer's number. He's cheap, and tough as nails, and he'll help her out.'

Christ, he's even further on the road to DEFCON 4 or 5 than I thought. I'm just about to tell him, gently but firmly, that he doesn't have a lawyer, when Grace speaks.

'It's really good of you, Jamie, but I don't think he'll be able to do very much to help me. It's a divorce lawyer I need, I'm afraid, not a criminal lawyer.'

What the hell? I mean, I know the White Christmases are lethal – look at Mum, fast asleep now, over there on the sofa – and I know Jamie's keen to impress posh, ethereal Grace with his bad-boy ways. But pretending he's got criminal lawyers on his speed dial? Has the booze triggered a psychotic break, or something?

'Grace, I'm sorry, you've not met Jamie before, but

sometimes it's best to take him with a pinch of salt!' I let out a little laugh. 'He's teasing you, and he shouldn't. This is a serious situation Grace is in, J. She really does need a lawyer. You mustn't waste her time pretending you know one.'

'Well, *obviously* I know one, Bella!' Jamie glares at me through slightly glazed eyes. 'And he's fucking good, too. I would never have got probation as early as I did if it weren't for him.'

This time my laugh is louder. 'What are you talking about, probation?'

'Probation, babe. From prison. For my GBH conviction.'

The living room suddenly seems to get very, very small, and very, very hot. 'GBH?'

'Come on, babe, you know all about this!' But there's a panicky look in Jamie's eyes. It's absurd to think of this right now, but it's a bit like the look he gets when I accuse him of farting in bed; he claims he hasn't, and then the terrible toxic smell starts to creep towards us, unavoidable evidence that he's tried to pull a fast one. Except right now, it's a hell of a lot guiltier-looking. 'You know I did seven months, for so-called assaulting my auntie's landlord in Kilburn . . . Hey, there's no need to look at me like I've just shot Bambi!' he laughs, but there's a hollow sound to it. 'And it's not like it sounds.' He turns to Grace, either because he wants to convince her that he's not a hardened violent criminal, or because he can't look me in the eye. 'This bloke gave as good as he got. And he'd been causing nothing but grief for my Auntie Eileen for months by the time I finally lost it with him. Always threatening to put up her rent, and never coming round to fix any of the lousy old appliances he'd saddled her with . . .'

'Sure. Um . . . it sounds awful.' Grace is looking embarrassed, and extremely uncomfortable. 'I might just go and get a bit of food, actually, if it's OK by you?'

As she slips away, Jamie looks at me again. 'All right, all right, maybe I haven't mentioned it to you. But it was three years before we met, at least! And it's not like it really *matters*.'

'Not like it really matters?' I echo. 'But I told you . . .' *Didn't* I tell him? '. . . when we were first talking about adoption, that we'd have to go through all kinds of police records checks. That they'd probably trawl through every parking ticket and fender-bender but that it would only be a problem if either of us had any kind of serious criminal conviction. You know. Like grievous bodily harm. Or something.'

Jamie swallows. 'Oh. Right. Shit. I don't remember you saying that.'

'No. No, you wouldn't, would you?' I feel my fists clench into tight, lethal balls and think, just for one moment, about drawing back one of them and smashing it into Jamie's face. Shattering a few of his teeth, perhaps. To go along with my dreams. 'You wouldn't remember, because you were probably doing something really important at the time. Like watching

Manchester United. Or recovering from a hangover.'

'Right. Yeah. Sorry, babe. Might have been.'

I take a deep breath. 'I mean, this isn't a small thing we're talking about here. We'll have to tell Samantha, and I don't think –'

'Who's Samantha?'

I'm just about to scream at him, at the top of my lungs, *For the hundredth time, she's our fucking adoption social worker*, when the doorbell rings.

This reminds me that I have a roomful of people here, most of whom are shamelessly eavesdropping on my conversation with Jamie, and that Dev is probably the one ringing the front doorbell.

'I need to get that.' I stumble away from Jamie and out into the corridor.

The last thing I need is Polly following me.

'Bells! Bella, stop.' She puts her hand on my shoulder before I've even reached the front door. 'I heard that. I mean, I heard some of it . . . this is crazy. You can't stay with him now! Not if you ever want to adopt a baby! No adoption agency in the land is going to look twice at you, with a prospective father who's been in prison – in *prison*, Bella! – for violent crime.'

'Polly, not this again.' I push her hand away, then turn to face her, plastering a smile over my face that I know for a fact isn't coming anywhere close to reaching my eyes. I'm willing myself to forget about Jamie, just for a few minutes, just while I get Polly and Dev talking. 'Let me get the door, OK?'

'Oh, come on, it'll just be some manky carol singers,

or something. Ignore it. You're upset.'

'I'm not upset. I'm fine!' I make sure my smile is even wider – God, my cheeks ache – as I reach to open the front door.

Thank God something is going right this evening. The way things are, it might well have been some manky carol singers. But it isn't. As planned, it's Dev.

He's looking very handsome, and very nervous, smartly and sweetly dressed up in a dark suit, with a check scarf and a blue coat folded over his arm.

'Bella!' he says. And then, noticing her behind me, 'Poll.' His Adam's apple lifts and lowers. 'Um. Happy Christmas.'

Polly is staring at him like he's the Ghost of Christmas Past. 'What are you doing here?' she whispers.

'Bella invited me. Didn't she . . . didn't she tell you?'

'No. She didn't tell me.'

'Well! There's no point in standing out there freezing!' I usher him indoors. 'Come on in, get warm.'

'I can't believe this,' Polly says. 'I can't believe you've done this, Bella.'

'Done what?' I can see Grace, hovering nervously in the living-room doorway, and I motion for her to come over. I have the feeling I might need a little bit of backup. 'Look, I just thought – *me and Grace* just thought – you might like to catch up with Dev, it being Christmas and everything.'

'You planned this too?' Polly spins round to look at Grace.

'No! It was Bella's idea.' Grace – or should I call her *Judas*? – looks like she wishes the floor would open up and swallow her whole. 'I mean, I knew about it, but I didn't plan it. But now that he's here . . . I mean, you were supposed to be getting married a week from now,' she adds lamely. 'Don't you think it's a bit silly to have let things get to the point where you won't even talk to him?'

'If she doesn't want to talk to me,' Dev interjects, doing his best not to look like a broken man, 'then it's fine. I'll just leave, and –'

'No. No, *I'll* leave.' There's a sob in Polly's voice. She starts pushing past Dev. Then she does a very, very odd thing. As she passes him, she makes a sudden grab for him, holding him tightly to her for three seconds . . . four . . . five . . .

It doesn't last. His own arms come up, after a moment of shock, to go around her. Which is when she lets go of him, moves for the front door, and slams it behind her.

I want Dev to go after her, but he refuses. He looks too shell-shocked to be of much use, anyway. My second choice is for me to go, alone, but Grace insists on coming with me.

We catch up with Polly as she wrestles with the tricky catch on the gate at the bottom of my front path.

'Leave me alone!' she commands.

'Polly, please, come back inside.'

'I cannot *believe* you did that to me!' Ignoring her

own professed desire to be left alone, she turns round to face us. In the unflattering orange streetlight, her face looks hollow, her cheeks sunken. 'I told you – I told both of you – just to forget about the idea of me and Dev being together! And what do you do? You scheme and plot together to dangle him under my nose!'

'We didn't scheme. Or plot,' Grace begins.

'And why would I believe anything you say?' Polly rounds on her. 'You didn't even tell me you were seeing Locanda Locatelli guy!'

'I . . . I haven't been . . .'

'Don't lie! Bella knows all about it. Just another one of the ways in which you two are oh-so-cosy together these days, apparently. I mean, who'd have ever thought the two of you would *band together* like this?' Her voice is heavy with sarcasm. 'The dynamic duo, putting aside twenty years of animosity, just to save poor little Polly! Well, it's easy, isn't it, to come up with a clever little plan to bring about the precious wedding you're both so keen on me having? Far easier than either of you sorting out the mess you're making of your own lives.'

Neither Grace nor I say anything. I suspect that, like me, she doesn't have the faintest idea what to say.

'I should never have come home,' Polly is saying, turning back to the gate and managing to flip the tricky catch this time. 'I should never have tried to make anything right with both of you. I just wanted to stop feeling so *guilty*. And then, maybe, I could have made things work with Dev –' She breaks off. She's looking over my shoulder, and I suddenly realise that there is noise and activity behind us.

When I turn round, I see that it's Anna. She's flanked by Poor Pete on one side, and Dev on the other, and she's holding her stomach, doubled over in pain. My first thought is that she should never have been eating so many of those sausage rolls. But then I realise that Anna's cheeks are tear-stained, and that Pete is looking stricken. Something is very much more serious here than a dodgy tummy from over-enthusiasm on the sausage roll front.

'We're getting her into the car,' Dev says, in his calm, steady doctor's voice, 'and taking her to the hospital. It's very likely that she's having a miscarriage.'

I stare at the three of them. 'But . . . she's not even pregnant.'

Dev's face – and thank God, I think he's the only one that's heard me – tells me that I'm wrong.

So I dart forward to help them with Anna, putting my arm round her as Pete fumbles for his car keys, and Dev gets the passenger door open, and then we all start gently loading her into her seat and fastening her seatbelt, before getting into the car ourselves.

I see Grace's shocked face, where she's still standing on the garden path, as Poor Pete pulls away from the kerb.

And it's only then that I realise that Polly has gone.

*

When my taxi finally pulls up outside the flat, bringing me home from the hospital, it's two o'clock in the morning. Christmas morning. Yay. Happy Christmas.

Though, actually, it is a happy Christmas, in one way. One very important way.

Because Anna really is pregnant. More to the point, she really is *still* pregnant. The horrible, frightening suspected miscarriage was, in fact, a combination of perfectly ordinary early-pregnancy spotting and – I *knew* it – far too many sausage rolls.

Anna burst into tears when she heard, and I think Pete was just about ready to kiss Dev, who slipped away quietly after being the one to tell them the good news. They're keeping her in hospital overnight, just to be safe, but with any luck she should be home for Christmas.

'Here we are, then, love,' says my driver, as I get out of the taxi and start shoving a twenty-pound note towards him. He waves it away. 'Nah. It's on me. You look like you've had a pretty rough night. Things bad at the hospital, were they?'

As always, the small kindness makes my eyes start to water. 'No . . . no, things weren't bad at the hospital at all. They were very, very good at the hospital. My best friend is pregnant.'

'Oh, well! That's nice, love. You must be thrilled for her.'

'Yes, I am. I really, really am. It's . . .' I glance up at the windows of my flat. They're dark, but I can see a flickering strobe-like light from – what else? – the Wii. 'It's here, actually, where the problem is.'

'Right . . .' He's lost a bit of interest, I can tell. Either that, or he just wants to get back into the West End and pick up Christmas Eve revellers who won't get all teary-eyed on him and make him feel obliged to cancel their fares. 'Well. Christmas is always a difficult time, isn't it? Brings a lot of emotions to the surface. Best thing is, go inside, crack open a nice bottle of wine, and hope Father Christmas makes everything better when you wake up. Yeah?'

I nod, and manage a smile, and watch him as he trundles off along the road, in the direction of Shepherd's Bush roundabout.

Thank God for Brian, with whom I kept in touch from the hospital, and whom I know has cleared away the food and drink and, even more importantly, cleared away Mum. He texted an hour or so ago to say they were back at their hotel and they'd be round late morning tomorrow for presents and Christmas lunch. So at least the flat looks clean and tidy as I let myself in.

There's nothing for it, really, but to go straight into the living room. But I stop, before I go in, because I can hear voices. And not the weird, electronic tones of the announcer on the Wii, but real voices. Jamie's, for one. And Liam's, for another.

'You remember how it was, mate,' Jamie is saying. 'And all right, GBH *sounds* really, really bad. But the other guy was an arsehole.'

'Bella isn't trying to adopt a child with the other

guy.' This is Liam. 'You really are a bit of a fucking fool, Jamie. What were you thinking, not telling her?'

'I didn't think it would ever really matter. I didn't think it would ever be an issue.'

'You thought you could get out of the police checks?' Liam sounds astonished.

Jamie doesn't say anything for a moment. There's just the plinky-plonk of the Wii. Then he says, 'I thought I could get out of the adoption.'

It feels like someone's just punched me very hard in the stomach. It doesn't hurt any less when I realise that, on some level, I knew it was coming.

When I've got over enough of the feeling of being winded, I peer through the half-open living-room door. I can see Jamie, slumped on the sofa, with a dejected look on his face; as if Manchester United have just lost a game. I think because, to Jamie, upsetting me *is* like Manchester United have just lost a game. It's not something he enjoys, or something he wants to happen. It's just no more of a big deal than that.

'Then you should have told her that,' says Liam, whose face I can't see.

'Look, it isn't like I *planned* it. I didn't sit down and think, hey, my girlfriend wants to adopt a kid, but I don't, so maybe I'll just keep quiet about it and hope it goes away . . .' Jamie tails off. 'I just don't know, now that it's staring me in the face, if it's something I'm really all that up for.'

'Christ, Jamie, listen to yourself!' There's a little bit of affection mixed in with a lot of irritation in Liam's voice. 'Don't you ever look at your life, and realise how lucky you are? To have a woman like Bella – an amazing, funny, beautiful woman like Bella – and to throw that away because you're not really *all that up* for making a proper life with her? When you know that's a thing that a lot of people would kill for?'

I don't move a muscle. I don't even breathe.

What does Liam mean by this?

Oh, wait a moment. I get it. He means Kerry. What he's really saying – even if he's using my name – is that *Kerry* was an amazing, funny, beautiful woman. That his life with her was just stolen in a flash, and nobody should take anything like that for granted.

Jamie's answer is to get to his feet, yawn, and stretch. 'Yeah, well, I'm too knackered to think about any of this tonight. I'm going to crash.'

Which means that any moment, he'll be walking right past me in the hallway.

I'm not ready for that encounter right now. I just can't do it. I don't even care that it's freezing cold outside, or that it's gone two o'clock on Christmas morning. I'm going for a walk. A long, long walk, until Jamie is fast asleep, and I can slip in to my side of the bed without waking him.

I move swiftly and silently to the front door, open it, and pull it shut with an almost inaudible click behind me.

Grace

Friday 25 December

When the electricity cuts off, at one thirty on Christmas Day, with a turkey in the oven and five pans of vegetables ready to go onto the hob, there's a small part of me that wonders if Charlie has put in a call to the power company and deliberately arranged the power cut, just to spite me.

The call I put in of my own, however, assures me via a soulless automated voice message, that in fact it's three whole streets that are out of power, that they are doing everything they can to fix the problem as fast as possible, and that I should call back for regular updates. So I stop thinking it's anything to do with Charlie.

Unless, of course, he's so focused on hating me, from the friend's flat he's staying in up in West Hampstead, that the power of his righteous anger has caused a small part of the National Grid to short-circuit.

When I hang up on the soulless automated voice, I try calling Polly, for at least the tenth time today. I desperately want to apologise for upsetting her last night, and I desperately need to hear a kind voice right now.

Her phone cuts straight to voicemail, for at least the tenth time today. So I leave a pathetically jokey message, asking her if she has any idea how to cook a turkey in a cold oven, and wondering if she's up for coming round and getting horribly drunk later on tonight. I'm just ending the call when I hear the front door open, and Charlie letting himself in.

He greets me with a look of twisted disgust on his face that's enough to make me wonder if I'm right about the power cut after all.

'Where are the boys?' is all he says to me, as he carries a bag of presents in, not bothering to wipe his feet on the doormat.

'They're in the garden. Percy is showing Robbie how to work the electric car your parents sent him.'

'Well, tell them to come in, for Christ's sake! I came over to spend Christmas Day with them, not stand around in a freezing cold garden trying to work a stupid toy.'

I don't say that actually, the only reason I suggested they go out into the garden was because Charlie was due to arrive almost two hours ago, and I thought a run-around out there might distract them from the fact he was late.

'Sure. I'll call them in. They should probably have a snack, anyway. Lunch is going to be delayed, because there's a power cut, and –'

'This is all your department, Grace,' he interrupts me coldly. 'I'm sorry, but I don't have all that much interest in your home-making trials and tribulations any more.' He pushes past me, determined to go out into the chilly garden now that I've expressed a reason of my own to bring the boys indoors. 'That can all be Saad Amar's concern, now.'

'Charlie, I've told you, it's all over with him!' Told him every day this past week, in pathetically begging text messages and emails that I'd be ashamed to send if I weren't all maxed out on the shame front. And if I weren't trying to save the only family my children have ever known. 'I'm not going to see him again! It was a huge mistake. *Huge*. And I'm so, so sorry.'

'You're right, it was a huge mistake. And you should be sorry.' Charlie's using the icy, clipped tone that accompanies my hysterical one these days – when he actually decides to speak to me at all, that is. 'You'll be even more sorry when Valentine has finished wiping the floor with you.'

The incongruously named Valentine is his freshly (re)appointed divorce lawyer, and the bogeyman Charlie has been scaring me with this past week.

'Oh, and just in case you were thinking of going out and having a little spending spree in the sales tomorrow, you should know that I'll be handing in my notice to MMA once the holidays are over – I mean, I don't know how I can be expected to work for my ex-wife's lover – so money is going to be pretty tight for you, I'm afraid. Even before Valentine has proposed a suitable settlement.'

I don't know why he thinks I've been planning shopping sprees. Or why he thinks he can scare me with looming penury. I mean, I'm scared enough of everything else for that to be pretty low down on my list right now.

'Oh God, Charlie, please don't leave MMA.'

'Why? So that you can feel less like you've destroyed my life?'

'No! Because you enjoy your job, and you're good at it, and –'

'Well, maybe you should have thought of that,' he says, a sneer taking up residence on his lips, 'before you opened your legs for my boss.'

Even if he weren't already heading for the back garden, I'd have absolutely nothing I could say to that.

The point is, he's right. I didn't think of anything. I refused to think of anything. Charlie's job. The effect on the boys. All I thought about – selfishly, *stupidly* – was Saad, and how incredible he made me feel.

To be honest, a whole lot of what I'm still thinking about – now just plain moronically – is Saad. Though this is partly just because it's taking so much effort to ignore his calls, and his texts, and – waiting for me when I got back home from Bella's disastrous party last night – an actual letter, shoved through the letter box. I opened it before I realised what it was, only to see that it was a version of the handmade card I made for Saad all those weeks ago. He'd photocopied my drawing of the Starbucks-drinking Van Gogh cow, and added, in the background, his own rather wobbly and endearingly rubbish drawings of two figures that I think were meant to be me and him, holding hands and smiling at each other. It made my heart hurt, just looking at it. Which is why I burned it, without reading the long letter inside. Burned my hand too, incidentally, which made me understand a little bit about what self-harm might be all about. The searing pain that shot through my finger, followed by the extreme soreness as I've chopped the veg and basted the turkey today, feel like penance for my terrible sin. I'd burn it again, five times over, if it would help ease the pain I've caused everybody else. I'd start wearing a hair shirt, and one of those horrible bonkers metal spike things the mad monk wears in the Da Vinci Code, and wake up in the middle of the night to scourge myself for three hours before sunrise, if it would turn the clock back to . . .

Well, to when? To the time before I started having an affair with Saad, so that I could stop it before it had even begun?

Or just to the time before Charlie found out?

The truly terrible thing is that despite all my agonies of regret, and the suffocating weight of guilt about what I've done to my family, I'm not sure I could put my hand on my heart and say I wish I'd never done what I did with Saad. That's how truly happy he made me.

'Mummy!' It's Robbie and Hector, pressing their noses up against the glass at the side of the front door. They've come round through the side gate into the front garden, which is only going to enrage Charlie even more, both because they're not supposed to know how to open the side gate (thanks for that, Percy) and because they've clearly run off the moment he's gone out there. Mind you, if he's doing the same with the electric car as he did with a remote-control plane last Christmas – taking it over, refusing to allow them to have a go in case they damage it, and barking at them when they get in the way – I can't exactly blame them. 'Mummy, Mummy, Santa Claus came!' Hector sings at me, as I open the door to let them in.

'I know, darling. Are you happy with the things he brought you?' By which, of course, I mean, are you happy, full stop? Do you mind that I've blighted your childhood by forcing your dad to divorce me? Has the fact that I've practically bankrupted myself (OK, practically bankrupted Charlie, but thanks to the fanatical Valentine, the end result will be the same) buying extra toys and games and chocolate made your Christmas as good as I always want it to be? 'Is the electric car good fun?'

'Yes, but that was from *Grandma and Grandpa*,' Robbie explains, with the weary patience he's picked up from Percy this past week. '*Santa* brought us different things. Santa brought me a water pistol, and a baseball mitt, and a Spongebob Squarepants annual . . .'

'We should really say thank you,' Hector adds, more serious than ever.

'Yes, that's a lovely idea. When Christmas is over, we'll write and say thank you to Santa. Now, don't the two of you want to go out and play with Daddy for a bit?'

They look reluctant.

'We're cold and hungry now,' Robbie informs me.

'Well, maybe you can have something to eat, and warm up a bit, and *then* go outside and play with Daddy.' I force a smile onto my face, trying to sound as positive as the slew of Coping with Divorce and Not Totally Screwing Up Your Children books I got from Amazon have bossily instructed me to. 'He's come all the way from North London to have lunch and play with you today!'

'Santa came all the way from the North *Pole*,' Hector says. 'I think we should have lunch with *him* instead.'

When I marshal them into the kitchen for a snack – homemade gingerbread men (only slightly burned) that I baked at four o'clock this morning! I'm not the world's worst mother after all! – I can see Percy and Charlie through the window. They're standing about ten feet apart, on opposite sides of the garden, while Charlie operates the electric car. They're not talking.

They don't talk much all day, in fact. Lunch, when it eventually hits the table at four thirty, is a pretty dismal affair, and not only because as soon as the power came back on, I had to heat-blast the turkey to within an inch of its life (or should that be death?), so that it's gone appallingly dry and chewy. Nor is it because the roast potatoes haven't really recovered from their slow start and have soaked up masses of oil to become soggy and leaden. Nor because I'm just a rubbish cook, who hasn't even managed to serve up a vegetable, root or crucifer, that isn't either under- or over-done.

It's because Charlie is pinch-lipped and silent at one end of the table, Percy morose and monosyllabic at the other, leaving Robbie bewildered, me desperate, and Hector still chattering on and on about inviting Santa for lunch, to anyone who will listen.

I think we're all relieved when a decent amount of time has passed and Charlie can take his leave of us without having to feel that he's done anything at all, unlike me, to Ruin Christmas.

Though actually, in the grand scheme of things, this is pretty ironic. Because from my point of view, Charlie has ruined plenty of Christmases. Hector's first Christmas, for example, when I was still permanently chained to the washing machine and the breast pump, and Charlie suddenly announced (on the twenty-third of December) that his parents had decided to come over to meet the baby, and would I mind *making* the mince pies this year rather than buying them from the Finest selection in Tesco, because they'd be so disappointed if they felt I wasn't doing a proper English Christmas. Or the first Christmas we had together, with his sister in Chicago, before the boys came along, when Charlie got his American and English sizes back to front, bought me a slinky negligee that was two sizes too small, and then spent the rest of the day wondering out loud if I should really be eating so much of that pecan pie, or drinking so much of that eggnog, as though I was fat rather than he being dim enough not to check the sizes.

Still, I know those things pale into insignificance in the wake of my crime.

Anyway, while he buttons his coat in the hall, he mutters threats at me about lawyers' letters, and how the courts take a dim view of a mother's adultery. He's so stoked up with righteous fury that my fresh round of apologies runs off him like water off a duck's back.

'Words are pretty meaningless,' he tells me, just before he stalks out towards the waiting cab that will take him back to West Hampstead, 'coming from a *liar* and a *cheat*.'

I just about make it through the boys' bathtime without bursting into tears, tuck them up into bed with promises of a walk to see the deer in Richmond Park tomorrow, and then I head downstairs again. I'm planning on pouring myself the largest gin and tonic the world has ever seen, desperately trying to call Polly again, and, if she doesn't answer, going out into the back garden and howling into the night air until at least a tiny part of this utter misery lifts itself from my shoulders.

I've forgotten – because he's been so quiet all day – about Percy.

He's sitting at the kitchen table, plugged simultaneously into his iPod and his iPad, while also sending a text message on his iPhone. Part of me wonders if I should start calling him iPercy.

He looks up, smiles, and – this is an honour indeed – takes both plugs of his iPod out of his ears. 'Hi.'

'Hi, Perce.' I think I may have to forgo the world's largest gin and tonic until he's in bed. My life may be falling apart but I'm not sure it's OK to demonstrate, to a teenage boy with a documented liking for pot, that mind-altering substances are the best way to deal with a bad situation. Toast, maybe, is the soft solution. 'I'm just going to make myself a bit of toast. Do you want any? Or anything else? A turkey sandwich? A jacket potato?'

'Yeah, toast would be good.' He watches me while I get the bread out and put it in the toaster. 'Thanks for the lunch, and everything. I hope Dad wasn't too mean to you.'

Something about his voice makes me turn round and look at him. He's got the strangest expression on his face, and I suddenly realise that this must be hideous for him, too. I've been so focused on Robbie and Hector that I've forgotten that this is the second divorce in Percy's young life. Another thing for me to feel sick with guilt about.

'Perce, you mustn't worry about things like that!' My mind flits to a bit of the psychobabble I read in one of the bossy divorce books from my new Amazon stash. 'I really want you to understand that even though things might be a little bit rocky between me and your dad for a while, everything will settle down in the end. And that I'll still always be here for you, no matter what happens.'

'You mean, when you're not my stepmother any more?'

'Oh, Percy. I'll always be your stepmother.'

'Good.' He grins, fleetingly. 'Because lots of the guys at school saw you when you dropped me off at the start of term, and they all think I've got the fittest stepmother in the world.'

'Right. Er . . . that's nice.'

His grin is replaced by a scowl. 'I seriously don't want Celia dropping me off at school, ever. There's no way I'm ever going to think of her as my stepmother. Not like you.'

I accidentally press the pop-up button on the toaster, then reflexively grab the hot toast as it shoots upwards, burning my already-burned hand again. '*Sorry?*'

'Celia. Dad's girlfriend. It's OK, Grace. You don't have to protect me from this stuff. I know all about her.'

Then how come I don't?

'Are you talking,' I say faintly, 'about your dad's secretary at work?' The one Malcolm Morley's wife thought was a 'silly little thing', the blonde in the short skirt? 'That Celia?'

'Yeah. That Celia.' Percy kicks the chair leg in front of him, moodily. 'First his secretary, then his girlfriend. For months and months. Your friend Thomas told me, that afternoon he met me at Paddington. I wasn't supposed to mention it to anyone, but I figured now Dad wants to get divorced from you, and everything, it would just be weird if I pretended I didn't know. Wouldn't it?'

'Yes . . . it would . . .'

'Anyway, I hope you're not too upset about it, Grace. You know you're miles better off without Dad, anyway, don't you? The same way Mum's been better off without him. The same way *I'm* better off without him. I mean, I'd be a basket case by now if I'd had to live with him the whole time I was growing up.' He lets out a little grunt of laughter. 'Hey, maybe this Celia cow has done Robbie and Hector a favour the same way you did me a favour, taking Dad out of the picture a bit . . . Is that them thumping around up there now?' he adds as we're suddenly interrupted by a thud from above, which is Robbie's bedroom. 'D'you want me to go up and check on them while you butter the toast?'

'No, I'll go.'

But my legs are wobbling so much as I climb the stairs that I'm almost worried they won't carry me.

Is this true? Actually, forget that. This *is* true. I know it's true.

All those late nights 'at the office', the 'client dinners', the meetings he just couldn't reschedule to come to his son's carol concert. His slavish devotion to late-night emailing on his BlackBerry. His total lack of interest in me, even when I was throwing myself at him in that stupid cheerleader outfit.

But more to the point, there's the intangible stuff too. The fact that, even though I didn't even talk to

Celia at that party – because Saad steered me away from her – I do recall that she's exactly the kind of pretty, mousy, extremely young little thing I was when Charlie first met me.

I wonder if she's the 'friend' he's staying with in West Hampstead.

I wonder how lucky he must have felt when he caught me out having a fling of my own.

I wonder if he's enjoyed coldly punishing me quite as much as he has, over the last week, because he's projecting onto me some deep-seated guilt of his own.

I wonder, though, if Charlie is actually capable of feeling guilt.

I'm in a bit of a daze as I open the door to Robbie's room, so I'm taken aback to see that he's out of his bed and that Hector is there with him. They're both huddled up together at the window, peeking out from the robot-patterned curtains to look down onto the street below.

'Do you think he'll come out?' Hector is whispering.

'He might,' says Robbie. 'He still has to give Mummy some presents . . . Oh, hello, Mummy,' he adds, noticing my presence as I come up behind them. 'We couldn't sleep because we're still too excited about Santa.'

'Robbie, darling, Santa has gone away now.' This might upset them; I must try to focus. 'What I mean is, he's gone away for another year. Back home to the North Pole. But he'll come back next Christmas, if you're both very good.'

'But he's still *here*,' Hector insists. He grabs my hand and pulls me closer to the window, pushing back the curtain so that I can see clearly. 'Look! Santa!'

He's pointing at Saad's shiny blue Bentley, which is parked on the opposite side of the street.

'That was the car Santa came in last time, wasn't it, Mummy?' Robbie looks up at me, slightly uncertain now, and checking. 'When he brought you the pretty shoes?'

'Yes.' My voice is a weird croak. 'Uh . . . is this the Santa you've been talking about today, boys?'

'*Yes.*' Hector is impatient. 'He's been here *all day*. We haven't seen him, but we know he's inside. Just *waiting*.'

'We don't know,' Robbie adds, 'what he is waiting for. But maybe he's lost, or something, Mummy. Maybe he needs directions back to the North Pole.'

'Maybe.' I start for the door. 'Mummy will just go and see what he wants, OK?'

'Tell him we've been very good!' Hector's voice floats after me, as I hurry down the stairs. 'And take a carrot for Rudolf!'

It's freezing outside now, with drizzle coming down that's only a degree or two away from turning into sleet. I'm unsuitably dressed in my jeans and thin sweater, not to mention the fact that I've only just remembered I'm not wearing shoes, just the comedy reindeer bedsocks that were Percy's Christmas present to me. So my feet are already soaking wet by the time I reach the Bentley, and tap on the window.

The back door opens immediately.

'No! Get back in!' I shove Thomas back into the car, clambering in myself before Robbie and Hector, who I'm quite sure are still watching, can see that 'Santa' isn't wearing full festive red-and-ermine regalia, but a heavy black coat and a rather natty Burberry check scarf.

And before the car's other occupant – Saad, of course – can think about getting out, either.

'Grace!' He leans forward from where he's sitting on the back seat, takes my hands and pulls me down to sit next to him. 'Are you all right? You're freezing! Would you like some coffee? Thomas, pour Grace some coffee. Or would you like something stronger?' he adds, as Thomas, bent double, starts shuffling around in a huge picnic basket that's on the floor of the vehicle. 'We have some pretty good fifty-year-old single malt, or Thomas has been desperate for a chance to crack open the Baileys. And we've got McDonald's leftovers, too, though they're probably a little bit cold by now.'

'I don't want a drink! Or McDonald's leftovers! I want to know what you're doing here.' I stare right at him, which is more difficult than I thought it would be. Because he looks so truly *lovely*. He's all muffled up in a big black ski jacket, plus a new-looking Burberry scarf that – I have a suspicion – might have been a Christmas present from Thomas. His hair is sticking up a bit on one side, as though he's been dozing in an uncomfortable position, and there are the faintest dark circles under his ink-black eyes. He looks in need of a good night's sleep. And, like I already said, truly lovely. But I can't let myself get distracted by that now. 'Have you been here all day? What in God's name were you thinking? With Charlie coming for Christmas, and everything . . .'

'Thomas, could you get into the front and give us a moment alone?' Saad puts out a hand to stop Thomas from rootling around looking for his bottle of Baileys.

'No, wait, you have to get out the other side,' I tell Thomas, as, with an expression of infinite patience, he clambers for the door. 'My two little boys are watching from upstairs, and they're waiting for a glimpse of Santa Claus,' I add apologetically. 'Would you mind being really, really careful and getting into the front without them seeing you?'

'Certainly, Mrs Cos – Grace.' He nods at me. 'I will ensure that I am invisible from all possible sightlines from the house.'

For the first time, I actually trust him. After all, I don't think his telling Percy about Charlie's affair with Celia was a malicious thing. I think he was doing what Saad wanted him to do. I think the information was supposed to filter back to me, eventually.

I wait for Thomas to have slid silently out of the back of the car and behind the black panel that separates us from the front before I say, 'So. Charlie's been having an affair with his secretary.'

Saad swallows. 'You know?'

'You wanted me to know.'

'Yes. No. Well, yes.' He lets out a long, exhausted sigh. 'Look, I don't know what I wanted, Grace. All I know is that everyone at the office knew about Celia, that I knew about Celia, and that it's been killing me that you didn't know about Celia. Especially when you kept feeling so guilty about what we were doing. When Charlie has been at it for months.'

'For years, I think, probably.' My mind is racing back to a couple of Charlie's former secretaries and young female colleagues at Farrell Christie Dench, his old firm. The funny looks they'd give me when I'd turn up for office Christmas parties. The way Charlie was suddenly managed out of the firm when a new boss took over: a tough, no-nonsense, middle-aged woman boss who perhaps didn't take kindly to Charlie's extra-office activities. The way *she* looked at me, at the one office party when I met her, with a kind of confused, pitying expression on her face, that I misread for disapproval of my stay-at-home-mother status. 'But it still doesn't mean it was OK for me to cheat on him.'

'OK, maybe not. But it certainly means you don't have to feel quite so torn up with guilt about it. And it certainly means he can stop acting so bloody superior to you. I mean, I saw his face when he left the house earlier, Grace, and he looked so fucking *pleased* with himself, I could have got out of the car and knocked his front teeth out.'

I smother a laugh. I can't help it. Partly at the image of Charlie with no front teeth, partly at the vision of

Saad peeking up over the edge of the car window to spy on the house all afternoon like some kind of lunatic cop on a stakeout, and partly just because I can feel low-level hysteria creeping in. 'Was that what you came round for? To sit outside the house waiting for Charlie, so you could smash his teeth in?'

'No!' Saad runs a hand though his hair, giving even more oomph to the sticking-up bit. 'I wasn't even sure if Charlie was going to be coming, until I saw him arrive. Of course that's not why I came. It's just . . . look, you haven't been returning my calls, or my texts, and I knew you wouldn't even have read my letter, and I've been worrying about you. And I can't stand it. I can't stand not being able to see you, and talk to you, and hold you. So I just . . . came over. Maybe I didn't think it through enough.'

I gesture at the picnic basket. 'It looks like you thought it through enough to bring supplies.'

'That was Thomas's idea. As soon as he knew I wasn't going to be talked out of it. I think he knew that as soon as I got here, I wouldn't want to go anywhere else.'

'But it's Christmas Day.' I mean, didn't he want to spend it with his family, or with some fellow billionaire friends? In his beautiful house, or at a fabulous hotel, or on whatever private island the Amars collectively own? Instead of sitting in a freezing car on one of the shabbier streets in Fulham, drinking whisky and eating cold Chicken McNuggets with his slightly obsessive housekeeper?

Now he looks at me, and it's as if he's read my mind. 'Grace, you don't understand. Christmas or no Christmas, I don't have anywhere better to be than here.'

The small explosion of happiness I feel inside is the first thing I've felt in days that hasn't hurt.

It's what propels me the few inches across the back seat towards Saad, and what makes me start to kiss him like I've never kissed him before. His lips feel incredible. His arms, wrapped tightly around me, feel even better. And for the first time in twenty years, I really do believe in Santa Claus.

Bella

Friday 25 December
As hideous Christmases go, this one has been right up there with the best of them.

Mum has been hungover ever since she and Brian arrived just before midday, a very (very) long eight hours ago. She's been sitting about the flat looking like a wet weekend and complaining: that it's too cold/warm/damp/stuffy; that the smell of cooking is making her feel sick; that Brian is giving her a headache with the noise of gently prising open roasted chestnuts and scooping out the soft flesh; that the Queen's yellow suit is so bright it's hurting her eyes; that the goose is too rich; that the brandy butter is too buttery. And too brandied. And Christmas pudding has enough calories in it anyway, without adding lumps of booze-soaked fat.

It's a wonder, really, that any of us got through our own bowls of Christmas pudding without dropping down dead from lard-induced heart attacks. Or leaning across the table and setting fire to my mother's eyebrows with the box of matches that was brought in to flame the pudding.

I came close, by the way. Several times. Such as

when Mum decided to reserve her only pleasant words of the day for Jamie, cooing at him as she handed over her barely touched plate of perfectly roasted goose and her uneaten portion of Christmas pudding, and urging him to 'eat up, eat up, God knows you need the strength to cope with Bella!'

Mind you, Jamie's been pretty thick with her, too. Offering her his tried-and-tested hangover tips (never mind that she'd rather burn off her *own* eyebrows than eat a fried ham-and-cheese sandwich, or drink a raw egg in a pint of Guinness) and sitting with her in front of the TV most of the afternoon, agreeing that the Queen looks like a canary in a wig and that Roger Moore is a better Bond than Sean Connery could ever have hoped to be, and raving about the bottle of whisky and the aftershave she bought him rather than admitting that he's never worn aftershave a day in his life and that whisky gives him diarrhoea.

Though I'm pretty sure the only reason Jamie's putting in so much time with Mum is that it's a sure-fire way of avoiding me. Which I know he's doing, because he hasn't said more than three words to me since he got up this morning ('Happy Christmas, Bells') and because every time I go into a room, he finds an excuse to leave it.

Still, I can hardly complain about him avoiding me. Let's face it, I'm avoiding him, too. Why else did I wander the frozen streets of Shepherd's Bush until two o'clock this morning? Why else was I weak with relief when I finally crept back in through the front door to see that the living-room lights were off, and that there wasn't even any thin TV light flickering from underneath the door of our bedroom?

Liam's bedroom light *was* still on, incidentally. It did cross my mind that maybe he was waiting up for me, just to be sure that I got back OK. Especially as, by the time I'd gone into the kitchen for a glass of water and then come back out into the hallway again, his bedroom light had gone off.

But probably he was just staying up to read, or something, and only realised the time when he heard the front door shut and looked at his clock to see what time I was crawling in. Hence the sudden lights-out. Nothing to do with being worried about me at all.

Still, bless him either way for being as stoical as he has been today, in the face of Mum's hangover hellishness and me and Jamie circling each other like wary wild animals. This can't have been the Christmas he was hoping for, even if he had known he'd be stuck in London rather than with his beloved daughters. Actually, he's ended up spending most of the day in the kitchen, chatting to Brian and offering to help with menial chopping and peeling tasks, while Mum and Jamie have cosied up in front of the telly and I've spent what felt like hours on end sitting in front of my dressing table, staring at myself in the mirror and wondering if I should give up on becoming a mother – let's face it, someone in charge of the universe seems to think that's a pretty bad idea – or give up on Jamie.

Oh, and trying to get hold of Polly. That's been my

other main activity of the day. Not made any easier by the fact that she's not answering her phone. According to Brian she called him and Mum this morning to wish them a happy Christmas and told them she'd decided, under the circumstances (of me *This Is Your Life*-ing her with her ex-fiancé, I suppose), that she'd spend the day with friends instead. Which 'friends', I've no idea. I'd have tried calling Grace to see if she's gone there, but I assume Polly is almost as annoyed with her as she is with me. Either way, and whoever she's with, it's just another thing that's contributing to my miserable Christmas Day.

It's a mixture of relief (no more Mum!) and panic (no more stalling over what to do about Jamie!) when Brian finally announces they're leaving, a little after eight o'clock.

'Now, there were only a couple of slices of the goose left over, but I know you always like to try to turn them into a bit of a savoury pie, so I've put them in some foil in the fridge,' he's saying to me, as we stand by the front door and he starts trying to help Mum into her coat. 'And please tell Anna I'd love her recipe for that Christmas pudding, won't you?'

'Oh, for heaven's sake, Brian, Anna's going to have better things to do over the next few weeks than pass around recipes!' Mum bats his help away and slips her coat over her shoulders, wearing it like some Garbo-esque cape. 'Tell her from me, Bella, that the thing she'll want to focus some serious attention on in the first three months is making sure she doesn't just *balloon*. You know, women *think* they can suddenly eat for two, but really it's only a very few extra calories they need to nourish an unborn baby. And Anna's already carrying quite a spare tyre around her tummy and hips, so if she's not incredibly careful –'

'Yes, Mum. I'll tell Anna that while carrying the baby she's almost driven herself insane to conceive, she'd better watch out that her middle doesn't get fat and flabby.'

'Not just her middle!' Mum completely misses my dripping sarcasm. 'Pregnancy does dreadful things to your thighs – I never had an ounce of cellulite until I was expecting you – and she won't want her face to get all bloated, either. She'll regret it, when she wants nice photos taken of her and the baby at the christening. Oh, and if you're going to be a godmother, darling, *please* try to think enough in advance and pick out something nice to wear. Black trousers are *so* inappropriate for a nice church christening, and it's not as if they do very much for your figure, either.'

Bad as it's already been, Christmas has already plummeted a few further notches down the Disaster scale by the time Brian has got Mum out of the flat, into the car, and safely headed towards the M4 to Wiltshire.

But as soon as they're gone, I realise that I'd rather stand at the front door letting in a draught of cold air and listening to Mum's bitching all night than go and talk to Jamie.

'Babe.'

Oh. He's beaten me to it.

When I turn round, he's standing in our bedroom doorway, with his well-practised puppy-dog expression on his face and a small, flat, Christmassy-wrapped parcel in his hand.

'We haven't given each other our presents yet,' he says.

It's true, we haven't. I've completely forgotten about the gifts I've bought for him: a posh leather Filofax for him to record all his new Keenan Landscapes appointments in (ha!), and one of those electronic photo frames that I thought one day soon he might like to put pictures of our new son or daughter in. They're still in their carrier bags, at the bottom of my wardrobe. I'd have wrapped them late last night, over a rum-laced hot chocolate, if I hadn't been out wandering the streets instead.

I head for the bedroom myself just as I notice the living-room door closing gently shut. Liam, giving us our privacy.

'And look, I know you're still upset with me about yesterday,' Jamie carries on, following me and looking pleased that I've come into the bedroom, 'but you have to know, babe, that I really wasn't trying to keep it a secret from you. It honestly slipped my mind, the whole prison thing.'

'Understandable.'

'Exactly!' He's the second person in the last few minutes not to pick up on my sarcasm. 'And like I said, it's not something I'm too proud of. Not something I'd ever go around talking about!'

'Even to your girlfriend.'

'Even to my girlfriend,' he agrees, solemnly. He sits down on the bed and pats it for me to sit next to him. For some reason, I do. He puts an arm around my shoulders. 'Anyway, I've been waiting all day to apologise to you about it, let you know how bad I feel. But I hope you notice that I've done my best to help you out today – you know, pull my weight with your mum and stuff.'

'*That's* what you've been doing?' I blink at him.

His chocolatey eyes blink back at me. 'Absolutely! You deserve a nice Christmas, Bells. You deserve the best.'

I can't help myself. I lean into the crook of his arm, letting my weight fall against him. It feels so nice. Gorgeous Jamie, big and strong, with his arms around me. It's the kind of feeling that could make me start to wonder why I'd ever risk giving him up in favour of adopting a child. Or rather, *trying* to adopt a child. Let's face it, even if I didn't have an ex-convict for a boyfriend, there's no guarantee that my adoption would work out. There could be all kinds of other reasons why I'd be turned down. All right, nothing as concrete as failing the police checks, but you never know, do you? If there's one thing I should have learned from my life, it's that the best-laid plans have a nasty tendency to go pear-shaped. I could end up without Jamie *and* without a child.

Wouldn't it be better just to settle for Jamie?

'So, happy Christmas, babe.' He hands me the tiny,

flat parcel. 'Go on! Open it,' he adds, in a can't-wait-to-see-the-look-on-your-face kind of voice. 'I really hope this is something that'll make you realise how committed I am to our future together.'

I pull at the tape, unfold the red-and-green wrapping, and look at the present inside.

It's a red plastic two-card wallet, a bit like the one I used to have for my Oyster Card before I stopped going on the tube and started going everywhere in my van.

'It's . . . for credit cards?'

'No!' Jamie laughs, grabs the wallet from me and flips it open. 'It's your very own Manchester United season ticket!'

So it is. Inside the wallet, on the left-hand side, is a small plastic card featuring the club's famous red crest and the words 'Manchester United Football Club, 2011–2012 Season'.

'And don't worry, I've got one for myself, of course! Oh, and before you start worrying that I've spent too much, the season's already a few months in so I got the pair of them for only eight hundred! From that new mate of mine over in South Kensington. Small problem, they're not seats next to each other – actually, they're eighteen rows apart – but I didn't think you'd mind that, Bells. Gorgeous girl like you, you'll make a load of friends at Old Trafford before you've even taken your seat! Anyway, we'll be travelling up and down together, of course, and we can meet for a drink at half-time.'

'But most of the matches are on weekends.' I've pulled out of his embrace now, and I'm staring at him.

'See? You're learning more about football already!'

'Weekends when I work. When my clients have their parties, and their lunches, and their buffet suppers. Saturdays and Sundays.'

'But you're your own boss, Bells! You can take off one day every other weekend, can't you? Especially now you're not going to have to be worrying about fitting in your working hours around a small kid.'

'What do you mean?'

'Well, it's like you said yesterday, isn't it? We don't stand all that much chance of adopting, what with my past history.' There's a slightly hopeful tinge to his voice; I can't believe I didn't notice it there when he talked about the adoption before. Because it *was* there. It was definitely there, all along. 'I mean, you would have had a lot less time for work if you'd had a kid to look after, anyway. Why not just look at it that way?'

I take a long, steadying breath. 'So what you're saying is that a bi-monthly trip up the M6 to Manchester is just as good a way for me to use my time as looking after our child?'

'Well, we could take the M1, if you preferred. Stop off at this nice pub I know in –'

'And that after a decade of me wanting a child, and years of planning to adopt a child, I should drop the dream just like that, without so much as a backwards glance? Because my boyfriend has a criminal record he didn't tell me about, and because he thinks a few trips to Old Trafford are a good substitute for parenthood?'

Jamie shuffles his feet. He stares at the floor, sheepishly. 'Well, I thought I was your fiancé, not just your boyfriend,' he says. 'But if you're having second thoughts about that . . .'

I let out a giggle. It takes me by surprise as much as it obviously takes Jamie by surprise. I mean, let's face it, this is no laughing matter. Or is it?

'Hey, this isn't funny, you know,' Jamie says indignantly.

'It is a little bit funny.' I'm still giggling. 'You buying a United season ticket for someone who could barely tell you the difference between football and rugby. Me buying you a Filofax for your non-existent gardening appointments and a photo frame for pictures of a child you never wanted.'

'I never said . . .' He stops. 'I'll get gardening appointments, you know,' he mumbles, after a moment. 'These things just take time.'

I feel a sudden rush of affection for him. Because he hasn't denied everything I just said; he hasn't contradicted what I said about a child. It's probably the most honest he's ever been about it. It feels as if some kind of pressure valve inside me has been gently, carefully released, leaving me about a ton lighter in the process.

'That wasn't my point,' I say, putting my hand lightly on his knee. 'I wasn't meaning to be rude about your gardening business. I only meant that we were buying presents for the wrong people. You bought a present for a woman who's happy to spend her weekends travelling to football games, and drinking in pubs. And I bought presents for a man who wants a nice steady job and a tight little family. But the trouble is, J, that I'm not that woman. You're not that man. And I just think,' I carry on, as he finally turns to look at me, 'that both of us would be better off trying to find that woman and that man. Or even going it alone. Rather than stumbling on together and both missing out on the things we really want in our lives.'

Jamie's full, soft mouth falls open, just slightly. 'Are you *dumping* me?'

'No, Jamie, I'm not. I'm freeing you. And I think you need to free me. Because honestly, as Christmas presents go, it's the best thing we could possibly give each other.'

There aren't any tears; no recriminations. OK, there aren't all that many more giggles, either. But as breakups on Christmas Night go, I think this one is about as civilised and painless as it comes.

If anything – if I weren't still feeling the pressure-valve relief and the sudden loss of all the weight I've been carrying (metaphysical, sadly, not actual; my demolition of Brian's roast goose has put paid to any possibility of that) – I might even be a tiny bit insulted that Jamie has shuffled out of my life without much of a fight. But I've no right to be insulted, seeing as I'm the one who gave him the push to set him shuffling. And seeing as Jamie shuffles into pretty much everything he does, without an agenda, or real commitment, or that much enthusiasm. He's taken his leave of me with pretty much the same *I mean, why the fuck not?* attitude with which he suggested our engagement.

He has at least, bless him, tried to put the faintest patina of respectability on things by disappearing to the pub to 'drown his sorrows'. Even though I think he'll hardly be surprised to find that his sorrows are excellent swimmers, practically Olympic gold-medal standard at the backstroke and butterfly. He's said he'll sleep on the sofa when he gets back, and move in with one of The Boys tomorrow.

I feel like I could do with a long, strong drink myself – Brian's leftover booze is calling me – but first of all I wash my face, scrub off my mascara, and change into my pyjamas. My old, comfy, checked ones with the loose elastic and missing buttons, that is, rather than the slippery black satin ones Mum's just given me as my Christmas present. Mum's choice of nightwear looks more suitable for greeting gentleman callers at the door of a Shanghai whorehouse than for drinking a schooner of cream sherry in front of rubbish late-night Christmas TV, which is how I intend to spend my first couple of hours as a singleton.

I've assumed that Liam has accompanied Jamie to the pub, because I heard the two of them exchanging a few inaudible words in the living room, followed by lots of heavy footsteps to the front door, followed by total silence. I set one foot outside my bedroom door before I realise that I'm wrong.

Liam is half-crouched right outside, in the act of setting down a tray of something. When he sees my (grotty, unloved) bare feet, he straightens up so fast I'm surprised he doesn't get the bends.

'Hey! Sorry! I wasn't lurking out here or anything. I was just leaving you that.'

'That' refers to the tray he's put down, my favourite slatted wooden one, loaded up with a mug of tea, Jamie's new bottle of whisky, a wodge of holly-print napkins and the ceramic basin containing the remains of Anna's Christmas pudding.

'I wasn't sure,' he carries on awkwardly, 'if you wanted a hot drink, a forty per cent proof drink, a good cry or a stodge blow-out. I mean, I haven't been dumped by anyone in a very, very long time, so I'm afraid I'm not too sure of the protocols.'

I stare at him. 'Jamie said he'd dumped *me*?'

'Er, yeah.' Liam muses on this for a moment, scratching his head. 'But then, come to think of it, Jamie also once said that our school football coach told him that if he'd not messed up his ankle when he was thirteen he would have been talent-scouted by Manchester United and had a career on the left wing to rival Ryan Giggs. So he does have a tendency to talk a vast amount of incredible bollocks.'

'That he does.' And I sort of don't really care. About what Jamie said about who dumped whom, that is. I've far more important things to think about right now than my pride.

Like the fact that Liam seems more concerned about taking care of me than going out for a pint with his newly single mate.

Like the fact that being in such close proximity to him in the boxy hallway is for some reason making my chest go all thuddy.

Like the fact that my own chest – at least, one side of it – is making a bid for freedom from between the two halves of my pyjama top where there aren't any buttons to fasten it. Which must be why Liam's gaze has travelled twenty centimetres south of my chin, and why he's turning rather red.

'Oh, crap!' I yelp, covering myself up the moment I realise I'm accidentally flashing him. 'God, I'm sorry.'

'Don't be.' He takes a couple of hasty steps backwards. 'I'll just . . . er . . . leave you to select your refreshment . . .'

My heart, which was the thing causing all that thudding a moment ago, has sunk. I'm just so disappointed that we're back here again: an awkward, uncomfortable encounter, once more featuring naked body parts. And it's not even as if Liam looked at all . . . well, at all *pleased* to encounter my left boob. Though why would he, I suppose, given that it's always been the droopier of the two, and that it's not exactly flattered by the grungy grey of my ancient pyjamas?

'. . . and I wasn't looking, by the way,' he's carrying on, turning more red than ever. 'Well, I *did* look – I mean, obviously it caught my eye – but I wasn't *staring*. I wouldn't want you to think that I was, you know, eyeing you up. Especially not under the circumstances.'

'The circumstances?'

'Yeah. That you've just broken up with someone. Which means, of course, that you're available. Not that it would have been OK to stare at your breasts if you *weren't* available!' he adds frantically. 'It's just that . . . well, it's different, of course, now that you are.'

'Now that I am, er, what?'

He stops backing away. 'Available,' he says.

There's a bit of a silence. It isn't an awkward one this time. It's filled, after a moment or two, in my head at least, by the return of that thuddy noise. Because now he actually is staring at me. And I'm staring right back at him.

'Do you really,' I ask, through a weirdly dry mouth, 'think I'm available?'

'Oh God, I'm sorry, Bella, I didn't mean to offend you. Look, I know you're not really available. You've only broken up with Jamie fifteen minutes ago. And he's a mate of mine, of course.'

'But if he weren't. And if I'd broken up with him longer than fifteen minutes ago.' Jesus, I really don't know what's happening to me. Even the Sahara-like sensation in my mouth isn't stopping me from talking. 'Then would you think I was available?'

He doesn't reply for a moment. Then he says,

slowly, 'You're asking me if I wonder if you're available *to me*.'

'Yes.'

'Then yes. Yes, Bella. I am wondering that.'

'I see. Well, that's . . . significant.' *That's significant?* How have I managed to turn this into what sounds like a business negotiation?

'And what about me?' Liam puts one arm up against the wall, in what is probably an attempt to look casual. Actually, it makes him look rather sexy. 'I mean, I don't know if you've ever wondered about *my* availability.'

Oh, good, so it's not just me, then. He's as bad at the slushy stuff as I am. If I've just made it sound like a business negotiation, he's just made it sound as though he's putting out a tender for some kind of unpleasant job that I need doing. Having the drains unblocked, perhaps, or scouring the oven.

'Actually you don't need to answer that.' He takes his arm down from the wall, giving up any attempt to look casual and looking as though he feels rather foolish all of a sudden. 'I know I'm not all that much of a catch. There's my girls, and there's Kerry – well, there *was* Kerry – and I still don't have a job to my name over here, although the signs were really good from that second interview at Google, and I know I'm not exactly an Adonis, especially when I leave it too long without getting my back waxed – Kerry always used to nag me about that –'

'Liam, stop. Body hair or no body hair, you're a

catch, OK? You're a serious catch.'

He takes a breath. 'Well, so are you. I mean, not that you need to worry about body hair. Not that you need to worry about your body at all, in fact. It's perfect. *You're* perfect.' He takes a step in my direction. 'I don't know if I should say this, Bella. You've only just broken up with Jamie. You're vulnerable. The last thing I want is to take advantage.'

'Well, say it anyway.' I grin at him. 'Then we can debate whether I'm too vulnerable for it or not.'

He takes another, bigger step, so that he's right in front of me. 'OK, small confession.' He smiles now too. 'It's not so much something I wanted to say as something I wanted to do.'

OK. This is it. I turn my face up to him.

But he doesn't kiss me. He leans down, wraps his arms around me, and holds me for a long, long moment in the warmest, most comfortable hug I've ever had in my life. *Then* he kisses me.

I honestly don't know how much time passes before I realise that, behind us in the bedroom, my phone has started to ring.

I wouldn't answer it – nothing on earth could be more important than Liam's kisses right now – but it's Polly's ringtone. And under the circumstances I'm going to have to make an early exception.

'I'm so sorry, I have to get that.' I pull reluctantly away. 'It's my sister.'

'No problem.' He grins down at me. He looks – and the expression has never felt more apt – as if all his

Christmases have come at once. 'There's plenty more where that came from.'

Now *that* I like the sound of. Because the early round of kisses was fantastic enough to make me a tiny bit trembly as I grab my phone. 'Poll?'

'Bella?'

'Polly, I've been trying you all day! Look, are you OK? Brian said you told him you were going to friends for the day, but I didn't think you'd have gone to Grace's, not after yesterday, and I couldn't think who else to –'

'I spent it with Dev.'

I almost drop the phone. 'With *Dev*?'

'Yes.' She giggles, sounding like the years have fallen away and she's eighteen again. Sounding like Polly again. 'Or should I call him . . .' she pauses, dramatically, '. . . my fiancé?'

'What?'

'We're getting married, Bella! On New Year's Eve, just like we planned. You had to be the first one to know.'

Is she joking? She doesn't *sound* like she's joking.

'But Polly, how . . . I mean, when . . .?'

'He called me last night, after your party, and I wasn't going to pick up, but then I did, and we talked. We talked for hours and hours, and . . . look, all that matters is this. Everything's OK.' Her voice cracks, ever so slightly, with joyful, almost disbelieving tears. 'Everything's OK, and we're getting married after all!'

Grace

Wednesday 30 December

I did give Robbie and Hector the choice of whether they come with me to Wiltshire for Polly's wedding tomorrow, or whether they spend the time at Vanessa's. Though they were quite excited by the idea of getting to see Auntie Polly 'looking like a beautiful Christmas angel', and sorely tempted by the prospect of seeing the donkeys in the fields near Mummy's old house, eventually staying at Vanessa's won.

This isn't, I hardly need to say, anything to do with the lure of Vanessa herself. It's because they'll get to spend another couple of nights worshipping at the altar of Percy, plus the chance to play with their baby sisters. Sorry, their baby *half*-sisters.

Not that Vanessa made that distinction, for once, when we spoke on the phone to arrange the visit. In fact, she's been super-nice to me, by her standards, ever since she found out about the divorce, and it was her suggestion, even, that the boys go and stay.

Perhaps it really is true that in times of crisis, you find out who your real friends are. And that you shouldn't be too surprised if one of your real friends turns out to be your husband's ex-wife.

I'm doubly grateful for Vanessa's kindness, because Charlie is 'too busy to take the boys'. Busy flat-hunting with Celia, he eventually admitted. He has to get settled in somewhere before he starts his new job at her father's brokerage firm in a couple of weeks' time. Turns out, happily for Charlie, that Celia's family are super-posh, not exactly short of a bob or two and, from the sounds of it, desperate to give their daughter's liaison with a (twice) married man a patina of respectability by setting them up in a swanky mansion-block apartment in Chelsea, as close to Peter Jones as is humanly possible. Although I haven't spoken to Charlie at much length this past week – he's more comfortable, since I confronted him about Celia on Boxing Day, doing everything through Valentine the lawyer – I've got the impression that bringing Charlie into the family firm is a big part of Celia's family's plan, as well. Something that makes me wonder if he hadn't already decided to leave MMA long before he found out about my relationship with Saad.

Either way, I'm glad about the job, and glad about the flat in Chelsea. I don't want Charlie to be unhappy, for the boys' sake as much as anything else. And I'm desperately hoping that Percy is right about life as Charlie's son being easier without having to actually live with him. As well as desperately hoping that his current state of being 'too busy' to see the boys wears off at some point. And hoping that Celia, who seems harmless enough, tries as hard to keep Charlie involved in Robbie and Hector's lives as I did with Percy.

Hoping, too, that for the sake of stability in everyone's lives, Celia isn't dumped for a newer, younger model by the time she hits twenty-eight, with a couple of children of her own.

'Totally naïve,' is Vanessa's pronouncement on these hopes, when I drop Robbie and Hector, with their overnight bags, at her door in time for lunch. They've already shot inside to find Percy, with barely a backwards glance.

'Honestly, Grace, don't be a *total* simpleton. Yes, of *course* this Celia girl will have a sell-by date with Charlie. *All* Charlie's relationships have sell-by dates. The man is biologically incapable of withstanding the seven-year itch. If you want my opinion,' she adds, in the tone of a woman who will give it to me whether I want it or not, 'he's biologically incapable of withstanding a seven-*month* itch. You weren't the first of his dalliances, when he was married to me, you know.'

'No. Well – um – that helps, Vanessa.' To be fair to her, it's not like she hasn't hinted darkly at this the entire time I've known her, with all her insinuations about Charlie 'boffing' all over London. Which makes me feel like even more of a prize chump, for getting all starry-eyed about Charlie in the first place. And then for marrying him. And then for having two children with him. 'Thank you. And thank you again for having the boys to stay.'

'It's my pleasure.' She eyes me suspiciously. 'I must

say, Grace, you do look very *nice*. Had your hair done, have you, for this wedding?'

'Well, yes, I am one of the bridesmaids.' I give a little laugh, and start backing away down the steps. 'Got to look respectable!'

'And your skin is all glowy and fresh.'

'Er, yes, just tried out a brand-new facial: three different kinds of oxygen, pumped into your face, while you lie in a, um . . . hyperbaric chamber.' This sounds vaguely enough like a Bliss facial I read about in a magazine at the hairdresser's this morning. But it's not convincing Vanessa. So I add, 'And I've been on a bit of a diet and exercise regime, ever since Christmas, of course. You know, what with trying to shake off the festive pounds, and with the wedding coming up and everything. Got to fit into my bridesmaid frock!'

'Mm.' Vanessa, despite never being one to underestimate the importance of shaking off the festive poundage, still looks unconvinced. 'Well. It's good to see you looking so well on it.'

'It?'

'This marvellous new regime of yours, I mean. Anyway, you probably need to get going.' She nods down at my wheelie suitcase. 'You're getting a taxi to the station, I assume?'

'That's the plan.'

Actually, this isn't the plan at all. The plan, in fact, is for Saad to pick me up, somewhere along Vanessa's road, and drive me, not just to the station, but all the way down to Wiltshire. Which is exceptionally generous of him – playing chauffeur for the day – seeing as he isn't actually going to come to the wedding with me. I just think it's a bit soon to be introducing him to Polly and her family as my . . . well, whatever he is, now.

Is it too soon to say 'boyfriend'?

'For heaven's sake, just how excited *are* you about being a bridesmaid? You can hardly stop smiling!' Vanessa accuses me. 'Now, about the boys staying over. Please feel assured that I have every confidence in my brand-new nanny. She's a marvellous Belarusian girl, just joined us before Christmas. I assume you'd like her to get the boys into bed promptly at seven thirty p.m. ? And obviously I assume neither of them has any fussy eating habits? Anything that might make Katya's job more difficult?'

Oh God, I'm going to accidentally see off another of Vanessa's nannies, aren't I? Ten minutes of Robbie refusing to eat any breakfast but eggs Benedict, and Hector gleefully inspecting the contents of each and every nappy and running through the latest pet names he's given his head lice, and the poor girl will be on the very next flight back to Minsk.

But it's a bit late for me to worry about any of that. So I just shake my head, and smile, and ask Vanessa to give the boys a big kiss from me, and then I start lugging my wheelie case back down her freshly swept front steps and garden path, and in the direction of Parsons Green, where Saad will collect me on the corner.

I've only gone a few yards when I hear my name being sung out from a little way along the road.

'Gra-ace!'

It's Chief Miranda. Actually, it's Chief Miranda plus two more of the Mirandas – I think one of them (Caroline?) is the one with the chalet in Verbiers, and the other one is the mother of the truly unpleasant Sebastian who emptied Robbie's lunchbox over his head on his second day of school. All three of them are dressed in spanking-new tracksuits and MBT trainers, and evidently coming to the end of a power walk.

'Oh, hi, Miranda. Hi – um – ladies. Happy New Year to you.'

'And happy New Year to you!' Chief Miranda says, before adding, 'Or *is* it?'

'Well, I'm just off to my best friend's wedding, and the sun is shining, so . . .'

'It's quite all right, Grace.' She puts her head on one side, in a show of simpering sympathy. 'We do all know what's happened. Charlie leaving you. I heard about it from Vanessa over Christmas.'

Of course she did.

'You poor, *poor* thing,' she carries on, before turning to the other Mirandas, almost as though she's forgotten I'm here for a moment. 'It's for a *younger woman*, did I mention? And from a terribly wealthy background too. Her father is the Wilkes in Wilkes Jonas Betteridge, isn't that right, Grace?'

'I've no idea who her father is,' I say.

'Oh, well, of *course* you don't want to think about

those kind of details too much. Especially someone with your artistic temperament. It must all be just so upsetting for you.'

'Will you get to keep the house, do you know?' Caroline-Miranda pipes up. 'It's just that my parents-in-law are thinking of moving to the area, and they don't want anywhere quite as big as ours. You're in one of the small terraces, on Crediton Road, aren't you? Can you tell me, have you extended into the loft space, because –'

'Caroline!' Chief Miranda looks shocked and thrilled in equal measure. 'You can't go asking poor Grace if she's going to lose her house, not when she's only just lost her husband!'

'He didn't die, or anything!' I protest. 'And really, I'm absolutely fine. Thank you for your . . .' *Prurient interest? Gleeful nosy-parkering? Unashamed thrill at the karma that has turned me into the dumped, older wife for a change?* '. . . concern.'

'Well, you know, if there's anything we can do . . . ? I mean, it isn't going to be as easy as you think, Grace, life as a single mother. Now that you're not quite as young as you were, and with one failed marriage behind you . . .'

Chief Miranda stops, distracted by the noise of a nearby car engine. She's even more distracted – we all are – when it turns out to be a sleek, gleaming dark green Aston Martin, pulling up in the space closest to us. And she's positively open-mouthed when Saad opens the driver's door and climbs out.

'Hello, ladies! Sorry to interrupt your jog!' He smiles around at everyone, then comes right up to me, takes my case from my hand, and leans down to plant a firm kiss on my lips. 'Ready to go, Grace?'

Right.

Well, the cat's well and truly out of the bag now. And I'd rather receive the Mirandas' scorn and envy than their jubilant 'sympathy'. I'm far more accustomed to the former, let's face it, than the latter.

I go on tiptoe to kiss him back. 'Absolutely, totally ready! It was good to see you all,' I add, turning round to smile at the Mirandas while Saad takes my case to the boot. They're open-mouthed, practically guppy-like, in astonishment. 'Caroline, I'll let you know, about the house, shall I?'

'Uh . . . wha . . . ah . . .'

'Great! Well, happy New Year again!'

'Happy New Year,' Chief Miranda manages, rather faintly.

They're still staring, not returning my cheery wave, as Saad and I drive away towards Parsons Green.

'I love this,' says Saad, as we drive smoothly along the ever-narrowing country roads, towards my home village. 'Seeing where you grew up. Where you come from.'

'Yes, well, I hope you won't be disappointed.' Now that we're nearly here, I'm a little embarrassed about Saad seeing *where I grew up, where I come from.*

Compared with his own exotic childhood homes, in all the places he's told me about – Beirut, New York, and Paris – Little Lavington is bound to be a let-down. It's a bit of a let-down by any standards, to be honest. There are forty-ish houses, one small church, a corner shop that sells the day before yesterday's papers (if you're lucky) and anyway is only open two and a half days a week, and a fenced-in village green that for some reason has become home to two seriously bored-looking donkeys. 'It isn't exactly teeming with life and vitality. Oh, hey, slow down a bit before this bend,' I add, my fingers automatically tightening on the leather seat as we approach the particularly nasty blind corner, on the way into the village. 'The one with the big oak tree.'

'You mean, the one with about half an oak tree.' Saad slows down, peering with curiosity at what is, indeed, a rather mangled remainder of the huge oak tree that used to be there. 'Looks like a few people have taken chunks out of that in their time.'

'Yes. Polly's sister being one of them.'

'Ouch.' Saad winces. 'That had to have hurt.'

'Mm.'

He glances over at me. 'You OK?'

'Yes, absolutely. It's just . . . well, it's a big thing. Polly finally getting married. Especially after everything that's happened.'

'All the fuss and cancellation, you mean?'

'Yes.' In the wing mirror on my side, I can still see the oak tree – Bella's oak tree, as I've rather perversely thought of it for the last ten years – vanishing into the distance behind us.

'So, has Polly explained what it was that changed her mind about marrying this guy?'

'I'm still not completely sure I know what it was that made her change her mind about *not* marrying him in the first place!' I'm not about to go into the things Polly said outside Bella's flat on Christmas Eve. That stuff about feeling guilty. Which was the first time I began to think I might know what the whole drama was about.

'Safer not to ask too many questions until after the wedding, perhaps.' Saad grins at me.

'Exactly.' Luckily now I have to give him directions through the village, to get to the Atkinses' house, which is a handy way of diverting the conversation off this topic. 'Take a left turn onto Main Street,' I tell him, 'and don't be fooled by the fact that it looks about as *main* as – oh shit.'

Polly is actually outside the house, waiting for us. Which completely screws up my plans to keep Saad's presence on the down-low.

'Is that the bride-to-be?' Saad asks, pulling the car up onto the kerb outside the house, as Polly lets out a shriek of excitement and starts running towards us.

'Yes, look, I'm really sorry, I didn't mean for there to be any big introductions . . .'

But it's too late. Polly has already pulled my door open and is throwing her arms around me.

'Gracie! You're here! Isn't this amazing? My

wedding, after everything that's happened! And as for you . . .' She stands back to let me get out of the car, and to have a look at the car herself – and at Saad, who's clambering out of the other side. Her eyes widen and she shoots me an *oh my God* look. 'You must be Saad!'

'And you must be Polly.' He leans in to give her a kiss on each cheek. As well he might, seeing as Polly is looking back to her old self, poured into spray-on jeans and a little cardi that hugs her every curve. Weirdly, though, I don't even feel the smallest pang of jealousy. Funny how it takes a relationship with an international playboy to make you feel so secure. 'It's great to meet you.'

'It's great to meet *you*. Now, please, both of you, come inside out of the cold and –'

'Saad isn't staying,' I say hastily. 'I mean, he has to get back to London pretty much right away. Don't you?' I turn to Saad, who's looking at me with amusement.

'Well, I do have a late meeting . . .'

'Exactly. He has a late meeting.'

Polly looks disappointed. 'But he could come back, couldn't he, after the meeting? Or tomorrow? In time for the wedding.'

'Er, no, no, I don't think –'

'But there's plenty of room!'

Plenty of room isn't really the point. Saad isn't going to want to spend the best part of two days at the wedding of a couple he doesn't even know. In the middle of nowhere. Cooped up in an ordinary little house that's roughly the same square footage as his bedroom suite. Sleeping in a bedroom that's smaller than his dressing room. Sharing a bathroom, for God's sake, that probably has the same rickety old shower that I remember from long-ago sleepovers, where your odds of suffering a boiling-water burn are about even with the chances of getting chilblains, and the odds of enjoying a pleasurable bathing experience are ten million to one. Why would Saad want to be doing any of that, when he could be whisking back up the motorway in his fabulous car to his fabulous house, with its acres of space and spectacular furnishings and its fabulous (and fully functioning) bathroom?

Which is why I practically fall over when I hear him saying to Polly, 'Hey, if it's no trouble, I'd really love to come to the wedding. I mean, I do have to get back to London right now, unfortunately. But I can pick up some of my stuff while I'm there and head back later tonight.'

'It's no trouble at all!' She beams at him; at both of us, in fact, while I open and shut my mouth like a startled goldfish. 'We've done this at such short notice that we need all the extra guests we can get. And you'll stay in the same room as Grace, of course,' she adds, shooting a knowing grin in my direction, 'so you won't even upset my sister's careful plans for who's sleeping where.'

'Great!' Saad reaches for my hand and gives it a squeeze. 'That OK with you, Grace? If I make it back here by around midnight?'

I'm about to answer when there's a shrill ring from Polly's mobile, and while she answers it (to give rather hopeless train instructions to a relative who appears to be planning to come down from Northumberland) I take the opportunity to collar Saad.

'You don't have to do this, you know!' I hiss at him.

'Do what?'

'Come to the wedding. I mean, you'll be horribly bored. And uncomfortable, too, if you stay the night. I mean, there's only one bathroom, and the shower's like something from the Old Testament, and you won't have your super-kingsize bed with the lovely Frette sheets, and –'

'Only one bathroom? Hmm.' He appears to muse. 'Does that mean it would be most efficient for me to share my shower with someone? You, for example?'

The prospect of sharing a shower with Saad, even under water that's either boiling or containing solid chunks of ice, is enough to distract me for a moment.

'And this bed you're talking about,' he carries on. 'Is it so small that there's a risk I could fall out and hurt myself? And does that mean I'd have to hold onto you for dear life all night?'

Again, the prospect of snuggling up with Saad all night – the first whole night, it occurs to me, that we've ever been able to share together – prevents me from forming a sentence.

'You think I'm only happy when I'm staying somewhere palatial? That 17 Main Street, Little Lavington is too shabby for me?'

'It's a bit shabby for pretty much anyone,' I mumble, embarrassed that he's seen through me. 'I'm being serious about the shower.'

'I'll survive it. Or maybe I'll just bring some diamond-encrusted wet wipes with me from London and avoid showering altogether.' He smiles at me. 'Come on, Grace. It'll be our first night together. I'd sleep in a haystack and wash in a muddy puddle if it meant the chance to spend an entire night with you. Though I realise that sounds a bit like I might be planning to also spend the night with those two donkeys back there on the green.'

I smile back. How can I help it? 'Look, if you're sure you won't be bored . . . and you don't mind driving the whole round trip all over again –'

'I'm never bored with you, Grace.' He leans down to give me a swift kiss, and as he does so, he whispers in my ear. 'But just in case, why don't you think up a few interesting things for us to do in that cramped little bed you've told me so much about? And I'll put some serious thought into the matter, too.'

'Go, go,' I croak, practically pushing him into the car and closing his door for him. 'The sooner you're on your way, the sooner you'll be back.'

I watch him drive away along Main Street, and as I turn back to Polly I see that she's now off the phone and grinning at me.

'Oh, *Gracie*. He's *ridiculous*.'

I know from the tone of her voice that this is A Good Thing. 'I know. I'm so happy.'

'You look it.'

'And so do you!' This is – thank God – finally true. 'But look, tell me how everything's going here. Did you manage to get your dress sorted out in time? How many people have said they can make it?' I'm assuming a fair few, from the fact that I can see a small marquee half-erected in the Atkinses' back garden, but before Polly can start filling me in on the details, Bella emerges from the side door of the house.

She's dressed in old jeans and a spattered apron, and there's a stressed-out frown on her face. She's holding a vast ceramic bowl of something chocolatey in the crook of one arm, and a stainless-steel whisk in the other hand.

'Poll? For Christ's sake, will you get in here and tell Mum she absolutely *cannot* wear the dress she's just brought back from Bristol?'

'Oh Lord, she's not bought something white, has she?'

'No. It's black. And *backless*.'

'I'll have you know, Bella Jayne Atkins, that the salesgirls at House of Fraser were lost for words when I came out of the changing room!' Marilyn has opened up the bathroom window, on the first floor, and is peering out over us, clutching a bit of lacy black fabric to her chest. It reminds me that there's one thing I didn't warn Saad about, something far more dangerous than the ancient shower: Polly's man-eating mother. 'They said I looked *just* like Hilary Swank when she wore that low-back dress to the Oscars,' she carries on, 'even if I am twenty years older than her.'

'*Twenty!*' Bella snorts.

'And it's not as if I even need to wear a bra, or anything, unlike *some* people . . .'

'Mum, look, let me just come up and see it on you, and then we can decide whether or not the dress will go with the wedding's general *look*, OK?' Polly squeezes my hand as she starts through the side door into the house. 'Grace, mind if I leave you to your own devices for a few minutes?'

'It'll be a bit longer than that,' Bella hisses at her. 'You're going to have to take Mum to Devizes before the shops all shut and forcibly get her to buy a suitable outfit. For fuck's sake, all she had to do was find a bloody pastel-coloured suit, or something! But no, she has to turn up to her own daughter's wedding dressed as Morticia fucking Addams!'

'Bells, calm down.' Polly is already on her way towards the stairs. 'It'll all be fine. I promise.'

Wonderful. I'm left alone in the hallway with a gently steaming Bella.

'Hi, Grace,' she says. 'And sorry. I suppose you weren't anticipating an arrival into World War Three.'

'It's fine,' I say, before realising that this might have sounded as though I was agreeing that it *is* World War Three. 'I mean, I know what weddings can be like! Especially having them at home. You're doing such an amazing job, Bella, at this kind of short notice, catering for . . . how many people is it going to be?'

'Seventy-six confirmed. Might be a few last-minute additions.'

'Oh, yes, um, one of those will be my . . . er . . . a friend of mine. If you don't mind, that is?'

'A friend?'

'Yes, but he's quite happy to share a bed with me. A room, I mean! What I mean is, you won't have to worry about sheets or towels or anything, if it's OK for him to stay the night . . . It was Polly's suggestion,' I finally say, faltering under her gimlet stare. 'I can tell him not to come back, if it's easier for you.'

'Oh, no, no, I mean, for heaven's sake, what difference does one more make?' she says, not sounding terribly hospitable about it. But then Bella isn't one of life's natural hosts, albeit that she makes her living out of it. Still, it's the food part that's her forte, and she's already stalking back to her natural habitat, the kitchen, where an entire production line is in place. There are fish kettles poaching things on the gas hob, and casserole dishes simmering on the Aga, and mounds and mounds of freshly peeled vegetables, waiting to go into other casserole dishes, that put my Christmas Day efforts to shame.

Polly's dad, Brian, is stacking trays of pastry rounds into the freezer, and looking almost as scared of Bella as I am.

'Grace, hello! Cup of tea? Piece of shortbread?'

'Oh, no, there's no need for that,' I tell him, before Bella can jump in and bark at him, sergeant-major style, that he's no time to be making cups of tea or putting out plates of shortbread. 'Honestly! Actually, I'd really just like to help. I mean, I'm not the greatest cook in the world, but if there's anything I can be doing in the marquee, or answering the phone . . .'

'Well, I suppose you could be making a start on cutting down some of the holly and ivy from the garden,' Bella says, looking dubious about my talents. 'We need enough to decorate the church and the tables in the marquee.'

Oh shit, I'd hoped for something low-key, physically undemanding and indoors.

'But of course, if you'd rather, I don't know, go and paint your toenails, or something . . .'

'Not at all!' I sense more than just a hint of disdain in Bella's tone. 'Holly and ivy it is! Could I just pop my things upstairs first, get them out of your way? And then I'll come straight back down and get cracking.'

'Sure. I'll show you up.'

'Bella,' I laugh, 'there's no need for that. I mean, I've stayed here a million times before!'

'Well, it's the first time you've stayed in my old room, so let me show you up.'

This time, I don't even attempt to argue.

Bella's old bedroom is a couple of doors along from Polly's, on the upstairs corridor. I've remembered it as painted in a chilly shade of pale blue, with a slightly dingy beige carpet, but either Marilyn and Brian have redecorated or my memories are completely wrong, because the walls are actually cream and there are wooden floorboards instead of a carpet. The bed is going to be a squeeze, though: a small double that makes me think Saad's suggestion of holding onto each other to avoid spilling out onto the floor was more apt than he realised.

'This is great, Bella, thanks so much! I'll just get my dress out and hang it up, and then –'

'Let me help,' she says unexpectedly. And not especially helpfully, either, because her hands are coated with a dusting of flour and whatever chocolatey thing it was she was mixing in that big ceramic bowl. A mousse, by the looks of it, or perhaps some kind of cocoa-y cake filling. Either way, not a thing I'd particularly like to get all over my dove-grey bridesmaid dress.

'Really, Bella, I don't want to keep you. You're so busy –'

'No, it's fine.' She reaches into the wardrobe for a hanger as I start to pull my dress out of my case. 'I'm sorry about what happened with you and your husband, by the way. I hope this wedding isn't going to be too difficult for you. I mean, obviously now you're bringing your *friend*, it might be a bit easier. But I know weddings are hard, when you've been through a breakup.'

'Thanks.' I don't want to talk about my failed marriage with Bella, despite the fact her tone of regret is a good deal more genuine than the Mirandas' was earlier. 'I'm just really pleased that Polly rethought everything in the end.'

'Yes.' Bella fixes me with a hard stare. 'Look, this is

probably none of my business, but how did you manage to make her realise she didn't need to feel so guilty any more?'

I drop my dress and have to bend over to pick it up before it gets any fluff on it. 'Sorry, I don't know what you mean.'

'Well, I'm assuming you spoke to her that night after she ran off from my Christmas Eve party. I mean, how else would she have realised she didn't need to sabotage her own happiness, just because of feeling so guilty about you?'

I stare at her like she's speaking Greek. Because as far as I'm concerned, she might as well be.

'Bella, I honestly have no idea what you're talking about. Why would Polly feel guilty about anything to do with me?' *And not guilty about anything to do with you, for example?*

'Because of what happened between her and Charlie, of course. And the fact that she didn't tell you about it.'

I feel like I'm spinning into a parallel universe. I sit down, very suddenly, on the edge of the bed. '*What* happened between her and Charlie?'

'Oh God, you really don't know?' Bella's eyes have flown wide. '*Shit*. I just assumed Polly came clean, and that's what made her feel OK about allowing herself to be happy with Dev.'

'Came clean about what?' I practically shriek. I've stopped being scared of Bella now, and all I'm scared about is what she's got to say.

'OK, look, it was totally one-sided. And it was years and years and *years* ago.' Bella is more uncomfortable and panicky than I think I've ever seen her look. 'Right after you'd just got married, in fact. Charlie asked Polly out for a drink, pretending he had some question to ask her about a twenty-first birthday present for you, and then when she got there, it turned out to be just this embarrassing, crude attempt to get her to sleep with him.'

I blink at her. 'And . . .?'

'And what? You were only just married, for heaven's sake! Don't you think that's *appalling*?'

'Yes, yes, of course, but I don't understand why Polly had to feel so awful about it.'

'Because she dillydallied about whether or not she should say anything to you. She thought you'd be livid with her and refuse to believe she'd not reciprocated. And then before she'd made up her mind what to do about it, you'd gone and got yourself pregnant with your eldest. Which just killed her. I mean, she honestly felt responsible for ruining your life, just for not telling you sooner so you could leave him . . .' She tails off as I start to laugh. 'What?'

'That's *all*?' I feel weak with relief.

I honestly thought she was about to tell me something much, much worse than that. I honestly thought she was about to tell me that Polly had slept with Charlie. Because if she had, I'm not sure it would have made all that much difference that it was, as she said, *years and years and years ago*.

Or that I'm not even with Charlie any more.

'What do you mean, that's all?' Bella's eyebrows crunch into a frown. 'Your husband – OK, your soon-to-be-ex husband – trying it on with your best friend? And her never telling you about it? That means *nothing* to you?'

'No, it's not that it means nothing. It's just that there are so many worse things it could have been.'

'What does that mean?'

'Um, well, she could have given in to his creepy advances. Or ended up having a full-blown affair with him, or something.'

'Yeah, like that would happen.' Bella lets out one of her most derisive snorts. 'Like that's something Polly would ever do to you.'

Now that I think my legs are sturdy enough to stand up again, I get up and busy myself unpacking my shoes. I'm going to be wearing my Jimmy Choos with the bridesmaid's dress tomorrow. The first time I've worn them out in public.

Bella watches me for a moment or two, shaking her head. 'Wow. You're really, really calm about this. And this is something Polly's been torturing herself with for years.'

I can't help resenting her implication that I'm somehow to blame for this. 'Look, it kills me that Polly's been torturing herself and keeping a secret! But if she'd just told me, I could have set her straight in an instant. That she's got nothing to feel bad about. Whether or not I'd still been stuck with Charlie. And if you think it'll make any difference to her enjoyment of her wedding day, I'll tell her right now!'

Just as I say this, in fact, Polly's voice becomes audible out on the landing. 'No, I don't think we can get back to Bristol before House of Fraser closes, Mum,' she's saying, 'but we can make it to Devizes in time before Reflections shuts, as long as we leave right now . . . Bells? Bella? Are you up here?'

'In my room!' Bella calls, shooting me a look that tells me I'm not to say anything at all about our current conversation. 'Success?' she asks, as Polly sticks her head round the door.

'Yes, if *success* means Mum agreeing to try and find something different to wear. No, if it means Mum not going into a massive sulk.'

'I'm not *in a massive sulk*,' Marilyn's voice comes through – sulkily – from the hallway. 'I just think it's *interesting* that both my daughters seem to want me to look like a washed-up old frump, while they both get to look ravishing for the day. Oh, hello, Grace, darling,' she adds, poking her head through the bedroom door next to Polly's. 'Will you come into town with us, and help me pick something that my daughters won't disapprove of? You're so elegant, Grace –' a rather triumphant and spiteful look in Bella's direction – 'that I'm sure *you* won't let me walk away with anything unflattering.'

I agree that I'll head to town with Polly and Marilyn – well, anything's got to be better than staying around the house to trim holly and ivy, and get the third degree from Bella – and ask for five minutes to change into something a bit warmer and run a comb through my hair.

The three Atkinses all get out of my way to let me do this in peace, and I'm just looking at myself in the wardrobe mirror and trying to zhuzh up my hair a bit when there's the briefest of knocks on the door and Bella, without waiting for a reply, comes back into the room again. She's got a quizzical, puzzled expression on her face.

'You're saying that Polly *didn't* tell you about this thing with Charlie, right?' she asks, not even bothering to apologise for intruding, or offer any small talk about why she's come back. 'After what she said on Christmas Eve? Before she called up the next day and told you everything was OK and she was getting married after all?'

'Exactly, Bella. She didn't tell me about it.'

'Then what changed?'

'Sorry?'

'Well, *something* changed, in between her running off on Christmas Eve and her big announcement on Christmas Day. I just assumed it was that she'd told you about Charlie, got it all off her chest and realised she was being silly to sabotage her own life just because of something she never told you.' She chews her lip. 'But if it wasn't that, what was it?'

I close the wardrobe door and turn round to face her. 'I don't know, Bella. And I don't think we need to know. The main thing is that she's getting married tomorrow, to a wonderful man whom she loves with all her heart. Isn't it?'

'Yes. Yes, I suppose that's the main thing.'

As I follow her downstairs, where Polly and her mum are waiting for me, I can't help thinking that Bella doesn't believe this is the main thing at all.

Later on, a little after midnight, I get a text from Saad saying he's just pulled up outside. So I clamber out of the small, slightly lumpy bed and go downstairs to let him in.

But as I head down the stairs, I realise that not everyone is asleep.

There's a slightly eerie glow coming from the living room, where all the lights are off, but where I can see, thanks to the eerie glow, that Bella is sitting on the sofa, a laptop open in front of her.

When she hears the creak on the stairs, she spins round, as though I've caught her in the middle of opening a jar of ready-made béarnaise, or using cheapo cooking chocolate instead of Valrhona 66%.

'Sorry, Bella, I didn't mean to scare you!'

She just stares at me blankly for a moment or two, not saying anything. When she does speak, she says, 'I was just checking a few emails and stuff.'

'Sure! Well, I was just going to let my friend in, if that's OK?'

'What? Oh, yes. Yes, it's fine.' She gets to her feet, very suddenly, and makes for the stairs, pushing past me as she goes up them. 'I just have to go and find something. Something important,' she mumbles.

A moment later, she's disappeared into Polly's old room, and shut the door behind her.

Well, that was weird. But then, I've never really understood Bella Atkins. And I'm fairly sure the feeling is mutual.

Anyway, it's not the time, now, to wonder about what she's doing. Because Saad is waiting for me, shivering on the doorstep.

'Hello, beautiful,' he says as I open the door. He leans down to kiss me, and despite the freezing air he's bringing in with him, his lips are surprisingly warm. 'How's that cramped bed been working out for you?'

'It's OK.' I lock the dead-bolt behind him. 'Though of course,' I add, as I start to lead him up the stairs, 'it'll be much better now that you're here.'

From: PollyWollyDoodle@hotmail.com
To: Julia247@yahoo.com
Date: 25 December 2011
Subject: Happy Christmas!

Julia

I did it. Jesus, I really did it. Yesterday, when I took Dev's call, I ended up telling him everything. And I mean *everything*.

And you know what, Julia, it was just like you said it would be. He didn't hang up in disgust. He didn't do anything in disgust. He just listened, and then when I (finally) stopped talking he asked if he could come over. I don't know what land-speed record his taxi broke, but he was at my flat twenty minutes later, and as soon as I opened the door he just kind of . . . *folded* me into this huge hug. Then he held me for ages and ages, while I howled, and he kept telling me in his lovely, kind, Dr Dev voice that it was all going to be all right.

And it's exactly like you said. Dev knowing about it all – and more to the point, understanding it all – has taken more weight off me than I could possibly have imagined.

So guess what. Deep breath and a drum roll, please . . . I'm going to marry him! He's asked me, all over again – asked the *real* Polly, not the 'perfect' Polly he thought he was getting, but the real Polly that he still, apparently, adores – and I've never said yes to anything faster in my life.

I have about a million calls to make now – I've called Bella already, but I still have to tell Grace, and our parents . . . oh, and 130 disgruntled wedding guests, I suppose – so I'd better stop this email now. But I just wanted to say thank you, Julia, for everything. I'll be in touch as soon as I can.

P x

From: PollyWollyDoodle@hotmail.com
To: Julia247@yahoo.com
Date: 30 December 2011
Subject: Here comes the bride . . .

Julia

It's madness here. Complete and utter madness. Though not, thank God, the kind of madness *you're* used to dealing with on a day-to-day basis. Just wedding madness. Nothing more harmful than that. (Though if you do ever think of transferring your practice to England, my mother might be a prime target for your psychotherapeutic services. While we're on the subject of proper madness, I mean.)

I really wish you *were* in England, though, just for tomorrow. Because I'd love you to see the end result of all your hard work, and the fact that you never wrote me off. Still, I understand that you couldn't fly over at such short notice. And I suppose it would have been difficult for you to blend in. '*Lovely to meet you, Cousin Vicky. Aren't you the one Polly told me about in one of our early counselling sessions together, the one who told Polly that snogging other people's boyfriends was OK as long as you didn't get caught? Oooh, yes, I'd love a smoked salmon canapé, thank you!'*

Like this wedding needs any more drama, after everything it's already been through!

Anyway, I just thought I'd drop you a quick line, even though I've been expressly instructed by my sister that I need to get an early night. But I'll be away on honeymoon after this, and then I've got to move all my worldly goods into the Wimbledon house, so it might be a few weeks before we can get back to our phone sessions. And I'm wondering, actually, if I might not need quite so many sessions as before. Now that I can talk to Dev, and tell him my fears about everything you and I have discussed, *ad nauseam*, for the past few months, it doesn't feel like I'm cracking up any more. Like I told you in my last email, he was so understanding about everything. He understands why I was panicking about settling down to a blissfully happy marriage, and lots and lots of beautiful children, when the two people I care about most in the world (apart from Dev, that is) don't get to have those things.

But this is the weirdest thing, Julia: after all this time worrying, and stressing, and beating myself up, it looks like Grace and Bella *are* going to get those things after all. The blissful relationship, in Grace's case, now that she's finally free of Cheaty Charlie, and looking absurdly happy with the gorgeous guy that (not blowing my own trumpet or anything) I urged her, weeks ago, to take as her lover.

And in Bella's case (please, please God) maybe the beautiful children.

I mean, she hasn't really spoken to me about it much, but her annoying boyfriend, Jamie, is definitely off the scene. He's not coming to the wedding, and when I asked Bella why, she just kind of shrugged and said that they weren't seeing each other any more, and that even if they were, he probably wouldn't have made it to the wedding, because there'd probably have been a 'big game' on, or something. And while I'm sad for her that her two-year relationship has ended (though I have to be honest, she doesn't seem all that sad about it herself) at least this really gives her the chance to focus on the adoption, either alone or with another, more serious man. I'm crossing every single digit I have that it works out for her.

And if it doesn't – well, as Dev said, when we talked about it on Christmas Eve – I'm just going to have to put every ounce of my energies into allowing her to become the most amazing aunt.

I know. I can't believe it either. That I'm sitting here, in my old bedroom, the night before my wedding, and that I'm actually talking about things like having children. That I don't feel sick with guilt, any more, that I can do that when

Bella can't. That Dev has made me realise that, despite what I've been telling myself, it isn't *really* my fault that Bella can't.

It's so strange to think that this is the very bedroom I was in on that horrendous night ten years ago when Dad came barging in, white as a ghost, to tell me that Bella had been in an accident and that we had to get to the hospital before, probably, she died. The very bed; the very duvet; the very pillows, even. (My mother isn't a big one for bothering to refresh her household items. There are mildew cultures on the shower curtain in her bathroom that are older than I am.)

And you know that letter I've told you about, Julia? The one I was in the process of writing, at the very moment that Dad barged in with the news about the accident? Well, that's in here, too. In this silly old shoebox, under my bed, where I used to store all my precious things – my diaries, and old friendship bracelets from Grace, and other letters, too, from boys I fancied, or the little notelets I'd get from Bella after she first moved to Bristol, mostly instructing me to do my homework and make sure I always ate breakfast. But of course this particular letter was one I was writing to Bella for a change. One I would have sent her, too, if it hadn't been for what happened just as I was finishing it.

I know you've always been a big one for 'perspective', Julia. I know you think it's important that people look backwards to moments in their past, so that we get a sense of why we are where we are, and hopefully how far we've come. So I pulled the shoebox out, a few minutes ago, because with your wisdom in mind I thought it might be good for me to reread the letter. Look back to the scared, silly little girl who wrote it, and realise what a mature, sensible woman I've become.

But I couldn't read it. I couldn't even open the envelope.

I just think, Julia, that some things are best left buried. I've unearthed them enough to come clean to Dev. But I'm not sure what good it would do to unearth them any further. To bring them blinking into the daylight.

You might think it's living a lie. But I'd rather live a lie for ever, I think, than risk telling the truth and destroying my relationship with my sister.

So I've put the letter back. Back in the shoebox, back under the bed. When I've moved all my old stuff to the house in Wimbledon, I'll decide finally what to do with it. Burn it, perhaps. Lock it away, more probably. Pass it onto my children one day, maybe, as a lesson about what NOT to do with their lives. The mistakes it's not OK to make.

I've gone on for far too long, as usual. Scared of Bella coming up to bed herself before I'm asleep and laying into me for ignoring her instructions about the early night! She's still hard at it in the kitchen, bless her, getting all the food prepped for the Big Day tomorrow. So I think the least I can do is follow her instructions, and turn out the light.

P x

3 August 2001

Dear Bella,

This is the hardest letter I've ever had to write to you.

Actually, come to think of it, it's just about the only letter I've ever had to write to you. I think I might have sent you the occasional postcard, like that Easter a few years back when me, Mum and Dad went to Woolacombe and you stayed at home to revise for your GCSEs. In fact, I'm pretty sure I sent you a postcard almost every day that week, because we kept eating the most amazing cream teas and I desperately wanted to tell you about them. And obviously I've sent you plenty of emails, especially since you've moved to Bristol and I haven't got as much credit as I need on my mobile. Letters, though, not so much. Letters are tricky. But I've got something to tell you and I think it's going to be easier to explain it in a letter than tell it to your face.

Plus there's the fact that I'm a pathetic coward, I suppose.

Bella, I've done the most awful thing.

I've slept with Christian.

Oh God, actually, it's even worse than that. I've *been sleeping* with Christian. More than once. It's happened four or five times, in fact, over the last few weeks. The first time – and I don't know if this is going to help at all; somehow I doubt it – I was very, very drunk indeed. You remember that weekend, after our exams, when me and Grace came to stay with you? Well, that's when it was. You were working late at the restaurant the night we arrived, and we were going to go out clubbing right away, but Christian said he'd cook for us while we had a couple of glasses of wine. And I think we lost track of time, not to mention how much we were drinking. Because somehow it suddenly ended up being past midnight, and we hadn't gone out clubbing at all, and Grace was passed out on the sofa in the living room, and Christian was kissing me. And then we were in the guest bedroom, and he was doing more than just kissing me.

I'm not sure if I really wanted it. On the other hand – and I'm trying to be honest with you here, even though I know it's probably far too little, far too late – I definitely didn't want to stop him. I don't think I knew I *could* stop him. And I didn't even really know what was happening until it had already happened.

Which isn't me trying to offer up some feeble excuse, by the way. 'Oh, I was so drunk, I didn't know what I was doing.' That sounds like Mum, after she's hit the G&Ts on a Sunday lunchtime and then ploughed her way through two platefuls of Dad's lasagne and three portions of tiramisu. Followed by hours of self-loathing before she finally works out who she's going to blame it on (usually you, or whoever it was who gave her the second G&T) and then starts recriminating outwards instead of inwards. All right, I may not have known what I was doing that first time, but I certainly knew exactly what I was doing the next time. And the times after that.

Look, I don't really think I should go into any more details. Not until I get the courage to actually face you in person. I feel sick even writing any of this down, knowing how much it's going to hurt you. And even though I know it would be a terrible, terrible lie, I wouldn't tell you unless I had to. I wouldn't inflict that kind of pain on you. But I have to tell you, Bells, because Christian has . . . well, he's not letting this go. Not letting *me* go, I mean. He's phoning me all the time, and now he's started leaving messages saying that he can't be with you now that this has happened between us. And he's going to call off the wedding.

Look, Bella, I desperately want that to happen. I *desperately* don't want you to marry him. What I've done to you, by sleeping with him, is horribly, horribly wrong, but he did it to you too. So no, I don't want him to marry you. But I don't want him to call off the wedding. I want *you* to call off the wedding.

This is why I have to tell you.

And if that means you never, ever speak to me again, well, maybe it's worth it. Just so you can understand that you're not the one who's done anything wrong. It's your horrible fiancé. And your even more horrible sister.

When you've read this letter, which I'm going to post to you first thing in the morning, please call me. Call me and scream at me. Better yet, come home and scream at me. Throw things at me; hit me, even, if you want. But just, please, don't . . . don't misunderstand me. Don't think that I meant to do this. Don't think I wouldn't undo it if I could. Don't think I'm not sorry.

I really hope that one day, you'll

Bella

Thursday 31 December

Polly's wedding day. It's bright and sunny.

Of course it is. What things in my sister's life aren't bright and sunny?

All morning, I've moved through the tasks I've had to do like a zombie.

Up at six thirty to make a start on the mise-en-place for the canapés.

By eight thirty, letting the florist into the marquee to do the centrepieces, and dealing with the fact that said marquee has sprung a leak overnight, dribbling last night's heavy showers all down over the seat at the top table where – who else? – I was supposed to sit.

By nine, dashing across the village to St Michael's to make sure everything's ready over there, from making sure the right hymn numbers are up to finishing off the holly and ivy decorations that Grace was supposed to do yesterday before she went swanning off shopping with Mum and Polly instead.

By ten, back to the kitchen to help Brian with the dishes for the cold section of the buffet – poached salmon, posh homemade pork pie, four different kinds of salad, despite the fact I thought we'd agreed on just a rocket-and-Parmesan and a classic Waldorf.

By eleven thirty, everything coming to a grinding halt to deal with the fallout from Anji, the hair and makeup girl's, suggestion that maybe Mum would like to try a special light-diffusing foundation that works particularly well with mature skin.

By twelve fifteen, finally calming down poor shaken Anji enough that she can make a start on Polly's hair and makeup, while I jump in the (ice-cold) shower.

By twelve thirty, starting my own hair and makeup, because the car is coming to pick us up at one fifteen and there isn't time, after Mum's temper tantrum, for Anji to do hair and makeup for me and Grace as well.

Now, at twelve forty-five, sitting on the bed in Polly's old room, dressed in my dove-grey prom dress and new LK Bennett sale-purchase shoes, staring at my newly made-up face in the mirror, and thinking.

No, scratch that. I'm not thinking. I can't think. My head's not clear enough to think. All I can do right now is *feel*.

Which is why, when there's a knock on the door and Grace sticks her head round it, I almost jump a mile.

'Sorry,' she says, coming into the room.

She looks stunning and super-model-like, as always, in her own dove-grey dress – she went for the drapey, above-the-knee version, the one for skinny-minnies with endless legs but (look, I have to find *some* way to feel better about standing next to her) no proper boobs – and the showy-off pair of Jimmy Choo shoes I saw her unpacking yesterday. I got the feeling, from the way she kind of clutched them to her chest when she got them out of the suitcase, that they might have been a present from her pretty-boy fancy man. The fancy man, incidentally, who turned up late last night and has spent all morning charming the pants off Mum (admittedly it's not like he had to make much effort, with looks like his) and mucking in, in a rather annoyingly confident and cheerful way, with any helpful odd job he could possibly find. For the last hour or so he's been using that absurdly swanky sports car of his to ferry some of the random relatives from the train station to the church. I've already received two excitable phone calls from the Durham cousins asking who the hot chauffeur is, and if there's any chance he's single.

It's no wonder, I suppose, that Grace seems so spectacularly unaffected by her horrible husband cheating on her. We'd all like a husband to cheat on us if we ended up with a prime specimen like that.

'I just came in to see if you needed any help with the heated rollers,' Grace adds.

'No.' I've ignored the heated rollers, in fact, in favour of putting my hair up.

'But I thought Polly wanted us to leave our hair down, to match her?'

'Yes. But I'm putting mine up.'

'Right. Um, are you sure? Because Polly hasn't been Bride-zilla-ish about anything, really, and if she wants us to wear our hair down, it's not really too much to ask . . .'

'Maybe not. But I'm already vertically challenged

next to you and Polly. And I don't think piling my hair on top of my head to add a couple of precious inches to my height is too much to ask.'

'No, no, of course. Well! You look great, anyway, Bella. The hair up really suits you! So, I'm just going to go and see how Polly's doing with the finishing touches to her makeup, if you don't need me for anything else?'

I shake my head.

'Good!' She turns back to the door, then stops. 'Um, Bella, don't snap at me or anything, but . . . well, are you OK?'

I don't snap at her. I just stare at her, without saying anything at all.

'I mean, I know you've hardly had a moment to yourself all morning,' she carries on, 'but now it's all about to kick off and I suppose I thought you'd be a bit more excited! About the car, and the church, and watching Poll walk down the aisle in her dress, and the big party in the marquee with all your amazing food . . .'

'I found the letter.'

'What letter?'

'This letter.' I reach under the bed, where I dug it out of one of Polly's old shoe-boxes, labelled 'Important and Precious Stuff', while Polly herself snored loudly above me, late last night. I root in the shoe-box, pull it out and hand it to her. 'The one Polly wrote me the night I had my car accident. The one telling me about her and Christian.'

Her blue eyes widen, displaying alarm that has obviously been ten years in the making. She opens her mouth as if she's about to start babbling and denying things, but then she closes it again. She takes the letter, glances down at it, and says, 'Oh. That letter.'

'Yes.'

There's another silence.

'How did you find out about it?'

'I've been reading Polly's emails.' It seems a tiny thing to admit, now. 'She writes to her counsellor, this woman called Julia, back in New York.'

'I didn't know she was seeing a coun –' Grace bites back her words, as if she knows that the only response she'll get from me is, *Well,* I *didn't know my little sister slept with my fiancé*. 'Sorry. Carry on.'

'There's not much to carry on with. It's just that. I've been reading her emails. That's how I found out about the letter. In an email I read last night.'

'Right. Right. OK.' Grace looks at a total loss to know what to say. She swallows, hard. 'Bella, I'm so sorry.'

'About what? That I found the letter? That I found it the night before the wedding? That Polly wrote the letter at all? That she slept with Christian? That that's why he dumped me, and that's why I got in the car that night, and that's why I was crying so much I smashed into that bloody oak tree, and that's why . . . ?'

My voice cracks. I think I need to stop talking.

In the silence that follows, Grace does a thing that truly astonishes me. She crosses the room, sits down next to me on Polly's old bed, and puts one of her cool, perfectly manicured hands on top of mine. Short of the huge, enveloping bear hug from Liam that I really, really want at this moment, it's the most comforting thing anyone could possibly do for me.

'It wasn't the way you think,' she says, softly, after a few minutes.

'How do you know what I think? I don't even know what I think.'

'It wasn't her. I mean, yes, of course, she went along with it. But it was him. It was all him. I mean, she was only seventeen, and he was . . .' She shrugs. 'He was Christian.'

Yes. Christian. Charismatic. Good-looking. Ten years older than Polly, when he took her to bed.

'And I don't know if this will help at all, but it didn't last long.'

'Christian never did.'

Grace lets out a laugh, then stops herself, as if she doesn't know whether it's OK to take it as a joke or not. 'I mean, things were over pretty quickly between them. It was . . .' she seems to be thinking about how she can say this in a way that doesn't make me think she's being blasé, '. . . only a handful of occasions.'

'Did she come down to Bristol to see him?'

'Mm.' I can tell she's torn between protecting Polly's secret and – perhaps as someone who's been cheated on herself recently – telling me what I need to know. 'But not at your flat, not after the first time. They'd meet at his brother's, or at a Holiday Inn. I think

Christian thought he was impressing her, taking her to a hotel.'

Yes, he would have done.

And I can imagine that Polly would have been duly impressed. The way I was when I first met Christian. The way you are when you can't quite believe that this gorgeous man is gazing into your eyes, and flirting with you. And the way that, temporarily at least, you start to see in yourself what he's telling you he sees in you.

'Honestly, though, Bella, she got her act together pretty fast. Not fast enough, maybe, but as soon as it really dawned on her what she was doing, she ended it.'

'And he wouldn't accept that she'd ended it.'

She looks surprised that I know, and then obviously remembers that I've read the letter. 'Exactly. Which was when Polly and I decided she was going to have to tell you. Which was when she wrote this.' She holds up the letter. 'And she would have sent it, too, if it hadn't been for . . .'

'My accident.'

'Yes. Your accident.'

I remember now, as clearly as if it was just yesterday, waking up in the hospital right after the emergency surgery. Waking up to Polly, sitting next to my bed. Her eyes were red and puffy, her face deathly white and streaked with the indigo mascara she favoured back then. I remember that she was holding my hand, the way Grace is doing now, and that the moment I opened my eyes, she whispered, 'I'm sorry, Bella. I'm so, so sorry.'

If I could turn the clock back ten years to that moment, would I demand of her, like I've just demanded of Grace, exactly what it is she's sorry about? Sorry about sleeping with Christian; about Christian breaking up with me; about me waking up in a hospital bed with no chance, ever, of having a baby?

Or would I keep holding her hand and tell her that it's all OK?

'Because it wasn't her fault.'

Wait – was that me who just said that? I suppose it must have been.

'It wasn't Polly's fault.' Definitely me this time. I can feel my mouth moving around the syllables. It's a little bit like I've flicked onto some kind of autopilot. Like my brain has slipped into override – finding letters, words, whole sentences, even, that after all those years of trying to find someone or something to blame for my accident, I would never have thought I could say. But here I am, saying them. And more to the point, meaning them.

'My accident wasn't Polly's fault. How could it have been? Was she the one who made me get in the car? Was she the one who made me keep going, even though I knew I was driving dangerously?'

'Well, no,' says Grace, 'of course not. But –'

'I could have pulled over, howled for an hour in a lay-by, and then carried on without ending up tangled with the tree. Or maybe I would still have ended up tangled with the tree. Maybe I would have blinked at the wrong moment, or been dazzled by a headlight, or swerved to avoid a squirrel. Who knows? I don't. Polly certainly doesn't. In fact, now I come to think of it, it's a little bit typical of her that she'd assume she *does* know things like that.' I can feel a wry smile inching across my face. 'That the universe has her sufficiently at the centre of it to make all things within it, good and bad, mostly down to Polly.'

A flicker of a smile crosses Grace's face as well. 'Fair point. But whatever the reason, she tortured herself with it. She already felt horrible enough about betraying you like she did . . .'

'She didn't betray me. Well, OK, maybe she did betray me, a bit.'

Grace pulls an awkward face. 'She slept with your fiancé.'

'She was seventeen.' It's that brain-override thing again. 'And Christian was ten years older than her. Yes, she was a fool, but we've all been fools when it comes to unsuitable men. For crying out loud, I'm almost twice the age now that Polly was then, and I'm not exactly immune to stupid relationships myself. Wasting my time with someone, even though I know it's got no future. I've betrayed myself just as much as Polly betrayed me.'

Grace doesn't say anything for a moment. Then she says, 'None of my business, I know, but are you talking about Jamie? Because I couldn't help noticing he's not here for the wedding.'

'Yes.'

'I'm really sorry.'

'Don't be.' I turn to look at her. 'That's sort of my point. If Polly hadn't done what she did, I might still be stuck with Christian. Then I would never have met Jamie. And if I hadn't met Jamie, I would never have met . . .' I hesitate.

'Liam?'

I'm shocked. 'You know about me and Liam?'

But nobody knows about me and Liam. I quite specifically haven't mentioned a single word about Liam to anyone. Not to Anna, because I'm mindful of the fact that her doctor has told her not to get herself worked up or over-excited about anything. Not to Polly, because I didn't want to detract her attention from doing anything more arduous than walking down an aisle and just *getting bloody married*.

And, I suppose, because I want to keep whatever it is that Liam and I have a little bit protected from the outside world for now. And because if there *is* going to be a serious future between us – and I know it's absurdly early days, but I really think that maybe there is – then the very first people that should know about it are his daughters, Sally and Chloe, whom he's with back home in Cork, for New Year's Eve, right now. Who, if everything works out with the third-round interview he had the other day, should be coming to join him in London as soon as possible in the next few weeks.

'I know there was another gorgeous Irishman at

your party on Christmas Eve,' Grace is saying, 'who couldn't take his eyes off you. And I know his name was Liam. I'm just putting two and two together. I've no idea if I'm making four.'

I grin at her. 'You're making four.'

There's a flurry of noise in the corridor outside, before the bedroom door suddenly opens.

Polly is standing in the doorway, wearing her wedding dress. It's a simple, ivory sheath that I helped her pick out only a couple of days ago, with a shimmer of crystals on the bodice and long, romantic fluted sleeves, to keep out the December chill. Her hair is loose, in glossy waves over her shoulders, and it's adorned with a single cream rose, to match the ones in the bouquet she's holding.

She looks perfectly, completely beautiful.

I grab the letter from Grace's hand and slip it, surreptitiously, under the pillow.

'Guys! The car's arrived! And I need you to tell me if the makeup is too much. I'm not keen on the eye-shadow, but Mum says it'll look good in the photos, and . . .' Polly stares at us, as it seems suddenly to dawn on her that we're sitting next to each other on the bed, and looking . . . I don't know . . . companionable, I suppose, for once. 'What's going on in here?'

'Nothing. Nothing at all.' I get to my feet. 'Grace was just helping me with my hair. I decided to put it up, actually, if that's OK with you.'

'Yes, of course, it's fine . . . you look gorgeous, Bells. You too, Gracie.' She glances between the pair of us, her confusion giving way to something different. 'I can't tell you, both of you, how glad I am that you're my bridesmaids.' She takes a deep, suddenly wobbly breath. 'That you've both done so much for me, that you're so happy for me, even though . . . even though . . .'

I take a step forward, put my arms round her, and squeeze her very tightly. 'We're not just happy for you, Dood,' I say quietly, but so that Grace can hear as well. 'We're happy, full stop. Both of us. OK?'

Polly gulps, squeezes me back, and then pulls away just as the car lets out a hoot on the street below. 'Shit! Oh God, that doesn't sound very bridal, does it? I mean, *bother*. We need to get going! Are you both ready? Tell me honestly, about the eyeshadow. No, it's too much, it's too much,' she suddenly yelps, catching a glimpse of herself in the mirror on the back of the door. 'Dev will think he's marrying a walking cosmetics counter . . .'

She hurtles back to the bathroom, graceful in her long dress, to get Anji to tone down the eyeshadow.

'I'll go and tell the car we're on our way down.' Grace gets up and walks to the door. She stops beside me, as she gets there, and looks at me. 'And . . . um . . . the letter?'

I already know exactly what I'm going to do about the letter. I go back to the bed, take it out from under the pillow, then lean down and put it in the shoe-box, hidden away again where it came from.

After all, Polly's forgiven herself, enough to marry

Dev and be happy, at least. And as for me . . . well, it's like I said to Grace, there's nothing I feel the need to forgive her for.

'My life is good,' I tell Grace, as I straighten up to look at her. 'Actually, it's pretty great. And there's no need for the past to get in the way of the future.'

'So . . . it's our secret?'

I nod. 'Well who'd have ever thought you and me would share a secret?'

A wide smile lights up her impassive, perfect face. She opens her mouth to say something, just as the car hoots again below. 'All right, all right, we're coming! See you down there, Bella.'

After she's left the room, it's very quiet for a moment.

Then I hear the buzz of my mobile, from inside the satin clutch bag I've left on Polly's dressing table.

When I open the bag up and take out my phone, I can see that it's a new text message. Two new text messages, in fact – both of them from Liam.

The first one is just words: *Me and the girls on the beach at Barleycove. We think you'd love it here. L xx*

The second one is a photo. It must have been taken by a kind passer-by, because Liam is in it himself. He's looking freezing, and wind-swept, and very, very happy, with the Atlantic Ocean in the background and his arms around a pair of little dark-haired girls, standing in front of him.

The two sisters are smiling at me, and waving.

ALSO AVAILABLE IN ARROW

Confetti Confidential

Holly McQueen

Isabel Bookbinder dreams of pearly white weddings, happy brides, handsome grooms. And champagne towers that don't topple over. She dreams of the perfect wedding. But not for herself . . . For her clients, of course.

It's all about bride management as far as Isabel's concerned. Even when she misplaces a couple of brides and loses her job working for wedding guru Pippa Everitt, Isabel isn't disheartened. She throws herself straight into launching *Isabel Bookbinder, Individual Weddings*.

But, nothing in Isabel's life is ever straightforward, and despite her best efforts, things don't go quite according to plan . . .

'I quite fell in love with Isabel. Funny, charming and accident prone, she is the perfect heroine for today' Penny Vincenzi

'Like catching a snippet of gossip in the girls' loos and deciding you want to carry on listening . . . As frivolous deckchair escapism . . . it certainly does the job' *Daily Mail*

'I think Isabel and I were twins separated at birth. I love her!' Katie Fforde

arrow books

ALSO AVAILABLE IN ARROW

The Fabulously Fashionable Life of Isabel Bookbinder

Holly McQueen

When aspiring designer Isabel Bookbinder bags a job with Nancy 'Fashion Aristocracy' Tavistock, she's sure her career is finally on track. Dazzlingly glamorous, this is a world that she feels truly passionate about – after all, she knows her Geiger from her Louboutin, her Primark from her Prada, and she's *always* poring over fashion magazines. Well, ok, the fashion pages of *heat.*

So, learning from the very best, the future's looking bright for Isabel Bookbinder: Top International Fashion Designer. Within days she's putting the final touches to her debut collection, has dreamt up a perfume line, *Isabelissimo*, and is very nearly a friend of John Galliano. And on top of that she might even have fallen in love.

Yet nothing ever runs smoothly for Isabel and fabulously fashionable as her life is, it soon seems to be spiralling a little ou[illegible] of her control . . .

'I think Isabel and I were twins seperated at birth. I love her!'
Katie Fforde

'Marvellously funny' Jilly Cooper

'Does exactly what it says on the tin: if you like Sophie Kinsella's Shopaholic books and you miss Bridget Jones, then meet Isabel'
Louise Bagshawe, *Mail on Sunday*

arrow books